THREADBARE

THE TRAVELING SHOW

Alex D. Mers

BY ALEXANDRA DEMERS

For all of my teachers.

I dedicate this book to the people who read to me, who listened to my first stories, and even to those who said, "Put that book away, and take out your math." This is for the teachers who raised me, for the one who lent her beautiful name to this book, and for the one I married. Thank you.

TABLE OF CONTENTS

Prologue: The Cage..7
1 The Optimist..13
2 The Errand...25
3 The Family...46
4 The Costume..78
5 The Ride...95
6 The Search..109
7 The Gift..123
8 The Stranger..137
9 The Condemned...165
10 The Discovery..179
11 The Party..195
12 The Rehearsal..225
13 The Vision...243
14 The Prison...261
15 The Rebels...285
16 The Plan...317
17 The Festival...329
Epilogue: The Gun..355
Acknowledgments:...361

PROLOGUE: THE CAGE

May 17th, 1945
Pearisville (formerly Greenville), South Carolina

Sangria barely had enough room to breathe. Head between her ankles, her entire body was crammed into a cage suspended four feet off of the ground. Even if she could move, she didn't dare try to readjust. Any movement would make the cage swing.

How in the world did I end up here?

Sangria took in what little she could of the dark room. The dry smell of dust and scattered straw made her eyes itch. Heavy, canvas walls blocked most of the light and sounds from outside, but they could never block the screams. She would hear them almost every night, coming closer and closer until at last, it was her turn.

I hate the screams. I hate the gawkers. I hate the jeers. I hate this place.

Sangria licked her lips. Juan should have let out his familiar, anguished howl by now. She had been hanging for much longer than ever before, and she was beginning to get a little worried. She wished she could look at her watch or move her ankles far enough apart to hear what was going on outside. Suddenly, she heard a rustle of paper.

"Hey," she whispered. "*Hey!* How much longer do I have to sit like this? Are they coming soon or not?"

"You're next," a young man's voice answered softly from a far corner. Sangria thought that he had one of those accents that made anything spoken in a whisper sound intimate. He suppressed a little cough and added, "Settle down in there or else you'll start swinging."

"You need to repair this cage as soon as I'm out, René," she growled. "I've got a huge wire poking me in the side. I will hold you responsible if it tears my costume."

Instead of an answer, she heard another flutter of paper.

"Are you ignoring me?" she hissed.

"Of course not, *chérie*. Fix your cage. Got it."

"What are you doing back there?"

"Reading."

"Reading what?"

"*Bon sang*, you're talkative tonight," he murmured. "Perhaps I ought to make the cage a little smaller, *non*?"

"What did you say, Bozo?" Sangria rattled the tiny door and the cage bobbed from side to side.

"I said Nick must be captivating the crowd again." René chuckled and reached out to steady her confines. "So I'm reading the newspaper until everybody gets here."

There was a pause, and since there was still no sign of her tormentors, Sangria raspberried in boredom. "Well? What's the news say?"

René angled the paper so that the print was illuminated by a strip of light coming from a gap in the canvas walls. "The widow of a local hero was arrested by inquestors. Seems that she's been sent to prison in Nieuwestad."

Sangria used the bars on her cage to scratch her nose. "What for?"

"What else? Participating in the insurrection." He moved the paper through the strip of light, highlighting the important parts. "She was married to a Favored Citizen, but he died in the war. She lost her fortune and lived in hiding until the inquestors dragged her from her home." He sighed and scanned a grocery ad for bargains. "*La pauvre.* The war took everything from her."

"Odd that Inkies would nab a Favored Citizen." Sangria felt a sneeze coming on, and she sniffed it back defiantly. "They're practically American royalty."

"Well, it's not so odd considering this woman was an immigrant," René explained bitterly. "Not even her husband's status could save her in the end."

Sangria rolled her eyes. "Since when did you give a fig about politics?"

"Since when was sympathy political?" he shot back.

Sangria's retort was cut off by a triple-knock on the wall.

"That's your cue." René tossed his newspaper aside and flew off of his stool. He pulled the fly hand-over-hand as fast as he could, raising the curtain with a whir. "Time to untie the Knot-Freak."

The room flooded with yellow light, and Sangria heard a woman's muted scream. Her insides roiled.

Whatever happened to the gasps of wonder?

She couldn't see the crowd, but she judged by the sounds of surprise that there must have been a group of ten or fifteen people standing in the dark outside. Audiences were always stunned by the way she managed to fit into a birdcage, perfectly framing her doll-like face with her arms and legs.

René hid from the crowd behind the curtain, but the stage lights caught the edge of his rough hand as he gently set a needle down onto her record. The dented old phonograph played the eerie opening violin strains of "Danse Macabre," and Sangria began to move out. She only had enough time in her performance to display the extent of her flexibility, so she moved in perfect sync with the music. One arm slid from the small opening first, then the rest of her torso. She gripped the chain that suspended her cage and freed her legs. Turning to the side, she dipped backwards so that her head touched her bottom as she stood. She deepened the bend until her head reached her ankles again, her arms outstretched for balance with practiced grace.

"Now there's a bendy bird I'd love to stuff," came a quip from the audience followed by sparse chuckles.

Sangria snapped up straight and glared into the darkness. "*Who said that?*"

"Can you wrap your gams clear around, Knot-Freak?" the heckler called back.

"I'm a trained dancer and concert violinist!" she shouted before René dropped the curtain like a rock. Sangria clawed beneath the tattered canvas and scrambled out. "You're a goat-mothered bumpkin who's gotta pay money before he can lay eyes on a real woman! Which one of us really belongs in the cage, huh?"

She felt René's firm grip on her elbows, drawing her back.

"Where you going, Birdy?" the man in the audience hooted. "Tell your wrangler that I haven't got my nickel's worth yet!"

"Come and get it, you hillbilly bastard!" Sangria thrashed against René and his hands clamped down on her like manacles. "Get up here so I can choke you to death with my ankles and sell tickets at your funeral!"

René managed to pull her behind the curtain again. She was incredibly strong for somebody so petite, and he didn't release her until she stopped struggling.

"That was certainly the most excitement we've had in awhile," he said breathlessly, fanning himself with his wide-brimmed hat. Sangria fixed him with a green glare. "That man was out of line, *chérie*. Marmi won't blame you for getting upset."

Sangria sniffed and wiped her eyes. "I have had enough," she mumbled, backing away from him. "I can't take this anymore."

"What do you mean? You're not talking about leaving, are you?" René tilted his head. "*Chérie*, you can't."

Sangria bit her lip and frowned at her backdrop instead of answering him. Her set was a silhouette of a tree with dozens of tin birds that flew out of it on their own. It was inspired by Balinese shadow puppets, and René had spent months crafting it from scrap down to the most minute detail. Joined with her music and performance, the result was a breathtaking scene that was unusual for such a small traveling show.

They both turned at the sound of coins falling into her lock-box outside.

"Hear that?" he smiled, rubbing her shoulder. "She can threaten somebody with a humiliating death, and everyone will still love the Knot-Freak."

What René hoped would encourage Sangria had instead drove her into outrage. "Don't you get it, you moron? I did not train my entire life just to be ogled for pocket change at some filthy little mudshow!" Shoving past René with a furious sob, she cried, "Damn them all and damn you, too! I will never be the Knot-Freak again!"

CHAPTER 1: THE OPTIMIST

May 18th, 1945
Cold River, South Carolina

Amandine Stewart was an optimist. Even as she was forcefully escorted from her home, she tried to imagine what adventures awaited her now that she was homeless.

"You are doing your country a great service," said the assistant who tugged her along by the elbow, but he only repeated what the Administrator had said in the den.

Amandine hardly agreed, though she wasn't about to admit that out loud. She took in what she could of the tall corridor instead, taking a final mental picture of the place that had once been her childhood home. She noted the thin scratch in the wallpaper beside the library door, the result of cannon fire during an epic, imaginary naval battle between herself and the maid. The maid had disappeared with the rest of the household staff years ago, long before anyone in the government showed any interest in the Stewart family.

The girl hesitated for just a moment as she passed the staircase and reached for the banister. Her father put his hand here before he left, back when the wooden surface was still smooth and polished. Now it was grimy from neglect and marred by the scratches her mother left when she was dragged away. Fingertips tracing the gash, Amandine realized that this was the last place each member of the Stewart family touched before they left this house for good. She was jarred from her thoughts when the assistant gave her a shove between her shoulders.

"Have a good day," he barked. "Hail to the Republic!" And with that, the double doors slammed shut behind her.

Amandine smoothed her blue silk dress and looked around. The sun warmed the crisp air after a recent spring rain. It was the kind of day where she once might have liked to take some books outside or play tennis, but the hills surrounding the great house had returned to wilderness. Unkempt shrubs bloomed, and the lawns—once a smooth, striped emerald— were now waist-deep and full of weeds.

Amandine descended the steps from the house just as three government trucks circled the cobblestone courtyard. Tailgates dropped with a bang, and soldiers unloaded boxes and furniture with trained uniformity.

They're certainly excited to move in, she thought, keeping out of their way. *They didn't even wait for the ink to dry.*

Since the soldiers weren't paying her any attention, she took the opportunity to reclaim her bicycle. She had to free the garage door from a wall of vines, but she found her bike precisely where she left it three years ago, hanging on the wall above her father's dusty Deluxe Roadster.

Amandine was nearly ready to go. She pumped air into the tires, secured her suitcase to the bike with a length of twine, and double-checked her coat pocket for the envelope full of crisp, blue, New American Republic dollars that the Administrator had given her in exchange for her property. As an afterthought, she kept a single bill from the envelope and hid the rest inside her dress front until she got a chance to conceal it somewhere safer. Satisfied, she walked the bike out the back and kicked the door shut behind her.

She pushed off of the cobblestone and buzzed past the preoccupied soldiers. She offered a quick glance over her shoulder to the red-brick Georgian house, where the marble statues of Mercury and Arachne that flanked the doorway were already being swapped for a pair of dour-looking gryphons.

"Bye, house," she murmured. Amandine wanted to wave, but a sharp twinge deep in her chest stopped her. She gripped the handlebars until her fingers turned white, and the feeling seeped away. With a deep breath, she smiled at the sun-dappled road ahead. She didn't dwell on the fact that her house—and all that remained of her life before the war—was now the governing administrator's offices. She only hoped Mr. White at the bakery could make her a sandwich for the road.

Administrator Peter Graft puffed his chest with pride as he toured the new premises. Securing the Stewart house had been quite a piece of luck, and he was confident that his new offices were now the finest in the state. He explored the master bedroom upstairs, imagining it as a lounge or smoking room where he could entertain his superiors. He went to the window to admire the view of the countryside, but when he drew back the curtains, the smug expression vanished from his face.

A black sedan, trimmed in chrome and glistening like a beetle, rolled right into the middle of the courtyard where the Administrator's men were unloading. Graft's throat felt tight. He wiped his sweating palms on his blue jacket and paced the room. If he had any question about exactly who was paying him a visit, his men's reaction removed all doubt. All at once, they dropped whatever they were carrying and stood at attention.

"*Attention!* Inquestor present!"

A man stepped from the car and straightened his impeccably tailored black uniform. He scanned the courtyard, and suddenly his head jerked up towards the house. Graft stumbled back out of sight. He had no idea what an inquestor was doing here, but he knew better than to keep his guest waiting. Breathing hard, he wiped his receding hair back and went down to meet him.

Inquestors were the New American Republic's response to the civil unrest that ripped across the country after the 1932 election. Distinguished by their black high officer's uniforms and the silver catamount insignia on their shoulder, they prowled communities everywhere, working above the law to root out anyone who flouted the NAR's authority. Some of the most notorious insurrectionists were concealed within NAR ranks, and Graft dearly hoped that his impulsive property purchase didn't put him under suspicion. Nothing could save him if an inquestor had him in his sights.

Those jealous bastards up at the Pearisville office must have called him, he thought to himself. *I bet they thought if they couldn't have the Stewart place, nobody should. I'll show them! I'll deal with the Inky first and then oh, I'll show them good!*

By the time Graft made it downstairs, the officer was already in the foyer, examining the grand room around him. "Inquestor!" He tried to sound cheerful, but his voice trembled. "Welcome! I'm Administrator Peter Graft."

The man turned on his heels. He was a little smaller and much younger than any high officer Graft had ever seen. He couldn't have been any older than twenty-five, and mischief glittered in his dark eyes.

"Inquestor Marcus Carver. Pleased to meet you." He dropped his rigid posture and shook Graft's hand as if they were old friends. "I hope I'm not catching you at a bad time. Your boys look busy outside."

The Administrator was caught off guard by the Inquestor's greeting, and he had to clear his throat. "I apologize. I'm afraid we're in the middle of a move, and our offices are not operational at the moment."

"Oh, I understand. I won't take up much of your time." Carver gestured with an open hand to the parlor. "I only have a few questions. Before we begin, would you mind if we sat down together?"

"Of course not, Inquestor," he chuckled nervously. "After you."

Grinning, Carver gripped Graft's shoulder and forced him towards the doorway with a hard slap to the back. "No, Administrator. After you. I insist!"

The Inquestor followed closely, staying just out of Graft's peripheral vision as he led them to a set of couches arranged before the grand fireplace. Instead of sitting down, Carver glanced inside the fireplace and ran his fingers along the green marble mantle before taking a deep breath. He seemed disappointed.

"Have you been here before, Inquestor?" Graft asked, sitting down.

"Yes." Carver folded his hands behind his back and rocked on his heels. "Oh, yes, I certainly have. Did you say you just bought this building?"

"I... did not, sir."

"Someone outside must have said it," he shrugged. "Did you buy it today?"

"Just now, sir."

Everything about the Inquestor's attitude betrayed his frustration. "It's a shame this house will be turned into offices. This room was so nice for taking coffee." He went to where an elegant sideboard used to stand between two picture windows and prodded the indents in the rug with his polished shoe. "I don't suppose you've got the means to fix coffee yet, do you?"

The Administrator was about to call for some, but Carver held up his hand.

"Don't trouble yourself unless you've already got a pot going. I was just reminiscing about the last time I visited here." He sat across from Graft and shouted in surprise when the deep cushions of the new couch nearly swallowed him. "What a gas!" he cackled. "The lady of the house made such a fine cup of coffee, wouldn't you say?"

"I wouldn't know," came Graft's guarded reply. "She didn't offer me any and hardly seemed old enough to know how to brew it properly herself."

Carver's expression clouded in confusion as he attempted to sit up straight. "I was talking about the girl's mother, Caroline Stewart."

"Never heard of her." Graft shook his head. "My dealings were with the girl only."

"Didn't she seem a bit young to be quite so... affluent?" Carver swept his arm across the room. His gaze caught on something high up on the opposite end of the parlor, and Graft had to turn to see what captured his attention. It was an oil painting of the Stewart family wearing their Sunday best in that very parlor. The father was an imposing man who stood protectively behind his seated wife and the cherubic baby girl in her lap. Though his expression was fairly neutral, Graft got the impression that he was glaring at him, almost as if he was daring him to disrupt the happy life he had made for himself.

"Her paperwork was in order," Graft explained, drawing the Inquestor's focus back. "Since she was seventeen, she was legally entitled to all of her family's property. After the war, it didn't amount to much beyond this house, an empty textile factory ten miles from here, and another empty store in town."

"You bought all of it?" Carver hitched a brow. "How on earth did you approve the funds?"

"It was completely within my office's budget, sir," he explained. "The girl was willing to accept my initial offer on the condition that I buy all of her property and pay cash. Frankly, it seemed like she was in a hurry to leave town."

The Inquestor tapped his fingers together as he absorbed these facts. "Were those her only conditions?"

"Yes, sir."

"Did you make any conditions of your own? Perhaps a little incentive to keep the price so low?"

Graft blinked. "No, sir. It was all approved by my legal administrator and detailed in the contract. I can retrieve it for you right—"

"I just think it's funny that you'd buy so much useless property instead of just sending the girl to the replacement home and confiscating it all," Carver interrupted, but then waved the thought aside. "But never mind that. Chasing up girls for the home isn't your department. Did Amandine tell you what happened to her parents?"

Graft was relieved that he could finally provide some answers to the Inquestor. "Her father served in both wars. Killed in action a little over two years ago, I believe." "Interesting." Carver took out a notepad from his pocket and began writing furiously. "Branch and rank?"

"Navy. He was captain of the NARS Osiris, lost in the Atlantic." Graft's good memory had always served him well, and he was glad it didn't fail him now despite his anxiety.

"And her mother?" Carver pressed. He used such a peculiar emphasis that Graft suspected this was the heart of the matter.

"She didn't say. I assumed she died as well. Fever epidemic, or something."

Carver laughed inwardly and put his notebook away. "No, she didn't."

Graft was afraid of this. The Inquestor knew much more than he was letting on. "Is it this Caroline you're after, sir?"

"No, not anymore," he replied, his smile unwavering. "I popped by for a visit... oh, I suppose it was two months ago now? She invited me in, fixed me a coffee right where we're sitting, and after we had a chat about what she'd been up to, I hit her."

He drew his gun, a nickel-plated 1911 with a gleaming pearl grip, and the Administrator recoiled in shock.

"I hit her over the head again and again with this pistol for trying to feed me a load of hokum about how she was just a war hero's widow. You see, she was a rebel fighter. And not just any fighter. No, I've got her linked directly to the leaders." He burst out with wild laughter as he played with his gun, pulling back the hammer and releasing it slowly.

Click-click. Click.

Click-click. Click.

"You mean... she was *the* Caroline Stewart? The one they locked up for working with Tall-Me and Cleo?" Graft desperately wanted the Inquestor to put the gun away. "But... if you have Caroline already, then you must be after the girl."

"I am!" He caught his breath and wiped at a tear.

"But the girl was a shut-in. Why didn't you just arrest her with her mother?"

21

"You must not have been in your position long, Administrator," Carver's tone suddenly dropped to a low and dangerous growl.

Click-click.

"Otherwise you would know it is not a good idea to pry an inquestor for confidential information, and you've already done so three times."

"I— I'm sorry, Inquestor," Graft stammered.

"Oh, what the hell? I'll tell you anyway." Carver's cheerful demeanor returned without a trace of his momentary hostility. "It was an oversight! I was just so giddy about Caroline, I didn't even stop to think about the girl upstairs. Serves me right. A stitch in time saves nine, and now I've got a couple of loose ends to tie up if I ever want to see the end of this investigation. This is where you come in, Administrator." He leaned forward and lowered his voice to an excited whisper. "Did you know that this was a rebel safe house when you bought it? Come on now! You can tell me!" He punched him lightly in the arm. "Tell me just like little miss Amandine told you."

"She didn't tell me anything," he rasped, watching the gun intently for any sudden movements. Carver still hadn't let the hammer down.

"Horse feathers!" The Inquestor laughed again as if Graft was playing a hilarious trick on him. "I know you have a way with young ladies."

Startled, he finally looked up from the gun to Carver. "Sir?"

"You're a popular customer over at the replacement home," he said, shaking a finger at him. "All those young widows and orphaned daughters—they all need somebody to care for them. I hear you do that *very* well."

Graft paled. How could the Inquestor have possibly known about that? He never visited the same replacement home twice. He never left a clue or used his real name. A flash of his badge was all it took to grant him unfettered access to a menagerie of eligible, desperate women.

"All of those girls with rebel ties..." Carver was motionless and wide-eyed, like a snake about to strike. "And they're all missing. Nowhere to be found."

"No, sir! Please, let me—"

"Now the daughter of a murderess runs free with a pocketful of taxpayers' cash while you look after her safe house. I wonder what the boys in blue will uncover if I turn them loose in that 'empty' factory."

Graft saw the end of the gun move in his direction. In a panic, he cried, "*The girl left fifteen minutes ago!* She said she was heading to Nieuwestad to see her mother! That's all I know, Inquestor! I swear it!"

Carver seemed startled by this outburst. He looked down at his gun, and with an embarrassed laugh, he finally let down the hammer and turned the weapon over in his hand.

"Nieuwestad, you say?" He stood and replaced his hat over his glossy black hair. "Thank you. That is most helpful."

Was that all? the Administrator thought. He took a ragged breath and rose unsteadily to his feet. "Will there be anything else, Inquestor?"

Carver recovered his formality and bowed. "No, thank you. I just about have what I was after, so I will let you get back to work and see myself out. Hail to the Republic."

The moment the Inquestor was out of the parlor, Graft slumped down on the couch and buried his face in his hands. His entire body shook as he reflected on how narrowly he avoided trouble.

"Such a shame about this house," he heard Carver say from directly behind him. His blood turned to ice when he heard the sound he'd never hoped to hear again.

Click-click.

"It's so luxurious. I feel just awful every time I have to make a mess in here."

CHAPTER 2: THE ERRAND

"One cheese sandwich, coming right up, Miss Stewart," the baker said, dropping new coins into her outstretched palm. "There. I think that is supposed to be proper change, though you'd better count again for me."

Amandine examined them in her palm for a moment. "I'm so glad they made the dimes bigger than the nickels now. It makes sense since they're worth more."

The baker prepared her order, watching her carefully while she browsed the humble cakes on display. He didn't recognize Amandine when she first stepped into his shop. She was a wisp of the schoolgirl that she used to be, but her familiar order and glowing smile endured throughout the years of hardship.

He rolled the bag shut and passed it over the counter. "Mr. White, do you know if our post office has reopened yet?" She stuffed the bag under her coat. "I need to get a letter to my mother and tell her that I sold the estate."

"You sold the Stewart place?" Mr. White exclaimed in surprise. "Is that what brings you down from the big house after so long?"

"That's right," she chirped. "But if folks ask, you can tell them I was driven out by a three year-long hankering for a cheese sandwich."

Mr. White laughed on his way to the refrigerator. "I think Pearisville is the closest town that still gets regular mail." He returned with a cold soda in a green glass bottle. "This is for the road. I reckon Cold River won't be seeing much more of the Stewart family, so take this with my best wishes."

"Thanks, Mr. White," she said. "I'm certainly going to miss your cheese sandwiches."

"Any idea where you're going?"

"Nieuwestad."

"Nieuwestad, *New York*? Land sakes, that's a very long way. Are you going for your mother?"

"Yes, sir. I figured that I'd work to pay my way and save my nickels for *maman's* defense," she explained.

Like most people in Cold River, Mr. White knew the Stewarts well, and it saddened him to see that this was how it ended for their family in this town. "It's a damned shame what happened to Caroline," he grunted. "I remember when Willy brought her from France back in twenty-two. Everybody was worried that she wouldn't get along out here in the sticks."

"Really?" Amandine perked.

"It's true," he said. "You could tell she was a high-class lady. She didn't talk much at first, but she ended up being even easier to get on with than your stubborn dad. He was a good man, but that pride got the best of him sometimes. Caroline, on the other hand, was an angel. Didn't matter if you were a king or a cotton-picker; she'd treat you with the same kindness."

"That sounds about right," Amandine murmured. She didn't realize that she had started squeezing the long, silver locket around her neck until the hinge bit into her palm. "Well, I had better be on my way, sir. Got a lot of miles to cover."

"When you get to Pearisville, look for my cousin Nathaniel's store on the near side of town, just past the bridge. It's White's, same as mine. If you tell him that I sent you, he might give you a meal for some work." Before she left, the baker added earnestly, "You be careful now, young lady."

Amandine waved, and the door chimed brightly behind her. *Goodbyes aren't so bad if you've got bells to say them for you,* she decided, popping the cap off of her soda bottle and mounting her bike.

There was still plenty of time left in the day for the long ride to Pearisville, so Amandine decided to take the road through town. She cruised down the empty, littered main street one last time, past broken windows that made the vacant stores gape open like caves.

Contrary to what the NAR party had promised, nothing looked like the shimmering, Utopian pictures they passed around during The Depression, and the war had only made things worse. There was no bounty of food, only ration cards. There were no happy, smiling families, just men sent to serve before they could finish school and women whisked away to replacement homes if they had nobody to care for them. Still, Amandine thought things weren't so bad. At least people could eat again, even if it was heavily regulated by government storehouses, and the streets weren't an open war zone anymore.

She glided around ruts and potholes. *Of all the things the NAR party said they'd fix, I suppose they never said anything about the roads.*

Amandine was glad to see that the only place that didn't have a single broken window was Master Elegance, the two-storied brownstone store that once drew the eastern elite to the rural town of Cold River. She didn't know if vandals avoided Master Elegance because of its visibility at the corner of a prominent intersection or out of respect of its former owner. She smiled at her own reflection that seemed to roll right through the dusty, gilded mirrors and toppled mannequins inside.

Beneath layers of anti-government graffiti, Amandine could still make out the cheery message on the sign out of town: PLEASE VISIT COLD RIVER AGAIN SOON.

Maybe someday. She knew better than to try and wave again. *Today, Nieuwestad calls.*

Amandine didn't encounter many other travelers on the road to Pearisville, but those who did pass her saw a girl visibly affected by the war in her frailty. She was a small, skinny thing wearing a man's jacket over an old, drop-waist dress, and her curly, brown hair was cropped short beneath a gray cloche hat. Since she believed that venturing out on her own was a very special occasion, she put on her last pair of stockings, but they were made for a much healthier woman and sagged around her thin legs. If somebody were to judge her by her appearance, Amandine hardly resembled someone who had once been heiress to a fabric fortune.

"Some people might say that Fortune is fickle, coming and going when you least expect it," Amandine remembered her father telling her once. "But I say that just because Fortune's turned her back on you doesn't mean you're powerless. You've got to bring her back around yourself. Don't ever just sit by as long as you can still stand on your own two feet."

Will Stewart had tried to instill his hardworking, pragmatic ideals on his daughter since the day she was born; after all, he was proof that with squared shoulders and determination, no problem was insurmountable. He would remind her that when he was called to fight in the Great War, he worked hard and made himself into a captain. When he came home to find his father's business in shambles, he turned the dilapidated storefront into a fine textile factory and world-renowned clothing label. He even refused to take the Depression lying down. As the country suffered a decade of poverty and political unrest, he protected not only his family and business but the entire rural community of Cold River by securing a contract making uniforms for the newly elected NAR party.

"Everything will be alright, Button," Will had said, inviting young Amandine to see the stack of opened mail on his desk. They were all thank-you letters from his employees, praising him for not cutting a single job while so many other people in the country had lost everything. Will looked from the letters to the new uniform sketches pinned to his wall. He proudly touched his favorite design: a slender black suit. "It's not haute couture anymore, but it's the dignity and pride of service to our country."

At fourteen, Amandine got to experience fickle fortune herself when her father's world of carefree comfort collapsed around her. The second World War was someone else's concern, a far-off problem, until it took Will away and never brought him home. Without his direction, the factory closed, too. She wanted to do as her father said and turn her own luck around, but when the NAR found themselves fighting for the losing side in the war, everything turned worse than it ever had been during the Depression. Sickness wiped out entire towns, money became worthless, and every day became a grueling hunt for food. Rumors spread that women were being bought and sold in replacement homes, a government welfare program meant to aid unwed mothers. The practice was apparently so lucrative that corrupt administrators had begun to abduct young women, even girls, who didn't have men to defend them. Because of this, Caroline had warned her daughter against ever leaving the house, and Amandine reluctantly agreed.

The girl tried not to let her confinement bother her too much. She decided that if her circumstances were beyond her control, she could always change her outlook. Ignoring the hunger pangs in her stomach, she gleaned a little happiness from sewing projects and spending time in their library. In a way, those things made her father feel a little closer.

Will had been gone for nearly a year, when one day starvation finally drove Amandine from the house and into the wilderness. As she rooted around the cold earth beneath the pecan trees, she spotted a tiny speck of yellow in a clearing and discovered a patch of newly sprouted dandelions. Hands quaking with joy, she gathered as much as she could find and ran back to their dark, empty mansion.

"Look, *maman*," she beamed, rinsing the leaves in icy water. "Our luck has finally turned."

Caroline scowled at the bowl of weeds in the sink, her gaunt face set as hard as stone. "Indeed, *ma jolie*. I think this is only the beginning."

She was right. For the next two years, Caroline left Amandine alone in the house frequently, but she always returned with a sack of food. It wasn't much at first; just enough to fit in a canister she hid in the dumbwaiter, but it was better than weeds and wormy pecans. Amandine tried to ask where the food came from, but the only answer Caroline gave her was "a friend at the storehouse." Gradually, the bags got a little bigger and sometimes they came with luxury items like chocolate, blocks of butter, and, curiously, real silk stockings.

As Amandine feared, their turn of good luck didn't last long. One night while she was reading in her room, she heard a commotion downstairs. From her vantage point on the dark landing, she could see into the parlor where an officer in black had Caroline pinned to the floor. Horrified, she tried to make sense of what she was seeing when four armed policemen burst in through the front door.

"In here, fellas," she heard the Inquestor call. "She won't fight you. I doubt she can even stand up after the little bump I just gave her."

Blood ran down Caroline's battered face, and she grabbed at the banister. Her wide, frantic eyes found Amandine hidden in the dark, and she made a split second decision. Caroline let go of the banister. The officers tackled her to the ground, but not before she cried, "Please, I've done nothing wrong! I was just getting food! *Fais attention à lui!* Let me go! My husband was a Favored Citizen! I was just so hungry... *s'il vous plaît, fais attention!*"

It was a warning Amandine had heard all of her life. Whenever she left a hot iron unattended or climbed too high on the library ladder, it was always "*Amandine, fais attention!*" Now they were her mother' last words to her, broken up so that officers would think that she was just begging in French.

Watch out for him! Please, be careful!

"Good work, Inquestor," one of the officers said. "This has got to be the biggest bust in history. We've crippled the insurrection."

"Don't start counting chickens," the Inquestor replied, making a hasty exit. "Get her to the station and throw her in with the others until I can get more agents and transport arranged to Nieuwestad. It ain't over 'til *every* one of them is in the ground."

The door boomed shut and hours passed before Amandine emerged, trembling, from her hiding place. Not knowing what else to do, she set about washing the bloodstains from the rug. As she scrubbed at the pitch-black spots by lamplight, Amandine realized that she had always taken a passive approach to her father's advice. She couldn't affect change by simply willing it to go the way she wanted; a smile and a positive attitude wouldn't be enough to bring her mother back. Tossing frothy brown water off the back porch and into the night, Amandine knew that she had to get Caroline out.

A few weeks later when Amandine was appraising the last few valuable trinkets in the house, the local governing administrator himself appeared at her door and complimented her magnificent house.

Hello again, Fortune, she thought to herself, welcoming Peter Graft into the parlor. *I hope you stick around a little longer this time.*

All of these events brought Amandine to where she was now, pedaling down a rugged path to recover her mother. She didn't know what she would say when she finally reached the prison; she didn't even know how she would get there. All she knew for certain was that she had to try.

That afternoon, she came out of the forested country to the river and saw the town of Pearisville on the other side. The old bridge had been a casualty of the civil conflict, and its burnt remains crumbled into the gushing current. Amandine searched for a place to cross and spotted a narrow, temporary bridge made of rope and chains nearby.

She pedaled across, mindful of the irregular gaps in the scrap-wood slats. Her cloche hat narrowed her view like a horse's blinders, so she didn't see the delivery truck roll onto the opposite end of the bridge until she felt a rumble in her handlebars.

"Hey!" She waved her arm and swerved to a stop. "Look out, mister!"

The driver either didn't see her or simply didn't care. Amandine had no choice but to abandon her bike and scramble over the rope railing to avoid being hit. The truck knocked the bike over the edge, but Amandine managed to grab the handle of her suitcase before it fell. The twine that secured it to the back couldn't hold and she watched in dismay as her bicycle splashed into the rushing brown waters below.

Amandine tossed her suitcase back onto the bridge and climbed over, rubbing her chafed hands together while the truck sped away.

Oh golly, I've lost my bike. How in the world am I supposed to get to Nieuwestad now?

She squeezed her belongings to her chest.

Keep on the sunny side, Amandine. 'Count your blessings, name them one by one.' One, you ain't hurt. Two, you saved your suitcase. Three, maybe this new Mr. White can make you another cheese sandwich for supper.

That was all she needed to collect herself, and she quickly lugged her suitcase across the bridge before another car came.

Pearisville was recovering well, considering it had been the site of a particularly bloody conflict between the rebels and the police only a year before. Children played in the streets unsupervised, housewives did their shopping, and a cafe played patriotic music while it served its diners. Amandine let her nose guide her to the town bakery, a clean white building with lace curtains in the window and a printed pink sign that read, "CHOCOLATE CONFECTIONS! FIRST TIME SINCE THE WAR! ONLY AT WHITE'S."

She smiled when the door chimed, and a woman in a pink apron greeted her from behind a scrubbed countertop. "Welcome, young lady. How may I help you?"

Amandine liked bakeries. The warm smell of bread and sugar wrapped her in an olfactory blanket of comfort and brought her back to Saturday mornings before the war, when she'd wake up to the smell of cinnamon rolls and coffee downstairs. Amandine inhaled deeply before she replied.

"I just came from Cold River, ma'am, and I'm on my way to Nieuwestad. Mr. Clarence White there told me that I might get some work from Mr. Nathaniel White here."

Now that the woman knew that Amandine wasn't going to buy anything, the smile she put on for customers fell away. She paused to mull the idea over, thoughtfully touching her blonde set curls. "Did he? Well, I suppose we'll see about that. My name is Betsy White. Nathaniel's my husband." She looked Amandine over. "Are you a baker?"

"No, ma'am. I'm a tailor's daughter."

The baker's nails clicked with incredulity on the countertop. Amandine's clothes were well-kept and neat, but decades out of fashion.

"And where are your parents?"

"My father was killed in action, and my mother is in the Nieuwestad Prison of War Criminals. I'm on my way to get her released," Amandine replied.

Mrs. White inhaled deeply. "Bless your heart."

Amandine cringed. She must have looked very pitiful or sounded very stupid to have earned a condescending response like that.

"And what's your name, sugar?"

Amandine began to get the feeling that Mrs. White didn't want the daughter of a tailor or an accused criminal to work for her, but she didn't let the smile on her face falter. "My name is Amandine Stewart, ma'am. It's a pleasure to make your acquaintance."

Mrs. White's face moved with recognition. "Stewart, you say? Of the fabric factory in Cold River? And the design label?"

"Yes. Well, I was."

"Well, I do declare!" The baker brightened. "I loved your fabrics. Never bought any of your dresses myself, but I used your material to make all of my curtains and towels before the war, and they still hold their color like new." She paused before asking carefully, "But whatever happened? Last I heard, Mr. Stewart was commissioned by the government to make all of the servicemen's uniforms."

"It's true, but he answered the call about three years ago." Amandine shrugged and rubbed the edge of her coat between her fingers. "Guess they needed a sailor more than a tailor. We lost him, and *maman* couldn't keep the business without him."

"Oh, bless your heart!" This time the phrase was soft as meringue, and Mrs. White reached for Amandine's hat. "Take this off. Hang your things and come into the kitchen. I have just the job to suit you." She swapped her coat for an apron and led the girl into the back room. "You came at the right time. My husband is out running errands, and I was just working on a big chocolate order."

"Your kitchen looks very nice." The girl admired the clean, enameled ovens and linoleum floor that had been scrubbed so much, they were beginning to show wear down to the black layer beneath. "Golly, it looks like it's right out of a Good Housekeeping ad."

Mrs. White moved a wooden stool in front of a table stacked high with boxes and tissue paper. "It's part of White's purity guarantee. While other bakeries cut their flour with plaster and baked their bricks in hollowed out oil drums, we always baked real bread in a proper kitchen. We made sure to clean everyday, even when there wasn't a flake of soap to be found."

Amandine glanced at the bar of soap she had just picked up at the sink. She quickly put it back into the graniteware soapdish and lathered the residue until it bubbled between her fingers.

"How did you manage to stay open when flour was worth its weight in gold?" She dried her hands on a towel made from a familiar pink material.

"It was tricky for awhile. I suspect our regular supplier might have been dealing in black market flour." Mrs. White quickly considered what she had just said before adding, "But it's not likely. He probably had a business connection at the storehouse."

"Really? I hope it wasn't the same guy my mother knew, because I think that's how she got mistaken for an insurrectionist." Amandine sat on the stool and examined the supplies in front of her. "Hogwash! *Maman* loved jazz and fashion. She didn't give a fig about politics. That was Dad's favorite topic, and he was a favored citizen of the NAR. All of this was just a big misunderstanding which I will straighten out as soon as I get to Nieuwestad."

Mrs. White squinted at the odd girl for some time. When the pause began to drag on for too long, Amandine turned on the swiveling stool and chirped, "Want me to box up these chocolates, ma'am?"

Mrs. White sighed. "Yes, sugar. Let me show you how to do it." She arranged the treats in pretty paper cups and pink tissue paper.

"Looks easy enough."

"Ah, but presentation is key." Mrs. White tied the lid shut with a white ribbon. She set the completed box aside. "There you have it. Now, I'll be making chocolates right behind you if you have any questions. I need ten boxes of a dozen packed for the order, plus a few more to put into the window."

Amandine saluted and got to work. She found that packing chocolates wasn't too different from the more familiar task of packing garment boxes, so her eyes strayed from her hands to her surroundings. She scanned the shelves of spices, utensils, and miscellany and noticed an old radio as she knotted the bow on her first box.

"May I turn on some music?" Amandine asked over her shoulder.

Mrs. White pulled a face. "I don't much care for the marches. Fifteen minutes of that same old *parum-pum-pum,* and I start to feel like I've turned into a mixing machine. My husband keeps that in here to listen to the news."

Amandine switched on the radio. Its face glowed yellow and piccolo tweeted out a patriotic melody beneath the cheery voice of a radio personality.

"—listening to 'How We Are In The NAR!' Coming up: he's becoming such a hot topic, I'm almost afraid to touch him! Hear how everybody's new favorite inquestor single-handedly—"

The voice slipped into static. Twisting the tuning knob very carefully, Amandine found the signal she was looking for on a low frequency and tapped her Mary-Jane in time to the old dance record.

Mrs. White's mouth fell open in shock. "That's a pirate station."

"This station is good," the girl said as if she hadn't heard her. "*Maman* and I listened to this after we had to turn all of our dance records in for food rations."

"Turn it off."

"Beg your pardon?"

"Jazz is illegal! Turn that off at once!" Mrs. White flew at the radio, but her hand stopped on the dial. She froze, listening.

Amandine beamed, oblivious. "This one's a swell number, isn't it?"

Mrs. White vanished from the bakery, lost to a summer night long ago. The air buzzed with bugs and electricity, and her new bob haircut tickled her cheeks. She swayed in time to the Twelfth Street Rag, hoping somebody would ask her for a dance when she felt a shy tap on her shoulder.

"This song was playing at the church social where I met my husband," she whispered, still clinging to a night when she danced until her legs ached, and the feverish kiss he stole in the choir loft tasted like lemonade. She smiled and turned the volume up ever so slightly. "It feels like a lifetime ago."

"It's much more fun to work to this kind of music, don't you think?" Amandine perched on her stool and continued packing as if she had done it her entire life. Offhandedly, she added, "Something's burning, ma'am," and Mrs. White dashed for the neglected pot of chocolate.

The two continued working, driven by energetic swing until the disc jockey came on. Amandine flung a paper cup aside and clapped her hands. "It's DJMA! My absolute favorite radio host!"

"Not Marc Antony." Mrs. White's gaze shifted between the front door and the open kitchen window. "We haven't been listening to Tall-Me and Cleo's station this whole time, have we?"

"Shh!" Amandine fluttered her hand urgently. "This is a real treat. He almost never comes on during the day."

DJ Marc Antony was an irreverent radio personality with a golden, transatlantic voice. Broadcasting from wandering locations, his signal was bounced from pirate station to station, reaching his mysterious network of freedom fighters across the country.

"Hello, everybody! My name is Marc Antony, and you are listening to the best station on the radio; the only one that will satisfy you ducky shin-crackers anymore, K-Patriot, 550!" He spoke in rapid, run-on sentences that sometimes exploded in volume without warning. "That's not true. I made it up. Watch the boys in blue and my good old friends the inquestors try to find my signal out there, anyways. You're wasting your time, Inkies, because nobody can find Marc Antony! I'm everywhere! A phantom of the airwaves! No, the only people this guy has his door open to is Tall-Me and Cleo. And guess what? They're in the news again!"

DJMA hummed idly and rustled his papers while he searched for the article he wanted to talk about. "'Rebel Leader Cleo Goes To Trial,' it says. Ouch. The day they nabbed her was a miserable day for the movement! I was so blue, I thought about stringing myself up by my headset, but then I

41

remembered that my sound technician would likely take up my mantle, and he doesn't know jazz from a jingle. Don't worry, folks, Marc Antony will persevere! I must, because who else is going to fight for the music?

"Gotta hand it to 'em, though. That was probably the biggest bust the inquestors ever pulled off. They got a lot of our red brothers and sisters that day, and in typical NAR fashion, they dragged in a lot of innocent bystanders, too. Poor folks that were just in the wrong place at the wrong time. I bet catching Cleo and her crew got someone promoted. Oh, look! They printed an awful picture of her. Cleo is an absolute fox, ladies and gentlemen. Don't let the paper tell you otherwise. She's so smoking hot, so beautiful, so fierce and terrifying, they'd have to doctor these photos in order to make her look bad. Sorry, folks. Ol' Marc's got it bad for Cleo. Anyway, I'm going to move on before I storm the prison myself and bust her out. Next headline... 'Tall-Me Threatens To Destroy Hospital.' Oh, now I doubt that very much. I don't know Tall-Me like *I know Cleo—*"

He lowered his voice to a suggestive purr, which made Amandine and Mrs. White giggle behind their wrists.

"—But I can bet he's not talking about St. James Infirmary. Let me see here..." he paused and mumbled as he scanned the article. "Uh-huh, thought so! The so-called hospital happens to be a disease research facility run by one of those Overcast Krauts. I know this because I have several reliable sources. 'Why, Marc Antony!' you may say. 'You're holed up in a super-secret location! How reliable can your sources be?' Well, I sprung my sources out of the mad scientist's lab myself! Me and Cleo! Well, actually, it was Cleo and her crew who did the springing, while I watched the door and manned the radio. *I am very good at manning the radio,*" he emphasized defensively. "Anyways, at this 'hospital,' they cut into people while they're still awake, torture them, shoot them up full of disease and just when they run out of usefulness, they get propped up in a field like a bunch of leprous scarecrows and used for target practice! Tall-Me is right to make that his next priority. What kind of sicko, blue or not, could do—"

The bell above the door to the shop chimed and Amandine reflexively flicked off the radio.

Mrs. White wiped her hands on a towel before she picked up the extra boxes of chocolate and floated out to greet the customer.

"Welcome! How may I help you?"

Amandine slid off of her perch and peered into the shop where a young man with long, dark hair fumbled with something behind the counter.

"Good afternoon, *madame*. I would like to buy some bread," he said, his voice trickling out in a warm French accent. Its familiar sound reminded Amandine of her mother, and she positioned herself to get a better look at this visitor. "I know it is late in the day, but I'll take whatever you have left. I would also like to pick up the special order for Mrs. Thatch."

"Of course," Mrs. White said cheerfully. "You are welcome to set your parcels on the counter for a moment while we select which breads you like."

43

"Thank you, *madame*." He hefted several large shopping bags onto the counter and managed to get what he was after: his wallet. "I need ten loaves."

"Ten?" Mrs. White repeated, flashing all ten fingers. The young man spoke very clearly, but Amandine supposed that Mrs. White was the kind of person who would inadvertently imitate and belittle anybody with an accent.

"Yes, *madame*. I hope it's not an imposition."

"No, that's good. That will clean us out for the day." Mrs. White beckoned to Amandine, and she carried out the towering order of chocolates.

When he saw the stack of boxes, he took a step back and blinked in surprise. "*Ooh là là.* That's a lot." He chuckled nervously. "I thought when Carmelita said a few boxes— I am sorry, I will have to return for this."

"Nonsense," Mrs. White said, taking the cash and food permit he produced from his wallet. She stamped the permit and handed it back with his change. "My assistant here can help you."

"I would be grateful," the young man said kindly.

Their eyes met, his bright gray to her brown, and Amandine knew in that instant that she liked him very much. Maybe it was just wishful thinking, but it seemed like he was looking at her in the same way. He reminded her of a character from an adventure story, like a pirate or gypsy prince; lean, tanned, and scarred from hard work, and dressed in a hodgepodge of worn, foreign clothing. Despite his humble appearance, he was roguishly handsome. She had never seen anyone like him, but then again, she hadn't seen a young man her age in years either.

"What is your name, *mademoiselle*?"

"Amandine," she replied, bagging the chocolates.

"*Enchanté*." He touched the brim of his beat-up hat. "Amandine, what a beautiful French name you have."

"Thank you." She shook open more bags while Mrs. White filled them with random loaves of bread. "What's yours?"

"René."

"Are you hosting a last-minute dinner party, Mr. René?" The girl nodded at all of his sacks of food.

"It's for my family," he explained. "There are seventeen of us, so I suppose you could say every night is a dinner party."

"Surely you could've recruited a little sister or brother to help you carry all this," Mrs. White put in.

"You know siblings," he smiled. "Some of them would rather starve than help me." He scooped up his packages, and Amandine grabbed the rest. "Thank you for the bread and for lending me this charming helper."

"Please return her in one piece." Mrs. White held the door for them as they tottered out. "I want that apron back."

CHAPTER 3: THE FAMILY

"I am sorry," René said, leading them off the cracked pavement and onto a dirt trail. "I should have mentioned earlier. We need to head out of town a ways."

Amandine's arms quivered from the weight of the bags, but she was determined to carry them by herself. "I don't mind the walk," she said. "I didn't get out much during the war."

"My family had the same problem, but we're happy to be working once again." He managed his load with ease and peered around his groceries at the girl beside him. "So what did you do if you didn't get out?"

"I read a lot," she replied. "I'd sew up just about anything I could get my hands on, too. Didn't want to fall out of practice. I'm from a family of tailors, you see."

"Interesting. I could use a tailor." He kicked his leg out to the side to show her where the hem of his pinstriped trousers ended high above his ankles. "Maybe we could arrange a trade. I am pretty handy. Do you need anything fixed?"

"My bike could have used a proper tune-up this morning," she sighed helplessly. "But it's at the bottom of the river now."

He gave her a curious expression. It wavered for a moment between a smile and a frown as he tried to decide if she was poking fun at him. Finally, he laughed; it was the sunniest, most musical sound she had ever heard.

The more she looked at him, especially now that he was really smiling, the more enamored she became. She decided to outright ask him something she suspected and secretly hoped.

"Excuse me for being frank, but... are you a rebel?"

René's smile faded, though he wasn't shocked or offended. Lightly, he said, "No. Most of my family detests politics. I am a pacifist."

"You mean you have no opinions one way or the other?" she asked.

"Oh, I have opinions. It's just not always safe to express them."

Now it was René's turn to study Amandine. It was unusual and oftentimes dangerous to openly discuss one's opinion of the civil conflict, but she didn't seem like the type to make trouble. She struck him as something innocent and fragile. She was like someone's irreplaceable treasure, hidden away and carefully guarded throughout the war, weakened but otherwise undamaged by dark times. He liked her. He felt drawn to her as one might feel towards a stray kitten, so he thought he'd take a risk and be honest.

"There are good things to be found on each side, but unfortunately there are bad things as well. The NAR gives us order, infrastructure, and food, but at a very high cost. The rebels fight for our total freedom, but it seems that whenever

47

they show up, a lot of innocent people get hurt. What would their success bring so soon after the war? More starvation and unrest? Another Depression? Total anarchy?" Amandine mulled this over, and he went on. "I've met a few rebels in my travels. They only want to do what they feel is right. Do you know any?"

She shook her head.

René changed the subject and indicated the dusty path ahead with a thrust of his chin. "See the clearing just past the trees? That's our camp."

"Camp?" For some reason, Amandine imagined that he lived in a crowded farmhouse or a crumbling family plantation. "What happened to your house?"

"Believe it or not, I am not actually from Pearisville," he teased. "I live on the road."

"You're homeless, too?"

"No, not exactly." He halted mid-step. "Wait. What do mean 'homeless, too?'"

Before she could answer, Amandine saw an enormous woman come hurtling from the treeline. She was globular, likely over four hundred pounds, and her tiny hands fluttered to keep her balance as she ran. Even from this distance, Amandine could see that she was very pretty. Her skin was smooth and pale, which contrasted dramatically with her dark hair set in perfect finger waves. Her dress was violet silk, but much like René's, it was worn and old.

"Oh, hello," René said as she slowed to a halt. "This is *Madame* Carmelita Valentina Coronado Thatch."

"*¡Finalmente!*" Carmelita huffed. "You were gone for so long. I should have sent one of the Russians with you. Those two have been arguing all day, and it's driving me crazy." She touched her dainty wrist to her forehead and swooned, "I need to sit down."

Carmelita plopped down in the grass and beat the air with a lace fan she pulled from her dress front, all the while staring expectantly at René."

"*Madame*, this is Amandine," he said. "She has your order."

Almost as quick as she sat down, Carmelita was up again and reaching for the bags of chocolate. "Thank you, Amandine. You are an angel! *¡Un milagro!*"

"Do you enjoy chocolates, ma'am?" Amandine asked as the woman delved into her first box. She managed to do so quickly but neatly.

"It is not for me," she explained between pieces. "It is for my baby. He has made me crave nothing else, and I've been saving for weeks to get him real chocolate."

"A baby!" Amandine exclaimed. "How wonderful! Congratulations, ma'am."

In truth, she would have never been able to tell that Carmelita was pregnant, but to say so would have been impolite.

Carmelita gathered up all of her boxes and started back towards the trees where she came from. "Excuse me. I have overexerted myself, so I am going home to rest before I faint. It was nice to meet you, *Armandita*."

René chuckled and continued along the path.

"It must be nice to have people from all over the world in your family," Amandine said, reaching up to take some of his bags. "French, Spaniards, Russians..."

"Presently, I am the only Frenchman," he said. "We have some from here in America, Cameroon, Côte d'Ivoire, Mexico, India, and China, too."

Amandine began to understand that his family wasn't the traditional kind. They were nomadic outcasts, picked up from all over the world. Perhaps it was a lonely way to live, never being part of a community, but René didn't seem like the tragic type at all. She concluded that he must live quite an adventurous life.

They arrived at the camp clearing which was surrounded by a variety of colorful, beat-up vehicles. Rusted trucks had their cargo strapped down beneath heavy canvas sheets, and seven travel trailers were arranged like a ring of tiny houses, complete with clotheslines and outdoor furniture. A white tent was set back into the trees, and a temporary kitchen was put up near the central fire pit.

Carmelita collapsed into an extra-wide lawn chair under the shade of her blue trailer. Painted on the side was a caricature of herself and a person who was part man and part woman, split right down the middle. Above the characters, bold lettering read, "ALIVE, JAW-DROPPING HUMAN FREAKS! CARMELITA THE FAT-LADY AND NICK-OLETTE, THE HALF-MAN!"

René led her to the fire pit where two identical men were squatting and bickering about the best way to arrange the kindling. They abandoned their task when they spotted René.

"Russians?" Amandine asked before they reached them.

"Yes. How could you tell?"

She indicated a nearby yellow trailer which featured two fire-juggling clowns and the words, "FROM THE MOSCOW BALLET, ACROBATIC TWINS SASHA AND PIOTR PASTERNAKOV!"

One of the Russians clapped René hard on the back and nearly knocked the paper bags out of his hands. "There is our favorite little errand-boy," he said loudly.

"What took you so long with the food, huh?" shouted the other.

"I bet I can guess what kept him," said the first with a double-tilt of his head in Amandine's direction. They shot each other a conspiratorial look and broke out into wild snickering.

The pair were perfectly identical in every way, from their shaved heads and thick eyebrows that nearly hid their small blue eyes, down to the ragged clothes they wore. Only after watching them for a moment did Amandine finally notice a difference; one had a blurry, gray tattoo of a sailing galleon that showed beneath his shirt, and his brother had a leaping stag.

"You should have gone with him to help, Piotr." Sasha pushed his brother's shoulder. "You see what trouble René gets up to when he's on his own."

"I was washing the pots," Piotr snapped, striking him in return.

"No, *I* washed the pots! You sit there like an idiot while I always do the work!"

51

René saw an opportunity to escape when they started arguing and shoving each other again. He maneuvered around them, completely forgotten, and set the groceries on the scarred kitchen table.

While Amandine arranged the grocery bags, she stole a few curious glances at each trailer. The camp was cozy, tidy, and except for the three others, it appeared to be empty.

"Where is everyone?" she asked.

"They are probably out in the forest or in their trailers." René dusted his hands and stretched his aching arms. "You usually won't see anyone until they smell dinner."

There was a pause, filled with the sounds of the forest and two simultaneous, bilingual tirades. Amandine turned to leave, but something made her want to take her time.

"Well, it was nice to meet you, René," she said, taking small steps backwards. "I had better get on back to the bakery."

"Please stay," René insisted, and she leaped to his side again. "That is, please stay for a few moments longer. I have a few specific orders to deliver around camp and could use some help." He rummaged through the shopping bags until he found what he needed. "Follow me and perhaps you can see what traveling life is like."

He walked across the camp towards a black delivery truck which had no caricatures, only serious gold lettering that read, "ANTONIO CORONADO, MASTER OF ILLUSION." René knocked on the side and peered into the cab, but the illusionist was nowhere to be found.

"*Señor?*" he called.

A loud bang ripped through the air, sending birds bursting from the trees, and René made his way further into the forest towards the sound. A mysterious, handsome gentleman in a fine tuxedo stood at the edge of a creek below, scowling at something above him.

"Antonio!" René slipped on the grass as he hurried down the slope. "What in the world are you doing?"

"Just the man I need," Coronado mumbled, running his hand over his black, silver-streaked hair. "René, your timing is impeccable. My damn bird won't come down from that tree." He glared at the reluctant dove, hand outstretched, and commanded, "*¡Ven aquí!*"

"You can't practice with doves *and* gunpowder." René rolled up his sleeves and lifted himself up into the lowest branches. "The ladies were mortified after the last time they did your laundry. Speaking of ladies, meet my new friend Amandine. She has your order."

Coronado frowned at the girl, but she didn't let his cold nature bother her. She presented all three packages, not knowing which was his. He chose the second one with the pharmacy label, and hefted it several times before he pocketed it.

"This does not feel sufficient," he complained.

René leapt down, white dove in hand. "The medicine was at the pharmacy, but the chemicals you wanted are still controlled substances. I get a lot of unwanted attention when I ask for them, you know." He handed the bird to Coronado, and it vanished with a flourish from its master. "I suppose the NAR is worried about rebels making bombs."

"I am not making bombs." Coronado headed back up the hill, and the other two turned to follow. "I am working on something for the festival. I want a new display that will put people on the edge of their seats."

"It makes sense now," Amandine chimed in. "You're all with a circus!"

Her comment made Coronado freeze. He whirled on her and leaned in so close that she could smell wine and sulfur on him.

"I don't work for a circus, *señorita*," he growled. "I am not some card-flicking magician. I am a *master* of illusion! What I do could keep you up at night, wondering how in the name of heaven I have achieved the impossible. I was a headlining act across Europe! I performed for kings and sold-out crowds!"

"Easy, Antonio." René wedged himself between them. "I never told her who we are. Who *you* are. I am sure she got that idea from the Russians."

He huffed and stormed back towards his truck, coat tails fluttering behind him. "Have they started dinner yet?"

"If they'll ever stop fighting," René rolled his eyes.

Coronado cast the back doors of his truck open wide, revealing shelves upon shelves of miscellaneous boxes and multicolored glass bottles that tinkled together when he climbed inside. It resembled a cluttered little apothecary with a cot and trunk squeezed into the back corner. He tossed out two empty birdcages to René.

"Clean these, won't you?"

"Certainly." René didn't clean them so much as he shook them out and scraped out the soiled newspaper lining with a stick.

Once he'd put his parcel away, the illusionist emerged from his truck again with a palmful of change. The young man passed the cages back and accepted his tip from Coronado with a nod of thanks.

René divided the change in half and gave Amandine a share before continuing on to the white tent at the head of the camp. As they passed the fire again, she noticed the Russians had started chopping vegetables but decided to settle their argument with a game of five-finger fillet instead.

They stopped at the tent's red carpet door, and René ran his hand across the copper wind chime that hung outside.

"Marmi?" he called. "I'm back."

"Come in, René," said a deep voice from within. "We're all finished here."

Suddenly the door whipped open, and a furious little woman blocked the way. "No! You can't come in until I'm done!" She smeared the makeup that pooled beneath her wet pear-green eyes, and she sized up Amandine. "Who's the fuddy-duddy?" Without waiting for a response, she disappeared back inside.

"Is that Marmi?" Amandine whispered. After her last introduction, she didn't want to accidentally offend anybody again.

"That's Sangria Groviglio, our contortionist." René held the heavy oriental rug aside and ushered her in. "*This* is Marmi."

If Amandine imagined René as a gypsy prince, then there was no doubt that Marmi was the queen. Wearing many colorful robes, her cocoa skin was ornamented with a hundred chains, beads, and faux gems from her headscarf to her bare feet. She was lounging in a folding chair with a smoldering pipe in hand, holding an air of wisdom and authority, though her age was difficult to guess.

Amandine marveled at her exotic beauty and wondered if her facial piercings hurt very much.

Sangria paced the dusty carpet floor. She was petite, lean, muscular as a cat, and curiously, she seemed to be dressed in only her underwear. "Why can't I be in the festival show?" she demanded, completely ignoring Amandine and René's presence.

Marmi played with the smoke that floated from her pipe and spoke in a peculiar English accent. "I never said you couldn't. You have yet to show me how your act can be incorporated into it. I don't see anything new, Sangria. You will remain a freak-act until you can either cooperate with the others or show me something new."

Sangria let out a sound between a snarl and a sob. René put a hand on her bare shoulder, but she promptly shrugged him off.

"Don't touch me, you moron!"

He backed off respectfully and held out her parcel that contained several glossy fashion magazines. Sangria snatched them up and stormed out of the tent.

"Just where do you think you're going?" Marmi snapped. "René isn't your personal slave. Pay him what he's due."

Sangria yanked her purse out of the front of her corset. She threw several coins at him and fled the tent with her hands over her face. "I'm not a freak," she muttered miserably. "I should be the star."

They listened to her light footsteps retreat before Marmi released a heavy sigh. "I apologize." She rubbed her temples, which sent stacks of bangles sliding down her slender arm. "Sangria ought to know how to behave herself when we have guests."

"This is Amandine." René made introductions again while he picked up the change from the dirt. "She works at the bakery and helped me carry everything back."

"A pleasure, ma'am." Amandine felt it necessary to curtsy in Marmi's imposing presence.

"Welcome, child." The matriarch showed a gold tooth at the back of her soft, white smile. "I am Madame Marmi. I hope René tipped you for your assistance."

"Yes, ma'am," she answered.

"Very good. Please bring me my order."

René handed her a brown paper sack that had been stamped with the name of a tobacconist. Amandine placed it on the folding table at Marmi's side, all the while feeling the strangely heavy weight of the matriarch's gaze.

"I sense something about you, child. You seem... uprooted. You don't live here." Marmi gestured in the general direction of Pearisville.

"No, ma'am," she answered politely. "Just passing through."

"I see." Marmi continued to study her with narrowed, yellow eyes. "But you're traveling alone. You don't even have any siblings."

Amandine wondered how Marmi could have possibly known that. "No, ma'am. I don't have anyone except for my mother anymore, and she's all the way up in Nieuwestad."

The woman shook her head, jewelry chiming. "This is most unsafe." She jabbed emphatically at the door with her pipe. "Sangria tried to make it alone, but she came to us in awful shape. Goodness knows the horrors she endured on the road. It was very fortunate that we found her."

"And we were very fortunate that she could play the violin and tie herself into a knot," René put in kindly. "She's an excellent performer, and she pulls in the most money."

"Indeed," Marmi took a long draw from her slender pipe. "If you're determined to get to Nieuwestad, you had better find a way to get there quickly, child." She jerked her chin down once with finality.

"Yes, ma'am," Amandine agreed. "That is why I'm working now— to pay my way."

"It's a shame she can't work her trade on the road," René spoke up suddenly. "She tells me that she's an expert dressmaker from a family of tailors. Just look at how well-maintained her old clothes are. They are probably older than she is."

He looked straight into her eyes for the briefest moment; Amandine blushed. Nobody had ever looked at her that way before, and she didn't know what it meant.

"Your skills are wasted on delivery errands," he said, smiling.

Marmi let a puff of smoke escape her nose. "A tailor, you say." She stared into the cloud and raised a ringed eyebrow as if it had told her something interesting. "*A costumer, perhaps.*"

"Yes, ma'am. I learned to sew from my father before the war."

There was a pause while Marmi repacked her pipe with new tobacco and lit it again. This time, her golden stare bore into René.

René tried a bolder approach. "Perhaps she could come with us. As you said, it is very dangerous for a young lady to travel alone."

"René hasn't yet told you about what we do here," Marmi said, changing the subject.

"No, ma'am." Amandine noticed that Marmi had a peculiar way of never asking any questions. "And Mister Coronado got angry when I said you were a circus."

Marmi let out a low, throaty laugh. "Perhaps we were once, many years ago. We used to have so many performers, and we traveled all over the world. These days, I'm afraid we have been reduced to little more than a mud show." She absently picked at the fringe on her purple sash.

"I am sorry, *madame*. This may not be the best time to bring this up, but..." René pulled a folded piece of paper from his pocket and showed it to Marmi. "I found this still tacked to a post in town. Johnstone was here two weeks ago."

Marmi glanced at the sign once and made a noise of disgust. "So that louse is headed to Nieuwestad, too."

She thrust the paper at Amandine. It was a full-color poster for a different traveling show. A jolly showmaster had his arms spread wide over a line of posing showgirls while a row of monsters at the bottom of the page reached up from the shadows.

"He's our competition," René explained.

"Oh, I would hardly call him competition." Marmi gnawed on her pipe. "He's a crook. His shows are nothing but lights and half-naked girls."

"Naked girls?" Amandine gasped. "Why would anybody take an obscene act to the capital city?"

"For the festival?" René tilted his head. "You know, the Freedom Festival? It's been all over the papers and the radio."

Amandine had never heard of it, but she nodded anyway. She believed that DJMA would rather chew tacks than promote anything like the Freedom Festival on his station.

Marmi went on. "The Freedom Festival in Nieuwestad is an official celebration of the end of the war overseas. They are calling for performers of all sorts, and I have secured us the stage in the city center on the second day. We need fresh ideas for a bigger, better presentation. Although I ultimately make the decisions about what gets put into the show, Coronado is in charge. He has been working most diligently with René to improve the colored lights and invent some new fire-tricks."

René beamed.

"We certainly need a seamstress, but I can't afford to take on just anyone," she concluded. "You will have to prove your skill."

"I can draw, cut, and sew a dress in a single day," Amandine exclaimed, overjoyed by the thought of working and traveling with company. "I promise, you won't be disappointed!"

"I will decide," Marmi said with a dismissive wave of her hand. "Come back later tonight, child."

They left the tent, and René grinned from ear to ear. "Pardon me for putting you out like that," he said. "But I am so glad you accepted. We haven't had a proper costumer in years."

Sangria appeared from the other side of the tent where she had been eavesdropping and pointed an accusing finger at René. "I see *exactly* what you're up to! Marmi is off her cob for letting you have your way." She turned her finger on Amandine. "And you! You don't know what you're getting yourself into."

Amandine shook her head. "You're right. I don't. It will be a new experience, that's for certain."

Sangria glowered. "Anybody ever tell you that that optimism makes you sound like a dummy?"

"I love her optimism," René said, giving the contortionist a condescending pat on the head. She swatted his hand away. "Between Marmi's worries and Antonio's... *creative blockage*, I think it's just the attitude we need to get this show rolling."

"And where do you expect to keep her?" Sangria sniffed, scrutinizing the newcomer. "I doubt she comes with her own trailer."

René shrugged. "*Chérie*, you know that is Marmi's decision. She will choose a trailer that still has space."

Sangria's face fell in horror. "No! I won't stand for it! She's not staying with me!"

René smirked and returned to their guest. "I am sure your employer is expecting you. You had better hurry back, but please join us for dinner." He checked his pockets. "Did I already split the tips?"

"Yes, thank you," Amandine nodded.

He handed her another coin. "This is from me personally. Thank you for—" He stopped as if he had forgotten why Amandine was there.

"For the groceries?" she guessed.

René took off his hat and absently preened the red feather tucked into the band. "I was going to say, 'for your company.'"

"Yes, I'm sure her conversations were riveting," Sangria grumbled. "Now get lost, Raggedy Ann."

Amandine thanked René again and made her way back to town with a feeling of exhilaration swelling in her chest. She wanted to cheer but knew that wouldn't be proper since Sangria and René were still within earshot. Instead, she looked across the camp again with a new perspective; this was going to be her new, temporary home. Just as René has said, more people appeared the closer it got to dinnertime. There was another pair of tall and muscular men with beautiful midnight skin, speaking French and rearranging heavy stage equipment into a storage truck. A woman covered from neck to ankles in tattoos sat alone by the fire, smoking a cigarette and reading the newspaper.

Nobody paid attention to Amandine as she left the camp, counting her tip. She had earned nearly a dollar, which was a generous amount for such a little job. She added a bounce to her step, thinking of how her fortune was already taking a turn for the better.

When Amandine returned to the bakery, the sign had been turned to "CLOSED," but the door had been left unlocked, so she let herself in without setting off the bell. She was about to call out when she heard Mrs. White's voice coming from the kitchen.

"—no idea if she's touched or just naive. Everybody knows that rebel collaborators are considered traitors of the worst kind, and to be suspected of treason is just as bad as being guilty in the eyes of an inquestor."

"If Caroline Stewart really went into the Prison of War Criminals, then the only way she's coming out again is for public execution," said a man's voice. Amandine assumed that it was Mr. White, returned from his errands.

Amandine peered into the kitchen and saw the Whites leaning over the kneading table. Mrs. White looked sad. "But the poor thing has no place to go."

"That's what replacement homes are for," he said gruffly, shutting down her request before she even asked it.

"The girl would be safer there than on the road where she might cross paths with dangerous vagrants who might try to take advantage of her. There's no telling what a crooked cop or a bored inquestor might do, either. You ought to give her their address and—"

"I'm back," Amandine said, jangling the doorbell.

"There you are," Mrs. White exclaimed. She nudged her husband's arm and said, "This is the Stewart girl I hired to help with the big order."

Mr. White had his ledger open in front of him, and he acknowledged the girl with a single nod.

"I was afraid Casanova had whisked you away," Mrs. White said with a wink.

Amandine tugged on her necklace, embarrassed that her infatuation was so obvious. "In a way he did, ma'am."

"How do you mean?" she asked with sudden suspicion.

"I think I will join his family on their way to Nieuwestad. His... er, Marmi said it was dangerous for a girl to be traveling alone."

"Well, she's right about that," Mrs. White agreed. She gave Amandine a rag in a small, soapy bucket, and the girl pretended not to see the wide-eyed looks that the bakers shot each other while she cleaned the kitchen. "So, this young man's mother will look after you?"

"Yes, ma'am. She said I could earn my keep if I make them some new clothes. The war didn't leave them with much."

When Amandine finished cleaning the kitchen, Mr. White passed her two silver coins. "That's five hours' work at forty cents an hour," he said curtly. "Your pay for today is two dollars."

"Thank you, sir." She put away the last few baking sheets and added the money to her earnings from René. "Mrs. White, may I ask a favor?"

"Yes, sugar?"

"Could I trouble you for a cheese sandwich before I go?"

Mr. White looked after his wife imploringly. "Me too?"

"I don't know what it is about these sandwiches." She sighed and pulled several pieces of sliced bread from a cellophane bag. "You'll both spoil your dinner."

"This might be my last chance to enjoy my favorite snack," Amandine said brightly. "I'm sure they have cheese sandwiches up in Nieuwestad, but it won't be a *White's* cheese sandwich."

The baker's prickly temperament melted away at this and he smiled at the girl. "Did you know that Grandma White made these for us kids everyday after school?"

"You don't say," Amandine chirped. "I used to get them everyday after school, too!"

"I know my cousin sold these cheap to get rid of old bread." Mr. White watched his wife apply the condiments with a frown. "More mayonnaise, please. Perhaps we ought to start selling them here, too. Get an afterschool crowd of our own."

"These won't pull in an afterschool crowd," Mrs. White exclaimed. "*It's just bread and cheese!*"

"Bah. You just haven't learned to appreciate the delicious simplicity." Mr. White fondly pecked his wife on the temple. "Ask the girl. She'll tell you."

Amandine nodded in agreement. While she waited, a thought crossed her mind. "I was curious about something, ma'am. Have you seen any traveling shows in town recently?"

"Why, yes." She brandished her butterknife at her husband when he reached over her shoulder to recenter the cheese. "There was a show last night, but we missed it. We did see a rather interesting dance performance here almost two weeks ago, didn't we?"

"That's right," Mr. White nodded, locking their money in the safe beneath the counter. He struggled with it for a moment, and that was when Amandine finally noticed that Mr. White only had one arm.

"It was very new and different," she continued. "The music had a real rhythm that made you want to dance."

"Like jazz?" Amandine knew that Mrs. White was talking about Marmi's rival.

"No." She shot a stern look at the girl. "Nobody plays jazz. It's illegal."

Amandine smiled apologetically. "Something else, then?"

"Yes, it had a very heavy beat, like *bump-bump-cha-bump*. I didn't even realize that I was dancing until I accidentally knocked the popcorn out of Nathaniel's's hand. The performances were not very good. Nobody seemed very

66

enthusiastic, but the music was exciting. If this music were on the radio, I wouldn't get any work done. I would dance all day."

She handed out the cheese sandwiches. Mr. White finished his in four quick bites and smiled in gratitude as he wiped his hand on his apron.

"Thank you for the sandwich. And thank you for letting me work here today." Amandine put on her coat and picked up her suitcase.

"Be safe, Miss Stewart," the baker said. "And good luck."

She waved to the couple behind her, and the door chimed brightly again.

Outside, the sun was setting and the air was beginning to cool. Amandine could smell fires burning, which rekindled memories of better times at home. That reminded her of the reason she came to Pearisville in the first place, so she scanned the streets for a mailbox until she spotted one on the corner near the grocer's.

She pressed the envelope to her heart and thought of Caroline. Amandine hoped her mother was comfortable in prison and that a letter would bring her a little cheer if she was feeling lonesome. With a kiss to the wrinkled paper, she dropped the letter in the mailbox and trotted back down the road out of town.

It was twilight when she reached the camp partially hidden in the trees. She could see that a number of people were sitting around the fire, but outside of the circle near the road, a lone silhouetted figure played a resonator guitar.

René set the instrument down as soon as he saw her trotting up the path. "There you are." He took her suitcase for her. "You are just in time for dinner."

"You weren't waiting for me, were you?" she teased. "Why aren't you with the others?"

"Nobody likes my guitar-playing," he lied. He wiped his hair sheepishly and suddenly Amandine's infatuation didn't feel quite so embarrassing.

They entered the camp again, only this time, everyone stared. All together, they were an odd group of bizarre and foreign appearance. Aside from the people she had met already, she saw a diverse cluster of women, a thin man, a little person that she momentarily mistook for a child, an extremely hairy fellow, and a man in a ruffled blouse. René invited the girl to sit in a chair near Coronado and went to get her some dinner.

The illusionist was sitting alone at a folding table, thumbing through a notebook with a glass of wine in hand. He had changed out of his tuxedo into more comfortable clothes in somber colors, yet he still looked exceptionally sharp for someone who spent most of his time outdoors. He regarded Amandine with the same coldness.

"So you're here to stay, eh?"
"Yes, sir."

He lit a cigarette and asked through his teeth, "You do men's clothing?"

Amandine assumed that René had already spread the word about her purpose. "Yes, sir. That was my father's specialty, but I know a thing or two myself."

René reappeared with a bowl of stew, a cup of water, and a chunk of bread. Coronado laughed when he handed it to her, but the sound was laden with disparagement.

"Something funny?" René sat on the ground and plucked a jaunty melody on his guitar.

"How are you supposed to eat without your bowl?"

"I didn't think she had her own yet."

Coronado shook his head, amused. "And I suppose if she didn't bring her own tent, you'd share yours as well?"

"Nonsense." He kicked dirt in the illusionist's direction. "That's Sangria's job."

Meanwhile, the contortionist sat across the fire, staring at Amandine with a combination of disgust and fear.

Marmi was seated furthest from the food, slightly elevated from the others by the gentle incline of the ground. Her ornaments clinked like raindrops on glass when she stood at her impressive height of six feet.

"Everyone," she called out. "I would like you to meet our new seamstress. She will stay on with us from now until we reach Nieuwestad." She extended a hand towards Amandine, who quickly swallowed what she was eating and waved politely. "Tell everyone your name, child."

"My name is Amandine Stewart, and I'll be making your costumes." She heard Coronado grumble something about "*nothing but tattered rags to wear,*" so she added, "And regular clothes! I can make those, too."

Marmi nodded to René. "You have already met our stagehand. He can build, repair, and assist with anything that you require. Since I am busy preparing for the festival, please go to him before you come to me. Also—" She pointed to Sangria, who shrank back in her chair. "That is Sangria. You will be sharing her trailer."

The contortionist gripped her bowl and moaned in protest.

Marmi ignored her tantrum. "You can meet the others in your own time. Enjoy your supper, then get settled in right away. We leave early tomorrow."

Amandine nodded and tucked into her bowl. It was more food than she had eaten in years, and it tasted delicious. Tender meat, sweet carrots, onions, and buttery potatoes filled her with a warm feeling of comfort that only a hearty meal could provide. She returned her empty bowl to René while she chewed her bread.

He refilled his bowl for himself and plopped back onto the ground again. "Tell me," he said, using the back of his guitar as a table. "What do you need to start working on costumes?"

Coronado tapped on a blank page in his notebook with his pencil. "What makes you think I'd entrust such an important part of the new show to this girl? How do we know if she's any good when we haven't seen a *stitch* of proof?"

"Well," Amandine disregarded the grumpy illusionist. "I can sew fast enough by hand, but it would be much quicker if I had a machine."

"Purchasing an expensive electric machine is out of the question," Coronado exclaimed. "We'd have to hook it up to the generator, and the cost of fuel alone would—"

"I will see what I can come up with," René cut him off and gave him a wide-eyed look in warning. He didn't want the illusionist's attitude to leave a poor first impression on the girl, and fortunately, Coronado relented. He returned to his wine glass with a scoff.

Now that she was full, Amandine realized that she also felt very tired. She looked across the fire for Sangria, but the contortionist had vanished.

"She probably escaped to her trailer," Coronado said, following her gaze to the empty chair. "Needed to defend it from foreign invaders, I'd imagine."

"Come on." René stood up with his bowl in his hand. "We'll make sure she lets you in."

"I'm not going anywhere," Coronado growled. "I'm going to have another glass of wine while I finish my notes."

"That reminds me," René said, shaking his spoon. "I think I may have found a solution to our pyrotechnic problem."

"Really? And this solution, it came to you just now, did it?"

"Help me escort Amandine to her new trailer, and I will show you how I think we can get that display you wanted." He turned and started walking, shoveling stew into his mouth. "And birds!" he added with his mouth full. "It will be like a phoenix rising from the ashes with a flick of your wrist."

Coronado sighed, shut his notebook, and followed René while Amandine trotted behind.

Sangria's home was an old shepherd's hut, painted dark red with a depiction of a sultry, long-haired woman holding a violin in her lap. René knocked a cheerful cadence on the door.

"Sangria! *Ma chérie, s'il vous plaît*, open the door. Our new seamstress is out here, and she would like to share this cozy trailer with you."

"It *is* quite lovely," Amandine murmured, admiring the empty, painted flower box that was tacked beneath a clouded yellow window.

A shadow appeared at the door, and Sangria shouted, "I just spoke with Margaret and as it turns out, the other girls will be taking her in their trailer instead."

"Whatever you say," René shrugged. "Amandine, you will like Margaret. She's like a big sister to all of us, and she will make sure that you are comfortable." He winked at her, cleared his throat and said loudly, "Come on, *señor*. Let's introduce Amandine to her new roommates."

Suddenly, there came a small crash from within followed by shuffling, scraping, and the lock finally turning.

Sangria leaned in the doorway, examining her red nails with her small hips thrust out to one side. She wore a lacy nightdress beneath a black kimono and her long hair was let down to her waist. "Oh, Mister Coronado, you're here as well? How nice it is to see you."

"Sangria," was his disinterested reply.

René nudged the illusionist. "Antonio is here because he was truly concerned that his new friend settles in comfortably. Isn't that right, *señor*?"

"Nothing could concern me more," he sighed, impatient with René's little game.

The contortionist mirrored his sigh and gave her hair a casual toss. "Well, you know, sometimes Margaret smokes in the trailer. It's terribly unsafe and the smell will never get out of your clothes. Perhaps the dressmaker should stay with me. I think I might have some room on the floor."

Amandine didn't realize that she was supposed to respond. Sangria sighed even louder and dragged Amandine inside.

"*Fantastico.* I hope everybody's happy now." Coronado patted his pockets in search of a match for the unlit cigarette that dangled from his lips. René raised his hand, flicked the air, and the end of Coronado's cigarette magically flared to life.

The illusionist stared dumbfounded at the flame.

"How did you *do* that?"

"I told you I worked out a solution," René laughed. "I was lying about the birds, though." He let Coronado roll up his sleeve and examine every inch of his arms. As Coronado tugged him away to better study him in the light, René called out, "It seems we have a bit of work to do before we turn in. Good night, ladies!"

73

With that, the men were gone, and Sangria slammed the door behind them.

The wagon was tiny. It would have been cramped for a single person, but it had been adapted to fit two. Two beds, one above the other, made up a large portion of the back of the trailer. There was also a vanity table, barely wider than her lap, opposite a small wood stove and some storage space which contained piles upon piles of clothes.

Sangria sat on the bottom bed and brushed her hair while Amandine went for the top. The bed was made up with plump pillows and a dark patchwork quilt. Amandine was glad for this because she hadn't thought to bring any bedding of her own.

"Get off," Sangria hissed. "You sleep on the floor."

Amandine stopped and sat cross-legged on the mat in front of the pot-belly stove.

"For a dressmaker, you sure don't dress very well," Sangria hounded her. "You look like a flapper. Those clothes look like they might have been popular twenty or thirty years ago."

"They were," Amandine replied. "They belonged to my mother and were the only clothes left in the house that fit me." She smoothed the material of her ocean blue dress with pride. For such an old garment, it still served her well. "I admit, I didn't go out much during the war. I didn't realize that it had become fashionable to wear your underwear out in public."

"I don't wear my underwear out in public." Sangria clutched her kimono closed over her chest. "That was my costume. I have to wear something that won't restrict my movement."

Amandine pulled off her dress and stockings. She changed for the night into a simple white shift and covered herself with her father's jacket. She tried to settle in as comfortably as she could, but her suitcase was a poor substitute for a pillow, and she could still feel the knotted wood floor through the thin rug.

"Speaking of performances, I heard that you want to be the star of the festival show," Amandine said, attempting some friendly conversation.

"I can't imagine what you would know about our show, but you heard right. And I will be." She pitched her hairbrush into the vanity and slammed the drawer. "It's my only hope of ever getting out of this dump."

"What's stopping you?"

Sangria hesitated. She didn't want to divulge too much to the girl that she had already decided was her enemy, but just as Amandine had suspected, Sangria loved nothing more than talking about herself.

"Marmi is what's stopping me. She hates my act, but I don't know what she expects. I'm just as good a dancer as the other girls. Better, even. I've been trained my whole life."

"Perhaps it's the presentation itself, then."

"What in the world are you talking about?"

Amandine rolled onto her side and propped herself up on one arm while her roommate climbed into bed. "The spectacle. The display that captivates audiences. My father always told me '*Apparel oft proclaims the man*.'"

"I don't follow your meaning. I work hard to look my best, and I don't think my act can possibly be improved upon."

"You *are* beautiful," Amandine agreed. "Which makes me wonder why the wall outside is billing you as the 'Knot Freak.'"

Sangria winced. "I asked René to paint off the 'freak' part."

"Well, I think that with a few dramatic, inexpensive changes, you can become something else. Take the 'freak' part out of your show, and you could be the 'Love Knot.' An unobtainable object of attention and desire. A fantasy. An impossibility."

Amandine could tell that she had Sangria's attention.

"I know you don't want me here, but if you give me the chance to help you, I promise that the next time you talk to Marmi, she will make you a part of the new show."

Sangria hesitated. It sounded too good to be true. "How long would that take?"

Amandine twiddled her thumbs. "To make a whole new costume? Two hours, maybe."

There was a silence. Amandine knew that Sangria was considering her idea because she hadn't turned the lamp off yet.

Finally, she said, "So, theoretically, you can change my stage persona tonight?"

"Yes, but I can't do much without anything to work with. No fabric, lace, ribbons, make-up, nothing." Amandine sighed, and suddenly realized what she was doing. She was manipulating Sangria much like René did.

"I have some!" Sangria blurted. "Let's make a deal. You give me something to show Marmi in the morning before we leave, and I might be able to free up a bed for you."

Amandine shrugged. "I could use some place to unpack my things as well."

Sangria leaped out of bed and turned out a dresser drawer that was brimming with lacy underwear. "Is that good?"

Amandine sat up and stretched her arms over her head. "Delightful. This will also be a perfect opportunity to show Marmi what I am capable of." She threw her coat on over her shift and examined the clothes on the floor. "Alright, you said complete freedom of movement is necessary in your performance. You already have the right idea: less is best, but we really can't have you prancing around in your underwear anymore."

CHAPTER 4: THE COSTUME

The camp gradually came alive with the sun. After a comfortable night's sleep, Amandine stepped out into the morning chill in search of breakfast. She found Sasha tending the fire, sitting on a jerry can and drinking coffee from a tin cup.

"*Dobroye utro, shveyachka.*" He waved at her with his fire-poking stick. She noticed that he was dressed in only patched trousers and an undershirt.

"Aren't you cold?" Amandine shivered. Her brown crepe dress had no warmth to it at all, and she pulled her coat around herself a little more tightly.

"Russians never get cold," he boasted. He poured more coffee from the large kettle into his cup and held it out to her. "Coffee, *shveyachka*? It will help warm you."

"Thank you." She briefly considered asking for cream and sugar, but then thought better of it. Sipping the bitter brew, she asked, "Tell me, what does '*shveyachka*' mean?"

"In English?" He scratched his shaved head. "It means 'little lady who makes the clothes.'"

Just as Amandine decided that she liked her new nickname, a group of women appeared at the fireside. All four were wrapped in embroidered shawls and started ladling steaming oatmeal into their bowls.

"*Dobroye utro, damy!*" Sasha cried, but they mostly ignored him. "You will enjoy my special porridge. Piotr wasn't here to ruin it this time."

"What's so special about it?" the tattooed woman asked in a drowsy monotone.

Sasha went to where a damp dish towel was sitting on the kitchen table. With a theatrical flourish, he flicked it aside and revealed a bowl full of freshly rinsed wild raspberries. The ladies murmured in delight and picked the biggest, brightest berries to add to their oatmeal.

Sasha tugged on his suspenders proudly and beckoned. "*Lyuda*, bring everyone to meet the new girl."

Blowing and carefully nibbling spoonfuls of hot oats, the women came over to where Amandine was standing.

"*Schveyachka*, may I introduce the most beautiful ballerina to ever get kicked out of *Ballets Russes* and my future wife, Ludmilla Fedorovna Snizhenova."

"Lies. Every word," she said with a smile. Ludmilla was a wisp-like woman with white-blonde hair and small, pointed features. Her legs were incredibly long, and her movements were so graceful that she seemed weightless. She extended a hand with rosy fingertips, and Amandine was surprised when she shook her hand with a monstrously strong grip. She indicated the others with a graceful *port de bras*. "This is Margaret Mulryan. She is American, like you."

Margaret was the tattooed woman Amandine had noticed the day before. Her copper hair was set in rollers and a snarling dragon slithered out of the top of her slouchy men's sweater. She plucked her cigarette out of her mouth and mumbled, "Hullo."

"Margaret's a freak-act like Sangria and Carmelita," Ludmilla explained. "She got all of her tattoos from her last job."

"Made tea for an ink parlor," Margaret said before Amandine asked.

"She shares a trailer with Chitra Puri," Ludmilla went on, introducing another. "She's a dancer from Bombay."

"Good morning." Chitra's soft accent was like a stone dropping into still water. Her round face was the color of cinnamon, and her dark hair was braided into a rope that hung down to her hips. Amandine noted that although Chitra was wearing a traditional green saree and a gold ring in her nose, she wore an old blouse and trousers beneath.

"Finally, this is May Song from Shanghai. We share that pink trailer over there." Ludmilla pointed to their home, which had caricatures of the two dancing over blue chrysanthemums painted over it.

May said nothing. She dipped her head to acknowledge the introduction, but kept her dark eyes solemnly downcast at her worn cotton pants. Amandine wondered if she was a mute or only very shy. She stood with her hair hanging like a straight, black curtain in front of her face, bent over and frozen, until the conversation continued without her.

Sasha threw a thick arm around Ludmilla's shoulders. In a stage-whisper, he said, "I noticed that *shveyachka* doesn't have any dishes to take her meals with. Do you suppose you could...?"

Ludmilla nodded and pushed her own enamel bowl and spoon into Amandine's hands.

"I can't take your breakfast," Amandine exclaimed.

"Take it," Ludmilla insisted. "Keep it until you get your own. I have another set. You are one of us now, and it is important that you understand that we are family. Even with her awful attitude, we consider Sangria our sister."

Sasha hooked Ludmilla around the waist this time, drawing her even closer. She tolerated his attentions with a weary smile. "And I am Papa, and you are Mama!"

Just then, Piotr returned from washing in the creek, and he slapped his brother repeatedly until he released the ballerina. "*Lyuda maya*, is this man bothering you?"

Sasha's retort was cut off when he noticed something across the camp, and his face screwed up in confusion. The others turned to see what was wrong.

Sangria had emerged, dressed in the improvised costume Amandine had made the night before. Her hair was chopped short in a severe straight bob, and her face was painted with bold kumadori makeup. She wore a striped corset with the bones removed and the front cut out in the shape of a heart, baring her stomach. The rest of her limbs were wrapped in scraps of black lace, mesh, ribbons, and her shadowy new look was completed with a pair of gloves and ballet slippers.

Sangria approached the group coolly and gave a little turn, posing against the kitchen table like a pin-up model.

When her presence was met with stunned silence, she jerked her shoulders up and demanded, "*Well?*"

"It would look better at night with stage lighting," Amandine blurted.

Everyone turned their bewildered faces back to her, so she hurried to explain.

"I made that. I thought of Japanese kabuki theater for her makeup, and I wanted to do something seductive and a little scary. Let's face it, the way she can bend is a little of both." When no one responded, she nervously exclaimed, "It's for her festival audition!"

Chitra spoke first in a hushed, worried tone. "What will Marmi say?"

"That's exactly what I intend to find out." With a lift of her chin, Sangria sashayed off to Marmi's tent.

Amandine drummed her nails onto the side of her bowl for a few seconds before she timidly asked, "So… do you like it?"

"*Shveyachka,*" Ludmilla beamed. "When can you start on *our* costumes?"

Inside the white tent, Marmi dropped her pipe in disbelief. She leaned forward in her chair with her fingers laced over her mouth as she watched Sangria demonstrate her movements in her new costume, doing complete backbends, splits and even sitting on her own head. All the while, nobody spoke until the wind chime jangled.

"Marmi! I have your tea," René called out. He backed through the door carefully, guarding the tray he carried, but he nearly dropped it in astonishment when he finally turned around and saw somebody coiled like a snake on the floor.

It took him quite a while before he finally recognized the other person in the tent as Sangria. She had become something darker, more sinister, and yet so captivating. René couldn't understand it; the only thing that had changed was her clothes, but there was something different in her eyes as well. She turned her stare up at him, and her red lips curled with newfound confidence and triumph. That look made René's stomach turn, and he suddenly wanted to leave.

Setting the tray at Marmi's side, he picked up her pipe from the carpet and said, "If that is all, *madame*, I will make sure everyone is ready to move out." Without waiting for a response, he made a hasty exit from the tent.

Once he was outside, René scanned the camp for Amandine. He saw the dancers heading back towards their trailers, knocking on doors to wake the others as they passed. Piotr was tasting the oatmeal that Sasha made and promptly spit it out, earning a bombardment of insults. Carmelita was making her customary morning shuffle for the privacy of the trees. Finally, he spotted Amandine sitting on the steps of her trailer, eating her breakfast and looking over some notes she had taken in a leatherbound blue journal.

When she saw him nearly running to her, Amandine felt a rush that warmed her insides quicker than the cup of coffee. Giddy, she asked, "Where's the fire, René?"

He fumbled for words before he finally said, "You did that to Sangria, didn't you?"

The girl blushed and poked at her oatmeal until the raspberries left pink streaks in the bowl.

"Aha!" René exclaimed. "I knew there was something special about you! I knew it the moment I saw you!" He pointed excitedly to the head of the camp. "I was just in the tent with Marmi, and she is either just as amazed as I am by her transformation... or very angry. But I don't really think she is angry."

Just then, Sangria rushed past them. She barely avoided colliding with Amandine as she dove inside and slammed the door so hard that it shook the entire trailer.

Just then, Marmi emerged from her tent and beckoned to the bewildered dressmaker. Amandine promptly jammed her journal into her pocket and hurried over with René not far behind.

"Yes, ma'am?"

"I am impressed," Marmi said. "You took an angry girl in her underwear and in one night turned her into a... I don't know what she is, but I want to see more."

Marmi sipped her rooibos tea and looked Amandine over from her short, messy curls to the stockings bunched around her calves.

"If you continue to produce similar results, I would like you to work closely with Coronado on the new show.

However, that will have to wait until we stop. For now, all of us must prepare to move right away."

Marmi gave René a nod and returned to her tent to pack.

"*Ç'est génial!*" René lifted his hand like he was going to pat Amandine's shoulder, but he changed his mind mid-gesture and wiped his hair back instead.

"That doesn't sound at all bad." Amandine frowned at the red trailer again. "Though I wonder what got Sangria all worked up. I'd better check on her."

"Right." René rubbed his hands together. "We have to get going in about twenty minutes. You don't have to worry about much. Just make sure all of your things are inside the trailer and somebody will come hitch you."

He laughed nervously, gave a small wave, and jogged off towards Coronado's truck.

Inside the trailer, Sangria was sitting calmly at her vanity. She glanced over at Amandine and resumed wiping off her dramatic makeup with a damp cloth as if nothing was wrong.

"You've changed clothes already," Amandine said, noting her roommate's belted black dress.

"Well, I can't strut around in my costume all day," Sangria sighed, wringing out her washcloth. "We have to move."

"Did Marmi like what you showed her?"

"Oh yes." Sangria poked through the cosmetics spread out on the vanity. "In fact, she asked me to consult with Mister

Coronado about finding a role for me to play in the show when we stop."

"That's great news!" Amandine clapped her hands. "It's exactly what we wanted! You had me all worried, acting all serious like that."

The contortionist ignored her and sketched in her eyebrows. "Can you do me a favor?"

Amandine wasn't sure why Sangria wanted to avoid the subject, but she let it go for the time being. "Sure. What do you need?"

"Could you please go get my breakfast while I finish getting ready?"

"Of course!"Amandine scooped up the Japanese bowl sitting by the stove. "Anything for the star."

She left Sangria blushing so deeply, that her cheeks nearly turned purple.

"Bystryee! Bystryee!" Piotr shouted at the others who had come late for breakfast. "Hurry up and eat! The Frenchman says we only have fifteen minutes until we move." He seemed to be in no rush himself, however, as he casually swept oats and coffee grounds from the kitchen table.

Carmelita was helping herself to seconds when Amandine trotted over to the campfire.

"Armandina!" she exclaimed. "I am so glad you're staying on with us. Come meet my husband."

"Amandine," she corrected her gently. People often mispronounced her name, but she enjoyed this particular

86

variation. "It's a French name, though I think the Spanish version is just lovely, too."

"*Ai*, French, French and more French," Carmelita complained. "French everywhere and not another soul who can speak *Español.*"

"No one, darling," said the person at her side. "Except for you, me, your brother, and Juan." He extended a hand in Amandine's direction. "I haven't introduced myself yet. I'm Nick Thatch, the Half-Man. You've already met my wife."

Amandine shook his hand. "Pleasure to meet you, sir. Or do you prefer 'ma'am?'"

Nick laughed in an exaggerated baritone. It was true, even when he wasn't performing, one half of him was considerably more feminine that the other. His right side looked strong and handsome, like the American soldier in the recruitment ads, with short brown hair, half of a mustache, and muscular definition. His left side had much longer hair in half of a victory roll, a shaped eyebrow, and hairless limbs.

"I am entirely a gentleman, despite what my trailer says."

"Your left side is very pretty, though," Amandine gushed, already excited by the idea of designing a costume for Nick.

"My husband does very well for someone who isn't really a freak," Carmelita said. "He was discharged early into the war and traveled around as a handyman for hire. He found our fire one night and asked for work. We already had René to do the fixing, of course, so the girls and I got creative and dressed Nico up like this. Now he's one of our most popular freak-acts after Sangria."

Nick shrugged his shoulders in a way that said, "That's just how it is."

"It was a pleasure meeting you, sir," Amandine said. "But you'll have to excuse me. I need to get Sangria her breakfast before we go."

"Sangria and Antonio are the two biggest egos in camp," Nick warned. "Don't let either one of them boss you around."

Amandine started back to her trailer, but she paused to watch Coronado's truck fly across the clearing in reverse. It struck the red shepherd's hut with a bang and rocked it violently from side to side.

Sangria's head popped out of the window. She was already well into a colorful, metaphoric curse, but when she realized that it was Coronado's truck that hit her, she disappeared back inside again.

René hopped out from the driver's seat and sucked air between his teeth as he inspected the damage. Coronado looked as unhappy as ever, smoking on the passenger's side.

"¡Ten cuidado! ¿Qué sucede contigo?" he scolded him. "Eyes on the mirrors!"

"Sorry." René hitched the trailer. "That was a bit closer than I thought."

All at once, Amandine understood Sangria's odd behavior. She had seen her mother moon around the house before she was arrested, and the way Caroline clammed up when confronted looked exactly like what Sangria was doing now. This new knowledge made Amandine grin to herself, and she waved to the surly illusionist.

Unsurprisingly, Coronado only grunted in reply.

Amandine climbed inside and set Sangria's food on the vanity. "Are you alright?" she asked, kneeling to help pick up her scattered makeup.

"Perfectly fine." Sangria put everything away in their drawer. "Just a little confused. Mister Coronado doesn't usually hitch me."

"René was driving," Amandine said helpfully. Once everything was cleaned up, she retrieved her sewing kit from her belongings and climbed up onto her top bunk.

"Well, that explains everything," Sangria exclaimed, collapsing on her bed with her breakfast. "That idiot Frenchman has been skipping around the camp like a fool in love. It's as if you were the last girl in the world."

"I thought he seemed rather keen on you, despite your hostility," she replied and heard Sangria sputter her oatmeal below. "But... do you really think René likes me?" Amandine felt her face go hot. "That would be marvelous."

"Don't get all excited," Sangria growled, composing herself. "I don't know anything about that. All I know is that yesterday I see him leave to do the shopping, acting like his usual insufferably boring self, and the next thing I know, he's fawning over you and telling everyone to go out of their way to make you feel welcome."

"How sweet of him," Amandine beamed. Once she made sure that Sangria wasn't looking, she pulled her envelope of cash from the inside of her dress and ripped the lining out of her father's jacket. She stitched several bills at a time to the inside of the coat, hiding her work beneath several incomplete quilt blocks. If Sangria looked up at what she was doing, all she would see was that Amandine was making good progress on a colorful quilt top that she intended to give her mother upon their reunion.

"Get over yourself," the contortionist said coldly. "René's a wolf. The only reason he's behaving this way is obviously because he feels sorry for you. Though I suppose it's only natural. A wolf has to eat, even if all he can catch are shrews. I mean, it's not like he could be with any of us."

Amandine knew what Sangria was trying to do. The contortionist might have consented to share sleeping space, but that didn't mean that she suddenly liked their arrangement. After all, she had her costume and her place in the new show. There was no reason to keep Amandine around, so she doubled her efforts to drive her away. What Sangria couldn't have known was that she was about to get a taste of the infamous Stewart stubbornness, because Amandine had resolved to stick around and conquer her roommate with kindness.

"Why couldn't René be with any of you?" Amandine asked patiently.

"He's the youngest guy in camp. All of the other women are in their thirties or forties."

"You aren't thirty or forty."

"*I'm twenty*, and I wouldn't touch that greasy idiot with a ten-foot pole." Sangria shuddered and lowered her voice to a whisper. "In any case, it just isn't that way with us.

Everyone is like a family. It could never be, and to even consider it—"

"But what about Nick and Carmelita?" Amandine interjected.

"Nick was an outsider. Carmelita has been with us for as long as her brother Antonio has."

"Well then, what about you and Mr. Coronado?" Amandine asked, flipping the conversation on its head. Even without seeing, she knew right away she'd found another one of Sangria's many sensitive spots.

"You and your incessant questions!" Sangria stood to glare at her, and Amandine made a show of examining a completed quilt block, back to front. "What do you think you know about that, anyway?"

"Oh, it just seems that you are very tough to everyone here, even to Marmi, but not to Mr. Coronado." Amandine pretended to find a mistake in her stitching. Lightly, she added, "You were happy to let me sleep outside until he showed up."

Sangria sat down again in silence, though there was a lot of noise coming from outside. Engines were starting, Marmi's tent was thrown into the back of a truck with a whump, and the Russians were arguing about who's turn it was to drive.

When Sangria spoke again, her voice had grown very small. "It couldn't be, because he doesn't pay any attention to me."

"Sure it could." Amandine closed up the jacket with a lightning-fast whip-stitch. "You two are pretty similar. You're both assertive, talented performers, and you like to wear a lot of black. The only little difference is your age." She giggled. "I mean, he looks old enough to be your father."

The contortionist growled. "The age difference doesn't mean anything, only that he's much more worldly and experienced than any other dumb boy."

Amandine suspected that she was talking about René again, but she chose not to challenge that remark. "It looks like he will have to start paying attention to you if Marmi wants you to be in the festival show with him. You just have to let him know that you're interested."

"It would not be appropriate because of his wife, Estefania," she answered evasively. "Rumor has it that something terrible happened to her in Moscow. Antonio was headlining an international tour when it happened. Carmelita is the only other person who knows about it, but she hasn't told a soul. I heard it was so awful, she shut herself away and ate and ate and ate... that's how she got so big. She was traumatized! Anyway, if it upset Carmelita that much, it must have devastated him."

"You need to spend more time on the sunny side of the street." Amandine tied off her thread and hung over the edge of the bunk like a monkey. "You're in the show now. You can spend more time with your sweetie. Things are already looking up."

Sangria choked on her coffee. "Wait a minute! I never said I was sweet on Antonio!"

Amandine rolled her eyes and pulled herself back up into her bunk to put her things away. "Whatever you say. My dad really liked the handkerchiefs *maman* embroidered for him. Maybe you can try that for Mister Coronado." She pictured it with a smile. "You can sew 'A.C.' with a little dove on it."

There was a knock at the door. "Are you ladies ready to go?" René called out.

Amandine hopped off of the bed with her hands clenched tight to keep them from shaking. "We're ready!"

René took a step back when she opened the door, taking in her modest but attractive appearance. "Pardon my surprise," he said tenderly. "You look...very pretty."

Sangria made an exaggerated gagging noise.

"I am sorry." He bashfully kicked a rock away from the bottom step of the trailer. "That was a bit bold of me."

"Not at all." Amandine beamed. "Really. It was a nice thing to say."

"I came here to ask you if you'd like to do something fun."

"Absolutely." Even if René asked her to help him peel a thousand potatoes, Amandine knew she would still enjoy every moment.

"You bonehead," Sangria snapped. "You don't even know what it is yet."

René chuckled. "She's right. It's a little dangerous."

Amandine waved the notion away. "That's what makes it fun."

"*Parfait*," he said. "Follow me."

Amandine grabbed her coat, hat, gloves, and sunglasses, and once she'd put everything on, René reached for her hand. Even through her glove, his touch sent an electric jolt throughout her whole body that made her jump in surprise. She snorted loudly with nervous laughter.

"What are you doing, anyway?" Sangria asked René. "I thought we're leaving. Won't you be driving?"

"Not this time," he replied. "Antonio's pulling you."

Amandine tipped her sunglasses down and gave her roommate a crafty wink. "Maybe he'd appreciate a little company. You can talk about the show."

"*No!*" Sangria barked. "That is, um… that is, I was going to stay here and… practice my embroidery."

"Right." Amandine tapped the side of her nose. "Help yourself to my sewing kit."

With that, they left the contortionist puzzling over a needle and floss.

CHAPTER 5: THE RIDE

René put on his beat-up gambler hat and knotted an old bandana around his neck. "After you," he said, sweeping his arm towards a small ladder attached to the back of Coronado's truck.

Amandine climbed up to the luggage rack on top. René's duffel bag made a comfortable cushion to sit on while Coronado's trunk served as a sturdy backrest. Once he'd helped her up, René knocked on the roof of the cab to let the driver know they were ready to go.

Coronado flicked a cigarette butt out of the window, and the truck began to pull out of the clearing. They were the last in a strange, noisy, and colorful procession. From where Amandine could see, it appeared that only the men were driving, towing the women in their trailers. Marmi's tent was loaded into the flatbed truck that led the group north.

"Did Marmi say which town we'll stop at next?" Amandine asked. She wondered how much good her pre-war road map would have done her had she still been traveling alone.

"I don't know. I don't think even she knows until we're there, but she hasn't led us wrong yet."

The truck rocked and lurched as it climbed out of the wooded area and onto the road. Amandine squeaked when the truck pitched to one side and nearly tossed her off.

"Careful!" René caught her around the shoulders. "You alright?"

"Yeah!" It took every ounce of her control to keep from squealing again.

He released his gentle hold on her and angled his hat against the sun, letting the morning light catch the little trinkets attached to the band. "So I see that Sangria kept you busy last night. How did you sleep?"

"Real well," she replied. She decided not to tell him about Sangria's attempt to drive her away. "Her trailer sure is cozy. Which one's yours?"

"I don't have one. I keep a little tent outside of Antonio's truck."

"He won't let you in either?"

"Like Sangria, Antonio values his privacy," René explained with a shrug. "But I don't mind it. He's not as unkind as he likes to appear. I get the cab to myself all winter."

The procession drove through town, and Amandine was thrilled to see Mr. White cleaning the windows outside of his shop. He saw her in the reflection in the glass and turned to wave with his washrag as they passed.

They drove out of sight, and Amandine said wistfully, "In another life, I think I would have been a baker. I bet I could make some beautiful cakes if I only learned how that darned piping bag works."

"You could, if you wanted." René folded his arms behind his head and settled in a bit more comfortably. "Why not? Nothing is stopping you. Or did you already have plans after this?"

Amandine shook her head. "Not really. When I was small I knew I'd work for my father, but then he died and our business closed. Then I thought that maybe I could start a new business with my mother, but then she was taken away. Now I just want to free her." She paused, giving this question some thought. "Perhaps if Nieuwestad is nice, I'll stay there and open a boutique *and* a pastry shop."

"A danish with your dress?" he said, amused. "I like it. I'm sure you can find a market for that sort of thing in a place like Nieuwestad."

"But what about you?" she asked. "What do you do? Are you only a handyman, or do you have an act too?"

"I just run the shows. I don't perform." René chuckled. "I tried a few years ago when we had animals. I wasn't too bad at trick-riding or sharp-shooting, but I am just not as natural on stage as the others."

Amandine pictured him in costume, squeezing between the dancers for space at the vanity. "You have a horse?"

"I used to," he said a little sadly. "I had a gentle mare named Bonbon. She was the color of caramel, you see. I was still a boy when Sasha and Piotr told me that she ran away, but now I'm fairly certain that she was slaughtered for food." He kicked some dried bird-droppings off of the roof. "That winter was a very difficult, hungry time."

Amandine tried to nod sympathetically, but she had to protect her skirt from the breeze as the procession picked up speed. "Have you always wanted to work for a traveling show?" she asked, clamping the extra fabric between her knees.

"Not exactly. I just fell into it, and it suited me."

"What do you really want to do then?"

René made a face. He didn't know whether or not to tell her the truth. Shaking his head, he said, "No. It's nothing. Silly, in fact."

"Don't say that. I really want to know."

"You'll laugh at me."

"I won't!" She nudged his shoulder with hers. "Not if it's important to you."

"Alright." He pulled an orange from his pocket and began peeling it, tossing the rind over the side of the truck. "What I really want... what I've dreamed of since I was a child is... to be a cowboy."

"You don't say." Amandine glanced at his tell-tale hat and bandana.

"It's the reason why I joined Marmi in the first place. I heard that she was headed to America, so I had to find a way to make myself useful so that she'd take me along."

"We're driving north-east," she noted. "If you want to be a cowboy, you had better turn around and go west."

"I know, but Nieuwestad is our destination." He split the orange in half for them to share. "If I ever leave the traveling life, there is nothing I would rather do than chase cattle and break horses out on my own ranch."

While she didn't know anything about ranching, Amandine did remember a little about cotton farms from shadowing her father. The day they visited the gins, she saw a laborer get heat stroke and fall into the machinery. The whole experience left a very poor impression of agriculture on her.

"It sounds like very difficult and miserable work."

"I don't care if the work knocks me dead," he said, dreaming. "It would be all mine. I can defend my land from bandits and wild animals. I can ride back to camp after a long day, wash up in the creek, and eat a dutch-oven dinner around the fire with other cowboys."

Amandine suspected that his perception of cowboy life came primarily from adventure serials. "I think I hear a 'but' coming."

"But," he smiled and chewed on an orange wedge. "Marmi has lost a huge number of performers. After all she's done for me, I don't have the heart to leave her with so few people left."

"Did that Johnstone fellow take them all?" she asked, playing with a leafy twig that had fallen on the roof.

"Yes. The poor fools. He bribed them with fantastical amounts of money. He promised them things beyond his means, like high wages and their own private trailers. To a group of outsiders, starved and deprived by the war, it was impossible for them to pass such a chance."

"I take it that's not what happened."

"No," he scowled. "Juan, one of our freak-acts, came back almost immediately. He said that the living conditions weren't even fit for animals. Everyone was responsible for their own food and shopping, which can be a real problem for the freak-acts that can't go into town on their own. He also said that the ticket sales went straight into Johnstone's pocket, not to the care and keeping of the group." René shook his head and sighed loudly, driving away the troublesome thoughts. "What none of us can understand is how he still manages to be so widely successful."

Amandine perked up. "I asked the Whites about that. They saw his show and said it was his music."

"Is it?" René's smile returned. He was impressed that that she was already trying to be so helpful.

"Yes! So all you have to do is find the guy doing his music, offer him a million bucks and a castle on the moon, and you've got Johnstone beat."

René laughed, and once again the sound filled Amandine with joy. "Whatever the case may be, Marmi won't be content until she can take care of our family and keep it together forever."

We have that in common, she thought, pressing her locket in her hand.

Nathaniel White had to prop the door open with his shoe in order to carry the wash bucket and broom back inside the bakery. Normally Moses was quick enough to help, but Nathaniel could see his assistant's head bobbing on the other side of the small crowd of housewives that clustered at the counter.

"Sorry about the door, Mr. White," the young man said, stamping a food permit and counting out change. "Reckon everybody smelled the rhubarb all at once."

"Don't you worry about me, Moses. You just take care of Mrs. DeLaney there." He crab-walked around his customers, careful not to hit anybody with the broom clamped under his arm. "See if you can convince her to make her famous pudding with some of our apple bread."

"Your apple bread never lasts long enough to make it into pudding," tittered the little old woman at the counter.

"Mr. White, do you have a moment to talk about cakes?" said another customer, lightly catching him by the shirt where an arm should have been. The action caught them both by surprise, and she released him so fast, a spider may as well have crawled out from beneath his pinned sleeve. "You did such a swell job on the Bishop's anniversary cake. I was wondering if you could whip up something like that for my sister's wedding."

"I'd be delighted," Nathaniel said, wishing he had just gone through the back door with his dirty bucket instead. "Give me just a moment to check on my rhubarb pies, and then I'll be right with you."

Nathaniel pushed through the swinging half-doors back into the kitchen, leaving the murmur of customers and the chiming door for Moses to deal with. He put his cleaning supplies away in the closet, washed his hand, and dropped his apron over his head. With the edge of the counter's help, he managed to get it tied behind his back just as a buzzer went off. Inside the oven, red juices burbled through the gaps in the golden, latticed pie crusts, and Nathaniel took a deep breath of their sugary, tart scent.

"Mr. White," called Moses from the front.

"Just a moment more." He slid the pies out one by one onto the kneading table to cool.

"Mr. White, sir," he repeated a little more urgently.

Nathaniel realized that the store had gone strangely quiet. He shook off his oven mitt and pushed back into the shop.

To his astonishment, all of the customers had vanished. Instead, three police officers stood at the counter, and one held Moses at gunpoint. That is, Nathaniel thought that they were all police officers until a fourth in black appeared from behind them, holding a rhubarb turnover.

"I could smell these clear down by the bridge," the Inquestor said, grinning. "How much?"

"On the house," Nathaniel replied cautiously.

"Mighty kind of you." He bowed his head a little. "Inquestor Carver. Nathaniel White, I presume?"

"I am." Nathaniel stepped up beside Moses, who was staring down the barrel pointed at his nose. "What's the meaning of this, officers? What has Moses done?"

"Good question." The Inquestor crammed half of the turnover into his mouth and asked the officer, "You know something I don't, buddy?"

"Wherever there's trouble, there's always negroes," he growled. "And I don't like the look of this uppity half-breed."

102

"Who said anything about trouble? I'm just looking for a wandering fugitive." Carver dabbed at the corners of his mouth with his knuckles. "You. Moses, was it? Were you here yesterday?"

"Yes, sir," the young man said bravely. "Came in at 4:30 on the dot to start the dough, clocked out at 12:30, then I swept floors at the Pickwick until closing time."

Carver squinted at the ceiling and tapped his fingers together while he did some figuring in his head. "That checks out. You're free to go."

"What?" the room echoed. The police looked just as bewildered as Nathaniel and Moses.

"Go down, Moses! Way down in Egypt land!" Carver sang dramatically. He swept his arms wide, parting a path straight to the door. "That is, unless you'd prefer to stay and watch the police at work."

Moses exchanged a glance with his boss, and Nathaniel tipped his head towards the door. "Go on, now."

"But sir—"

"See if Betsy needs a hand with the shopping," he said, giving Moses a pointed look.

Moses nodded in understanding. He slipped around the officers as quickly as he could without breaking into a run. The door jangled shut, leaving Nathaniel completely alone with the NAR agents.

"Like I said, we're hunting for a vagrant," Carver continued. "Seen anybody pass through here, perhaps looking for work?"

The Stewart girl immediately sprang to mind, but after seeing how these men treated Moses for no reason at all, Nathaniel was not about to throw another child to the wolves. His wife had taken a liking to the girl, and technically speaking, he didn't know precisely why she was in town. She could have been visiting Shoeless Joe Jackson for all he knew.

"I'm afraid not, Inquestor," Nathaniel replied.

"You sure?" Carver's eyebrow sprang up. "This one had a pretty distinct look. About five-foot-six, brown hair worn down to the chin?"

Nathaniel's face didn't move.

"Blue silk dress? Seventeen year-old girl?" The Inquestor crossed the room with a ghost-like fluidity and before Nathaniel knew it, Carver's face was only inches from his. "Have you hired anybody who looks like that?"

"The only person I've hired to help is Moses," the baker said stiffly. "Six-foot-two, curly hair, baker's apron, eighteen year-old boy."

Carver leaned on the counter and evaluated Nathaniel through narrowed eyes, slowly chewing the last of his turnover. He licked pink rhubarb juice from his glove and smiled.

"*Moses.* You know, that reminds me of a little rhyme." Carver swirled his finger in the air and suddenly the police spread out and ransacked the bakery. They threw bread from the shelves and dumped all of the supplies behind the counter out onto the floor. The Inquestor sidestepped a flying box of truffles and recited over the noise, "'*Moses supposes his toeses are roses, but Moses supposes erroneously. Moses, he knowses his toeses aren't roses as Moses supposes his toeses to be.'"*

The police moved into the kitchen, and he heard the cymbalic crash of baking sheets hitting the floor.

Carver went on, "They use tongue-twisters like that in elocution classes. I never took elocution myself, but I hear they're necessary if you want a career in politics, film or…"

The police returned with something from the kitchen, and they slammed it down onto the counter.

"Radio!" Carver concluded gleefully. He let the police officer stretch the cord across the wall before he flicked it on.

"Write a little note on your toes,
Don't forget to dot the 'i,'
Look at what you wrote, goodness knows,
It's easy as pie!"

The jumping notes felt as damning as a funeral dirge. Suddenly, an officer appeared behind Nathaniel and cracked the back of his knees with his nightstick, bringing him down to the floor hard.

"You a jazz hound, Nathaniel White?" Carver cocked his head as the officer cuffed his wrist to his ankle. "Or did somebody else tune this radio to the rebels' station?"

"I don't have a clue what you're talking about," Nathaniel growled. "I'm an American citizen, dammit. *I served.* I don't have to answer to these Gestapo scare-tactics."

"Hey, you won't find any fans of Fritz among us." Carver pointed to his empty sleeve. "Are they the ones who took your arm?"

"I lost it in France to a British Bren," Nathaniel growled. "Back when the Krauts were still our best customers."

The police's eyes kept moving from Nathaniel to the Inquestor, waiting for another sign to move on him, but the Inquestor didn't drop his smile. Just then, there was a rustle in the kitchen, and Carver's curious gaze lifted towards it.

"Nathaniel, honey?" Betsy White's voice called from the back door.

Nathaniel blanched. Moses didn't find her in time.

"I got those strawberries and something else. Please don't be angry, but I stopped by the second-hand shop and found this beautiful Master Elegance dress and I *just had to*—" The rustling of her shopping bags stopped when she found the terrible mess in the kitchen.

"Nathaniel?" Her heels clicked hurriedly across the linoleum. "Moses? What in the name of—"

She burst through the kitchen door. She only had an instant to take in the sight of her shackled husband, four officers, and her shop in shambles before a blue officer knocked her back into the kitchen.

"Get your hands off of her!" Nathaniel cried. He tried to stand, but the cuffs made him pitch face-first into the floor. "Betsy!" He pushed his body towards the kitchen with all his might, but a forceful hand caught him by the collar and shoved him back up against the counter.

"No, no! No, stop!" Mrs. White cried from behind the swinging doors and Nathaniel could do nothing but stare in

106

horror as the other two police officers followed. "What do you want?" she demanded desperately. "*What do you want?*"

Carver did a Charleston-step across the bakery and helped himself to the last rhubarb turnover on the shelf. He took another bite and turned up the volume on the radio.

"*Let's to the Breakaway!*
Get hot and shake away!
It's got that snappiest syncopation!
Three times up on your heels!
Oh boy, how good it feels!
You'll get the happiest new sensation!"

"Stop! Please, don't do this," Betsy wailed. "Please... please..."

Suddenly, she screamed and Nathaniel launched himself towards the door again. He made it far enough this time to see his pies get swept off of the counter and boiling hot rhubarb exploded across the floor and splashed into his face. He cried out in agony, not from the burning syrup in his eyes, but from the hands that gripped his ankle and dragged him, powerless, back into the shop.

"Hey, what gives, buddy?" Carver growled. "We were in the middle of talking."

Nathaniel was not an emotional man. The night he crawled through the ruined French village, he didn't shed a tear for his comrades that littered the road or the tattered limb that dragged along uselessly beside him. He only thought of his Betsy, his sunny Southern Belle, and how badly he wanted to see her smiling face again. Throughout his recovery and long journey home, he worried that she wouldn't want a broken, crippled man, but to his great relief, she was the first to appear at the edge of the train platform, and his injury made it no less marvelous to hold her again.

Hot tears rolled down his blistering cheeks. Betsy had stopped screaming. Now there was nothing but her pained moans and "Let's Do The Breakaway" on the radio. He had endured so much in his thirty-five years, but never in his life had Nathaniel White ever felt so helpless.

"Now then—" The Inquestor squatted beside him and poked Nathaniel's sloping shoulder. "I'm looking for a vagrant. Seen anybody pass through here?" His wild grin was tinged pink with rhubarb. *"Perhaps somebody looking for work?"*

CHAPTER 6: THE SEARCH

The caravan continued on throughout the morning, and they stopped in a small town at noon to refuel the trucks. This process normally took about an hour, so Amandine and René climbed down from their lofty perch to see about lunch.

Sasha was slicing bread, ham and cheese to feed the small crowd that had gathered around him already. Piotr showed up shortly after everybody had a sandwich, carrying a bucket of cold, clean water he'd drawn from a pump. While she waited in line for a drink, Amandine was introduced to the other members of the group she hadn't met yet.

There was Christopher Halton, the thin man. Born with an intestinal condition that turned him skeletally thin, Christopher was a positive, humorous fellow who took every opportunity in the conversation to express his dislike for the NAR. She met Juan Flores, the dog-man. He was covered from head to foot in wiry, black hair which made him terribly shy. She was also introduced to Gregory Thomas, or Tiny Greg, who looked like a two-year-old child when he was in fact a thirty-three-year-old man. He shared a trailer with Juan and Christopher, and he slept in a fruit crate tucked under their bunks.

Finally, Amandine met Jean-Claude Dembélé from the Ivory Coast and Ambroise Kuohmoukouri from Cameroon. They were both tall, muscular men and Amandine was dismayed to see that they had to split their shirt sleeves in order to fit their bulging arms through.

"*S'il vous plait,*" Ambroise said. "Do you suppose you can make me something nice?"

Amandine paused to process his unfamiliar accent. His French was brusque, but the vowels in his English rolled beautifully like an unfurling bolt of velvet.

"Something colorful, if it's not too much trouble," he went on. "I want to take Margie to the pictures, but she says we shouldn't. She is such a modest girl, you see. She cares so much about appearances."

Amandine looked from Ambroise to Margaret, who was leaning against Ambroise's truck with a lit cigarette in one hand and a pair of colas she had bought from the service station dangling in the other.

"Of course," Amandine beamed. "I'd be delighted."

Marmi had just put away her road map when she spotted a police cruiser come up the road, and a black car materialized like a shadow right behind it. Marmi cursed. Her group was frequently stopped by the authorities, and it was always a humiliating ordeal. Just as she expected, the cars stopped just behind the caravan with their lights flashing and four men climbed out. Three wore blue and stalked towards her with their hands on their pistols, while one in black lingered behind.

"Your leader will come forward!" shouted a blue officer as if he were addressing a rowdy schoolyard.

Marmi stepped up. "You may speak to me," she said smoothly. She had swapped her robes for a floral sundress, and while the change made her appear harmless and ordinary, her height and carriage still alluded to her authority.

"A negress in charge, huh? Unlock your trucks," ordered the first officer. "Line your people up over there with their papers."

Although subjected to searches countless times, everyone still waited for Marmi's order. Wordlessly, she gestured to them and it was done.

The Inquestor finally strolled up to her. "I'm sorry for my colleague's enthusiasm," he said graciously, shielding his eyes from the sun to look up at her. "My boss saddled me with a load of lackeys, and all they want to do is show me how tough they can be."

Marmi said nothing. Instead she tried to read the peculiar Inquestor as she surrendered her papers to him.

"This is just a standard search. A little practice for the Inquestors of tomorrow. There's nothing to fear." Carver took her identification, his black eyes just as calculating as her gold ones. "As long as you've got nothing to hide."

René and Coronado made a beeline for the back of his truck. Amandine was digging in her coat for her own papers when Sangria cracked the trailer door.

"A search?" She frowned at the police lining everybody up along the side of the road.

"Are you worried?" Amandine asked. "René told me that this happens all the time."

Sangria put on a pair of sunglasses and descended the trailer steps like a movie star. "I'm only surprised it took this long."

Amandine and Sangria were joined at the end of the line by René and Coronado. They waited and watched while two officers ransacked the trucks, and one interrogated everyone in turn. As he made his way down the line, his every step was shadowed by the Inquestor.

Amandine thought the Inquestor looked a little short for a high officer, but of course it could have just been his careless posture that made him appear that way. In fact, the more she studied him, the more she realized that nothing about his attitude conveyed his status except for his black suit, similar to the uniform her father wore with total solemnity and pride. Amandine wondered what her father would have had to say about the flippant officer sauntering down the line towards her now.

"This seems rather unprofessional and downright unkind," Amandine muttered as one blue officer dumped out a drawerful of Caremlita's underwear and proceeded to wave her slip in front of the other like a flag. "And I bet a pocketful of

112

parrot feathers they won't even clean up after themselves. Whatever are they looking for?"

"Anything that might make them suspect that we're harboring rebels," Coronado said with contempt. "That could be explosive material, drugs, weapons, the French, banned music records, too much cash, or even too much food."

"Did you say 'the French?'" she asked in amazement.

The illusionist nodded, tapping a pack of cigarettes in his hand but not taking any. "It's not widely known, but we learned from these frequent searches that simply speaking French puts you beneath the worst scrutiny. I suspect it has something to do with old war-time prejudices. Nick said that the French Resistance would always attack American troops, even after the NAR switched sides. Now the French have a reputation for being sneaky, underhanded saboteurs, and they're always prime suspects for insurrectionists."

Amandine pondered this. Her mother's arrest was beginning to make more sense. "What about René?" she asked. "And Jean-Claude and Ambroise?"

"Please," Sangria scoffed. "You'd have to be crazy to start trouble with Jean-Claude and Ambroise."

She was right. The two men glowered at the officer who had emptied Marmi's tent onto the dirt until he put it back the way it was.

"And the medicine and explosives? But Mister Coronado, your truck is full of them!"

René gestured for Amandine to be quiet. The officer had finally come to Sangria, but to his disappointment, the

Inquestor took over from there. She held out her papers with a limp wrist and a giggle.

"Good afternoon, miss," he said, standing close. He hadn't read more than Sangria's name because he was busy looking the pretty, young performer over. "'*Sangria Groviglio.*' Well, that just rolls off of the tongue like poetry, doesn't it? Tell me, is that really your name?"

The contortionist nodded. "Yes, sir, it truly is. Miss Sangria Groviglio. What may I call you?"

"I'm Inquestor Carver." He tore his gaze away from her ample red lips long enough to finish skimming her documentation. "You're American. Perfect. This won't take long."

"I don't mind." Sangria slipped her sunglasses off and demurely nibbled on the earpiece. Amandine noticed that an extra button at the top of her dress had come undone. "I could stand here with you all day."

René rolled his eyes, and the Inquestor anxiously cleared his throat.

"I can't help but wonder what a lovely young woman such as yourself—" He finally noticed Amandine. "—And your charming friend here, are doing with this bunch of weirdos."

Amandine stared intently at Carver as she handed him her papers. She hadn't forgotten her mother's last warning to beware of inquestors, but this one was as good-looking as a silent film star and just as monochromatic, even in broad daylight. He had a stubborn smile that broke through each time he tried to look serious, and his eyebrows jumped with interest

114

whenever he listened. He felt friendly. What's more, he felt familiar, but Amandine couldn't even begin to guess where she might know him from.

"Oh, well, you see..." Sangria tucked her short hair behind her ear with a pout. "I was in a bad way during the war. Nobody wanted me, but these people took me in. It was very fortunate because I'm an excellent performer."

"What do you do?" Carver asked. Her papers detailed all of this, but they were hanging at his side, completely forgotten.

"Well, I can dance." She ticked off her talents on her fingers and pretended that they took great effort to remember. "I can play the violin. I can do a little gymnastics and acrobatics..." Like a dim light bulb flickering on, her face lit up and she pointed to her last finger. "I'm also a very adept contortionist."

"Golly gee, you *are* talented." Carver guffawed and dabbed the sweat off of his brow with his handkerchief. "I'm sorry you had to resort to this. You know, there are places you could go. Shelters called replacement homes for young, unattached women such as yourself. They give you honest work, a safe place to live, and they could even pair you with... *eligible* officers in need of a wife."

Sangria beamed as if she wanted nothing more in her life than a chance at marrying an inquestor. This seemed to please Carver, and he turned his attention to Amandine.

"Miss Stewart," he said. "Forgive me, I can't pronounce your name. Is it like Amanda? Rhymes with Caroline?"

115

"It's 'Aman-deen.' Rhymes with 'Caro-leen.'"

He paused and only one eyebrow jumped this time. "There is no profession listed here. No profession and no family makes you an excellent candidate for the replacement home."

"Actually, I just got hired yesterday by this group to make costumes," she said proudly. "It's my first real job."

Carver sighed melodically and returned their paperwork. He wrote down some information on his notepad before tearing off the page and holding it out to Amandine. "Take this. When you get close to a train, you ladies should take it to the city and contact these people. They will take better care of you."

Sangria took the paper instead, folded it carefully, and tucked it down inside the front of her dress. The Inquestor watched it vanish and turned bright red.

"Thank you ever so much, Inquestor." She took his gloved hand in both of hers. Leaning in close, she smiled victoriously at the simple power she held over him. "You have a marvelous day, now."

Carver encouraged the original officer to take over with a gesture when it was Coronado's turn. The illusionist confidently extended his papers. "It's really warming up today, isn't it, Inquestor?"

Carver ignored him; he was still staring at Sangria as she lazed against a tree, absently fanning her exposed collarbone with her papers.

The blue officer spoke. "Antonio Coronado, aged forty-two, medically trained by the Spanish army, in the country working as a magic-man..."

While Sangria's performance was perfect, Amandine noticed Coronado's eye twitch at this remark.

"You're related to the fat one?" the officer asked.

Composing himself, Coronado answered sweetly. "Yes. She's my younger sister."

The officer threw his papers back at him with disinterest. He moved in front of René, who gripped his hat in his hands and stared at the ground.

"You! Papers!"

Trembling, René pulled them from his pocket.

The officer scanned them suspiciously. Where everybody else's official photo was framed by a thin black line, René's was boxed in by a bright red bar. "Ren Person, aged nineteen— a Frenchman?" The officer's face changed to a mix of anger and triumph at this discovery.

"Officer, his name is René Personne and he is indeed a Frenchman," Coronado cut in, and René looked relieved that somebody else was speaking for him.

"Wow, a person of interest on your first search?" Carver jostled the police officer with his elbow. "You boys will be inquestors by the weekend."

Coronado laughed. "No, sir."

"Why is that funny?" the officer demanded.

Coronado shrugged. "The boy is an idiot, I'm afraid. Dumb as a hammer, but I keep him around because he can use one."

The officer glared skeptically at René. "Speak for yourself!"

René shot a look at Coronado, who gave him a permissive nod. He appeared to concentrate very hard. Finally, he mumbled, "*Oui?*"

"English," Coronado reminded him firmly.

"...yes."

"What are you doing in America, Frenchman?" the officer asked impatiently.

Coronado cut in again. "I brought him myself. You see, twelve years ago I was driving in Paris when the poor street urchin ran beneath my truck. His leg was crushed and his already meager intelligence suffered when his head struck the pavement. I am a good Christian, sir— a Catholic, of course— and I couldn't leave him in that state. I used my medical training to doctor him as best I could, but the damage was, as you can see, severe. See how he still favors one leg?"

René shifted his weight to one side before the officer looked and Carver snorted.

"I decided to take him in," Coronado continued. "I fed him, clothed him, and gave him honest work. I am responsible for this poor creature now. He would probably die in the streets if it weren't for me."

Just then, the searching officers reached Coronado's truck and tried the back doors, but they wouldn't budge. One stepped up onto the bumper to peer in the back window. "Inquestor!" he shouted. "This one is locked and packed to the gills with bottles and boxes! Could be drugs or other contraband."

118

Coronado laughed nervously and reached into his pocket. "My apologies. I thought I unlocked that."

The officers snatched the keys from him and flung open the doors. To their surprise, they found that except for a couple of dirty bird cages, the truck was completely empty.

In a white flash, Carver drew his pistol and held a genuinely petrified René at gunpoint. "Well?" he asked excitedly. "What's in there?"

They tapped the walls, checked the windows, and searched the truck all over again in bewilderment. "Nothing, Inquestor. It's empty."

The blue officer in charge signaled to the others. "Come on, let's go. This place is a damned circus."

Carver shrugged and holstered the gun.

"Actually, we're just a traveling show," Coronado said with mock-helpfulness and a wave. "Have a nice afternoon, officers. Hail to the Republic."

Carver was the only one who waved back. "Yeah! Hail and all that jazz!"

The blue officer tossed René's papers over his shoulder. Coronado picked them up and watched while the NAR agents went into the service station. As soon as the door closed behind them, he turned back to his companions with an unlit cigarette sticking out of his wide smile.

"I swear, René gets dumber every time Antonio tells that story." Sangria closed up her blouse and ripped Carver's note to shreds.

René stormed up to Coronado and snatched his papers back. "He pulled a gun on me, Antonio!"

Coronado shrugged.

"Searches are not the time for tricks," he fumed. "He could have shot me!"

"Cool down, *caballero*." Coronado stepped back and spread his arms in an invitation. "You've got a fast hand. You could have shot him back."

René shook his head and stooped to help everyone gather their scattered belongings from the ditch. "I'm not falling for it. You can't goad me into lighting your cigarette for you."

"Come on," Coronado was still wearing a smug grin. "Why waste a match when it's such a fun trick?"

René shook his head again, but then had a sudden change of mind. "Oh, fine. Have it your way." He pointed at Coronado with a snap.

Coronado smelled something burning, but it wasn't his cigarette. Searching, he discovered that the pocket that held his identification was on fire.

"*Dommage*," René shrugged and scooped up clothes from the tall grass. "I missed."

Carver trotted out of the service station, pleased as punch now that he had a thermos full of fresh coffee and a moon pie. He beckoned the other police officers into his car and all four piled into the Interceptor. The blue officers sat in silence for some time while Carver filled out some paperwork and ate his moon pie. They exchanged wary glances until finally the most senior police officer spoke up from the passenger's seat. "Inquestor, wasn't that the girl you were looking for?"

Carver took a long drink of coffee and hissed when the drink burned his tongue. "Sure was."

"Why didn't you arrest her?"

Carver didn't answer. Instead, he watched the performers pick up the last of their possessions from the ditch. The fat lady was weeping with humiliation while a man with half a moustache tried to comfort her. The Chinese woman finished folding the last of her enormous underthings and returned them with a double-bow before retreating to her own trailer further up the road.

"They're a suspicious-looking group," the Inquestor said to himself. He glanced at the officers in his backseat and added, "Wouldn't you say?"

"Extremely, sir," said one. "I think you ought to shoot them all and save yourself the time and paperwork."

"Shoot them? Me?" The Inquestor gasped. "Oh, no! I can't shoot. I'm probably the worst shot in the NAR. The foxy, blonde administrator who serves the Chief Inquestor his coffee can handle a gun better than me. And while I'm sure you eager-beavers think I'm always sending update reports to headquarters—" He fluttered his incomplete form at them before tossing it into the backseat. "Snuffing people always means more paperwork, not less."

"You're being modest," said the first. "I heard that they called you 'The Marksman' at the academy."

"My classmates were trying to be funny," Carver frowned. "I can't shoot the broad side of a barn. I mean, I try. I

121

go the range when I have time, but it doesn't seem to be helping. Take earlier, for example—"

He took out his sidearm with a spin and showed them his gleaming weapon. The nickel-plated 1911 was standard issue to all inquestors, used just as much for ornamentation as it was for defense.

"There was a crooked administrator back in Cold River," he explained. "It was right before I got stuck with you boys. He had his back to me, maybe six feet away. I had a clear shot, but I missed." Carver pretended to shoot all over the place. "He bolted and managed to slip past me. I finally nicked him on his way out the front door, but since I already unloaded my entire magazine I couldn't put him out of his misery. He bled out in the courtyard in front of all of his employees." He holstered his weapon and shuddered. "What a mess! That's why I prefer a more hands-on approach."

The officers were grinning at each other. "So let's get hands-on. Make 'em sing, just like those bakers."

Carver shook his head as he made his decision. "I'm going to follow this girl to Nieuwestad. I got a feeling she's going to lead us to something big."

CHAPTER 7: THE GIFT

The group stopped again outside of a small town several hours before sunset and the moment the trailers were parked, everyone had a routine. Jean-Claude and Ambroise put up Marmi's tent before they headed off to exercise. Sasha and Piotr unpacked their cooking equipment and went to draw water from a nearby stream. The dancers set about housekeeping, cleaning road dust from their tiny homes while the others were responsible for setting up furniture and gathering firewood.

Amandine followed suit and busied herself cleaning. As she wiped down the window, she spotted René heading down from Mamri's tent with his wallet and a stack of papers in hand, likely on his way into town again. She hoped he would invite her to join him, and no sooner did she think this when he veered off the path and headed straight towards her hut.

"Why, hello again." She waved with the cloth, sending a puff of dust in his direction. "What can I do for you?"

"As wonderful as it is to see you again so soon, I am actually looking for Sangria." René put his head in the doorway and found the contortionist lazing on her bunk. "I need you to come to town with me."

"Me?" Sangria glared over her magazine. "Why me and not your new favorite little rag doll?"

"Because..." He searched for a reason and decided to go with the truth. "Marmi said Amandine can't go with me unless we have a chaperone."

"*Aha!*" Sangria turned the page with a decisive slap. "Forget it."

"Hold on just a moment!" He hopped inside. There was barely enough room to breathe with the three of them in there, and René's sudden nearness made Amandine freeze. "We need to put on a show tomorrow night. Don't you want to go shopping with Amandine and update your costume? Remember, it's the *première*—" He pronounced the word in French for effect. "—Of the new and improved Love-Knot!"

Sangria scowled and tossed her magazine aside. "Damn it. You're right. Give me a few minutes to freshen up for town." She squeezed past them and sat at her vanity. Pushing him away by the seat of his pants, she shouted, "Begone!"

While they waited for Sangria to get ready, René set up a pair of folding chairs just outside the door. He invited Amandine to sit before he climbed back onto the roof and assembled the retractable awning.

"How lovely," Amandine said when he jumped down beside her again. "You've made a shady porch for this little house on wheels." She crossed her ankles and sat back with a deep breath. "All we need are some sweet-teas and rocking chairs, and this would be just like home before the war."

"Tell me about your home." René replaced his tools in the pouch he kept slung across his chest.

Amandine was bubbling with happy memories she wanted to share, but she stopped herself when she remembered something. "Hang on! I've told you plenty about me already. You know all about my family, where I'm from, and where I'm going. I realized this afternoon that I don't even know your name."

René didn't answer. Instead, he waited for her to ask a direct question.

At that moment Sangria, who had been eavesdropping again, appeared at the door. "You're kidding, right? It's 'René.'" She lingered on the top step so that she could look down her nose at Amandine. "*Ruh-nay*. It's probably the most common, boring French name after 'Jacques' or 'Pierre.' He goes by the equally dull last name of 'Personne.'"

The two rolled their eyes and started off. Sangria scampered after them and opened her red paper parasol. "I mean, how can you not know his name? Are you deaf, forgetful, or really just that stupid?"

René was about to snap back when Amandine touched his elbow. "Now, now," she interrupted. "I may not speak much French, but I learned enough to know that 'René Personne' means 'reborn' and 'nobody.'"

Sangria's mouth opened in surprise, but she clamped it shut angrily. "Oh, it is, is it?"

"It's true," René said, amused by being found out. "I am nobody. I was nobody in France, and now I am nobody here in America."

"Well, boo-hoo," Sangria snarled. "'Mister Nobody.' How appropriate!"

"I like it," Amandine assured him. "It makes you sound mysterious. Like the Rogue Rider."

"Rogue Rider?"

"Only the best western adventure to ever come from pulp-publishing," she nodded, suddenly noting all of the similarities René shared with the dime-novel hero.

Sangria wedged the two of them apart with her parasol, hitting René in the face. "Even that sounds better than your dumb made-up name."

"Your name is made-up, too," René argued, rubbing his cheek.

"Darling, nobody is who they say they are." Sangria cast her eyes upwards helplessly. "Not even the people you think you know best, apparently. In any case, I like the name I've given myself very much. I have no more ties to my old life, so no reason to keep my old name."

"Parentless, too?" Amandine asked sympathetically. "We have that in common."

"We have nothing in common," the contortionist growled, frustrated by Amandine's constant attempts to bond with her. "You had a wealthy, all-American hero for a father and some French criminal for a mother. My parents were on the bottom side of middle-class pre-war, trying everything and anything to just to look like they were rich. Even before things got really bad, they had spent so much money on outward appearances, we would eat whatever mother could boil on our fine china. They were raising me up to be an artist, suited to

126

entertain only the most elite audiences. Dance lessons, music lessons, gymnastic lessons... I had the very best education, but... no friends. No food." She scoffed sadly. "I thought I was hungry then."

Amandine looked to René, who looked like he was hearing this story for the first time as well. "But then the war began?"

Sangria nodded. A stopper had been pulled, and no matter how badly she wanted to replace it, she couldn't control what spilled out. "Yes, then the war began. My parents were more desperate than ever to keep up their charade. They were always bragging to their rich friends about all of their food and important friends who got them special privileges. It was all a lie. Soon their rich friends started going hungry like everybody else. One day while I was at my lessons, I learned that the neighbors came to our house and demanded to meet my parents' contacts. My parents were forced to come clean about their lie. They had no important friends. They had nothing. All we had to eat was a handful of dandelions my mother had gathered in secret that day."

Amandine remembered how glad she had once been to eat weeds. "I'm so sorry. Were your parents killed?"

"No, nothing so dramatic as that," Sangria grumbled. "They were laughed at. Humiliated. They were gone by the time I came home. When I got back, some very dangerous-looking vagrants had already moved into my house. They, uh... they tried to get me to stay, but I ran away. All I had were the clothes on my back and my violin."

Sangria sniffed once and stopped talking. It was impossible for Amandine to read her roommate's face from beneath her parasol, so she looked to René again.

"The Russians sometimes come with me on these errands," he said quietly. "Sasha happened to spot Sangria in an alley. Marmi and Antonio cared for her until she was better."

"I suppose all of my parents' play-acting turned out to be good for something," Sangria spoke up again. "Although sitting on my head in a dirty little traveling show is hardly the future they had in mind for me."

"It will turn around," René said, trying to comfort her. "Aside from the searches, we are doing much better than we ever had. We eat three times a day now, we get little improvements to our equipment here and there. Don't forget, if we win the competition at the festival, we will be rich."

"There's a competition?" Amandine asked just as they came upon the town. René paused, pulled a hammer from his toolkit with a flourish, and tacked a poster to a telephone pole.

"What did you think all this fuss over the show was for?" Sangria replied, becoming herself again. "What did you think we were headed for Nieuwestad for? The Freedom Festival is in three months, and we have to somehow compose, design, and rehearse an incredible act while scraping together a living along the way!"

"I am confident that Coronado is onto something," René said, passing the extra tacks and posters to Amandine while he put up another. "He's the only one of us who has ever

128

had his own show in a real theater. He knows what we need. We just have to get creative and find a way to make it happen."

"It's going to be a failure," Sangria groaned.

"We have an advantage over many of the performing groups," he went on. "We stuck together throughout the Depression and the war. Many other groups disbanded or shut down. All we need is... an edge." He tilted his head in Amandine's direction.

Amandine took all of this in while she chewed her bottom lip. There was so much more at stake than just a couple of tutus and tuxedos. She had never been entrusted with a project like this, so before that pervasive, destructive feeling called doubt crept into her mind, she imagined the grandest, most incredible costumes she could. She tried to think about unusual colors and exotic styles that would require a whole new means of dressmaking.

"Hurry up, bonehead!" Sangria shouted at her. The others had gone ahead of her a little ways, but Amandine could still hear her mumbling. "You see her freeze just now? It's like her brain shorted out."

"*Mon Dieu*, Sangria, shut up," René muttered.

René went into the various stores and bought what they needed, while Amandine continued to put up posters and Sangria supervised. People slowed as they passed by to stare at the dark and beautiful performer. As soon as someone's attention was snared, Amandine would wave and point to the posters she was hanging.

"MARMI'S MARVELS," it read, beneath a stylized print of Marmi in a gypsy costume. "SEE FREAKS THAT TERRIFY, EXOTIC DANCES THAT MYSTIFY, ILLUSIONS THAT STUPEFY. TOMORROW NIGHT. 25¢ for children, 35¢ for adults."

When they returned to camp, Amandine helped Sasha and Piotr unload the groceries. "What's for supper?"she asked.

"It had better not be stroganoff." Sangria elbowed past René to root around the paper bag for her new magazine.

Piotr grinned mischievously. "For you, *zanuda*, it will be delightful steak—"

"Pork shoulder." René deposited the cheap cut onto the kitchen table.

Piotr snorted. "A delightful pork shoulder gently cooked to tender perfection in a gourmet mushroom sauce topping a bed of pasta."

"In Russia, we call it... stroganoff!" Sasha kissed his fingers dramatically. Everyone within earshot cackled and Sangria stormed off to her trailer in a huff.

The night went on much as it had the night before, only this time René headed off to scavenge the junkyard while Amandine stayed behind with Coronado to have a look at his suit. He was so particular about the fit of his tuxedo that she must have measured him a dozen times. It had to accommodate certain tricks he wasn't willing to explain to her and even after all of his bellyaching, he wouldn't relinquish the suit so that she could actually work on it.

Amandine remembered how her father dealt with picky customers. He would nod, smile, show the client some detailed notes he'd taken, then do whatever he wanted in the end. It always seemed to work for him, she recalled fondly.

In the morning there was no rush to leave, and Amandine was free to begin her work. When she returned from washing up, breakfast had been cleaned from the kitchen table, and all of the women were using it to sort through piles of clothes. Ludmilla beckoned her over.

"Can you use any of this?" she asked, guiding her to the table's edge. "These are all of the old clothes we don't need. Some of these have nice lace, buttons or material that can be salvaged. What do you think?"

Amandine passed her hand over the fabric. The majority of it was horribly worn and stained. However, Ludmilla was right. A gleaming button here or a length of sturdy lace there stood out from the rest of the rags. She shook her head. "I'm sorry, but most of this is no good. I'm going to need something stronger. Something newer."

Ludmilla sighed. "We were afraid of that. Ah, well."

"We will come up with something," Chitra said helpfully, returning the clothes to a large laundry basket.

Amandine took the basket to her shaded folding chair outside of her trailer. She spent most of the morning ripping seams, pulling buttons, adding scraps of colorful fabric to her sewing kit while the others rehearsed for the performance that night.

Sangria rolled out of bed shortly before lunch time wearing a leotard, dance shoes, and a striped scarf over her hair. Stretching fluidly with her violin in hand, she sulked off into the trees to practice alone. She didn't acknowledge Amandine at all.

René didn't speak to Amandine all morning either like she had hoped he would. She spotted him crossing the camp several times with a troubled look on his face and black grease all over his hands. She figured that as the only handyman, he must have been extremely busy, so she left him to his work. That didn't keep her from watching his comings and goings, however, hoping each time he passed that he would stop and talk to her.

By noontime, Amandine had salvaged all she could from the basket. She was just picking up her workspace when René reappeared, still as filthy as he was before. He hesitated before wordlessly presenting her with some lumpy objects wrapped in his bandana.

"What's this?" Curious, she lifted the corner of the red paisley cloth.

"*I made you some dishes,*" he said quickly and a little too loudly. "Well, that is, I found some dishes in the dump. That is, I found the broken pieces and I..."

Amandine saw a little white china cup with a rosebud on the side. It had been broken, but then reattached to a completely different blue porcelain cup with the small brass handle from a candlestick fixed to the side. She turned it over in her hands, marveling at how smoothly the pieces fit together.

René was still fumbling. "I couldn't find any dishes nice enough, so I thought I'd make you a set from the nice pieces I could find..."

"They're so beautiful." She took up the small plate and bowl assembled like a colorful mosaic. "I absolutely love them."

"You do?" His shoulders dropped with relief. "That is, I thought I could make it look nice, but as I walked over here, I realized that you are a girl from a wealthy family who wouldn't — *shouldn't* eat off of broken dishes... from the dump."

On an impulse, she wanted to run into his arms. She didn't care that he was covered in grease and smelled like gasoline. No one had ever made her a gift like this before, and she wanted René to know that she would have chosen his broken dishes over her family's whole closet of silver. She looked around to see if anyone was watching and found Sasha and Piotr standing side by side, pointing at them. For once they were not arguing, but giggling suspiciously with each other.

Amandine sighed and set her unique dishes on top of her laundry basket. "Have you been working on those all morning?"

"Ah, no," he said. "I made those last night. I wanted to make sure the glue was dry before I gave them to you. Let me show you what I've been working on this morning."

He led her around the back of Coronado's truck where the Illusionist was sitting on an overturned crate, surrounded by a half-circle of candle stubs. He glanced up at the pair.

"I think I've got it," Coronado said proudly. With a flourish of his hand, he touched a wick, and a tiny yellow flame popped from his fingertip.

René nodded, impressed. "Now you just have to throw it." He wiped his black hands together, and they unexpectedly burst into two fireballs. He yelped and beat the flames out on his pants.

Coronado smirked. "That's what you get for trying to show off." He took René's hands and determined that he wasn't seriously hurt. Shooing him away, he said, "Fireballs give me an idea, though. Leave the magic to me and show the little lady what you've been working on."

He pointed at a giant mess of tools, wood, and scrap metal. In the midst of this chaos stood a junk-contraption that Amandine was very familiar with.

It was a treadle sewing machine, but it was unlike one she had ever seen before. The legs were mismatched and the treadle itself was fashioned from an overturned serving tray. The polished machine was set snugly into the table which had been rebuilt using wood from an orange crate.

"It's not finished," René explained, going to a bucket of water to wash his hands. "The table was split and completely rotted, so I replaced it. I replaced the old bent and broken legs, too. The machine itself was rusted solid, and that's what I was working on all morning. Just a lot of scrubbing and oiling. It's still missing several parts... like the belt that turns the wheel and... a little piece that goes inside the bottom there." He chuckled. "I don't even know what it's called in

French, let alone English. I pulled it out and it crumbled to dust."

Amandine gave the stop motion a turn, and the machine moved flawlessly, making a familiar soft *cha-cha-cha-cha* sound that reminded her of happier times. She pressed the treadle with her foot, watching the wheel make several smooth rotations.

The combined joy she felt over the dishes and the sewing machine was so strong she thought she would burst, so she took a deep breath to calm herself. Even after five measured breaths, she was still quivering with elation, and her silence was beginning to make René nervous.

"Thank you, René," she finally said. "I'm sorry for not saying so right away, but I'm speechless." She touched the table top which had been sanded and oiled, yet still bore the name of a fruit farm and a blossoming orange tree. "It's incredible. I bet nobody else in the whole world has a machine like this."

"I can make a belt easily enough." René rubbed his neck. "But I don't know where I can find the right... thing for the machine. If I knew what it looked like, I might be able to make the part..."

She examined the throat plate and determined what was missing. "You don't need to worry. It's a little metal spool for the thread called a bobbin. I have a bunch in my sewing kit."

She could hardly wait to use her new machine, but she wanted to spend time with René even more. "Why don't you take a break?" She pointed to the lawn chairs by Sangria's trailer. "I'll get your lunch for you. Go and sit in the shade."

Amandine picked up his dented tin dishes and bounced away before he could protest. He wasn't used to resting while a project still lay unfinished, but he did as she said. He tilted his chair against her trailer and pulled his hat down over his eyes. He had just begun to drift off when a shadow passed over him.

Sangria glowered with her fists on her hips. "Just what do you think you're doing, lazing around by my trailer?"

René dropped his hat over his eyes again. "Waiting for Amandine to bring me my lunch."

"The way you two have practically married after two days makes me sick." Sangria tipped him out of his seat with her bow. "I can't wait until we get to Nieuwestad, and we're rid of her."

CHAPTER 8: THE STRANGER

Amandine spent the rest of the afternoon making small repairs and alterations to the group's costumes by hand. She was appalled to see that Chitra's costume was held shut with safety pins, so she made an emergency trip to the five and dime for a zipper. On her way back, she passed a crate of tattered, used books in front of the booksellers. The bright yellow spine of a solitary Rogue Rider volume stood out to her like a beacon, stuffed between a cookbook and a repair manual. Half of the cover was missing, and she recalled that this particular tale ended in a cliffhanger, but she paid the cashier a penny for it and left the book inside René's tent for him to find later.

That evening while everyone else warmed up, Amandine was assigned to sell tickets. She put on her nicest mint green dress, wrapped her hair up in an ivory scarf, and sat at a folding table with a little cash box. People started arriving just before the sun set, and the line grew steadily while Amandine counted change, ripped tickets, and pointed the guests over to where the Russians were selling peanuts and popcorn. Snacks in hand, couples and families filled the long benches in front of their humble outdoor stage.

In the midst of this rush, Amandine tried to hide her surprise when a group of officers cut to the front of the line. She recognized the Inquestor right away, and his presence scared several people back to their cars.

She recovered her smile. "Lovely to see you again, officers. It will be a dollar and forty cents for your tickets."

"Miss Stewart," Carver said in a sing-song, disapproving tone. He leaned forward on the table, chin propped up on his hands. "When we last met, you neglected to tell me that your mother was imprisoned for treason, robbery, and brutal acts of violence against the NAR."

Amandine felt pinned by all of the faces that now stared at her. Defensively, she replied, "My mother may be French, but she's no rebel. *Maman* could sing 'Death Before Betraying My Home So Good to Me' sweeter than anybody you hear on the radio."

Carver laughed; he didn't buy it.

"What's my mother got to do with me, anyway?"

"Well, when you withhold crucial information like that, it makes you a highly suspicious character as well." He stared at her as if she were a child caught scribbling on the walls. "I don't know how you managed to avoid getting a red window on your papers with a record like hers. I don't know how you squeaked past the replacement home and rehabilitation programs either. It all strikes me as terribly—" His gaze drifted to someplace off in the middle distance before snapping back to hers. "—*Convenient* for you."

"I'm not hiding anything," Amandine said coolly. "I just make costumes for a traveling show." She saw another couple leave the line, and she knew she had to end this conversation before she lost any more customers. "Why don't you four enjoy the show on me?"

"What's this show all about?" Carver asked with genuine curiosity.

"I'm afraid I'm not the best salesgirl," she answered truthfully. "I don't actually know because I haven't seen it myself yet. I understand there will be strong men, acrobatics, magic, dancing…"

The way he was hanging on her every word gave her the impression that he was waiting for her to say something in particular. She took a wild guess. "I hear our contortionist is the most popular act in our freak show."

Carver laughed and said sincerely, "I like you, Miss Stewart."

If it wasn't for the knotted feeling in the pit of her stomach telling her not to trust him, Amandine might have liked him too. He still felt so familiar.

"I like you, so I feel inclined to warn you. You and your little show have just gained my undivided attention." He leaned in so close that she could smell his chypre aftershave over the camp odor of popcorn and generator exhaust. He lowered his voice to a murmur, and she found the sound to be surprisingly gentle and relaxing.

"You know, inquestors get a bum rap. Contrary to what you might believe, all we need is information. That's all I want. Just come along quietly and answer a few of my questions. We can go someplace private, maybe get a cup of coffee. We can be alone. Say the word, and I'll call off these gorillas."

He gestured to the trio in blue behind him who were fidgeting with anticipation. Amandine began to understand that all it would take was a single command from the Inquestor, and she could do nothing to resist them. She dropped her eyes and gripped her cash box as if it could somehow protect her. Carver noticed that even though Amandine had her head down, she was watching René test the stage lights from across the crowds. The Inquestor rested one hand on his mirror-bright pistol. "Come with me and we don't have to bother your friends."

Amandine felt the knot in her stomach tighten. She thought of harm coming to René, whose worst crime had been to extend a little kindness to her. *I have to be brave,* she told herself. *If I want to help maman, from now on, I must be brave.*

During her darkest times when fear began to close in, Amandine maintained her optimism by counting her blessings and letting their collective positivity beat back despair. Fortunately, she had a lot to be glad for. She thought of how she hadn't felt hunger in days. The Russians made delicious meals and always pushed second helpings on her. She thought of the smile that cracked through Sangria's tough exterior when she saw her new costume. She thought of her beautiful new dishes and sewing machine. She thought of René.

"Pardon me." Amandine looked up at Carver again, and her smile returned with all of the radiance her memories carried. "I'm very sorry, Inquestor, but I have work to do, and then I must be on my way. I'm afraid I can't go with you."

At first Carver tilted his head in confusion. He glanced over his shoulder at the officers behind him, then laughed in a resigned, hopeless way. "Well, how do you like that? We will be watching you very closely, Miss Stewart." He rummaged in his pocket for change and slid it across the table. "All of you."

"Enjoy!" Amandine ripped four tickets and waved.

"You chuckleheads owe me for the show," she heard Carver say to the others as they went to stand at the back of the audience. "Go buy me a popcorn and see if they got cherry cola."

Why would NAR agents be after me? Amandine thought. She felt very serious while she sold her last tickets. *I haven't done anything wrong. An administrator bought my house, for goodness' sake. If I were in some sort of trouble, wouldn't he have said something?*

She was startled from her thoughts when Marmi appeared behind her and pressed her painted hand to her shoulder. She was dressed for the show in voluminous robes decorated with rich embroidery, tiny bells, and stacks of fine jewelry.

"The police have returned," Marmi said suspiciously.

Amandine closed up the cash box and exhaled all of the tension she had been hiding from the last guests. "Yes, and I'm afraid it's my fault. They said they suspect me of trouble because my mother was a criminal—"

She paused, knowing full well that Marmi would be within her right to abandon her if she told the whole truth. She couldn't lie. She suspected that Marmi could see right through her if she tried, anyway.

"—And now they suspect all of you, too."

Marmi studied the officers and after a while, her face wrinkled in perplexity. "Odd. I can't make sense of what the Inquestor wants."

"Ma'am?"

"He wants you, that much is clear, but only as a means to get at something else…" Her voice trailed off, and she blinked rapidly. She looked from Amandine to René and then to the stage where she knew Sangria was preparing to play. Composing herself once more, Marmi put on a reassuring smile.

"Don't worry about the police for now, child. You just watch the show and start thinking about our costumes." She patted Amandine's cheek before getting into position behind the audience.

The stage lights dimmed, and Marmi moved up the center aisle while emotive violin music began playing from someplace backstage. She swayed as she walked, one arm carrying the bulk of her costume, the other moving gracefully before her. She turned when she reached the stage, humming and mumbling to the music before suddenly pointing to a man in the front row.

"You, sir! You're a carpenter," she declared.

The man glanced around, hoping that she was pointing at another carpenter sitting nearby. "That's right."

"You are worried about your livelihood," Marmi went on. "You brought your children out with you tonight because you didn't want them to worry too."

The little girls sitting on either side of him looked up at their father. He rubbed their twin braids and smiled sadly.

"Do not despair! Fortune will soon return and it will manifest in the form of a…" Marmi paused and waved her hand in front of her face as if to dispel some invisible fog. Finally, she laughed. "I hope you aren't superstitious! It will manifest in the form of a broken mirror. Watch for the signs, and your financial troubles will be over!"

The audience murmured in puzzlement.

Marmi pointed at someone else. "You, madam! You lost your man in the war. He wrote a final letter to you that was never sent. It is with his personal effects, held by a trusted comrade." She shut her eyes tightly and concentrated. "His name was... Clay?"

The woman gasped. "Yes! George Clayton! That was his best friend!"

"Find the man, and you will have your husband's last words to you."

The woman wept, and audience applauded again with more enthusiasm. Marmi bowed deeply, dropping her armful of weighty costume. "My name is Madame Marmi, and I bid you welcome. What I have just shown you is my gift of Infinite Sight. I see all: the past, the future, the living and the dead. It is but a taste of the wonders you will see here tonight, brought to you by some of the most skilled artists of the world!"

143

Amandine stopped listening because a pickup truck pulled into the lot and shined its headlights right at her. She shielded her eyes until he shut off the engine, and a man carrying a suitcase hopped from the cab.

A straggler, she thought, reopening her cash box as he strode towards her.

He was a handsome man in his mid-thirties with dark eyes and skin the color of gingerbread. His smile was perfect and genuine and everything about him, from the way he spoke to the way he moved, had a rhythm to it. It was as if he danced to a music that played only for him.

"Evening, *cher*," he said in a rich southern accent. "What's your name?"

"Amandine."

"I knew a girl named Amandine back in school. Everybody called her Mandy, so that's what I'm gonna call you." He tipped his hat. "How do you do, Miss Mandy? My name is Glorious Holloway."

The girl giggled; even his name was musical. "You're late for the show, but there is still room in the back. Thirty-five cents a ticket."

"As much as I love a good performance, I'm not actually here to see the show." He drummed his fingertips on his suitcase in a rapid cadence. "I'm looking for Madame Marmi. Is she around, by any chance?"

Amandine pointed to the stage where Marmi was presenting the twins for the opening act. "She's performing right now, but I can let her know you want to see her."

Glorious jingled his keys in his pocket and glanced back towards to road. "No, don't trouble her. I think I'll buy that ticket after all and speak to her after the show."

Amandine ripped a ticket for him and with another tip of his hat, he went to join the audience.

Now that her job was done, Amandine moved quietly around the cluster of trailers where the freak-acts were putting the finishing touches on their old costumes. Margaret was helping Carmelita get her jewelry on, while Tiny Greg stood on a stack of boxes in order to brush out the pelt of thick black hair on Juan's back to give him a wild, ferocious appearance. Nick turned from side to side in front of a long mirror, primping his feminine half. Amandine knew she wouldn't see René. It was his job to make sure the show ran smoothly, so she didn't want to interrupt him. Instead, she sought out the concession stand to grab a sack of popcorn. Salty snack and notebook in hand, she scaled a trailer to get a good view of the stage.

Sasha and Piotr didn't have a costume. In fact, they looked the same as they always did, just with a little bit of clown makeup. Their fire-juggling and acrobatic act was fast-paced and exciting. They thrilled the audience from their very first stunt, and the applause never seemed to stop.

The second act featured Jean-Claude's strong-man act. He wore a worn-out singlet that might have been a bright red and white stripe once upon a time, but it had faded to a dingy brown and gray. His act was paced a bit slower, and he did some flexing synchronized to the music before he lifted several audience volunteers on a plank across the shoulders.

"Man, oh man, I can barely lift myself out of bed in the morning, let alone four ladies and a fat guy." A voice from behind Amandine made her jump. Glorious was standing on the ladder, and he waved. "Sorry to startle you. Might I join you up here?

Amandine looked for Marmi, but she was nowhere to be found. "I don't really think you're allowed."

"May I stand on the ladder, then?" he asked. "That kitty-coat and his thugs are making me awful nervous. I'd like to try and stay out of their way."

"I know what you mean. They worry me, too." Amandine thought she might feel better with a little friendly company. "Sure, you can come up. The view is pretty good up here."

He climbed up and sat beside her, smiling gratefully when she offered her popcorn.

The dancers came next. Amandine wished she could hear the music from her vantage point because their movements were incredible. Their dance contained elements of ballet, traditional Indian dance and fluttering scarves in large, sweeping movements. Their costumes were in dire need of an update, and Amandine spent the majority of the act making quick notes and sketches. Glorious, on the other hand, was riveted by the performance, and he tapped his knee in time to the music in his head.

After the ladies, Ambroise had an interesting wild-man act where he danced in a grass skirt to a pounding drum beat. By the time he reached the end of his performance, he had

146

swallowed swords, spit fire, and finished with a war-cry, holding two flaming swords aloft to thunderous applause.

Coronado had the final act, and Amandine looked forward to this above all. He made birds appear out of thin air, lit small flames using René's new trick, and he even made Ludmilla vanish with a wave of a cloth and reappear instantly in the center of the audience. His magical performance was very good, but it didn't have the breathtaking impact she thought he wanted.

Marmi emerged from behind the stage curtain once more and thanked the audience for their attendance. She promised more excitement in the freak show and private fortune-tellings for only a dime more.

Glorious clapped as the show came to an end. "No intermission?"

"This is the intermission," the girl explained. "Sort of. I think the freak show is an optional tour."

"I like that idea." Glorious climbed down the ladder first, then offered his hand up to Amandine. "My last employer would parade his freaks out on stage, and it would often send ladies with delicate sensibilities into convulsions of terror."

Amandine wanted to ask Glorious about his last job, but she knew it was none of her business. "I think you can talk to Marmi now," she said. "I'll ask and see if she has a moment before she starts her readings. Follow me." She beckoned, leading him around the crowd to Marmi's tent.

Marmi granted her permission to enter and turned from her vanity in surprise when she saw a strange man follow her seamstress inside. Amandine made hasty introductions.

147

"This is Mr. Glorious Holloway, ma'am. He came in after the show started and said he wanted to speak with you."

"Welcome," Marmi said cautiously. "Amandine, the hem on my red gown has come loose. Please repair it."

The seamstress wasn't certain if the gown really needed repair. She didn't even have her sewing kit on her, but she quickly understood Marmi's request to mean that she wanted her to stay in the tent as long as a stranger was around. She obediently went to inspect the dark, heavy fabric while she pretended not to listen.

"Thank you, Madame Marmi," Glorious said, removing his hat. "I know showtime is a busy time for y'all, so I'll be short and to the point."

Marmi settled into her folding chair and lit her pipe, her eyes fixed on the visitor.

"I'm from Istrouma, down in Lou'siana. I was an electrician by day and a jazz piano player by night when Mr. Cornelius Johnstone offered me a load of money to play music for his shows."

Marmi's hard expression lit with clarity. "I've heard of you. You're the sole reason Johnstone's shows are achieving any measure of success."

"My reputation precedes me." Glorious bowed with a half-smile. "Well, you might have also heard that working for Johnstone is the pits. I don't want to take up your time with the story of why, but I heard whisperings that Johnstone was looking to get his droppers to rub me out. I wasn't too keen on a road-side dirt-nap, so I have come to offer you my services

148

as a musician, electrician, entertainer, stage-hand, whatever you need, in exchange for some protection from that man."

"You must think I am a fool." Marmi frowned. "Johnstone is cruel, but he's not an idiot. He wouldn't kill his golden goose."

"He would if he got his hands on a machine that could play my music for me." Glorious gently set down his suitcase and knelt to open it. Marmi arched an eyebrow at the peculiar mess of wires, switches, and tiny glass bulbs that protruded from it. "She may not look like much now, but this is Polly. She was going to be my costar in a musical act that's gonna change the way the NAR listens to music. She was going to win Johnstone the big prize at the festival, and he was willing to kill me for her." Still kneeling, he pushed the case towards Marmi's bare, painted feet like a devotee making an offering to a goddess. "Let me travel with you, madame, and on my honor, Polly is yours. Let me finish building her, and she will sing you to salvation."

"If you're so sure that your device will win, you ought to just could just enter in the festival by yourself," Marmi said.

Glorious reached inside his jacket and held out his identification. His photo was framed with a red bar.

Marmi glanced at it once and reevaluated him. "You didn't get that stringing lights in Istrouma."

"No, ma'am. I got that for daring to play jazz in N'Aurelian. As Johnstone was fond of reminding us, those red windows meant that we were all one phone call away from the backseat of an Interceptor."

"So he used inquestors to keep you in check." Marmi exhaled a ribbon of smoke that seemed to point straight to Amandine. "As I am sure you noticed, we've already got an inquestor on us. If I take you on, the only thing you could possibly offer me is more trouble."

Glorious remained kneeling. He had not yet run out of offerings. "I can help bring the others back."

Glancing up from her meaningless task, Amandine could tell that Glorious had struck a tender nerve. Marmi bit the mouthpiece on her pipe and used a gravelly voice to hide her emotion. "Tell me who wants to return."

"Everyone. The freaks, the acts, and even some of Johnstone's original people." He closed up his suitcase. "All I want is to join you. I was able to bring my own truck. I have everything I need to take care of myself, so I don't require much, just a job and a group of nice folks to travel with."

Marmi snarled, "I don't believe you."

"It's all the truth, ma'am. I swear it."

She jabbed her pipe in his direction. "You're hiding something. I can't see what it is, but it's dangerous, and you want to use it to coerce me."

Glorious turned his hat in his hands humbly. "You're right, ma'am. I haven't been completely upfront with you."

Amandine's mouth fell open a little in astonishment. Could Marmi's Infinite Sight be true? Could she really see all?

"Well, then!" Marmi snapped. "Out with it or out with you!

"I got the feeling that you might not trust me, what with my employment history and all, so I brought somebody to vouch for me." He replaced his hat, knowing that the conversation was quickly reaching its end. "Heard he was one of yours, so I brought him home. Baji Rao is sleeping in my truck."

"Rao?" This seemed to be the last thing Marmi expected to hear. It shocked her so badly that she spoke his name as a question, the first Amandine had ever heard. "I thought... I thought Rao was dead."

Eager to prove his goodwill, Glorious beckoned to her, and Marmi flew out of the tent behind him. Amandine abandoned the gown and followed. They moved quickly through the crowds, over to where the guests were parked.

Glorious drove an old, red, electrician's truck, and the back was loaded with boxes of lights, wires, and other pieces of scrap. Marmi looked into the cab. A huge figure covered in a moth-eaten woolen blanket was sleeping across the bench seat. She wrenched the door open and the figure stirred.

From Marmi's emotional reaction to Rao's return, Amandine expected to see a lost husband or brother. What appeared before them in the cab was a full-grown, ten-foot long, four-hundred-pound Bengal tiger. He lifted his head and stared at Marmi with his jaws agape, black tufted ears twitching in her direction. Suddenly, he pounced like a golden flash and flatted Marmi to the dirt.

Amandine shrieked.

A crowd circled around them to see what the trouble was. Sasha, Piotr, Jean-Claude, and Ambroise came charging through the throng, shouldering people aside. To Amandine's surprise, they didn't defend their matriarch. Instead, all four men dog-piled on the animal, crying out in Russian and French.

"Koshka vernulas!"

"Tu es un chaton méchant!"

Through the chaos, Amandine spotted Marmi half-pinned by this enormous cat, squeezing his neck and weeping into his fur while he rubbed his yellow teeth across her shoulder. "My sweet baby," she sobbed. "My ferocious Baji Rao, where have you been all this time?"

"Baji Rao ghar hai!" Chitra cried, and the dancers leaped into the pile on top of the tiger.

Marmi decided that she'd had enough as more of her cast-members threw themselves into the joyous reunion on the ground. Glorious took both of her arms and hauled her upright, but her long costume got stuck. Marmi was able to get free when the tiger rolled over to accept scratches on his belly.

René hurried over from the freak show. He squatted to ruffle the tiger's face between his hands, and Amandine noticed a bright yellow book tucked into his back pocket. "It's good to see you again, *mon ami*." He gave Rao's fur a violent tousle while the tiger chuffed and gently mouthed his forearm.

"What's going on here?" Coronado demanded once he finally made his dramatic appearance.

"Rao's come home," Marmi beamed. "And he brought a musician back with him."

Lily Aerfeldt had just locked the cafe door for the night. She was about to start cleaning the floors when she heard a tap at the front window. At first she didn't see anybody in the darkness, but as her eyes adjusted, she spotted a man waving to get her attention. She politely shook her head and pointed to the hours posted on the door. He pantomimed begging pitifully, and she was about to refuse him again until the streetlight happened to glint off of the silver catamount on his shoulder.

Lily dropped her broom and ran to unlock the door; she knew what happened to people that denied service to inquestors.

Twenty minutes passed, and all he had asked for was black coffee. She resumed cleaning the floor in silence, pausing every few minutes to refill his cup while he read a newspaper in the booth nearest the window. When that was finished, and she had nothing left to do but wait for the Inquestor to leave, she pretended to clean the counter again.

"Miss?"

Lily jumped.

"Sorry. I didn't catch your name."

"Aerfeldt, Inquestor, sir," she said, rubbing even harder at the laminate surface. She heard the booth squeak, and she glanced up to see that he had turned to face her.

"That's a mouthful. Got anything shorter?"

Quietly, she answered, "Lily, sir."

"Lily, if it's not too much trouble, would you mind bringing me more coffee?" He playfully shook his empty cup in her direction.

"Yes, Inquestor, sir." She reached for the nearly empty pot. At this rate, she'd need to brew him another. "Can I get anything else for you?"

"What have you got?" he asked.

"Well..." She tried to remember what was in the refrigerator. "The cook left a while ago, but I can whip up a sandwich. We always got pie or maybe a slice of leftover cake in the back."

"Actually, what I'd really appreciate is a little company."

She fumbled the coffee pot. "S-sir?"

"Please sit." He indicated the seat across from him. "Let's talk awhile."

Lily trembled as she slid into the booth. She touched her yellow hair nervously, coiling the end around her finger while she waited for his next demand. To her puzzlement, he seemed to be waiting for her to speak first.

"So, Inquestor... is there anything good in the newspaper?"

He chuckled. "You don't have to keep calling me that. 'Carver' will do."

"Mister... Carver?" she asked carefully.

"Miss Aerfeldt," he responded with a nod. He tipped the page downwards so she could see what he was reading. "In answer to your question, there's plenty of good stuff in the newspaper. Listen to this. You won't believe it." He cleared his

154

throat. "Dear Emmy, I got engaged to the girl of my dreams, but since then she has become another person. To put it bluntly, she has grown so fat, she's nearly added another person! I thought she was supposed to get plump long, *long* after we've been married. How do I get back the thin girl I proposed to? Help me! Dread to be Wed."

Carver glanced up to check Lily's response. She was confused, but she politely tried to keep her expression neutral.

"I think it's his own fault," he said, ignoring whatever Emmy had to say on the matter. "He's a young fellow, so it's very likely he's with the army. He has all of his NAR agent perks, including storehouse privileges. If her family was having a hard time getting food, he probably used that to win her over in the first place. This one is easy. Stop feeding your fiance, and she won't get fat."

He shook his head and scanned the page again. Tapping another letter, he exclaimed, "Here's one I can better relate to. 'Dear Emmy, my husband insists that I starch his shirts. Do I have to? I'm a welder, not a laundress. Signed, To Starch, Or Not To Starch?'" He pounded the table so hard, he made the flatware rattle. "Absolutely! A man's shirt should always be as crisp and starchy as a bag of potato chips!"

A giggle escaped from Lily, and a bit of tension seemed to vanish along with it. She thought perhaps all he wanted was a little friendly conversation, so she tried to treat him like a regular patron. She noted his perfect black suit. "I bet your wife spends ages taking care of your uniforms."

"I'm not married," he said, putting his paper away.

She wasn't sure where to focus her attention because each time she looked up from the table, he was watching her intently. While he didn't seem quite so threatening when he was giving his own take on the advice column, her instincts still told her to be wary.

"A bachelor?" she asked lightly.

"Unfortunately," he pouted. "I tried to get a girl to come out for coffee with me earlier, but she shut me down."

"Ouch," Lily said, feeling a little more at ease. "Tough luck."

"To make it worse, my boss is making me drag around a bunch of academy-hopefuls, and they saw the whole thing."

"How embarrassing." She was leaning forward now.

"Honestly, I think those goons scared her off."

"That's not it. I think it was—" She stopped abruptly, realizing that she was being too careless.

"It was what?" he pressed.

Timidly, she responded, "Maybe it's because you're an inquestor."

He frowned. "Do ladies not like inquestors?"

She grimaced and shook her head slowly.

Carver looked surprised. "Why not? I make good money. I have a nice apartment in Nieuwestad. I mean, just look at my beautiful car!" He pointed at the curvaceous Interceptor parked outside, gleaming beneath the streetlights. "It's the intimidating amount of laundry, isn't it? Unbelievable! The inquestors' strict grooming standards are ruining my love life!"

Lily giggled again and tried to reassure him. "It's not about all that."

"Then what is it?" he pleaded. "Tell me, because I have had just the absolute worst dumb luck in the romance department."

"Maybe you should write to Emmy." She tried to keep a straight face.

Carver burst out laughing. "I mean it!"

"Alright," she gave in. "How to put this? It's because they're afraid of you. They're afraid of what you do."

"Is that so?" The Inquestor's smile vanished, and his voice became measured and low. "And what, precisely, are *they* so afraid of? What, exactly, do *they* think I do?"

Her breath stopped in her throat.

"Are *you* afraid of me, Lily?" he demanded.

If she had offended the Inquestor, it was too late and no use to apologize. Her eyes dropped down to her lap, and she said nothing. Unexpectedly, he reached across the table and tilted her chin upwards with a finger.

"You shouldn't be," he chirped. "Go on, ask me anything."

She was unsure if he was being sincere. The person in front of her was odd, funny, and handsome: nothing like what she had expected an inquestor to be. As if reading her thoughts, he gave up all traces of his official formality and laid back in the booth.

"I'm an open book. I'll tell you anything you want to know about me, the inquestors, good laundry tips, the best coffee places on the east side of the country..." He trailed off, smiling warmly at her.

Lily had no idea what she could possibly ask him. The first question that came to mind was silly, but it was all she could think of.

"What's... your favorite color?"

"Red," he said seriously. "It's all I ever see."

She rearranged the salt and pepper shakers on the table. "Where're you from?"

"Arizona, pre-war. Now I'm in Nieuwestad when I'm not in the field."

"What brings you to the cafe tonight?"

"Needed some coffee, and this was the first place I found with its lights on." He smiled, amused by the way she slid a sugar packet across the tabletop just to keep her hands busy. "I came from a show just outside of town. I didn't see the whole thing, though. I left during the magic act."

"Why? No good?"

"No, it was really good for such a little production. I just couldn't figure out how his magic tricks worked, and that was making me angry." He sulked, clearly still irritated that he had been fooled. "Anyway, as soon as I was out of there, I got rid of the barnacles stuck to my stern and went to spend some time alone."

"And those barnacles, are they making it hard for you to do your job?"

He groaned and rubbed his temples. "Like you wouldn't believe. They're all about yelling and punching and making a mess of things. Don't get me wrong, they're good

158

agents. They're just what the NAR wants, but they're just what I *don't* want right now."

Lily had stopped her fidgeting, completely engrossed in this unexpected conversation with the Inquestor. When she first saw him, she was struck by his exemplary appearance and fearsome reputation. Now as it was growing late, she could start to see imperfections in him. His black hair was coming loose from its style, and he needed a shave. His dark eyes were tired but seemed content for the moment. Now that she had the courage to really look at him, she saw something she never expected to see in one of the most dangerous men in the NAR: vulnerability.

"What do you want right now?" she asked.

"I want to be left alone!" He lightly hit the table with the edge of his hand to emphasize each point. "I want to be free to do my job the way I want to do it. I want a raise! I want a vacation! But most of all..."

Carver dropped his voice a little. Her hand was resting on the table, and he took it cautiously. She didn't flinch or resist. To her own surprise, she smiled at his touch, finding it warm even through his glove.

"Most of all, I just want one person to share everything I have with, even if it's only for a little while."

They looked into each other's eyes.

"So," she said softly. "You don't really want to be alone."

Suddenly, the door slammed open, and the bell jangled wildly. Lily yanked her hand away and jumped out of her seat as one of Carver's blue shadows stalked up to the booth.

159

"Speak of the barnacle." Carver smiled sadly. He went for his mug and found it empty, so he folded his hands and waited for the officer to explain his presence.

"Pardon me, Inquestor," the officer said, using respectful words but a very disrespectful tone. "May I please speak with you?"

"Sure you can, Mister...?" He gestured for him to sit where Lily had just been.

"*Officer* Charles Norton," he said stiffly, taking the seat. "I have been traveling with you for nearly three days, Inquestor. I had hoped that you would at least remember my name."

"Sorry." Carver turned to the waitress and pointed at his mug. "Lily, could I trouble you for some more coffee?"

Her heart thundering, she nodded curtly and retreated behind the counter. She listened while she prepared a fresh pot.

"What can I do for you, Chuck?" Carver sighed.

"Inquestor, we were asked by our captain to assist you in your hunt for rebels. For our efforts, we were to gain some experience to better prepare us for the exam, and with any luck, gain your endorsement to the academy as well."

"Yep, I get it," he nodded mechanically. "You thought tagging along with me would give you an edge over all of the other hopefuls. Anyway, what's your beef?"

"*My beef,*" he growled. "Is that there is clearly something up with those side-show freaks, and that girl couldn't be redder if her throat was cut. Yet you're willing to trail them all the way back to Nieuwestad at a snail's pace just to see if it will yield something bigger?"

160

Norton expected the Inquestor to interject, but Carver didn't answer. He was preoccupied with scooting Lily's sugar packet across the table like a toy car.

"And that attempt at getting her to come quietly tonight was pathetic! Half the town saw it, and now nobody will respect the inquestors anymore. You should have beat an answer out of her in front of everybody! To top it all off, now those freaks know we're following them."

"I'm following them," Carver corrected him. "If you don't like the way I handle things, you can go back to Pearisville. I will not have your ego muck up my case."

"Your case?" he blustered.

"Yes." Carver straightened his posture, and the sugar packet vanished. "My aim isn't simply 'get the girl.' It's to put an end to the rebellion in the NAR."

"But what does she—?"

"It's not about her! You need to look at the bigger picture." He slid the folded newspaper across the table and tapped the front-page photograph to prove his point.

Surrounded by shackled men and women, Caroline Stewart glared into the camera beneath the headline.

"Is it coming together yet, Chuck?" Carver said patiently. "Pieces falling into place? Without her mother to protect her, where do you think the girl is going to go? Why is she headed to Nieuwestad in the company of a bunch of transient foreigners?"

"You think she's headed to another rebel safehouse?"

"I think she's heading to *the* rebel safehouse." Carver traced a square around the picture, boxing the prisoners in.

"The place where Tall-Me hangs his hat and Cleo kicks off her heels after a hard day's murder."

"But what use is some teenager to the rebel leaders?"

"Not sure, but if she's important to them, she's important to me. What I do know is that she lived in one of their safehouses, and that knowledge alone could be invaluable." The Inquestor laced his fingers together and stretched, cracking all of his knuckles at once. "Fortunately, I'm very good at getting people to talk."

Skimming the article, Norton didn't realize that his mouth had fallen open. He sputtered, "But the girl's an air-head! She didn't even recognize you!"

"An act. She was pretending, just like that dish was trying to misdirect me with her feminine wiles and that French kid pretended to be a gimpy mook." Carver paused and raised a quizzical eyebrow at Norton. "You didn't actually buy that bunk, did you?"

"Well, I thought that—"

"Oh, dear!" The Inquestor's face fell. "You did! Well, that's a real shame. I'll have to wire IHQ in the morning and let them know not to expect you at the testing center."

"Sir?" Norton's eye twitched.

"If you can't see through a few smart-assed teenagers, then I cannot in good faith give someone like you my endorsement. You don't need to pass any exam if all you want to do is beat up girls, freaks, and foreigners in public. You're better off staying with the police."

"I will take the exam with or without your endorsement," Norton tried to keep his voice level. "I don't

162

know how a nancing, off-the-cob... *buffoon* like you managed to pass it, but I have what it takes to wear the black and then some!"

"Listen here, jackass." Carver cast the newspaper aside in anger. "You can forget about the black. You can forget about the exam, because the only way you're ever going to see IHQ is in a Nieuwestad travel brochure. *I'm blacklisting you!*"

Norton blanched, and for a while the only sound in the cafe was the ticking wall clock and the gurgling coffee machine. His stunned silence didn't last, however, and Norton's anger soon seethed up and boiled out of control.

"If you don't get that girl," he snarled. "If you don't call the local blues and round up every last one of those freaks tonight, I will do it myself. I will show you how inquestors are supposed to handle traitors! Five minutes with me, and that scrawny brat will spill everything she knows about the rebels! The only red left in this town will be their blood all over those stupid trailers!" Spit flying, he bellowed, "*I will get results!*"

Norton tried to stare Carver down, but the Inquestor wouldn't engage him. He only regarded him with mild irritation until Lily returned with the coffee. Carver brightened when she refilled the cups, and he caught her wrist before she could bolt behind the counter again.

"Thank you, Lily." He rubbed the back of her hand with his thumb. "Earlier you mentioned pie. Could you please bring us a slice? I bet pie would cheer up my friend here while we work out a couple of little gripes."

She nodded, and after hesitating a moment longer, he released her.

Lily pushed through the swinging doors into the kitchen. Once she managed to unlock the cooler, she scanned their stock and tried to guess what flavor the Inquestor would like.

Red. He's probably a cherry kind of guy.

She cut him a generous slice from an unopened box and crowned it with a dollop of whipped cream. Satisfied with her charming presentation, she set the plates on a serving tray and backed through the double doors into the dining room again.

The sight before her made Lily drop both plates in horror. Blood was splattered across the booth and running down the front window. Carver smashed Norton's face with the handle of his 1911 again and again, and each blow whittled away at Norton's ability to resist.

"*'Nancing?'*" the Inquestor cried. "*'Off the cob?'* I'll show you 'off the cob!'" Casting the sticky weapon aside, he pounced over the table and caught Norton in a chokehold. Norton kicked and groped at the Inquestor as the last of his life was slowly crushed out of him. With a final jerk, Carver snapped his neck.

Carver met Lily's eyes in the reflection of the front window. He spun to face her and let Norton's body fall in a crumpled heap to the floor.

"I'm sorry about the mess," he said, smiling apologetically. He straightening his blood-soaked jacket, picked up his pistol, and stalked towards her. "And I'm very sorry you had to see that."

164

CHAPTER 9: THE CONDEMNED

Deep within the Nieuwestad Prison of War Criminals in a mostly vacant block, a man named John Merchant dug into the wall beneath his bunk. John was a slight, bookish man with a neatly groomed beard and presently, he was the cell's only occupant. Almost every prisoner, except for those captured with Cleo in the last big bust, had been taken to the city square the day before. As he scratched at the wall with a rudimentary pick, John tried not to think about how much time he had left before he made that trip himself.

He wiggled out from beneath the bunk and crouched to examine his work. Hours of careful, quiet digging resulted in a hole the size of a soup can. When he replaced the cement wall-front, the hiding place was nearly invisible. Using his hands, he swept the leftover crumbled concrete into his hat and got to his feet with a stretch. He hid his pick inside his bed frame and left the cell carrying his hat in his pocket and a large book under his arm.

John kept his head down while he walked briskly down the echoing corridor. There weren't many guards in the near-empty D-block, but John knew that it was best not to make eye-contact with one. They could give him a beating if they thought he looked threatening. Then again, they could beat him if they thought he was hiding something, too.

Predictably, the guard on duty shouted at him. "Merchant! What are you up to?"

"Library, sir," he said clearly, raising the book but not his eyes.

"That book too long for you?"

"Dumas was known for his adventures but not for his brevity, sir," he replied with a wry smile. "I was hoping they had that book of dirty poetry in 'cause I got my name on the waitlist."

The guard laughed and flipped his newspaper to the funny pages.

Located in the main corridor between blocks, the library was once no more than a broom closet. Over time, the prisoners had organized the space to hold the growing collection of books left behind by their predecessors. It was run on an honor system, and people had taken to writing their names on the inside cover of the books they borrowed as a way to leave their mark. Some of the more popular titles had names on both covers with lists stretching into the beginning chapters.

John opened the heavy tome to add his own name, and he found something curious. There was only one name written in sloppy blue ink, followed by a row of tally marks that stretched across the title page like a multi-colored picket fence. At first he was confused. Had one person really read this book over a hundred times? He wondered if he knew the book's original owner when he realized that the sloppy name was "Edmund Dantès."

John sighed. He left his mark, a solitary graphite slash, before he replaced the old book and retrieved the one he wanted.

The NAR wanted people to believe that this prison held the nation's worst traitors, thieves, and murderers, but John saw something else entirely. Taking the upper levels back to his own block, he saw a typical American community where men and women carried on as best they could until their time was up. In one cell, a man read the sports highlights aloud to his roommates. In the next, a husband and wife sat together on the bottom bunk, staring at a photograph in their hands. In another, a group of women set each other's hair with strips of a torn bed sheet and gossiped about a man with a reputation. Of course there were a few real criminals among them, but John knew if he took a sample of the crimes these people were going to die for, he would find such offenses as "possession of illicit diversions" and "agricultural larceny" before he found treason or murder.

John stopped to visit a friend who lived at the end of the row, and he found him playing cards with his cellmates.

"Hey, Dick!" John called out. Dick was a serious, sturdy man who farmed before he served in the army, and he was imprisoned for using both of his skill sets outside of the NAR's permission. Ignoring Dick's scowl, John looped one arm through the bars and thumbed the worn pages to the first poem. "I just got the book of dirty prose. What do you think of this? '*Come slowly— Eden, Lips unused to thee— Bashful— sip thy jasmines— As the fainting bee—*'"

Irritated, Dick reached beneath his bunk and threw something at him. "Get out of here with that filth, John! Don't you know I've been saved?"

John caught the coil of scrap-wire and apologized. "Oh, right. Sorry, pal. See you at the mess hall later?"

Dick nodded and returned to his game.

John went down to the lower levels and found another friend, Mel, daydreaming on his bunk and picking his teeth with a splintered matchstick. A firefighter pre-war, somebody thought it would be funny to issue him a flamethrower when he was drafted. Before he was arrested, Mel was the one Cleo called on after a storehouse was emptied or a replacement home was liberated so that those buildings could never be used again.

"Mel, you wanna hear something that'll make you blush?" John waved the book at him, getting his attention with one of the racy illustrations. "'*As I would free the white almond from the green husk, so I would strip your trappings off, Beloved. And fingering the smooth and polished kernel, I should see that in my hands glittered a gem beyond counting.*'"

"Trap-stripping, you say?" Mel sat up and took the book from John. He scanned the poem and returned it with a grin on his face. "I'm going to have to check that one out after you."

"Good luck," John answered dismally. "The waitlist is months long. I get the feeling we'll have all taken the last tour bus to Nieuwestad by then."

He opened his book as he walked away, and two paper clips and safety pin slid into his waiting palm.

John met his third friend, Bob, on his way to the yard with a group of others. "Hiya, Bob. Going outside?" he asked pleasantly. "Take my hat. It's warm out."

"Want to come out with us?" Bob casually pocketed the hat filled with chipped concrete. "I hear it's awfully lonesome up in D-block these days."

"Not today. I've got a new book."

"What is it?" Bob asked with feigned interest. While men like Mel and Dick served on the ground during the war, Bob was an ex-administrator. Before that, he taught classic literature and had his name on nearly every book in their broom-closet library already.

"You've read the Bible, right?" John said.

"You're funny, John. Ma couldn't drag me to church."

John rolled his eyes. Apparently Bob had an appreciation for theatrics as well. Surrounded by prying eyes and suspicious ears, John didn't think this was the appropriate time for improvisation, but he had no choice but to play along.

"I bet you wish you had. Listen to this! Song of Solomon." John read the passage with exuberance, but when he looked up to gauge reactions, he saw only looks of confusion.

Bob scratched his head. "'*Strengthen me with raisins?*' What does that even mean?"

"It's supposed to be dirty," John said. "Looks like your ma couldn't drag you to school either." Bob punched him in the shoulder, and John felt the heft of a wooden spool fall into the breast pocket of his red jumpsuit.

Just then, a group of guards came storming up to them with their nightsticks drawn. "No congregating in the corridor," one barked like the red Cerberus insignia on his shoulder. He grabbed John forcefully by the collar. "You there! What've you got?"

"A book, sir."

"What book? Read it!"

John opened a page at random and came upon a poem that fortunately didn't take much imagination for everyone present to interpret, especially not with the accompanying illustration.

"I'll be confiscating that." The guard snatched the book away. "Get back to your own block immediately."

John retreated to his cell, shaking from the thrill of nearly being caught. After all, he had what he was really after.

Later that night, hours after lights-out had been called, John laid quietly in his bunk. When he heard footsteps echoing through the empty hall, he rolled onto his side and pretended to sleep while he watched the door.

"You up?" Mel whispered. The silhouette of Dick and Bob appeared behind him.

"Yeah." John moved to the floor and the others joined him in a circle, sitting cross-legged. "I got it done, too. How about some light?"

Dick took out a small tobacco tin that had been filled with grease. A wick protruded from the top and Mel lit it with a match, setting the tiny lamp in the center of their circle. John crawled under his bed and went to retrieve what he had been hiding in the hole in his wall.

To an untrained eye, what he brought out looked like a pile of junk tacked to a scrap of wood. To these men, each war veterans and now imprisoned freedom-fighters, this was a foxhole radio.

"Does it work?" Dick asked.

"Of course it works," John snapped. "I wouldn't risk us all getting shot if it didn't."

"What do you think it's gonna be? Music or news?" Bob asked, leaning back on his hands. "My money's on music. DJMA loves him some swing."

"It had better be news," Dick grumbled. "Or what's the point?"

John connected a few loose wires, and then ever so faintly, they could hear static through the tin can speaker. They leaned in so close that they were nearly touching heads while John searched for the right signal.

"I knew this was a waste of time," Dick lamented after several minutes of fruitless static. "It doesn't work."

"We couldn't hear anything over your bellyaching anyway," Mel hissed. "John knows radios. If we can't get a signal, it's probably because DJMA threw a fit up at the station and broke something."

"Thank you," John said appreciatively and resumed his search. Smiles broke out on all of their faces when the small device finally picked up a bubbly clarinet solo on the rebel's pirate radio station.

"Ha! Music! I called it," Bob exclaimed, and the others shushed him.

They listened to the big band record in silence, tapping their fingers in time. For some, the music reminded them of nights after a successful raid when Marc Antony would sling record after hot record, Cleo would dance, and they'd all feast on the spoils of a busted storehouse. For others, it reminded them of simpler times before the war. Whatever memories it stirred up, it carried them away from the prison where release was synonymous with death. For those few, short, happy minutes, they were free.

"Here he comes," John whispered when the song concluded. "Finally."

"Hello, ladies, gentlemen, boys, and girls," DJMA cried with exuberance. "Rebels, freedom-fighters, disgruntled citizens, and the true-blue bozos trying to figure out where I am and how to decode my secret messages. *Et-gay offay ai-may ashun-stay!* I don't want to talk to you."

The prisoners chuckled. It felt good to hear their old comrade's voice again.

"Good evening! I'm DJMA, or Marc Antony for those of you tuning in for the first time. That record I just played for you was one of my personal favorites. It's lost its sleeve and label, though, so I can't tell you for certain what it was called or who played it. See, that's the problem with the world these days. I wanna get some good tunes, I gotta get 'em from a man who's been hiding 'em in his outhouse and used the sleeves for kindling years ago.

"I oughtta name this record before it's lost to history. Yup, I'm gonna do that right now. Here's a bit of tape. Here's a marker. I think it's called, 'Rhythm on the Radio' and the fella who sings it… golly, his name is right on the tip of my tongue. If I had a phone you could call, I'd give you my number so you could tell me what that song really was. Heck, if I gave out my number on the air, those blue bastards would be keeping the operators up all night trying to chat with yours truly.

"There's only one person I want calling me right now, and that's this doll I met in my travels last week. She was as cute as a button! I played up my best traits like my handsomeness, my singleness, and my popularity, but I don't think she bought it. It's so hard to meet nice girls when the blacks-and-blues keep sending all the free ones to replacement homes. How's a guy like me ever going to get some company up here? This station gets awfully lonely, especially without Cleo around. Somebody cheer me up and call this number. It's the President of the New American Republic, Alexander Fairchild's personal phone number. Dial it up now."

"D'you think it's really the President's number?" Bob whispered.

As if he had heard him, DJMA shouted, "It really is his number! One of my fans up in Nieuwestad sent it to me. I tried it out the other day and managed to get ahold of Fairchild

173

himself! Well, I just left a message with Old Alf for his wife. I told him to thank her for the lovely, romantic evening we shared, eating cheeseburgers and smashing mailboxes in a stolen Interceptor. I was hoping for an intimate tour of the presidential palace, but Alf needed a bedtime story so we had to cut the good times short. If you're listening, Gertie-Baby, do Marky a favor and drop in on the salon before our next date. Your moustache is impressive for a lady, but when we kiss it sure tickles something fierce."

Everyone was grinning and biting their tongues to stay silent, but poor Mel was nearly smothering himself to keep his laughter in control.

"But you're not here to listen to me brag about my prank calls. You want some news! I know my paper is around here somewhere, but this place is such a mess. I really need a lady up here. This station isn't the only thing that could use a feminine touch. Ah, here's my paper. Today's edition of the NAR Globe was hiding under my coffee. Here we go. It says... 'aircraft carrier sinks, all crew aboard presumed dead.' Wow, that's a big one! Was it our aircraft carrier? Yup. Sure was. The NARS Vulcan. Says here she was coming back from Europe and lost communications in the middle of the night. She was presumed missing until a fishing boat came across her wreckage. Now I don't know much about boats, but aircraft carriers are supposed to be the biggest, toughest floaters out there, right? I mean, you'd need a gun the size of the Fourteenth Street-Canarsie Line to make a dent in it, right? Well, the fine journalists at the Globe think it was Tall-Me!

"Oh, that Tall-Me! What a card! They say he's derailed trains, robbed banks, slaughtered countless NAR police forces, and now they say he's wrecking aircraft carriers? Does he have the kraken at his command? I suppose now he's got his own fleet of haunted pirate ships that just appear when his enemies need vanquishing? How does one little man, with maybe a couple of his red buddies tagging along, take out an aircraft carrier when he's busy raiding storehouses and liberating replacement homes here on dry land? Why are you so quick to accuse him, Globe, but you won't consider that maybe, just maybe, it's one of the many European nations we've pissed off? England? France? Germany, maybe? I don't know about you, but I certainly wouldn't appreciate it if I caught my supposed allies two-timing me. There are too many unanswered questions here, Globe. You need to brush up on your reporting. You wants some tips on journalism? Call me. Or don't. I don't have a phone.

"Now, ladies and gentlemen, I have never met Tall-Me in person, but if I did, I would like to shake this man's hand. If he did even half of the stuff he's accused of, well, that makes him a true American patriot in my book.

"What else is in the news today? Looks like we have battling headlines. The next one says 'top rebel leader Cleo found entirely guilty. Public execution by firing squad scheduled for Freedom Festival.'"

DJMA paused. They could hear papers shuffling across his desk and a clatter, which might have been a falling coffee cup.

"Sorry, folks. I know that the number one rule of radio is no dead air, but this one's hitting me a little hard. Unlike Tall-Me, I know Cleo. We've been close for years. If she hadn't insisted I stay at the station, I probably would have been captured with her and all of the others, too. She's one of the most... incredible women I have ever met. This picture they have of her is garbage. Probably manipulated. They made her look like this shriveled, weaselly little old lady. In reality, she is keen and lean. Her hair is beautiful— all soft and curly, like a giant, chocolate war-bonnet. She's got this beautiful dark voice and big beautiful eyes. I know, I said 'beautiful' a lot. I mean, that's why they called her Cleo. She was like the ancient queen with a commanding presence. That's why I go by Marc Antony now, too. She's got my heart, and I'd gladly die for her. I bet her whole crew feels the same way.

"You know, nobody else could shoot like her either. She had this gun, this humongous Sharps rifle of legend, that was nearly as tall as me, and she'd carry it around like a lady carries her purse. One time, I saw her shoot— hang on, I'm keeping that story to myself. You god-damned, dirty, blue bastards tuning in can keep guessing as to what exactly she's so good at shooting at. I'll give you a hint. You better keep your curtains shut!

"This next song I'm dedicating to Cleo. It's got some keen Egyptian themes in it, and you night-owls can really cut a rug to it, too." There was a clinking of glass. "I'm pouring myself a *special* coffee now. Cheers, Cleo. Don't reach for your snake yet, and I won't fall on my sword. Hang in there, boss!"

John had only listened to the song's introduction when his instincts alerted him to another presence. He looked over his shoulder and jumped a mile high when he saw a silhouette standing in the open doorway of his cell. Everyone scrambled to their feet.

Caroline Stewart laughed softly and leaned against the wall with her arms crossed. "Easy, gentlemen. It's only me." She took a hand-rolled cigarette from her pocket, and Bob lifted his tin lamp with trembling hands to light it for her.

"Christ, Cleo." John wiped the cold sweat from his brow. "I thought you were a guard."

She exhaled, smoke swirling around her long, wild mane of dark hair, and the glow from her cigarette made her mischievous eyes shine orange. "A little bird told me you made another radio. I never want to miss a broadcast. What's the news?"

"The Globe's reporting that Tall-Me sunk an aircraft carrier," Dick informed her.

She listened to the quiet, tinny music coming from the scrap radio while she smoked. After a while she said, "This is a good song."

"DJMA said it was for you. He read about your execution."

"I hate that he's so worried about me," Caroline purred. "But I am glad that he's still free and working with the others to get us out."

"You know this for certain, boss?"

"They must be."

"So... you're not worried?" John tried to read her face, but the grease lamp and distant hall light were too dim.

"If Tall-Me is taking out aircraft carriers, then what's a little concrete prison wall? Even if he doesn't get us out…" She tapped her ash carelessly onto the floor. "At least our death will be celebrated with fireworks."

The others regarded at her warily. "You seem optimistic."

"I've been trying to be more positive. Somebody very dear to me always was."

Mel suddenly remembered something. "Speaking of which, I saw this in the mailroom. It looked personal, so I snatched it up before it went to the screener." He pulled a tightly folded envelope from inside his shoe. "Sorry if it's a little damp."

Caroline shot a dual stream of smoke from her nostrils and quickly scanned the letter. Even in the darkness, the others could see the color drain from her face.

"Who's it from, boss?" Bob asked, leaning in. "Who would be crazy enough to write you and implicate themselves?"

Caroline swallowed the growing lump in her throat. "My daughter."

"Your daughter?" John repeated. "But she was supposed to be taken care of."

Her expression hardened with rage as she lit the letter with the end of her cigarette. "Get a message out to our friends. Somebody needs to find her before the inquestors do."

178

CHAPTER 10: THE DISCOVERY

Glorious soon proved to be exactly what the small traveling show needed; he was a performance genius with exceptional musical and technical talent. By the time they put on their next show, he completely rewired their stage lights so that they would run more efficiently, and he improvised catchy, new show music on a keyboard of his own invention. It was a fascinating little toy that he would hook up to a car battery and manipulate the buzzes, pops and whines into rhythms and melodies.

Glorious also had a genuine interest in the talents of others. Oftentimes he could be found watching the performers practice or shadowing René and Amandine while they worked, but the person who intrigued him most was the mysterious Sangria. He had seen her contortionist act, but he was far more curious about what she could do with her fiddle. He asked her to perform for him one morning, and she reluctantly agreed.

Unsurprisingly, she showed up hours after the appointed time. Glorious didn't seem to mind that she kept him waiting. He sat on the tailgate of his truck, tinkering with the innards of an upright piano while he listened to René play the guitar. Amandine was nearby, testing her sewing machine on some scrap fabric, and she paused to watch the impromptu performance.

"I thought you would have given up by now," the contortionist sniffed.

"Fat chance. I took the liberty of fetching your fiddle," Glorious said, handing Sangria her battered case. "I'd still very much like to hear you play me something."

Baffled, she demanded, "Play what?"

"Anything."

Sangria heaved a sigh and bent to unpack her violin. She strummed the strings, tuned them, and applied a few strokes of rosin to her bow. "You want something off the cuff?" she asked stiffly, placing her instrument under her chin.

"Natch." Glorious waved his hand at René. "Do that thing you were doing earlier, son. That thing with the rhythm."

René nodded and struck chords in a rapid, jaunty succession.

"That sounds an awful lot like gypsy jazz," Amandine said playfully, shaking a pair of scissors at him. "Somebody call the inquestors. We've got a reprobate among us."

René strummed even louder, daring her to do something about it.

"Look at the brass on Monsieur Personne!" Glorious laughed. "Listen here! Did y'all know that during the Renaissance, the church tried to ban the tritone? They tried to ban *harmony*? This prohibition on jazz is the same thing. All of the inquestors in the country can't stop the music, not if enough people want it."

"That's all fine and good," Sangria grumbled. "But a history lesson isn't going to help if an inquestor hears us now."

"I hope an inquestor hears us now because I ain't never seen one dance before." He slapped René on the back and turned on his keyboard to add an electronic beat. "What I've got planned for the festival is gonna be harder and stronger than jazz. It'll be faster and hotter than swing! But I'm just one man with a little electric music box. I got some really big dreams, and if I ever want to see those dreams come to life, I need some ingenuity, some creativity, and a little magic."

Sangria rolled her eyes. "Sounds like what you really need is a genie in a bottle."

"Don't need no genie. I got all of that and then some right here with y'all."

"Well, then what do you need me for?"

"Every sundae needs a cherry on top. Every crown needs a jewel. What I need is a star for my show." Glorious clasped his hands together in a theatrical plea. "So how about it, Miss G? Can you make my dreams come true?"

Sangria stared at the ground in silence. René continued to play, but after a while he glanced up at Glorious with doubt.

All at once, she launched into a complicated bariolage. Her whole body moved in time, twisting, bending, and even leaping to match the voice of every spontaneous note. Glorious gave a whoop as René changed the key. The challenge fired her up, so she sawed an even more elaborate flourish of notes across the strings.

Amandine stood slack-jawed at the performance before her. Sangria could dance as furiously as she played and her flexibility added a bizarre, spellbinding element to the display. Glorious wanted to see how far she could go. He turned the tempo up and watched as she started into a slow pirouette. She spun faster and faster until he cut off the beat, and Sangria performed a shocking death drop. She threw herself flat on her back and pulled a jagged, sustained tremolo up the neck of her violin.

At last, she dropped the instrument at her side and breathed hard.

"Now, that's cooking with gas!" Glorious cried, throwing his keyboard aside. "Miss Mandy, did you hear that? Did you *see* that?"

Amandine had frozen mid-stitch, bent over the table. She stood up with a laugh as soon as the surprise wore off. "Sangria, that was swell! I've never heard anything like that in my life!"

"Cat's outta the bag, Miss G! Ain't no turning back now!" Glorious leaped off of his tailgate and darted to Marmi's tent to tell her everything.

René offered a hand to help Sangria sit up. "*Quelle surprise.* You're much better at that than I thought."

"You think you know everything, but you don't." She warned him off with a swipe of her bow and noticed Coronado watching them from his truck.

The illusionist granted her a single nod and resumed feeding his doves.

The days that followed brought the group a little closer to Nieuwestad. It wasn't the most direct route, and they made very slow progress, but the less time they spent on the road gave them more time to develop their show for the Freedom Festival. Coronado was relieved to split creative control with Glorious, but he was surprised when the electrician insisted that they also involve René, Nick Thatch, and Amandine in the process. He reasoned that if they really wanted to astound the cosmopolitan audience, they would need the most incredible visual display that their collective talents could conceive.

Nick had a background in engineering, so he was directed to design a portable set that could incorporate moving parts that René was responsible for constructing. Once Coronado and Glorious had chosen themes for each act, Amandine was given control over the aesthetic.

While the others were able to work immediately, scavenging supplies and equipment from dumps, junkyards, and abandoned buildings, Amandine was left with only her ideas. She offered to scavenge with them, but Glorious said that if there was any place they should not cut corners, it was in the costumes. René agreed; he never came across satin or rhinestones at the dump anyway.

One dusty, dry afternoon, René went searching for Amandine and the twins pointed him towards the stream beyond the trailers. He found clotheslines stretched out in the sun, and he ducked past the swaying bedsheets and trousers towards the tinkling sounds of laughter. Amandine, Margaret, and May were at the washtub beside the water, sitting on stools in the shade. René was about to call out, but his voice caught at the sight of her.

Amandine's yellow dress was pinned up so that she could straddle the washtub and her hair was tied up beneath a blue scrap scarf. She sang a swing tune with Margaret, one with a *chaka-chaka* rhythm that they used to guide their scrubbing. "*Scrub me, mama, to the boogie beat,*" they sang and burst out laughing. René couldn't help laughing too. Amandine was so vibrant, so healthy, and so different from the frail thing he met at the bakery.

May was the only one who noticed him standing amongst the colorful, drying saris. The dancer raised an inquisitive eyebrow when he didn't announce himself, but as usual, she said nothing.

"Hello there," he said at last. Amandine gave a start.

"Howdy, stranger." She draped a wet shirt against the edge of the tub and waved. "I haven't seen you all morning."

"That's because Glorious and I were at the junkyard," René replied. He crouched by the stream and splashed cool water over his face.

"Find anything good?"

He took a long drink out of his hands before answering. "Oh, yes. We found something quite wonderful. You're going to love it."

"What is it?" She looked around excitedly. "Where is it?"

"We came back to get some extra help because it's big. Come with us, and we'll show you."

Margaret and May shooed Amandine away permissively. With a word of thanks, she stepped into a pair of short brown boots and followed René back to camp.

"I hope I'm not under-dressed," she said, retying her scarf into a bow above her ear.

"It's only the junkyard," René replied a little anxiously. Amandine caught him staring at her, and his gaze broke with an embarrassed cough.

She playfully nudged him with her elbow. "That rinse in the stream didn't really do the trick. I might have to take you and your laundry to the washboard when we get back." She nodded at all of the stains on his clothes.

"I am sorry if I smell." He tugged at the front of his shirt to let some air in. "I've been busy since the sun went up. First I had to fix Jean-Claude's radiator. Then Ludmilla asked if I would clean out her stovepipe. After that, I went to the junkyard with Glorious. He wants to build a... an electric instrument. He showed me his technical plans, and I can't even begin to describe it. Anyway, it can get a little dirty when you have to dig through garbage for the right pieces of scrap."

"You don't stink," she assured him. "Even if you did, you're entitled to it. I don't know anybody in this camp who works half as hard as you do."

Her silly compliment caught him off-guard and seeing him grin and fluster for a response made Amandine overcome with an urge. Mustering up all of her courage, she reached for his hand and her slender fingers slipped as easily as puzzle-pieces between his. René was so surprised by her impulsive gesture that he stopped dead in his tracks.

185

Softly, she said, "René, I'm... I'm so very fond of you, I can hardly control myself." Her spontaneity quickly gave way to mortification, and she stared at their clasped hands in horror. "I'm sorry, I don't know what came over me!"

She tried to let him go, but he held on tight.

"Amandine, I think of you every minute," he confessed. He had trapped all of his feelings behind a wall since the day he first laid eyes on her, and the dam had finally burst. "You even appear in my dreams. There used to be nothing I loved more than my work, but now everything I do feels like a chore that keeps me from spending time with you."

"Well, then." Her voice was small but full of hopeful joy. She moved closer until she was near enough to feel the summer heat radiating off of him. "It's out in the open."

"Everybody knows it already," he chuckled. "Even Glorious."

If Amandine were back home, she knew that the next course of action would be to tell all of her friends about her new beau and then wait for René to plan their first date. She imagined that her mother would like René very much, but her father might have been too quick to judge him by his appearance. "*Apparel oft proclaims the man,*" she could hear him say with gruff disapproval. Now that she was on her own, she had no idea who to tell or what to do.

She bit her lip and traced half-circles in the dust with her boot. "So what do we do now?"

"Now?" René glanced around to make sure nobody was near, then he tilted her chin up with his free hand and kissed her once very lightly on the lips. Amandine squeaked

186

and felt her skin prickle to the pounding pulse in her ears. It was all such a sweet shock; she wanted him to kiss her again, but he was already at arm's distance before she had even realized what had happened.

René gave her the kind of warm smile that made her heart quiver when he turned back towards camp. "Now, we go see that surprise I was telling you about."

Amandine bolted from his side as soon as her trailer was in sight "Gia!" she cried, stumbling up the stairs. Whether she liked it or not, Sangria would have to assume the role of her best friend because this development was impossible to keep to herself. The first thing every best friend needed was a nickname.

"Gia?" Sangria repeated. She was lounging on her bunk with her bare feet propped outside of the open window. "Nobody's ever called me that before."

"Gia," Amandine said breathlessly. "You won't believe what just happened! René kissed me!"

The contortionist didn't look up from her fashion magazine. "Finally made his move, did he? About time. You were driving everybody nuts with all your sighs and doe-eyes."

"And it wasn't just any kiss!" She went for her scrap bag to find something prettier to tie her hair up with. "It was my first kiss."

Sangria eyed Amandine critically. "It probably only happened because you've got ten miles of leg showing. Ever think about that, Suzie-floozy?"

"Gee, they should have called you 'the Underpants-In-A-Knot-Freak.'" Amandine stuck out her tongue and threw her

187

old scarf at her roommate. "You can be as sour as you want because nothing is going to get me down today."

"I'm not sour." Sangria gave a haughty sniff. "Do whatever you want with René. Sneak over to his tent after dark. Elope for all I care. Just don't let Marmi catch you."

"Why not?" She unpinned her dress and let the skirt swish down to her knees.

"Because the old prude won't like it, and there *will* be consequences. Just ask Margaret what happened when she started fooling around with Ambroise. If you're lucky, she'll chew your heads off and then keep you separated any way she can devise. If she's really mad, she'll kick one of you out." Sangria dog-eared a page and added in a singsong voice, "Can't imagine which of you she'd choose."

Amandine scoffed. She didn't want to think about Marmi, not when her first kiss still burned like molten gold in her memory. "I actually came here to ask if you want to come with me on a walk," she said, dismissing her roommate's scaremongering. "René said they found something at the junkyard, and he needs extra hands to bring it all back. Want to come?"

Surprisingly, Sangria didn't refuse. She put aside her magazine, slipped on a pair of shoes and put on a wide-brimmed black straw hat. "Sure. I was getting bored stiff just sitting here anyway. Let's go."

The two of them met René, Nick, Glorious, and Coronado at the road just outside of camp. Coronado wasn't surprised to see that Amandine was coming, but he did a double-take when he realized that Sangria had come out of hiding. Neither one of them looked directly at the other.

"Miss Mandy." Glorious touched the edge of his hat in greeting and showed her some supplies he had gathered up. "I got you some scissors and a few sacks. You're gonna need them where we're going."

"I can hardly wait to see," she said, taking René's offered arm. She expected Coronado to remark on their public display of affection, but the illusionist was staring at Nick.

"Perhaps Mr. Holloway forgot to mention it to you, but we're going to be scavenging in the junkyard. Would you like to change before we go?" Coronado referred to the pink house dress and ladies' loafers that his brother-in-law was wearing. "Or perhaps you'd rather stay and look after my sister?"

Nick gave the long half of his hair a confident flounce. "My trousers are in the wash and 'Lita's taking a nap before dinner. I think my dress is just fine for scavenging."

"You're a real keen Sheba, Nick." Glorious handed him an empty sack. "If you weren't already married, I'd take you out dancing."

"Thank you!" Nick beamed and tossed the sack over his shoulder like a feather boa.

"'If he weren't already married,'" Coronado muttered. "*Estoy rodeado de bichos raros.*"

They started off. Glorious made the walk pass quickly with stories about his job as an electrician and nightclub musician. He was so animated, he even had Coronado and Sangria laughing.

189

"*Pop! Wham!*" Glorious clapped his hands. "I smelled like Cajun barbecue for days, but I never forgot to wait for the ballast to cool down again."

"That's funny because we heard that working for Johnstone was a nightmare," Sangria said. "But you make it sound like that was the best job of your life."

Glorious' smile disappeared. "Oh, this was before Johnstone, Miss G. Long before. If I knew then what I know now, I would have run instead of signing on with that monster."

"I'm sorry," Amandine said. "We never should have brought him up."

Glorious was the first to notice that she was fondly pressing René's arm. He winked at his new friend and gave him a discreet thumbs up. "Don't apologize. Nobody could imagine how bad it really was."

"So, he didn't pay you or what?" Sangria blurted.

"Shoot, if only that's all it were," Glorious replied. "At first, I was the highest paid performer, but he cut off my funds when he figured out that I was sharing it with the freak-acts. Called me a thieving bootlip and said he wouldn't pay me again until I gave him some new music, but how can a man write when he's hungry and surrounded by suffering? I stopped trying. Everything I wrote for him was modular with the same ol' beat, but people seemed to like it all the same. He would use my music most every night and make those poor, starved girls dance. If they didn't dance well enough or if they'd sass him, he'd beat them. He'd sometimes beat them until they broke, then expect them to keep dancing. He'd make

190

them do it, too. He had a wagon full of every kind of drug, dope them up, and send them spinning."

Glorious paused and watched the way dust settled on his wingtip shoes before he went on. "A lot of these girls were looking out of red windows for one reason or another, if you know my meaning. One of them decided she'd had enough. Said she was leaving, so Johnstone called up an inquestor. Bless her soul, she was tough as nails. She wouldn't even back down from the inquestor. In the end, Inky shot her right there on the stage in front of everybody rehearsing." He wiped his brow, but it wasn't just the late afternoon heat that made him sweat. "You can imagine that we gave up trying to leave for awhile."

"How'd you get away?" Amandine asked, trying to turn the conversation in a more positive route. "How did you know to come to Marmi?"

Just as she had hoped, Glorious brightened a bit at this question. "The radio, actually. Heard some ham-guys say y'all were close, so I took a gamble and acted quick. I grabbed Polly, loaded my truck, got the tiger— because who's gonna stop a guy with a tiger?— and I sped off in the direction y'all came in. I just looked for the posters. I'm real glad I found all y'all, too, because I was nearly out of gas."

"We're glad to have you," Coronado said sincerely. "I was starting to get a little worried about how we were going to pull off our new show. I'm just an illusionist, not a musician. You have a God-given gift."

Glorious bowed in gratitude.

"How much farther?" Sangria whined, kicking an empty bottle aside and sending it clattering across the road.

René checked their surroundings. "I think we're getting close."

"I recognize that bush." Glorious sprang off of the road. "We're right on top of it. Here it is!"

He held back some branches, revealing an unused path with a grand wave of his arms. Past the overgrowth stood an abandoned, tin-sided building drowning in weeds. Nearly all of the high windows were broken and the sign above the bolted main door was missing several letters.

Nick appraised the place before them while he tied on a calico apron. "This isn't the junkyard. 'FREEMAN'S QUALITY FED.' I mean, 'feed.'"

The others frowned in confusion, but Amandine knew exactly what this meant. "A feed factory?" she squeaked. "*You found a feed factory?*"

"I don't get it." Sangria dropped her sunglasses down to her chin.

"Feed is sold in patterned sacks so that farm wives can turn them into clothes and quilts once they're empty," Amandine explained. She yanked on the locked door and tried to scramble up the rusty wall to a window. "There's gotta be a treasure trove of fabric in there!"

"I caught a glimpse of it through the window," Glorious said. "Bolts bigger than you."

Amandine got a hold on the window, but her legs pedaled uselessly without traction on the wall. She lost her grip, fell flat on her bottom, and René chuckled as he hurried over to help her up.

"Stand aside," Sangria commanded, taking off her hat and shoes. "Nick, if you'd be so kind?" Nick moved beneath the window, and Sangria climbed up his shoulders, rolling smoothly into the open window. After a moment, the door unbolted from the inside.

The building was dark and damp where a caved-in corner of the roof let nature inside. Rows of rusted machinery stood silent, and vines grew up all of the interior walls. Any feed there might have been was long gone, either eaten by wild animals or rotted away.

"Packaging is in a room off of the main building to the west," Glorious said, leading everyone through the darkness. He looked through the window in the first door and cast the portal wide open. "Bingo!"

Amandine darted inside and hopped from foot to foot. "Look at all of this!" she cried, arms outstretched to the bounty before her.

The massive bolts were stacked on a rack against the wall. There was so much fabric, they couldn't even roll it all back; they would have to cut off as much as they could carry. Glorious handed Amandine a pair of scissors, and she got to work.

By the time she was through, she had twelve large sacks stuffed with yards and yards of calico, gingham, check, floral, and graphic fabrics in all colors. Amandine was so excited, she chattered nonstop during the walk back about what she was going to make for everybody.

While Amandine was planning, Sangria lagged behind. The contortionist dropped her heavy sacks on the ground and stopped to take a rock out of her shoe when Coronado's shadow hovered over her.

"I can carry all of this," he said gruffly, adding her bags to his own.

She said nothing, not even a word of thanks. Walking side by side, the two returned to camp in silence.

CHAPTER 11: THE PARTY

Amandine was never so happy as when she was sewing. At first, she faltered with uncertainty because it felt as if an important part of her had withered away from disuse. She didn't realize how confined she had been doing simple repairs and alterations until she was once again set free to create. The moment she laid her first cut pieces together, her hands remembered their old skill, and she guided the sewing machine with confidence.

For weeks, the dressmaker worked tirelessly at her machine which she would set up in some shaded spot near where the men were working. While Nick oversaw construction of the set, Glorious and René worked on a strange musical instrument. It was about eight feet tall, as wide as a sofa, and required more electric and mechanical parts than a car. It made the most terrible, loud buzzing noise, but Glorious assured everyone that it would be an incredible, show-stopping invention worth waiting for. They just needed to be a little patient.

Sangria had no patience, but it had nothing to do with the machine. The moment Amandine unloaded her textile plunder from the feed factory, Sangria hounded her for dresses like the magazine photos she'd shove in her face. Sangria whined, threatened, and outright demanded that she make her clothes first, but the dressmaker wouldn't budge from her schedule. Amandine prioritized the people with special physiques because many of them had gone years, if not their entire lives, without clothes that fit.

Day by day, Sangria's despair grew as the fabric supply dwindled. It finally came down to the conventionally-shaped people in camp, and she had a pretty good idea how she ranked among them, especially after weeks of torment. In an act of desperation, Sangria tried the last thing she could think of: she tried to be kind.

It started with little favors. Sometimes she would help Amandine press her fabric or offer to get her meals for her. If Amandine didn't need any help, Sangria made feeble attempts at small-talk and in doing so, she discovered that they shared an interest in dance music and adventure movies. Whenever Amandine needed to go into town, Sangria started going with her without asking and even helped her get ready. She showed her how to put on makeup and fix her hair in rolls, something René was very quick to notice.

As she gave Ambroise's completed suit jacket a final press, Sangria realized that she hadn't thought of her own dresses all week. When the suit was delivered and Amandine detailed everything Sangria had done to help, the contortionist had to bite her lip to hide her smile. Perhaps spending time with Amandine wasn't so bad after all.

Just as Sangria thought about how she could bring up her dresses again, she awoke one morning and discovered something odd. Amandine's suitcase, which took up a lot of space on top of the dresser, was missing. Sangria threw on her kimono and poked around. Amandine's old clothes were still in the drawers, but her sewing kit and personal effects were gone. She slinked out of the trailer towards the fire. She knew if anybody would know the comings and goings of camp, it was the Russians. She crept up to where they were preparing dutch-oven bread and had to clear her throat several times to get their attention.

"Good morning," Sasha said, feigning surprise at her appearance. "Our humblest apologies. We're fresh out of lox for your eggs benedict."

Sangria frowned. "I'm looking for Amandine."

"Why? Lose a button?"

"No," she growled. "Her suitcase is gone. Have you seen her?"

"*Nyet,*" Piotr replied. "She's usually up early working on the clothes, but she never skips breakfast."

Sasha made a show of scanning the camp. "Come to think of it, I haven't seen René all morning either." The pair of them shared a curious look, then started giggling and muttering in Russian.

"What? What is it?" Sangria demanded.

"I was cleaning up dinner last night, and I saw that Amandine was counting her savings by the fire," Piotr said.

"And Chitra told me two days ago that René asked for one of her gold rings in exchange for fixing the suspension on her trailer," Sasha added. "Maybe our handyman ran away with our dressmaker."

"Eloped?" Sangria's face fell. "Why would they elope? Why now?"

"Good question." Sasha poked the fire with a stick. "Who could have put such an idea into their heads, I wonder?"

"Well, at least *shveyachka* was kind enough to make us all such nice clothes before she left." Piotr reached over to smartly adjust the collar on his brother's gingham check shirt. Sangria bolted back to her trailer and slammed the door shut, but she could still hear the Russians laughing at her.

Glorious spied the exchange on his way to the workspace behind the incomplete set, toting a crate full of scrap. "And they wonder why poor Miss G never comes out but to eat and perform," he grumbled, dropping his crate between his electric instrument and Amandine's sewing machine. Rooting around for suitable lengths of wire, he said, "Miss Mandy, the Russians are teasing your roommate again. Do you think maybe you should check on her? See if she's alright?"

He glanced over his shoulder when he didn't get a response. Amandine was unpacking the new, store-bought fabric she had hidden in her suitcase when René interrupted her with a kiss. He took her gently by the shoulders and drew her in across the sewing table until their lips touched. With a contented sigh she melted against him, still clutching three yards of gray plaid in her hands.

Glorious crossed his arms and twirled a pair of wire strippers in one hand while he waited. When it seemed that the teenagers wouldn't stop kissing without an intervention, he yanked Rene away by the collar.

"*Mais non!*" René whined, reaching for Amandine. She giggled and waved goodbye. "*Monsieur, je t'en supplie!*"

"*Allons-y*, hot stuff, *tout suite*." Glorious dropped him at his workbench. "Can't waste the morning fooling around. We gotta get this machine finished."

"What's the big hurry?" René took up his tool kit and crawled into the back of the machine. "Marmi says we have until Nieuwestad."

"Don't talk to me about what Marmi says!" Glorious pulled a wild tangle of scrap wire into his lap. "If Marmi finds out I let you canoodle with the dressmaker when I'm supposed to be chaperoning, she'll leave me and this pile of garbage on the side of the road."

Sangria was relieved when Amandine returned to their trailer that evening bearing a paper parcel of clothes. She was upset that the Russians had fooled her, but her anger soon changed to wonderment when she tried on her new gowns, each one fit perfectly to her design and color preferences.

"Worth the wait, wouldn't you say, gentlemen?" Glorious nudged René and Coronado on either side of him when the ladies arrived together at dinner. Everyone applauded, and Amandine made Sangria do a little turn in her new dress.

"Oh, I just adore that collar," Nick said enviously. He was sitting beside his wife who nodded in agreement while she arranged a napkin around her decolletage. "Those vertical pleats add inches to her. I look like a bean-pole in pleats."

Amandine hopped her chair close to René and said, "Pleats might not be for you, Nick, but my father taught me that peplums detract from height and also give the illusion of hips."

Nick sloshed his bowl. "You mean—?"

"She's making a dress for you too, you pantywaist," Coronado growled, grinding his fingers into his temples.

Carmelita gasped and slapped her brother with her slipper. "¡Tirate a un pozo!"

Sangria sat down at the table and found that her bowl was waiting for her, already filled with steaming cabbage borscht. When Amandine passed her the bread basket, she murmured, "You know, you don't have to keep doing this."

"Doing what?"

"Getting my supper. Trying to be nice."

"Wasn't me," Amandine whispered, nodding across the table.

Coronado pretended not to hear as he dusted a footprint from his new shirt.

The next week, Glorious and René summoned everyone to a special dinner to unveil their project. Sasha and Piotr wanted to serve something a little different than stew or stroganoff, so Chitra helped them make curry. Everybody wore their favorite new clothes, and Amandine even made herself a party dress for the occasion. She joined the other women at the kitchen table, swapping compliments while they filled their bowls and plates.

They watched as Glorious and René struggled to haul in their invention. It resembled a pipe-organ in both size and composition but it had many more lights, dials, and buttons protruding from it. It was built on wheels for mobility, but the wheels kept getting caught in the soft ground so all of the men came over to help. Tiny Greg appeared first, lifting with everything he had until he was surrounded by the others and completely hidden behind a cover of straining legs. The machine finally came out of the dirt when Jean-Claude joined in, and everyone got it into position before Marmi's tent.

Amandine had René's plate ready by the time he collapsed, exhausted, into the chair beside her.

"Working hard?" she asked, leaning over him.

René opened his eyes. He was glad to see her. "I was, but I'm done now. We can show the electric-polly... I mean, the electro-pandemonium... we can show the machine to everyone and finally have some good, loud music for our performances." He shook his head and chuckled at his own poor attempt to name their invention. "But I am not the only one who has been working hard. Everybody looks incredible, Amandine. I hardly recognize anyone in their new clothes."

Amandine was about to reply when the firelight caught his eyes and made her forget what she wanted to say. His eyes were the color of a winter sky, yet as warm and inviting as a cup of tea. Now that she thought of it, his lips looked awfully inviting too. Without thinking, she started leaning forward, anxious to accept his lips' invitation until Glorious' voice stirred her from her trance.

"Ain't no time for sleeping, son," he shouted across the campfire. "Eat your supper before it gets cold."

René sat up with a groan and reached for his plate. "Thank you for getting dinner for me," he said, scooping rice into his mouth. "I would've rather starved than leave my chair again."

"Anytime." She reached under her seat for a final parcel. "But it's not the only thing I got for you."

He froze at the sight of the bundle she held out to him. "You didn't," René said with his mouth full.

"I did." She proudly put it on his lap. "And... it's a little special. I was running low on feedsack, and I didn't expect everybody to actually pay me for the clothes I made, so I went to town a few days ago—"

René swallowed and silenced her with a gesture. "You used the money you've been saving for your mother on some fabric? On clothes? For me?"

Amandine's smile wavered and after a hesitation, she nodded. "Only a few extra yards for you and Gia." She didn't expect the harshness in René's voice, but she thought perhaps she misunderstood it. Sweetly, she urged him, "Open it!"

For as long as he could remember, René had only ever worn second-hand clothes. He had never owned a shirt that wasn't already stained, and his trousers rarely came without a patch. While he was always aware that his clothes were in poor shape, he never gave much thought towards his appearance as long as he was covered in the summer, warm in the winter, and everything survived another trip through the wringer.

The clothes he unwrapped in his lap were different. They were sturdy, clean, fit to his height, and made in colors chosen to suit him. Pulling out a red shirt from behind the others, he was struck by how subtly it resembled a certain fictional outlaw.

Suddenly, René noticed the dirt and grease that covered his hands, and he dropped the new shirt as if it burned him.

"I can't wear these," he said, yanking off his bandana and wiping his hands.

For the first time, Amandine's smile fell completely, and the look of hurt that replaced it made René wince.

"Why not?" Her voice escaped in a cracked whimper.

He pointed to himself and exclaimed, "Look at me! You see what sort of work I do. I can't accept this." He stared at the clothes. They even had shiny, new buttons. He didn't know buttons were supposed to shine. "This is too nice for the likes of me."

A shadow fell over him and Glorious appeared with his plate piled high.

"Son, you best shut your mouth," he snapped. "We're gonna formally present the machine we've been working on all month, and you wanna go before all of these well-dressed people looking like you just crawled out a coal-chute?" He plucked him out of his chair and confiscated his plate and parcel. "Go get yourself washed up in the stream, put this on..." He chose a navy shirt and a pair of slim, brown, pinstripe pants. "And throw those old rags in the fire when you get back!" With a kick, Glorious sent René out of camp and towards the stream.

Sangria snickered wildly; there was little she loved more than seeing René tormented.

"Damn fool boy," Glorious muttered, taking the vacant seat. He shook his finger at Amandine. "Don't you let his foolishness upset you, Miss Mandy."

"I'm not upset," the dressmaker said. After a deep breath, her smile returned.

"I reckon it's my fault," Glorious went on, tucking a napkin into his collar. "I wore him out. I've had him running from dump to dump and all over creation looking for parts to assemble. I mean, my daddy taught me how to run electricity like magic, but your René has a gift with machines. That young man is an artist. I couldn't have put this together without him." Glorious took a bite and shut his eyes in satisfaction. "Good gracious, this is delicious! I ain't never had curry before."

"It has a way of lingering," Coronado said with a grimace, examining a morsel on the end of his fork.

René returned by the time everyone else was finishing dinner. He looked ashamed as he tied his wet hair back. "I... I am sorry for my behavior," he apologized. "Nobody has ever given me anything so nice before, and I didn't know how to act. I don't think I deserve it, but that's no excuse." He knelt down by her chair and took both of Amandine's hands in his own. "Thank you. I mean it. These clothes really suit me. Thank you for taking such care to make me something special."

"You're welcome." Amandine leaned back and evaluating him from top to bottom. "You look pretty sharp, if I do say so myself. I was a little worried about the fit, but luckily you never noticed me taking measurements on the sly."

"Measurements?" He sat down when Glorious gave him his seat back. "When did you measure me? *How* did you measure me?"

Amandine only winked in reply.

Just then, the others noticed René's change of wardrobe. The Russians started a round of whistling and catcalling, which made René wish he could disappear behind his dinner plate.

Glorious slapped his shoulder. "Don't mind them. You eat. I'm gonna go fire up the machine and make a little speech. Maybe see if the Russians can serve up their treat."

"We have dessert?" Amandine asked, imagining colorful Russian *pastila*.

Piotr appeared with a case of bottles and gently shook one at her in offering. "Well, it *used* to be bread and sugar."

"Ladies and gentlemen," Glorious said, standing proudly beside his machine. "I want to begin by thanking y'all for welcoming me into your traveling-show family. Thank y'all for sharing your your work, your food, and your tailor." He hooked his thumbs into the suspenders under his new cream-colored suit. "I bet we're now the best dressed transients in the NAR, am I right?"

205

Everybody clapped, and Amandine stood to take a quick bow.

"I wanna return the favor. I wanna show you what is gonna win us the big cash prize at the Freedom Festival in Nieuwestad." His arm swept over the massive instrument. "This here machine is the result of some long, hard work from myself and your very own Monsieur Personne. You might have heard us making noise on it from time to time, but tonight we wanna put on a little recital for you. Tonight, I invite you to sit back and enjoy the music with refreshments generously provided by the Pasternakov brothers."

Amandine swirled the drink in her cup. It was the color of tea, but certainly didn't smell like it. "What is this stuff, René?"

He didn't answer. It looked like he was steeling himself against something unpleasant before he knocked his cup back, shuddered, and staggered off to fetch his guitar.

"Don't drink that rain-barrel swill, *mi cariña*." Coronado reached for Sangria's cup and tossed it's contents over his shoulder. "Try something a little easier on the palette. I've been drinking it all evening." The girls exchanged wide-eyed look while the tipsy illusionist refilled her cup with red wine.

Glorious started the generator, and it roared to life, belching a white cloud of exhaust. With a dramatic flair, he switched on the machine. The front display was illuminated in multicolored lights in decorative rows. The display across the top said "MARMI'S MARVELS" in yellow neon letters, and Glorious looked for her reaction.

206

Marmi normally tried to appear stern and impassive, but her eyes went wide at the incredible machine before her. With the press of a button, her name began flashing. As each letter lit in turn, her smile grew a little wider until she finally nodded to Glorious, eager to see more.

Satisfied, Glorious took his seat and gave his arms a little shake.

"I call it 'the electropolyharmonium.' Enjoy!"

He began by playing an upbeat, minor polka. He played it well, but the audience was already familiar with Glorious' musical talent. It was the machine they were interested in, and so far the only impressive thing about it was that the display above flashed lights in time to the music he played. When he finished, it earned a polite response.

Glorious pretended to be disappointed. "What's the matter? You thought Big Polly could do more? Oh, I suppose you folks want something that will knock your socks off. Fine! If this don't turn you on, then you ain't got no switches!"

He worked at his control panel and played several keys. Big Polly looped a bass beat with low flashing orange lights. It resonated like a pulse, and Chitra was the first to start tilting her head from side to side in time. Glorious added several chords, revealing to everyone's astonishment that the machine could imitate every instrument in a jazz band and that got every foot tapping. Ludmilla finished her drink and did a little shimmy with Sasha. Piotr took Chitra by the hand and enthusiastically mimicked her Indian style of dancing.

René reappeared and leaped up beside Glorious, who handed him a cable. He plugged it into his modified guitar and played a swinging gypsy-jazz melody that Glorious altered through Big Polly. He looped it, skipped it, then when the song seemed to have no place else to go, he turned the entire machine down to just the bass again.

"Yes, sir!" he yelled over the beat. "Big Polly's got an entire orchestra hiding under her skirt! But you know what's the very best thing about this machine?" With a push of several more buttons, the song returned to a climax. *"She can play herself!"*

Big Polly exploded with beautiful lights and exciting new music. René dropped his guitar, but his melody played on. He ran over to where Amandine was sitting, lifted her up off her feet and whirled her around the fire. Glorious claimed Marmi before she could protest, and even the half-sauced Coronado had Sangria by the hand.

They were all laughing and twirling, finally allowing themselves to let loose. Amandine was glad that she still remembered a few swing steps, and René could improvise well enough until he learned what she was doing. In no time at all, they were moving together naturally and exuberantly. She relished each time he pulled her close after she spun away, matching her kicks, steps and twists. Occasionally Glorious ran up to the machine to play a new tune, but the music never stopped. They danced until Amandine couldn't stand anymore.

"I can't dance another step," she laughed. She doubled over and gasped for breath. René went to help her straighten up, and she pretended that exhaustion made her lean into his arms.

"Would you like to sit down?" he asked.

She nodded, and he led them away. To her amusement, they moved further from their folding chairs by the fire and in the direction of Coronado's truck.

"Where are we going?"

"Someplace quieter."

"You aren't taking me back to your tent, are you?" She whispered mischievously and prodded him in the ribs. The way he jumped made Amandine snort.

"Not my tent!" he said shrilly. "There's barely enough room for me in there. I can't even sit up to read."

"Speaking of reading—" Amandine remembered her first gift. "How did you like the Rogue Rider?"

He made a face as if she had asked something offensive. "I didn't. It was awful."

"Horsefeathers!" She prodded him again. "You couldn't put it down. I saw you during shows, reading by the stage lights. It was the ending, wasn't it?"

René grit his teeth and exhaled hard through his nose. "It is so frustrating! If Jed would only tell Annie he's the Rogue Rider, she wouldn't have been fooled by the corrupt Sheriff."

"But he can never tell her who he really is, because to do so would put her in danger. It doesn't matter how much good Jedrick Anders does, because the Rogue Rider is still a criminal. He's an *outlaw*!"

"He's amazing," René confessed with a dreamy sigh.

"I'll keep an eye out for the next one in the series," she said. "And I promise you'll be happy with how that particular adventure ends."

"Tell me!"

"No. I won't spoil it."

"Tell me!" He gave her shoulders a little shake. "I have to know what happens next. Between that cliffhanger and seeing you in that dress, I feel like I am going crazy."

Amandine blushed. She reflexively touched her white skirt, dotted with hundreds of blooming roses. "You like my dress?"

He was glad he didn't have to steal a glance at her now. René looked at her from the bow in her hair, down the trail of round red buttons to where the full skirt ended just below her knees.

"I love your dress," he said as he drew her against him, feeling the warm cotton around her waist.

Amandine closed her eyes and slowly raised herself up on her toes. She waited for a kiss but to her disappointment, none came. When she opened her eyes again, René was scanning their surroundings. They were standing behind Coronado's truck, but were not completely out of sight of the fire.

"Come on," he said, pulling her away from the light. "This way."

"Oh, the impropriety," she giggled. "We don't even have our slipshod chaperone."

"Well, if you're worried about your virtue, we can always go to your trailer."

"The only thing I'm worried about is Marmi." With a stern poke in his direction, she added, "And you should be too."

"But I am," he exclaimed. "Marmi only wants what's best for us. It's just that…"

They stopped at the foot of her trailer, and he paused. He didn't want to push her into something she might not want, so he respectfully took a step back. Hands in his pockets, he bashfully concluded, "It's just that Marmi might see a lot, but she doesn't see everything."

Amandine tried to suppress the smile that pushed through her serious front. Red lips twitching, she coyly crossed her arms and nodded towards her door. "Anyway, how does my trailer safeguard my virtue when we're just as alone there as the forest?"

"Sangria will likely come looking as soon as she sees us gone," he said with a shrug and his roguish smirk. "And I know she would love nothing more than to spoil our evening."

He had a point, but it was a flimsy defense. Amandine decided that she didn't particularly care as she pulled him inside and shut the door behind him.

"Sorry about the state of this place," she said, stuffing messy piles of fabric into a sack to be reorganized later. "I wanted to give you your clothes before the party, and I barely finished them in time."

Once the place was tidy, she lit the lamp with shaking hands and sat down beside him on Sangria's bunk. She wondered if René could comfortably rest anywhere, because the bed didn't contain him any better than his tent did.

They stared at their own laps, unsure of what to do. Both of them had imagined what would happen if they were alone together, but now that the moment was here, all of their plans and confidence evaporated. Looking up at the same time, they wordlessly decided to lay down. They settled on the quilt facing each other, just close enough so that their bodies touched. Amandine tucked one arm under her headand laced the fingers on her other hand into René's.

For a while there was no sound but the thumping bass beat of Big Polly. They could barely see each other by the dim glow from the lamp and changing colored lights from outside.

René was unsure if he could convey how he felt in English, so he spoke first in French. His words were strained as he searched for the courage to say them. "*Quand je t'ai vu pour la première fois, c'était le coup de foudre. Je veux être avec toi pour toujours...* do you understand what I am saying?"

"*Oui*," she replied, making no attempt at a correct accent. It made him chuckle. "I understand."

"Is there something wrong?"

"No, René. Never. I adore you, too. Only..." she trailed off.

"Please, tell me," he pressed. "Was it because I was being an ass earlier?"

"No, of course not. It's much more serious than that. It's that... well, what do we do now?"

His concern was replaced with a sly look. "I can think of a few things," he said, moving closer.

She playfully pushed him back. "That's not what I meant. I mean, what happens when we finally reach Nieuwestad? The minute I get those costumes done, I need to leave and find my mother."

212

"The minute?" he asked. "Won't you at least stay until the festival and see the result of all of our hard work?"

"No, René, I'm sorry. I really don't have any time to lose. While I'm endlessly grateful to everyone for looking after me, I'm afraid I may be wasting too much time. I need to find her as soon as my agreement with Marmi is fulfilled."

"Then I'll go with you," he said, moving closer again.

This time she did not push him back. "If she's still in trouble, *maman* and I might have to lay low until this business goes away."

"I could look after you both."

She smiled, imagining how happy she would be to have the two people she cared for the most always at her side, but she knew it was impossible. "You could never do that. I would never ask you to do that. Everyone would be heartbroken if you left. They need you." He opened his mouth to argue, but she stopped him. "You might say handymen are a dime a dozen, but how many others could keep the trucks working, build and run the shows each night, design and construct 'electric-pandemoniums' and... and... throw fire?"

"Nick Thatch could do it," René said feebly. "Maybe."

"Nick can design a bridge, but he can't change a tire," she laughed. "No, René. It's you. Who else could be so needed, so loved, and so loyal as you?"

Amandine didn't like to see how much this conversation was troubling him, so she gently stroked his cheek. René took her hand and kissed her palm, holding it firmly to his lips.

"We don't have to talk about any of this now," she said, lowering her voice to a murmur. "We don't have to talk about anything."

"Yes," he answered softly, reaching for her. "*Que mes baisers soient les mots d'amour que je ne te dis pas.*"

Amandine didn't understand that particular phrase, but she quickly learned that she didn't have to. He pulled her whole body close as easily as if she were a pillow, one hand pressing her lower back and the other in her hair. Slowly, he brushed her lips once with his; testing her, exploring her before she drew him in the rest of the way, and they shared a passionate kiss. As her hands gripped his shoulders, she took a deep breath of him, smelling gasoline, woodsmoke, and line-dried cotton. His lips were soft but they pressed hard with urgency and he tasted like…

Curry.

Amandine laughed, overwhelmed with too much longing to care.

The way he touched her now and the way her body responded was unlike the static energy she experienced with him before. Now she felt an all-consuming need, a hunger from within every fiber that could only be satiated by René. She wanted him to kiss her more. She needed him to touch her everywhere. Any self-discipline or restraint she might have summoned up moments ago was slipping away faster than water through her fingers and soon she surrendered to him completely.

Sensing his control, René pinned her. This show of force drew a small sound from Amandine, and he stopped.

214

"I am sorry," he said. "Am I hurting you?"

"No," she whispered, breathless. "It's just that... I haven't done anything like this before, and... well, it feels incredible." Her leg moved up his side seemingly on its own, and René held it against his hip from back of her knee. "But we had better stop."

"Must we?" He sought control once more with another kiss. Amandine shuddered, stunned into submission again when she parted her lips, and he eagerly kissed her deeper. She savored this for as long as she could bear it before gently breaking away.

Pained, he asked, "Why?"

She didn't know how to explain the conflict within her. She didn't know how to say how badly she wanted to give herself to him, yet feared the consequences if she did. Marmi's strict position was very much like her father's; or at least, she imagined it would have been had Will Stewart been given the opportunity to express it. Caroline, on the other hand, made her opinion clear. Not long before she was arrested, she held Amandine's hands over the kitchen table and told her, "When you fall in love, *ma puce*, enjoy the thrill but always try to land gracefully."

Disrespecting Marmi would not be graceful. Being discovered in such an intimate scenario by Sangria on her own bunk wouldn't be graceful either. In voice that did a poor job of hiding her unwillingness, she said, "Not yet."

René sighed, knowing that she was right.

"Let's stay right here together," she whispered.

He laid back and held her in his arms, wondering how he could truly fulfill her request.

The next morning, René awoke in slow disbelief as a stripe of late morning sun came through the curtains and fell across a strange sight. He didn't recognize the room, the beauty in his arms, or even himself in his new clothes. Gradually, memories of the night before fell back into place and soon he remembered everything with a smile. He lifted his head from the pillow to check on Amandine.

The seamstress was still sleeping, curled against him and breathing softly into his shirt. Though he felt he could watch her sleep forever, he couldn't resist turning his face into her hair to take in her sweet, clean scent.

"Good morning," he said when she stirred. "But I must still be dreaming."

She smiled with her eyes still closed. "Could we both be dreaming at the same time?"

"It's not likely."

"How do you figure?" She stretched and clung to him a little tighter.

"It can't be real, because I never could have kissed you like that. I never could have held you close to me all night." He got a mischievous idea. "I think I am going to need some proof."

In an instant she climbed on top of him, sunk her fingers into his hair, and pulled him into a kiss. René liked that she took control, but he especially liked that he was free to touch her from this position. Her body arched, craving contact as his hands mapped out her form. Her shoulders fit into his palms, her ribs expanded with each deep breath, his hands could almost encircle her waist.

Amandine paused, lips hovering over his, when she felt his fingers reach the hem of her dress. He stopped as well; the cotton border may as well have been a brick wall without her permission.

"Now?" he asked softly. It wasn't a plea, nor was there any insistence in his voice. He dipped his head against her neck and waited, though he knew what her answer would be.

She granted a final kiss to his forehead and reluctantly moved away.

René sat up and casually dropped his hat over his lap while Amandine fixed her bow. He didn't want to sour the mood by picking up their conversation from the night before, so he changed the subject.

"What do you suppose happened to Sangria?" he asked lightly. "She never came back to kick us out of her bed."

Realizing he was right, Amandine leaped off of the bunk. "I don't know, but I have a pretty good idea!"

The camp was an absolute disaster. Dishes, tables, chairs, and bottles were strewn everywhere. René gasped when he found that Big Polly was still humming quietly. The generator had been left on all night and he rushed over to switch it off.

No one else appeared to be up yet, so the pair crept towards Coronado's truck. They peered into the cab and found the illusionist behind the wheel, snoring softly with a bottle of wine on one side of him and Sangria on the other, curled up like a kitten under his jacket.

Amandine nodded with approval. "About time."

"Marmi will certainly have a thing or two to say about that," René whispered, moving away quietly. "If she asks you about this, it's probably best if you say nothing."

"I am sealed up tighter than a drum." She zipped her lips and tapped her temple. "She won't even be able to read my mind because all I'll think about is quilt block patterns."

"Oh, really?" he said, amused. "Is that how it works?"

"Maybe," she chirped. "All joking aside, our divas should both be much easier to work with after this."

"Or worse," he frowned. "Much worse."

They tiptoed around the rest of the camp, peering in cabs and behind trailers. The others who were caught misbehaving were Ludmilla with Sasha, Margaret with Ambroise, and most surprising of all, Marmi and Glorious. They were propped up behind the electropolyharmonium; her head rested on his chest and his face was buried in her unraveling turban. Even in his sleep, Glorious looked very pleased with himself.

They stifled their laughter and wordlessly decided that they had better start breakfast. Amandine picked up the trash and dishes while René built a fire. Next she explored the food crate while he rolled up his sleeves and went to get water from the stream. She was mixing up batter when he returned, so he started coffee and the aroma wafted around camp.

Juan appeared first, yawning and scratching all the hair that was matted flat on one side.

"Buenos dias," René said from the dishwashing tub. He dried a cup and held it out to him. "Coffee?"

Amandine soon had a stack of pancakes and cornmeal bacon cooked up on platters. When she finally sat down to eat with René, they kept a respectable distance, but they couldn't help smiling to themselves. Warm, tingling feelings from the night before were still fresh in their minds.

By now, almost everyone was awake. Though the morning was clear and pleasant, no one stopped to chat by the fire. One by one, they retrieved their food and retreated to the privacy of their trailers, either too ashamed or hungover to face anybody else. If he hadn't been watching for her, René might have missed Marmi sneak back to her tent. He wanted to judge her mood, so he fixed a tray of food and tea for her as usual. With a wink to Amandine, he trotted up the hill after her.

Marmi let him in when he rang her chime. She had changed clothes already and was brushing her long, black hair at the vanity.

"I have pancakes with jam and tea," René said casually, stepping over the tiger that laid by her table. "Did you sleep well?"

"Better than you, I suspect." She swiped her corkscrew curls furiously. "The twins didn't cook this morning."

"Amandine did." He answered the question she didn't ask and set the tray by her chair. "She takes such good care of us. We will all be very sorry to see her go."

Marmi didn't have any patience for small-talk. She could guess what René had been up to the night before, but when she whirled in her seat to confront him, she knew in that instant that she was wrong. The truth was in his eyes. René was no scoundrel. Although he had changed much in the years since they met, the depth and sincerity in his eyes had always remained the same.

"I am sorry," she said, humbled.

"Don't be."

"No, I am." She reached for a colorful scarf and tucked her hair inside it. "I was ready to lash out at you for something a great number of us are probably guilty of. If there's anybody I should blame, it's that forked-tongued con-man Glorious! It's those damned Pasternakovs! I don't know what they put in my cup, but it wasn't like any *kvass* I've ever had."

"Don't blame anyone," he said gently. "Least of all yourself. Everybody had more fun last night than we've had in years. We should be glad for the chance to cut loose a little." He prepared her tea for her, straining the fragrant red water into her ceramic cup. "Speaking of which, there was something I wanted to talk to you about."

The tiger eyed Marmi's breakfast, and René jerked the tray off the table just as Rao nipped at the cornmeal bacon. "Rao! *Honte à toi!*" He pushed the tiger away with his foot.

"This is not for you! Go get Sasha. Sasha's got your breakfast."

"*Chale jao!*" Marmi clapped her hands in Rao's face and with an impatient huff, the tiger sauntered out of the tent. Marmi reached fore the tray, but the moment her fingertips touched René's, she nearly dropped it in shock. "You're thinking of going with her," she murmured, setting the tray aside.

René smiled and offered her tea.

Marmi took the cup, stared into its swirling contents for a moment, and decided she needed something stronger. "You want my permission."

René watched her pack her pipe and wondered if she could carry on their entire conversation by herself.

"Nevermind what I think, child," Marmi said with the pipe in her teeth. "The girl won't let you. She believes very much in the bonds of family. She doesn't want you to choose between her and us." She took several deep drags and her eyes slid out of focus as if she could see through the tent walls into something far beyond. "And there is something serious, much more sinister at the end of Amandine's path. She is coming to realize it herself, and she does not want us to have any part of it."

"I know," Rene said, frustrated. "I hate to say it. I hate to even think it, but she's doomed to fail. Amandine wants to hire a solicitor for her poor mother, but she'd be lucky if she could hire a cab with what we've paid her."

Marmi's focus returned to him, unwavering as if searching his very soul. He thought he'd save her the trouble of trying to read him.

"I want to know if she has another path. Perhaps a place with us." He met her gaze with confidence. "A place with me."

"I see. You want to know what your future together holds." Marmi reached for his hands and turned his palms up. She hummed while she traced the lines that cut through the rough surface like ploughed field. "Let me see here... your head line says you are creative and adventurous. Your life line tells me that you have strength and enthusiasm, but it breaks, meaning you will experience a sudden change in your life. But this isn't new. I've known all of this about you since Paris, back when your hands weren't quite so big."

"I thought I was being very mysterious in Paris," he chuckled.

"You were a child, René." She squeezed his fingers. "And now you know better than to try and fool Madame Marmi."

"If you weren't desperate to uncover my secrets, then why did you take me on?"

"Do you want to stand here all day and revisit the past?" She pinched his bristling cheek fondly. "Or do you want to talk about the future?"

"The future, please."

She tapped the crease in his palm that ran horizontally beneath his fingers. "Here... your heart line tells me you will fall deeply in love with one person."

222

René beamed, but she shot him a serious look that gave him pause.

"Perhaps Amandine is that person, perhaps she isn't. You're only nineteen, and we have thousands of miles ahead of us. Amandine's road ends in Nieuwestad."

René closed his hands. He knew that palm reading was a party trick; Marmi had said so herself many times. What he didn't know was why she was trying to use that on him now.

"But you know," he said. "You can tell me what will happen. You can tell me what to do." Desperately, he demanded, "I want a vision. I want you to use your Infinite Sight."

Marmi scoffed, but the despair in his voice made her reconsider. She relented and thoughtfully closed her eyes, but all she could see was the past. She saw a little boy hiding in the back of Coronado's truck, insisting he wasn't a thief, but an aspiring cowboy who needed to get to America. She saw herself twelve years younger and a little fuller-figured, charmed by the child's polite determination, but with no interest in an extra mouth to feed.

"Every child wants to run away to join the circus," Marmi told him. "And they all run back home to mama when my tiger tries to eat them."

"I'm not scared of tigers," young René said. "I'm not scared of bears or mountain lions either. You'll need somebody brave to chase them all off for you in America."

"I already have brave men who can *wrestle* bears. You have to go home, child. Your mama will miss you." She remembered the way his heavy little eyebrows dipped down in

223

disappointment and the way her heart softened a little to see it. "But I suppose my bear-wrestlers could use some help with dinner. Stay and eat with us, then at least you will have a story to tell when you get home."

Contented for the moment, young René pulled off his coat, rolled up his sleeves, and went to help the Russians serve up *coq au vin*. The boy never did tell Marmi where he came from, but the tag inside his jacket that read "*Propriété de l'Orphelinat de Notre Dame*" and the welts that criss-crossed up his forearms told her everything she needed to know.

Marmi opened her eyes in the present. Even as the young man stood eye-to-eye with her, she still saw a little boy hiding from his hurt and dreaming of a bright future. "My darling, beloved child. I can't tell you about the future, because both of you already know what it holds," she said at last. "You need to open your eyes and see it yourself, because I don't want to be the one to break your heart."

"Then tell me how to change it," he begged. "Tell me what to do!"

She shook her head firmly and released him. "Here is what you do: tell everyone to get ready to leave." She turned her back and waved him away. "We press on to Nieuwestad tonight, and we finish that show."

CHAPTER 12: THE REHEARSAL

It took all day and most of the night to reach the outskirts of New Work, New Jersey. The caravan was slow, but they made good time as the roads became smoother the closer they got to the city. Coronado's truck brought up the rear of the procession, and the illusionist drove with one arm out of the window, the other resting with a cigarette on the steering wheel.

"Can you believe this?" he said to his passenger. "These roads have lamps now. Nothing was lit the last time we came here."

René was silent. He hadn't spoken a word to anyone after delivering Marmi's instructions, and Coronado was worried about the way he had completely withdrawn.

"The city should be fun to explore, eh?" he went on, hoping to coax a response out of him. "I imagine there will be so much to do. Restaurants, dance halls, picture-shows… of course, it doesn't sound very interesting to me, but to a bunch of young people— I could chaperone you if you wanted to take the girls out."

The passing lamps had a hypnotic effect on René. It drowned out most of what Coronado was saying, and it dulled the aching sadness he had been feeling since that morning.

225

René had absolute faith in Marmi's insight, but he could sense that she knew something else that she did not want to tell him. It confirmed that a parting would be inevitable, but he couldn't understand why she wouldn't just say so.

Amandine knew this was coming, and she didn't need Infinite Sight, he thought, tugging his hat lower so that the lamplights stayed out of his eyes. *Yet how can she keep on smiling? Do I not mean as much to her as she means to me?*

Perhaps Marmi saw that Amandine didn't truly care for him, and she was trying to spare his feelings. The thought hurt him so badly that he didn't want to look at her. René feared his own reaction to seeing her radiant smile, knowing she would soon leave, and he could not follow.

Coronado tried again to get him to open up. "Speaking of the city, I feel like I can finally show my face in public again. I never could have imagined that something so sharp and comfortable could have come from a bag of chicken feed. I can hardly wait to see what our little dressmaker does when she gets her hands on some real material."

He glanced over to check his reaction. René usually lit up whenever Amandine came up in conversation, but this time he didn't respond at all. Coronado tried the last thing he could think of. "We all will certainly miss her when she goes."

René huffed and reached for the radio.

"...and now a word from our sponsors! Do you tire of being relentlessly persecuted for expressing your own beliefs? Do you think that it's wrong to use food to buy your obedience? Is red your favorite color?"

"The pirate station?" René said in surprise.

Coronado shrugged and tapped his ash out of the window. "Not everyone can be as passive as you, René."

"Then join the rebel ranks," DJMA exclaimed brightly. "You don't need a gun. You don't need to fight at all! All you need to do is stand up for what this country used to believe in. You used to have rights, so fight for them in any way you can. Raise your own food and share it with the needy. Do not attend the Freedom Festival. Spread the message on your very own pirate radio station. *Tell our President Alexander Fairchild exactly where he can stick it!* Stand beside all-American heroes like Tall-Me and Cleo. Turn red today!"

"Change the station," Coronado said through his cigarette, his eyes illuminated by headlights in his mirror.

"Absolutely not." René crossed his arms. "I want to know what's so interesting about this guy that he's even got you—"

"It's just a recorded message. They play it all the time," Coronado said sternly. "Change the station and turn the radio off. The police are following us again."

René snatched up the side-view mirror and angled it towards the road behind them. Just as Coronado said, a familiar Interceptor appeared a few yards from their bumper, matching their speed and making no attempt to pass.

"Their lights aren't on," the illusionist said after a while. His gaze darted from the road to his mirror. "They're not stopping us."

"That's because they're watching us," René said uneasily. "Do you suppose...?"

The truck in front of them moved off of the main road and Coronado turned to follow it. The Interceptor slowed and stopped just past the turn, watching as they dipped behind a hill and fell out of sight into the darkness.

René gripped his chest and gasped; he didn't know how long he hadn't been breathing.

"Relax, friend," Coronado said. In truth, he wasn't so calm himself, and his stiff voice betrayed that. "We're almost to camp."

René adjusted the side mirror until he could see the trailer. The girls must have been sleeping because every window was black.

"I wonder if Marmi saw them," Coronado grumbled. The pavement ended with a hard bump and soon the rough trail led them to their new campsite. "*Dios mio*, what is that woman thinking? A costume made of solid gold isn't worth the trouble this girl will bring down on our heads."

They assumed their usual parking formations, except Coronado now kept his truck hitched to Sangria's trailer. The illusionist cut off his engine and stayed put in the dark cab for some time, shaking as he lit another cigarette.

René fell silent once again.

Morning soon fell upon the new camp. Marmi had a knack for picking excellent spots to stop and this one was no exception. It was a wide, flat clearing surrounded by red oaks a short distance from a straight stretch of river. There was plenty of room for the group to finish painting the set, rehearse, and settle in for awhile.

The twins made a hearty skillet dish for breakfast to strengthen everyone for the day of work ahead. After eating their fill of potatoes, sausage, and eggs, Amandine and Sangria left their trailer together, dressed to go to town.

Amandine couldn't find any sign of René. It had been a whole day since they last spoke, and she already missed him terribly. She wanted to invite him to town. She wanted to share a soda or perhaps browse a used bookstore together, but mainly she wanted to shake the nagging feeling that he was suddenly avoiding her. Something didn't feel right. She sensed a tension in the camp that was so heavy, it was almost tangible.

She found Coronado first, climbing out of his truck with a crate full of chemicals. Amandine trotted over, but she hadn't even begun her greeting before he cut her off brusquely. "René's not here. I don't know where he went, but I imagine it has to do with the tremendous amount of work he has on his plate." He kicked the doors shut and glared at her. "You had better stop wasting time with him and get to what we hired you to do."

His hostility made Sangria gasp. "Now you see here!"

"It's okay, Gia." Amandine tugged her by the elbow. "He's right. We need to get started right away, and I really want you to come with me."

Sangria stared down Coronado until he returned to his business with a huff. "Jerk," she muttered as soon as he was out of earshot. "Insufferable ass!"

Amandine bit her lip; something was definitely wrong. She thought that maybe a little space would help everybody get themselves sorted, so she hurried to get her budget from Marmi and the last of Glorious' notes.

Glorious was firing up the electropolyharmonium on a low power setting, one better suited for rehearsals, while the dancers led the others in warm-up stretches.

"Miss Mandy! Miss G! Going shopping in the big city?" he asked cheerfully. Amandine was glad to see that at least he was unaffected by the pressure.

"Just to the closest fabric store," Sangria complained. "I don't know if I'll ever get the chance explore Nieuwestad proper."

"Well, you be safe and have fun," he said, pulling some papers from Big Polly's bench. "I won't keep you. You've got a long walk ahead of you. I hope my last couple of notes are clear." He handed them to Amandine with a wink. "But I really hope you're able to let loose and get creative."

"Thanks, Glorious." Amandine scanned the notes before putting them in her coat pocket. "Have a good rehearsal. We'll be back soon."

"Before or after lunch?"

"I'm not really sure." She shrugged. "Why do you ask?"

He pointed at Sangria. "Miss G needs to rehearse with us, too. She is the star, after all."

The contortionist was taken aback; she didn't think Glorious was serious about giving her a central role in the show. With a tiny smile, she said, "I suppose I might, if I'm not too tired."

Amandine and Sangria walked for nearly an hour before they arrived at the fabric store. It was a brown brick building near the edge of town with high, half-moon windows crowning the upper stories above the wide, open storefront. No sooner had the door bell announced their arrival when suddenly Amandine was hit by a distinct smell that made tears burn in her eyes before she even understood what was happening. Uncontrollable emotions bubbled up with every familiar breath of dust, cotton fibers, and dye. She choked. She never expected that stepping over a threshold in New Jersey would take her eight hundred miles and almost ten years back to Cold River, South Carolina. Amandine half-expected to see her mother ordering the stock boys around or her father bent over the cutting table.

"Hey." Sangria noticed her burst of emotion with a frown. "What's the matter with you?"

"Nothing." Amandine turned her face up and blinked rapidly. If she couldn't hold her tears back, maybe gravity could. "It's just... the smell of this place. All the cotton and dye. It reminds me of *maman* and dad. It reminds me of home."

"Nostalgia?" Sangria sighed and rolled her eyes. "Thank goodness. I don't think I've ever seen you express anything less than 'total exhilaration,' and I got a little worried."

231

"Has it ever happened to you?" Amandine asked, dabbing her eyes with her wrist. "Have you ever been hit with a really specific smell that took you back home?"

Sangria smiled. It was a thin, wry expression, but Amandine was glad to see that it was happening more frequently nonetheless.

"One time really stands out," she said. "The girls found a dance studio that we were free to practice in, and I thought, 'hey, this is a rare opportunity, maybe I'll join them.' The second I smelled the cigarettes, sweat, and rosin, I was eight years old again, standing at the barre while Madame Gniewek corrected my posture with a stick." She took out her lacy handkerchief and handed it to Amandine. "I did an about-face and locked myself in my trailer for a week."

The shopkeeper was happy to show them to the sort of fabric Amandine was looking for. As she followed him down the aisles, she let her fingertips bounce across the edges of the bolts until she felt the whisper of a familiar, delicate crepe. She paused. It was unmistakably Master Elegance fabric and she closed her eyes against the painful pinprick in her heart.

"Button." Will Stewart checked his wristwatch and beckoned. "This way. Keep up."

"I know the way, dad. I've never been lost in here," young Amandine replied. She tucked the edge of the peach fabric back into the bolt before running after her father. "I was just looking at some of the new stuff."

"One day you can look until you're sick." He pushed his fingers through her curls, making them stand on end. "After a day like today, I'm certainly tired of it."

"You can't be tired of fabric," Amandine said, evading him long enough to fix her hair. "It's our life."

"No," Will replied. "It's my life. Mine and your mother's. You don't have to be anchored to this if you don't want it. Everything here will one day be yours, and it has always been my intent that you use it to build the sort of life you want for your future family."

She thought for a moment. "But I don't know anything else."

"Well, you're still only a little girl. Wait until you're a teenager and you know everything." He pressed her to his side while they walked down a long, bright aisle of bolts. He let her go when Will's assistant found them and he traded his apron and measuring tape for his briefcase, hat, and jacket.

"But I like it here." The assistant snuck Amandine a caramel with a wink and hurried off just as quickly as he appeared. "I like the store, too." She pouted at Will who still didn't seem to believe her. "I can be a dressmaker just like you. I caught *maman* snooping in my sketchbook, and she said I was showing some real talent."

"Your mother is right. You do have talent." Will adjusted his fedora. "At your age, I couldn't even thread a needle."

Caroline appeared at the end of the row in a smart gray suit, waiting impatiently for them. "At your age, you still can't read the time. *Dépêche-toi!* We're late for supper. Anita will be furious."

"Nice to see you too, Caroline of mine." Will gave his wife a quick kiss on the lips, hoisted his giggling daughter under his arm like a cask, and started into a brisk trot. "Come on. We need to hurry and act very pathetic because we can't have Anita threatening to quit again. I don't know what I'd do without her fried chicken."

Amandine came out of her daydream when her stomach growled. Thinking about their cook brought her back to reality, standing in the middle of an aisle and hugging a bolt of shocking red silk. She looked for Sangria and found her next to the cutting table, gaping at the stacks of shining fabric that spilled out of their bolts like gems. The shopkeeper was carefully measuring and cutting while a stock boy added more bolts to the pile.

"I can't believe Marmi was squirreling away this kind of money for costumes," Sangria said with wonder. "I thought if she had her way, she'd have us all in bed sheets like she wears."

Amandine glanced over the shopkeeper's shoulder to get a look at the tally he was keeping. Setting the red bolt down with the rest of the fabric, she checked the envelope Marmi gave her. She swallowed hard. It wasn't nearly enough money. It would barely cover a few more yards of calico.

"Are you ladies going to a ball?" the old man asked, grasping his shears with tremoring hands. Once the blades touched the fabric, they slid with the steady guidance of a skilled professional. "A special Freedom Festival celebration, perhaps?"

"You got it." Sangria rubbed the edge of an embellished striped material, only for the shopkeeper to strike her knuckles with the handle of his scissors. She recoiled and pouted.

"Good," he said. "When a couple of country girls start buying all of my good material, I certainly hope they aren't using it to piece a quilt."

"How'd you figure we're country girls?" Sangria grumbled, rubbing her hand.

"It's the feedsack dresses." He put his scissors in his apron. "Don't get me wrong. They look mighty fine. I hope you get the same lady to make your ballgowns." He winked at Amandine and totaled up her purchase.

Amandine reached into her coat for money, searching for the hidden space at the edge of the lining under her left arm. She widened the gap with her fingers until her hand could fit, then she plucked out several bills that were tacked inside.

"That's not Marmi's money," Sangria said suspiciously. "Her bills are always wrinkled from sitting in that drawstring purse."

Amandine showed her the envelope that contained the costume budget and Sangria scoffed at what she found inside. "I knew it. Marmi didn't give you beans."

"I imagine it was as much as she could spare after getting us this far without performing," she said with a little hitch in her voice. She took a deep breath that summoned up a little more determination. "I imagine she expected me to 'mend and make do,' but I've mended and made do for years, and so have all of you. This is no time to cut corners. Glorious says if it goes over well, this show could change your fortunes forever, so we all need to do our very best." She waved at her blue and pink floral dress. "But I can only do so much with feedsack."

"Yeah, but what's it to you?" Sangria asked bitterly. "You're leaving soon. What do you care if the costumes are made from potato sacks?"

The dressmaker immediately thought of René, who always put the needs of others before his own. She hoped that if the show was successful, Marmi could afford to take better care of him. She pictured him sprawled out across the bench seat of his own truck, reading the latest volume of Rogue Rider, and thinking of her. Amandine would be long gone, but at least her efforts helped to make his life a little more comfortable.

"Marmi took me in on good faith, proving that there is still great kindness left in the world. I intend to pay it back the

236

best way I can." She reached for the satin and silk bundles, sorting them by project before she placed them in her bag. "Dad told me that this money was for me and my family. Not just for *maman*," Amandine pushed the square of fiery red silk and a box of sequins into Sangria's hands with a smile. "But for my new family too."

"Oh, can it, you sappy drip!" Sangria blushed and hurried out of the store while Amandine collected her change. As soon as she was outside, curiosity got the best of her, and she held the silk against her fair skin. It was bold and dramatic, like blood on snow. All at once, she could see Amandine's design, and she knew it would be the most beautiful thing on the stage.

When their shopping was finished, Amandine surprised Sangria by stopping at a cafe where the two of them ate a fried chicken lunch. It wasn't like Anita's back home, but it hit the spot all the same.

"This is fun," Sangria admitted, generously applying jelly to her dinner roll. "Though I can't help but wonder why you're taking me on a date and not your darling René."

Sangria saw Amandine's face twitch. Instead of prodding at the nerve like she might have a month ago, she frowned and tore into a chicken leg. "I was worried about that. I warned you he's nothing but a big, bad wolf."

"It's not like that," she defended him. "Nothing happened. I thought... I thought things were going well, but then he went up to speak to Marmi and... nothing."

"Maybe Marmi told him to lay off," Sangria mused while she sucked the meat off of the bone and started picking at another with her fingers. "Maybe she hypnotized him. Why else would he have broke it off with you if you didn't give him what he was after?"

"Stop it, Gia," Amandine demanded. "Why do you keep saying René is like that? Do you two have a history or something?"

"Ugh, me and the dirty Frenchman?" Sangria exclaimed. "Don't make me sick!"

"Why do you dislike him so much?"

Sangria ate more chicken to keep from having to answer right away. When she finally did, her face was curled with disgust. "René is just so... *nice*. He's *too* nice! It doesn't matter if I tell him to hit the road or call him names, he keeps coming back with that '*ma chérie*' and that stupid smirk." She pushed her plate of bones away. "No fellow is ever that nice unless he's after something."

Amandine felt glad when her familiar old optimism prevailed. "You know, there's another reason I don't think you've considered."

"Yeah?"

"He cares about you."

"Me?" Sangria's eyebrows disappeared into her bangs. "Why the hell would he care about me, especially after what I've put him through?"

"Because he knows you've been hurt," she said gently. "He might not have known exactly how, but I believe he's

238

sensitive enough to see that the starving girl Sasha found in the alley was suffering badly, inside and out."

The waiter cleared the empty plate, leaving Sangria to stare at the counter's laminate surface. The two sat in silence while Amandine finished her lunch, and the contortionist kicked around this new perspective in her head.

She looked up when she heard Amandine's utensils hit the plate. "Speaking of suffering, it's going to be all blood, sweat, and tears as soon as we get back to camp." Sangria sighed. "With Glorious in charge, I know we can put this show together... but it's going to be *really* hard."

"Gia, if there's anybody who can pull off what Glorious has in mind, it's you. Anyway, I'm sure he can spare us a few minutes more." Amandine waved to the cook behind the counter. "Excuse me, sir! Two chocolate shakes, please!"

"You ladies wan' whip cream? Cherries?" he asked, reaching for some glasses.

"Why, natch!" Sangria beamed.

The next two weeks were a blur of music, dances, fire, and color. Day by day, a new costume appeared on stage, and Coronado was the first to appear in a shining white tuxedo. He was pleased beyond words, and it showed in his renewed enthusiasm on stage. His new act had mastered fire-throwing, transforming everyday objects into doves, and making costume jewelry vanish and reappear on Sangria's body. He would secure a dazzling necklace around her throat, jeweled cuffs on her wrists and a glittering crown on her head, only for it to disappear with a pass of a silk kerchief. Back and forth, the gems would come and go, until Coronado fluttered his magnificent cape like a matador and Sangria herself blinked in and out of existence. It was all synchronized flawlessly to Glorious' music and the dancers' choreography.

Next, Marmi had a tiger-taming act. Her regal costume resembled a white orchid, touched with purple and dripping with gold. She would guide Rao with a small flail up stairs, through hoops, and even straight into the air. Rao could roar on command which added an element of danger to the act. Nobody in the audience could have suspected that after the performance, he laid belly-up on a rug backstage, waiting patiently to be scratched by anybody who passed.

The third part of the show came as a complete surprise. It was a song performed by May, who up until this point, Amandine had assumed was incapable of speech let alone vocal talent. Somehow, Glorious managed to uncover her bright, brassy voice that shined in the song he wrote for her.

It was one of those moments where Amandine had to stop her work and watch, unwilling to believe that she had any part in this incredible show taking shape before her eyes. The act opened with the dancers spilling out from a giant dragon's mouth. Ludmilla and Chitra shimmied to one side in orange costumes while Sangria and Margaret shimmied to the other in gold. May bounced up to the microphone in an electric blue dress and sang with fiery attitude.

"Don't grab your hat, try stickin' around,
We can have fun here, I don't wanna go to town.
I got a bottle of bubbles and my records are hot.
I wanna see if you're the guy who can take it or not!

"I wanna swing with my baby,
Keepin' all the neighbors up!
I wanna bounce with my honey,
never gonna let it stop!
When we've worn down the floors
And set the ceiling alight,
Let's take it back to your place
And keep it jumping all night!"

"Take my hand, hang your coat on the hook,
I wanna show you how a real lady can cook.
There's fire in my heels and hell down below.
Just say the word, baby, I'll be ready to go!"

Their dance featured energetic kicks, thrusts, and figure-eight hip movements. Sangria and Margaret had never danced with the others before, but as soon as they overcame the challenge of learning the choreography, they fell in with ease. Sangria had so much fun dancing in the chorus that sometimes she laughed uncontrollably during the climax of the act.

The finale began with Sangria playing her violin alone on a dark stage. Hers was the last costume Amandine had to make and for now the contortionist rehearsed in her leotard. She was joined by Coronado and when the two danced, they moved as one with absolutely riveting chemistry. All of the others appeared on stage as the music swelled, and Glorious furiously worked his machine, leading the entire show to its explosively spectacular conclusion.

Even after hearing the songs and seeing the dances dozens of times before, Amandine couldn't help but stand up and move. She only wished she weren't dancing alone.

CHAPTER 13: THE VISION

August 24, 1945
Somewhere outside of New Work (formerly Newark), New Jersey

It was the opening night of the Freedom Festival, but Marmi's Marvels weren't scheduled to perform until the next day. Everyone got up before the sun and set to work, either fine-tuning their acts or loading the trucks up with their giant, moving sets. This was it; this was going to be the biggest performance of their lives. For most, the mood lingered somewhere between excited and frantic.

René on the other hand, was completely miserable. He wanted to speak to Amandine so badly, but he couldn't even bring himself to look in her direction. She had set up her sewing table and a makeshift fitting room no more than twenty yards away from where he was disassembling the set, but the sight of her packed suitcase felt like a punch in the gut. He didn't know that she meant to leave until he saw it propped against the machine, waiting beside her coat and hat. She was ready to leave without giving him any warning. Did she even mean to say goodbye?

Despite wanting to avoid thoughts of her, he kept picturing the way she would frown when she concentrated, thoughtfully nibbling the pins in her mouth until at last her face lit up, and she was satisfied with her work. He was picturing it so perfectly that he stopped paying attention to what he was doing.

"Whoa, René! Watch that drill!" Glorious threw a bracket at him, and it bounced off of the brim of his hat. "We're taking the set apart, not scrapping it. Remember?"

René peeked beneath his drill. Instead of removing the screw, he accidentally drove it deeper, making a split in the wood about six inches long. He heaved a sigh and moved across the flat backdrop.

"Eh, sorry. I am glad one of us was paying attention."

Glorious grumbled as he dropped screws and brackets into his tool belt one by one. "Yeah, I been paying attention. I seen that you been down ever since we got here. No pep in your step, none of your fresh ideas or input. You just been moving from job to job like a machine." With a grimace, he regarded the damage. "A busted machine. You're so messed up, you ain't even talked to poor Miss Mandy."

René tried to focus on his work again. He managed to free the first panel, painted like a cloudy star-studded sky, but by the time he got halfway through the next panel, he got to thinking about the way Amandine's skirt flared when she danced, and he accidentally pinned the end of his finger beneath a screw. He jumped back on his heels and cursed.

"Bordel de merde!"

"Language, son. What's the matter? You cut yourself?" Glorious clicked his tongue and tore off a strip of electrical tape to use as a bandage. "Why don't you take a break?"

"I can work," René muttered, sucking on his finger.

"I insist." Glorious walked René off of the backdrop and nearly tossed him in Amandine's direction. "Take a break. Go see if Miss Mandy needs one, too. She's been at that machine for weeks, bless her heart."

René knew there was no fighting this; he needed face her before he ran out of time. He thought about what to say while he dragged his feet over to where Amandine was working.

Hello, Amandine, he thought. *How have you been? Busy? Me too.*

No.

I am sorry I have been avoiding you. Let's go for a walk and talk for a little while. You'll change your mind about leaving if I kiss you until you're dizzy.

Don't be stupid, René!

Amandine, you can't go. It's dangerous out there, and your mother is probably already dead. What if the Inquestor finds you? You'll end up in a replacement home or you'll get the scaffold. Stay with us, and we'll eventually go back to Europe, away from this terrible conflict. Please, mon coeur, I beg you. Please don't leave me!

He sighed again as his voice of reason fought a losing battle with his emotions.

Amandine was close now, holding up a ruby silk costume with shimmering rhinestones around the cut-out front.

245

She checked it over on all sides before she called out to Sangria, who was waiting in the fitting room.

Sangria popped out from behind the hanging sheets, bouncing with glee at the splendid costume held before her. She was about to snatch it from Amandine's hands when she stopped short with a troubled look on her face. She emerged in her kimono and Amandine collapsed, sobbing, in her arms.

It was a scene that stunned René; Sangria's cold demeanor had warmed to comfort her friend, and Amandine's enduring joy had finally broken.

Furious, Sangria's head shot up, and she scanned the camp like a predator. She spotted René, and her face curled up like a gargoyle when she realized that he had been watching them.

"I hope you're happy," she snarled before he could start apologizing. "Look at what you've done! You dote on her, you treat her like a princess, and then what? Not a word, not a glance for weeks! As soon as she gives you a kiss, you give her the cold shoulder! It's a good thing you didn't get any more than that, you dog!"

She lunged, her wide sleeves whipped back like wings, and she slapped him square across his face.

"So what happened, creep?" She pelted his chest and arms with her tiny fists. "She not good enough for you? You gonna shop for some cheaper skirts in the city?"

"Gia! Don't!" Amandine snatched her hands up before she could hit him again. "Please don't! It's alright."

Coronado appeared so quickly, he was still holding a dove. "I could hear you from across camp! What on earth is going on? Why is Amandine crying?"

Sangria spat on the ground at René's feet.

"What happened?" Coronado demanded, flinging the bird over his shoulder. Accustomed to this sort of treatment, the bird righted itself mid-air and flew back to his perch.

"Please, Amandine—" René dodged another knuckle punch from Sangria. "May I speak to you alone?"

"Yes, I think I have time." Amandine nodded and blew her nose into a hankie. To Coronado, she asked, *"Señor,* will you still be able to drive me into town?"

"Of course, but—" Sangria stopped Coronado's question with a jab of her elbow. Resigned, he sighed. "When will you be ready?"

"I want to see Gia in that costume once more, and then it's time for goodbyes," she answered. "Probably within the hour. I don't know how late they accept visitors at the prison."

René felt as if the ground had given out from beneath him. Time had run out. He had less than an hour, an hour that wasn't his alone.

He offered his hand, but Amandine coolly took his elbow instead. No sooner had they turned their backs when Sangria started recounting everything she knew about their troubled romance to Coronado, peppering it with insults against René's intelligence and character.

René led Amandine to the river's edge where the sound of coursing water was enough to deter any eavesdroppers. They stopped in a small clearing of soft grass beneath the whispering oaks. Under different circumstances, it could have been a very romantic spot.

"It's so good to see you again, René," Amandine chirped as if he hadn't been deliberately avoiding her. "I'm sorry for getting so emotional."

"Don't apologize." He ran both hands through his hair anxiously. "No, you must forgive me. I have been acting like a damn fool again, Amandine."

"Nonsense. I know you had important work to do."

For the first time, her cheerful front frustrated him. "Please don't do that. You know that's not what I meant."

Her smile faded.

"Why pretend?" he demanded. "You're clearly just as upset as I am."

"I'm not pretending," she said defensively. "I'm just trying to find the good in something that hurts so bad." Almost to herself, she added, "Perhaps it's better like this."

"What are you saying?"

"Perhaps it's better that you broke it off when you did." She kept her voice high and light to conceal the way it cracked. "I can't imagine what I'd be feeling now if we had really loved each other."

"You mean you don't?" he said in anguish. "You never did?"

Mon Dieu, Marmi was right.

She shook her head vigorously. "How could you say that, René? I thought I made it clear from the start that I was wild about you! You are the kindest, most talented, hardest-working person I have ever met, and you're as handsome as the Sheik of Araby to boot. The very thought of parting with you hurt so much, I thought about—" Amandine shrank back, ashamed. "I even considered leaving my mother for you."

René was stunned. Without thinking, he blurted out, "Well, why don't you?"

"Because you dumped me without so much as a word," she said coldly. "You don't treat somebody you love that way, René."

The truth stung him with shame. "Then I was wrong," René admitted. "I didn't know how you could still smile, knowing that you'd leave soon. I thought it meant that you didn't feel the way I did."

"I smiled because I was glad for the time that we had," she snapped and suddenly covered her mouth in surprise. Amandine wasn't used to expressing anger and her voice adopted Sangria's harsh tone all on its own. She tried to wind her emotions back like thread around a spool and demanded, "What made you think such a… such a *silly* thing?"

René stared at the tops of his beat-up oxfords as if he expected the answer to appear there. "Marmi said… rather, I thought Marmi was trying to tell me as much."

Amandine scoffed and watched the river lap up the sandy banks. "Marmi has incredible intuition. Magic or no, she sees things others can't, things she may not want to see herself. It puts her in a much greater position of responsibility than any of us could imagine." She picked up a stone and tossed it into the shallow water, scattering dozens of tiny minnows. "Can you imagine it? Having the knowledge, the power even, to possibly change someone's fate? It must be so difficult. She probably feigns ignorance just to keep from having to make those sorts of decisions."

"I believe you're right." René wondered why he hadn't considered it before.

"What if Marmi saw that I stayed, but the whole group got arrested by that creepy little inquestor?" She turned to give René the wide-eyed look that meant she was teasing him. "What if you left, but all of the trucks broke down in a blizzard, and everybody had to huddle around one of Coronado's fireballs to keep warm?"

"Wouldn't be the first time something like that's happened," he replied with a half-smile, joining her at her side. "I am so sorry, Amandine. I could have avoided all of this trouble if I had just talked to you." He felt a little more rational now that his fears were put to rest, so he asked, "So what shall we do? Will I go or will you stay?"

Amandine leaned against a tree trunk and played with the buttons on her cuff. "Neither."

"Have you thought of another option?"

"No." She bit her lip hard and furiously twisted her buttons. "I will go and you will stay, same as before."

"But—" He clenched his teeth. "I don't understand."

"Whatever she sees, whatever she knows, I believe Marmi is still right. This is the only way." She tried to collect her thoughts and explain. "The problem with looking on the sunny side is that people often think I don't look anywhere else. I'm not an idiot. I know now that my mother likely helped the rebels, but that won't stop me from trying to defend her."

She stopped her vicious attack on her buttons before she pulled them right off and tugged on her locket instead.

"If I manage to get *maman* out, we need to run. Innocent or not, we're right in the middle of this mess, and I don't think the inquestors will just let us go back to making dresses in Cold River. They'll come after us any way they can, and if I join you, they'll come after you too. You will never be free so long as I stay with you."

She searched his face for understanding. "The last few weeks have made it clear that it's better you stay away from my problems, safe with your family who needs you." She opened her locket to her parents' portraits, taken when they were newlyweds. "It's better that I try to save what's left of mine."

When their eyes met again, Rene saw that she was smiling, but the insincerity behind it saddened him. He reached for her hand. "It was not to be, *chérie*."

"I will miss you, René." She gave his hand a squeeze and noticed his hurt finger. "Oh, no. Are you alright?"

"I wasn't being very careful," he explained glumly.

She reached into her pocket and took out a tarnished silver thimble. "Maybe you need this more than I do." She closed it in his hand before he could refuse. "Keep it… to remember me by."

He didn't need a thimble to remember her, not when she left her mark on every member of his family. René already saw her in the way Coronado performed, ready to dazzle audiences like the super-star he used to be. He saw her in the way Sangria had finally broken free from her cage. He looked down at his own outfit, black and red just like the Rogue Rider. He couldn't even enjoy his new favorite adventure series without remembering that it was Amandine who shared it with him.

"May I ride with you to the prison?" he asked, rolling the trinket in his palm. "I would like to see you off and... say goodbye properly."

"Of course." Her smile now held a little genuine happiness. "I would like that very much."

A little while after they returned to camp, Amandine finally decided that she was satisfied with Sangria's costume. The contortionist pranced proudly around camp, glowing like a firebird and cartwheeling for anybody who would look. Her display drew everyone out, and they circled around Amandine to say their goodbyes. The dressmaker was crushed by embraces, covered with kisses, and showered with parting gifts.

"I have no doubt my music is gonna turn Nieuwestad on it's head," Glorious boasted while the Russians thrust a sack of *pirozhki* into the girl's arms. "But your costumes? They exceeded not only my expectations but my wildest dreams! I hope you open a proper shop someday where I can visit. I gotta look sharp if I'm gonna be performing in the biggest clubs and theaters in the country."

"Save me a front-row seat," she said, and Glorious hugged her fiercely.

Marmi descended from her tent with Baji Rao padding along by her side. "This is for you, darling child." She held something out to Amandine wrapped in her purple sash. "So that you will always remember this parting with fondness."

Amandine opened the little bundle and revealed Marmi's copper wind chime. She didn't recall ever telling anyone how she felt about bells, but she soon remembered that when it came to Marmi, she didn't have to.

"Oh, Marmi!" Amandine cried, throwing herself into her long arms. "Thank you for taking me in and looking after me. I will never forget this grand adventure I've had with all of you." She looked up at the towering woman to see black kohl pooling under her eyes. "Could I trouble you for a favor before I go?"

"Anything," Marmi said warmly, sunlight glinting off of the gold in her mouth.

"Could you give me a vision?"

Marmi blinked and everyone around them fell silent.

"No one here has ever asked for a vision before, child." She pulled away with a dry chuckle. "I don't think anyone believes it's real."

Rene frowned from where he was listening a little ways outside of the crowd.

"I would like one all the same," Amandine said firmly. "Right now."

"Surely there is something else I can do for you." Marmi was beginning to sound nervous. "Something that would better show my gratitude for such beautiful costumes than a silly old parlor trick."

"No," said Amandine. "If you won't do it as a favor, then do it as repayment."

Coronado plucked his cigarette out of his mouth. "Repayment?"

A murmur went up in the group surrounding them.

Marmi hesitated. She looked to Coronado, who's dark glare demanded an explanation. Even her kind and loyal René wouldn't look at her. She searched every face for a way out of Amandine's request, but nobody offered her an escape. She sighed and reached into her sleeve for her pipe. "As you wish, child."

Marmi took her time packing fresh tobacco into the bowl. Once it was lit, she took a deep breath, closed her eyes and let a fragrant stream of smoke tumble out of her mouth. She shuddered and took Amandine's hands in hers.

The camp was completely silent. It was nearly two minutes before Marmi finally spoke.

"I see a shining object in a black hand," she said in a strained voice. "Bright white, like a diamond or a mirror. I hear something. '*Kah.*' A name... It's a name that commands fear and respect. Now I see fire. I am engulfed in fire and two people are standing right in the middle of it. We're all burning alive."

Coronado exchanged a worried look with Glorious across the crowd.

Marmi began to tremble. "There are loud noises. Whining. Thunder, too? No, explosions. Gunshots!"

Amandine's eyes went wide as Marmi's hands crept back up her arms and clamped down around her face. Her grip got so tight that Amandine cried out and tried to peel her hands away, but her fingernails only dug deeper into her skin.

"It's... it's fireworks. Blood, gunshots, and fireworks. I see..."

Coronado and Glorious reached Marmi's side at the same time and ripped her hands away.

"The NAR!" she said hoarsely, shaking so hard she lost her balance. "NAR agents are here!"

Glorious wrapped her in a bear-hug, pinning her arms to her sides. "Hush, now. Ain't nobody here, baby."

"That Inquestor! The one who has been following us!"

Coronado gave a false chuckle and guided Amandine away. "Don't listen to her. All of that stuff is made up. It comes from her pipe just as much as it comes from her colorful imagination. I don't think she meant to frighten you." He steered her towards the truck, giving her shoulders a squeeze that was supposed to be reassuring.

Glorious led Marmi back to her tent with some difficulty. Marmi was still shaking so violently that she could barely stand without his help, and Rao, sensing that something was wrong, kept butting the back of their knees with his broad head. Once Glorious managed to get her back inside, everyone turned to stare at Amandine.

"I don't suppose that changed your mind about going, did it?" Sangria asked while she played with the buckle on her bag.

Amandine shook her head. "No. After all, it's just an act. Just a parlor trick."

255

Her optimism was becoming harder and harder to maintain. Amandine reached down deep within herself and summoned up what memories she had, but all she could think about was Marmi's premonition of blood and fire. She forced herself to think of René— and that only reminded her that she was leaving him forever.

A dim smile was all that Amandine could muster. "I'll bet she was just trying to scare me into staying."

"That's right," Coronado said, with no sense of belief in his voice. "Well? Shall we?"

Amandine picked up her suitcase. It felt so much heavier this time. "Goodbye, everyone. I will always watch for your posters." They all moved in for one last hug before Amandine, Coronado, René and Sangria climbed into the cab of the illusionist's truck and rolled out of camp.

The trip went by mostly in silence as the truck rattled across town. Predictably, Coronado smoked and listened to the radio. René polished the thimble Amandine gave him and attached it to his hat. Sangria tried to lighten the mood by talking about all of the fine stores she would have to visit once they won the prize money for their show. She admired the nice houses, remarking upon one in particular that resembled her own childhood home.

Soon the homes and stores gave way to fields again and they came upon a bizarre structure looming in the late afternoon light. An enormous black concrete block sat in the center of rolling green fields, like a giant die on a gaming table. There were no signs, but there was also no question that they had come to the right place.

Sangria stared up at the high walls that surrounded the building. "Is that it?"

"I think so." The sight made Coronado's skin prickle. "It's much bigger than I imagined."

There was an office building outside of the prison wall and some space for parking. A group of officers were consulting with the gatekeeper, so no one noticed when Coronado pulled in and parked amongst some other black trucks. Everyone piled out, and Sangria went first to her friend.

"You take care," she said firmly. "Be strong, and if it doesn't work out... well, I won't let anybody else take that extra bunk in my trailer."

"Thank you for letting me live with you, Gia." Amandine held her tight. "And thank you for being my friend. I'm going to miss you."

"I'll miss you too, Raggedy Ann."

She turned to Coronado. He gave her one of his rare smiles, and for the briefest moment, Amandine could see what Sangria found so attractive about him. "*Señor*, thank you so much for looking after me and pushing me to do my best. You remind me of my father... in a dark, angry sort of way."

He seemed pleased by this compliment, and he embraced her, kissing each cheek in farewell.

"Sweet Amandine, you have been a treasure," he said sincerely. "We will enjoy our new success thanks in great part to your incredible talents. God go with you, *muñequita*."

Amandine turned to René at last.

"We'll wait in the truck," Coronado said, flicking away his cigarette butt and ushering Sangria back inside.

Standing alone in the parking lot of a federal prison, Amandine and René reached for each other one last time. Amandine pressed her cheek to his soft, warm shirt and struggled to find the words to tell him everything she wanted to say.

I don't want to leave you.
I don't want this to be over.
I'm scared, René.

She stopped trying to put her feelings into words when he pulled her just far enough away so that they looked into each other's eyes: hers dark, his silver-bright, both brimming.

Hot tears streamed down both cheeks. She finally managed to say, "Is it crazy to hope that one day we can find each other again?"

René smiled gently and brushed her tears away with rough fingers. "I'm optimistic." He drew her in and slowly their lips met in a painful kiss goodbye.

When at last they parted, she lifted her suitcase and moved towards the office building, letting her hand stay in René's until it could no longer reach. Her heart ripped to pieces when her fingers finally slipped from his.

Amandine's throat locked. She wanted to look back. She wanted to run back. She dug as deeply as she could for a glimmer of hope, but her eyes were fixed on the terrible, black tomb before her.

Maman is in there. Maman is waiting for me.

She pushed through the squealing steel door into a reception area. Concrete benches were lined up before a long clerk's desk which was manned by officers in blue uniforms. There were no other civilians this late in the day, and everyone looked up at Amandine's arrival. Plucking up her courage, she stepped up to the desk.

"Can I help you, miss?" the officer asked, noting her suitcase with suspicion. "Do you need directions someplace?"

"Yes, I would like to visit my mother, please."

The officer blinked. "I'm afraid you'll have to wait until her shift is over. We can't allow civilians inside the prison."

"I'm sorry." Amandine touched her forehead in embarrassment. "I should have been more specific. My mother is a prisoner here. I would like to visit her, please, and then look into what avenues I can pursue to secure her release."

The officer stared at her, and all of the others were wearing matching expressions of disbelief. "Who exactly are you trying to see?"

"Caroline Heloise Brodeur Stewart, sir."

"Why, exactly, are you trying to secure her release?"

Amandine was struck dumb by this question. "Because... she's my mother."

There was a rustle of steel against leather as half a dozen gleaming pistols unholstered at once. Amandine froze and slowly raised her hands. "There's no need for that," she said, her voice trembling. "I don't want any trouble."

"Why do you want Cleo?"

"I didn't say anything about Cleo. I said Caroline. I want Caroline!" she exclaimed. "I want my mother!" Someone reached for her elbow, and she wrenched away on instinct. Suddenly, her arms were pinned against her sides.

Amandine screamed.

CHAPTER 14: THE PRISON

"For goodness' sake," Sangria growled. "Stop crying, René."

"I have to agree," Coronado said. The two seemed to have returned to their old selves, sitting irritably in the cab. "It isn't dignified."

René wiped his face with his bandana and tried to calm down with a deep breath.

"There you go." Coronado patted his back. "Get it together."

He pushed his hand away. "Did she really mean so little to you after all?" René demanded. "How can you two be so calm? So cold?"

"You're a fool if you think you're the only one upset by this," Coronado scoffed. "And I think you're a downright idiot for letting this happen."

"'*Letting this happen?*'" René repeated in outrage. "You have no idea what you're talking about, Antonio! I had no choice! She wanted to leave!" His hands clenched into fists, and he struck the dashboard helplessly. "What was I supposed to do? She wanted to leave..."

"I have experienced loss before, you know," Coronado said evenly, reaching into his jacket pocket. "The worst kind. When Estefania was gone, I..."

He paused and seemed to forget he was looking for his pack of cigarettes. He sat motionless, briefly lost in thought. "I thought I would never feel whole again. That I would never know anything but guilt and grief."

He found his box and tapped a cigarette into his waiting palm. He put it between his lips while he hunted for a match.

"I'll say it again, I think you're a damned idiot for letting her go. If I had any control over the matter, Estefania would still be here. I would have given my very life. You, on the other hand, wasted precious time moping about all of the 'what ifs' and throwing too much stock in the drug-addled ramblings of an old, fortune-telling fraud. You let poor Amandine walk straight into certain danger."

Coronado struck a match unsuccessfully.

"I don't feel any sympathy for you—"

He tried again, but it died before he could light his cigarette.

"—Only for that poor girl."

Sangria's gloved hand appeared over his shoulder, and she pushed the matches down. René saw the meaningful look that passed between them, and Coronado put his cigarettes away, obeying her wordless entreaty.

Suddenly, they heard a muffled scream from the prison office building, and all three jumped in their seats.

"That was Amandine!" Sangria exclaimed. "Oh, misery me! We need to help her!"

"Help? What do we do?" René's brain seemed to be at odds with his instinct. He knew he needed a plan, but his body had already sprung into action. He kicked the door open just as they heard the shriek of tires on pavement. An Interceptor spun to a stop in front of the prison doors, and three officers raced into the building with their guns drawn.

"That's the Inquestor." Coronado paled.

"What the hell's he still doing here?" Sangria demanded.

"They've been following us since South Carolina."

"*What?*" she screeched. "He's been following us this whole time? *And you knew?*"

"*Dios mio...*" Coronado deflected the punch she threw at his shoulder and pointed to the Interceptor. "They've been to camp!"

The others didn't immediately understand his meaning until they noticed long, deep scratches and a smashed out window in the driver's door.

René knew it was now or never. "I am going in," he shouted, grabbing his hat and sprinting for the building.

"*¡Maldita sea!*" Coronado pounded his hands into the steering wheel. He whirled on Sangria. "You stay here! Don't you even think of getting out of this truck!" He slapped on his fedora and hurried after René. "Hide in the back! Use one of the covered birdcages! *Don't let anyone see you!*"

Sangria watched them go, and her mouth curled into a wicked, red smile. "They won't see a thing," she purred, reaching for her bag.

Inside the office, Amandine struggled as hard as she could against all of the hands that grabbed her. Carver tried to get at her himself, but not a single frenzied blue officer noticed that there was an inquestor among them in the chaos.

"For Christ's sake, you blue bastards!" Carver yelled, cracking one prison guard in the ear with his 1911. "Do I need to announce my own presence? Stand down, dammit! She's mine! *I said stand down!"*

He gave a cry of frustration and fired three shots into the ceiling. Everyone froze and stared at the Inquestor as plaster rained down on their heads.

"Attention!" Carver barked and everyone snapped upright. "There's a goddamn inquestor present, so I'd appreciate it if you'd remember your place and *show me some goddamn respect!"*

He fixed his hat that had been knocked askew in the tussle and shot Amandine a calculating glance. With a gesture from his pistol, the two officers that accompanied him grabbed her by the arms.

"Thank you, gentlemen," Carver sighed. "Now that we have order once more, we can sort this mess out." He leaned over to the guard he had hit. "What did she do to warrant all six of you on her?"

The guard didn't appear to hear the question. He was swaying and staring vacantly at the "NO SPITTING" sign on the wall as red seeped from his ear. Another answered for him.

"She asked for Cleo, Inquestor, sir."

"Aha!" Carver used the hot barrel of his gun to turn Amandine's face up to his. "I'd expect nothing less from the daughter of the diabolical—" He stopped short. "Hang on. Did you say she *asked* for Cleo?"

"Yes, Inquestor, sir. She wanted to visit her and then try to get her released."

The gun came under her chin again, and he came close enough to look into her eyes, frantically searching them for some kind of sign. With growing incredulity, he pulled away. "You can't be serious." He gaped at his officers. "She can't be serious."

"A trick, Inquestor," said the one on her left arm.

Carver frowned. "I'm very disappointed, Miss Stewart. If that's all you wanted to do, you should have just said so when we first met and spared me all of this trouble. After what Cleo put me though, I expected so much more out of you."

"Who are you, Inquestor?" Amandine blurted. "Why have you really been following me?"

"Don't play dumb," he snapped. "It might have worked on your carnie-friends, but it won't work on me. I made the mistake of underestimating Cleo once, and she nearly killed me. I wouldn't be surprised if this little game you're

265

playing— just asking for your mother— is not really just a distraction for some bigger scheme."

"My mother is not Cleo! She's Caroline! She's just a dressmaker, like me!" Desperately, she repeated, "Who are you, Inquestor? How do I know you?"

"From the radio, I'd imagine," he said with a peculiar, crazed expression. It was as though she were the first person he had ever encountered who didn't already know who he was. "They're always talking about me on 'How We Are In The NAR.' I'm famous now, thanks to Cleo."

A murmur of "Inquestor Carver!" went up around the officers, and they brightened with recognition, but Amandine still scowled. Carver tried again with slow, deliberate words.

"I arrested your mother. I went to your safehouse and beat her into submission before the other inquestors even started their cars." He stood back with his arms spread, like a performer awaiting applause. "I'm a national hero!"

Amandine felt her stomach churn. *It was him. Carver was the inquestor at my house that night. This whole time he's been toying with me, hoping I would lead him to more rebels. Instead, I led him to Marmi. I led him to René. How could I have been so stupid?*

Her reaction angered him. "You can't honestly expect me to believe that you didn't know your mother was Cleo." Carver spun his pistol in annoyance, and it flashed white with each rapid rotation. "I thought your naivety was just a front. Cleo was so smart, so dangerous, and so cunning. But this?" He heaved a sigh, deflating like a tire. "The proverbial apple fell from the tree and rolled down the hill. Well, it's not the

266

exciting grand finale I was hoping for, but let's be optimistic. At least we won't come away from this empty-handed. You and I will both get what we wanted."

"What do you mean?" Amandine asked fearfully.

"*I mean,*" Carver snarled. "I get a raise for capturing Cleo's daughter and a circus-tent full of your rebel friends while you get to see your mother again."

"You can't imprison me," she cried. "I've done nothing wrong!"

"Imprison you?" He laughed, and the deep, heartless sound chilled her to her core. "No, it's far too late for that. You're going to be executed tonight in the city square right beside her. I'm sure you want to catch up first and tell her all about your pretty costumes and your new boyfriend, so I'll let you ride in the same truck together."

He beckoned with his gun and the officers at her arms began moving her towards the prison. "What?" she gasped, voiceless with terror. "Execute us?"

"Rolled away down the hill and landed in a cow pie," Carver muttered. "Somebody tell the warden that I've arrived and that he needs to change the lineup for the festivities tonight. Let's get a move on! The trucks are loading soon!"

Coronado and René burst into the building. All heads whipped in their direction and Amandine cried out in fear for her life.

"It's them!" shouted one of Carver's officers. He pistol-whipped Amandine to stop her screaming and her eyebrow split in a burst of blood.

"A trick! I knew it! I knew it, I knew it, I knew it!" Carver punched the air ecstatically. "*Rebel raid! Kill them!*"

A guard pulled the alarm. The room flashed red, and a siren wailed outside, rising and falling in pitch like a tidal wave across the entire prison. René and Coronado barely dove behind a bench in time to avoid a hail of bullets as chaos broke out once more.

"*¡Mierda!*" Coronado covered his head. "*¡Esta era una idea estúpida! ¡Maldita sea!*"

One of Carver's men wrapped an arm around Amandine's neck to get her under control. She kicked wildly and hit Carver's hand with a crack that sent his gun sailing across the room where it clattered to the floor at René's feet. The two cowering behind the benches stared at it.

"What are you waiting for?" Coronado yelled over the thunderous gunshots. "Save us! Shoot them!"

René slowly reached for the nickel-plated 1911 as their concrete cover crumbled around them. It was heavy and warm in his hand, shining like the sun. Gripping the handle, he used the windows to count the guards reflected in the glass, all lined up behind the desks.

Side by side, like soupcans on a fence, he thought. *I can do this. I can stop them. They're not men. They're villains.*

Just beyond the guards, almost out of sight in the glass, Amandine was being dragged by her neck from the room. She would have been nearly invisible, faint as a ghost, if it wasn't for the blood running in a bright, red stripe down the front of her dress. René paled. Fortune had offered him one last chance, and he was running out of time.

They aren't men. They're not. Just targets. Soupcans in uniforms.

To Coronado's horror, René stuffed the gun in his belt. He waited until the officers paused to reload before he held up both hands and rose to his feet.

"Damned pacifist," Coronado muttered miserably. "You've killed us. We're going to die!"

"He's surrendering," one officer declared.

René glared at his surroundings and swallowed hard. He looked from guard to guard until his eyes finally fell on Amandine. The girl was weakening and blinded by blood. She slowed her struggling and tried to figure out why nobody was shooting anymore. Fearing the worst, she meekly called his name.

"René?"

"He's alive." Carver shook out his injured hand and flexed his fingers. His tone was almost helpful. "He's given up."

René took a deep breath and suddenly both fists ignited at his sides. "Given up?" he cried. "Never! *I'll see you all burn in Hell first!*"

Fear, anger, and desperation drove him into a frenzy. His body lurched forward. He threw two giant fireballs at the covering officers, setting their desks ablaze. He leaped over the benches, yelling like a madman as fire poured from his outstretched hands. He felt another fireball go roaring past his head; Coronado had materialized beside him. The illusionist cackled and pitched fireballs with dramatic flair.

Raw, animal instinct kicked in when Amandine realized that the building was on fire. She thrashed violently against the Inquestor. He nearly had her to the prison gate when René jumped over the burning desks. Carver swung wide, but René was faster. He ducked and slammed his palm directly into his chest. The Inquestor's jacket exploded into flames. Carver shrieked and bolted deeper into the prison, beating and clawing at his burning clothes.

Amandine tried to stand up, but her shoes slipped on the bloody floor. René tossed her over his shoulder like a canvas tent as he dashed for the door.

Coronado was brawling with an agent when he saw the pair retreat. "*Bastardo!*" He ended the fight with a punch to his opponent's throat. He was about to head after them when he spotted a singed officer reaching for Amandine's suitcase by the front desk. Coronado whirled around, stomped on the lobster-red hand that was latched to the handle, and burst out the door with the suitcase over his head.

René threw Amandine into the truck and pushed her down onto the floor of the backseat. Coronado tossed her suitcase in on top of her and sunk down low behind the steering wheel.

"What are you waiting for?" René cried. "Drive!"

Coronado shook his head and reached over the seat to press René's head down as well. "If we start tearing out of here, they will see us for miles. Here, we are a black truck sitting amongst other black trucks. I think we stand a better chance at hiding."

"And the writing on the side?" Amandine peeked between her fingers covering her wounded eye. "This truck's got your name on it."

"They won't see any writing," Coronado said with a touch of pride. "And if they check, they won't see anything in the back, either. Nothing, except for Sangria." He glanced at the tiny window that separated the cab from the cargo area. "I hope."

"I don't like this, Antonio." René pulled out his handkerchief and held it tightly to Amandine's brow. "We're sitting in plain sight."

"Shut up and see to the girl, will you?" Coronado snapped. "I promise you, we are completely invisible. Just... don't move."

René sighed and rubbed his blackened hand across his face, leaving a smear of soot like war-paint over his eyes. "This might be a foolish question, but... are you alright?"

The moment he asked this, Amandine sobbed uncontrollably. She snorted back her tears and hiccuped, "I am now. Thank you."

"What happened?"

"I don't really know. I went in, gave my mother's name, then all of a sudden they pulled guns on me." She lifted the handkerchief and decided that her bleeding had slowed enough that she could try to clean herself up. "It was a nightmare. I was telling them, 'Caroline, I want Caroline,' and they kept saying, 'Cleo, she's after Cleo!'"

"Your mother is Cleo?" Coronado piped up again. "If that's true, she's not only a rebel fighter, but the one in charge.

She's second only to Tall-Me." He laughed dryly, passing them a canteen of water he always kept in the cab. He also passed a flask, but not before he took a swig of it first. "If I had known — if I had any idea your mother was Cleo, I never would have let you leave the camp. Quite frankly, I never would have let you join us in the first place."

René soaked the handkerchief in water and wiped her face clean. Once he had done that, he took the flask and dribbled some of its contents onto her split brow. She flinched.

"Sorry," René said sympathetically. "I know it hurts."

"It's alright." She touched his arm to reassure him. "It won't get infected now."

"You're going to want me to stitch that up," Coronado said. "It's split pretty wide. If I could get into the back, I could get my medical bag."

Amandine shook her head. "That's not happening."

"It must, otherwise—"

"No, I mean, you aren't stitching my face. I've seen the repairs you've made to your own clothes, and your stitches are about as straight as a question mark." She pulled her suitcase up beside her on the seat and rummaged for her sewing kit. "I'll do it myself."

René felt a little queasy at the thought of Amandine stitching herself. She sensed this, so she gave him her hand mirror to hold; he could help without having to look.

"You're welcome for that suitcase, by the way," Coronado said sarcastically, peering up over the dash. "You nearly left a load of information for the inquestors to track us down with."

"I figured it would burn to the ground with the rest of the building," René replied. "What's going on over there, anyway?"

"It seems the fire might have been put out. There's a lot less smoke coming from the windows, and nobody's running as fast as they were a few minutes ago. There is some business with men and trucks at the gate, however." He furrowed his brow and scanned the small crowd milling frantically at the gate. "I'll let you know as soon as I see something."

Amandine whimpered, winced, and stamped her feet, but she managed to get three perfectly straight, decorative stitches in.

"Blue?" René asked with amusement once he finally allowed himself to look.

"It was the first spool I picked up," she admitted. The adrenaline had finally begun to subside, and she tenderly took his hand, blood and soot intermingling between their fingers. "Thank you for coming back for me."

"I had to," he said. "Every second that passed, I felt like I had made the worst mistake of my life."

"René was crying," Coronado put in with a giggle.

"We stayed to see if maybe you were turned away," René went on, ignoring him. "I didn't imagine... I didn't want to believe that you'd be hurt."

"I did," the Illusionist interjected again. "Never mind being Cleo's only living relative, if you so much as use the same aftershave as Tall-Me, they'll throw you in this hole until the next public execution."

273

René let Amandine lay on the seat where she'd be a little more comfortable while he took the floor. "So Cleo is your mother," he mused. "You had no idea?"

"I had an idea that she dealt with some rebels, but not that she was their leader," came her baffled reply. "Honestly, I thought her biggest secret was that she had a new beau. She'd moon around the house sometimes, and she'd come home from her travels with stuff I don't think she'd buy for herself. I tried to talk to *maman* about it. I wanted to tell her that I thought it was alright to move on, but she acted very guilty and completely clammed up."

"Marc Antony is practically in love with her," Coronado said from the front. "Maybe he's the boyfriend. Maybe he's actually your father."

Amandine laughed at the absurdity. "There's no way. My father is dead. Marc Antony can't— there's no way DJMA is my father."

Coronado's eyes appeared over the seat, and he raised a dubious eyebrow.

"Okay, I know I was way off about my mother," she said. "But my father was a proud man. He was kind, but extremely serious when it came to sewing and sailing. He was a true blue American patriot to the core, and he died at sea six months after he left us. Marc Antony is the exact opposite of my father in every way. They don't even sound alike."

All of DJMA's broadcasts obsessing over Cleo fell into a new light now that she knew he was referring to her mother. Perhaps he really was the mysterious boyfriend.

"But now that you mention it, who is Marc Antony? Who is Tall-Me?" she said. "Do I know either one of them? Did they ever come by the house?"

"A popular theory is that Tall-Me doesn't actually exist," Coronado said. "He's a fictional character made up by Marc Antony and Cleo so that they can give credit to independant uprisings without implicating anybody. Nobody knows anything for certain about Tall-Me; not his real name, what he looks like, or where he's from. The things people claim he's done vary from the unlikely to the downright impossible. All we know for certain is that a man wired the police after robbing the storehouses in Nieuwestad and said, 'My name is Tall-Me, and I am the people's will,' before vanishing without a trace."

Tall-Me's first public attack happened long before Amandine ever suspected Caroline of any rebellious activities. She remembered it well because that day she was so hungry, she licked her finger and tried to pick up any crumbs that might have been hiding in the breadbox. She remembered envisioning the storehouse on the harbor, stocked stories high with flour, beans, and canned goods. DJMA made Tall-Me sound like a modern-day Robin Hood, robbing the rich to feed the poor of Nieuwestad.

Something occurred to her. "Do you suppose he meant 'Ptolemy?'"

"What?"

She lifted her head up. "Ptolemy. You know, since we have Antony and Cleopatra? Ptolemy Soter cleaned up Egypt

275

after Alexander the Great conquered it. I suppose that'd be President Fairchild, in this case."

"How do you know that?"

"Our library was loaded with history books. Dad caught the Egyptian fever back in the twenties, and he never really let it go." She used her fingernail to scratch dried blood off of the face of her locket and added, "That's also why my middle name is Helen."

"Well, 'Ptolemy' would make more sense than a weird code name like 'Tall-Me,'" Coronado said with another sardonic chuckle. He stopped short, suddenly alert. "They're starting to take people out."

Amandine and René sat up just high enough so that they could see too.

Guards surrounded chained men in red jumpsuits, running them single-file outside. Carver stood out from the crowd since he was missing his coat and hat. His clothes were singed, his black hair hung loose in his face, and he paced like a caged animal in front of the prisoners. He was soon joined by another important-looking officer in black.

"Another inquestor?" Amandine asked softly.

"I don't think so," Coronado replied. "Look at the red dog patch on his shoulder. He must be the warden."

The warden spoke seriously with Carver until two more guards appeared, pulling a prisoner by the arms. The prisoner was chained, hooded, and thrown to his knees before the high officers.

Carver yanked the hood away, and Caroline's wild hair spilled out.

"*Maman!*" Amandine squeaked.

Caroline was furious. She was shouting something, but they couldn't hear it in the truck over the sirens. Whatever she said, it clearly upset the NAR agents and amused the other inmates. She spat at her captors in defiance, earning a kick to the stomach from the warden that buckled her in two. The warden stepped on the back of her neck and leaned forward, crushing her face into the pavement.

He called for something, and a rifle appeared. It was Cleo's signature weapon, a 50-90 Sharps, and Carver eagerly grabbed it up. The Inquestor admired the etched walnut stock for a moment before he aimed the heavy gun at Caroline's head.

"Amandine, *por el amor de Dios*, don't look," Coronado rasped. "Please, *mi cariña*, look away."

No one moved; everyone stared, completely frozen in horror.

But Carver didn't shoot her. Instead he stood back with his arms crossed smugly around his new prize and the warden called for something else. A knife was brought to him. He wrapped Caroline's hair in his fist, forcibly lifted her to her knees, and sawed all of her dark hair off at the scalp. Amandine wept for her mother. The NAR agents cackled at her humiliating, shorn head. They wolf-whistled and pinched her while she tried to shuffle to her feet.

Suddenly, with a ferocity that Amandine had never seen before, Caroline pounced like a lion and bit the warden's nose. He screamed. He slashed at her with the knife and she fell back, her face split open from hairline to cheek.

277

Amandine wailed and threw herself at René.

"*Shh! Shh!*" He clutched her head against his chest. "Amandine, be calm! We will think of something!" He stared at Coronado. "Antonio, what do we do? We can't possibly take them all out!"

"No." He drummed his fingers anxiously on the steering wheel. "There are dozens of them, maybe a hundred, not including those who might already be in the trucks. I might be able to release the prisoners and perhaps they—"

He didn't have time to finish the thought. Caroline and all of the other prisoners were loaded up into the surrounding trucks, and several officers came jogging in their direction.

"Uh-oh." Coronado scooted down out of sight. He held up his fire-throwing hand at the ready, but the officers completely ignored them and climbed into the surrounding trucks. Coronado started his engine at the same time as the others, and he fell into the back of the line leaving the prison.

"Where are we going?" Amandine asked timidly.

"Freedom Festival, I'd guess." He swiped at his hairstyle so that it better matched the other guards. "I had forgotten until I saw them bring everyone out. They need her alive for the public execution tonight."

René's mouth fell open. "And... we're just going to attend?"

"*No, we aren't just going to*— look, at the very least, we are still hiding in plain sight. If the opportunity arises to escape or to help... somehow..." Coronado let the unlikely notion hang as he checked his mirrors. "Will somebody make sure Sangria is in the back?"

Amandine tapped on the wall in the same cheery rhythm she always used on their trailer door. There was a dull thud in response.

"Somebody's back there."

The convoy moved slowly down the road, and the blaring sirens and searchlights scanning the fields surrounding the prison soon faded into the distance behind them. Police cruisers fell into place between each of the trucks, and a mounted patrol galloped alongside them.

Coronado cursed a long, vulgar string of profanities in Spanish, punctuating his tirade with blows to the steering wheel. Sneaking away would be impossible now.

"I hope you have that gun handy, René." Coronado lit another cigarette with a snap and pointed to his mirror. "We've got horses on either side, and that damned Inquestor just pulled up behind us again!"

René was unable to see from the back without sticking his head out of the window. "Does he recognize us?"

Suddenly, there came a thunderous pounding from the roof. Coronado yelped and nearly drove the truck off the road when Sangria dropped onto the hood. She wore a bandit mask and the black, tattered scrap costume that Amandine made on her first day in camp. Ribbons and netting whipped wildly around her; she gave a dainty wave with her fingertips before climbing back onto the roof again.

"What in God's name is she doing?" Coronado craned his neck. "She looks ridiculous!"

Sangria sprinted down the length of the truck and slammed an empty birdcage straight into Carver's windshield.

279

The glass exploded, and the car swerved sharply off of the road, barreling sideways down the hill.

Everything happened in an instant. René used the gun to bash out the window beside him, and he sprang like a coiled snake onto the mounted rider to their left. As soon as René was clear, Coronado swerved hard right and knocked the other rider to the ditch. He checked his mirrors again and saw that the Interceptor had come to rest upside down with smoke pouring out of the hood. The Inquestor was nowhere in sight.

René waved to Coronado, pointed to the front of the procession, and kicked the horse into a hard gallop.

"What is he doing?" Amandine cried. "He'll be seen! He'll be shot!"

Just as she said this, René vanished from the saddle, clinging to the far side of the horse with the skill of a trained trick-rider.

Sangria reappeared fluidly on the hood and pantomimed turning a key in a lock.

"Why the hell did she bring that absurd outfit? A jailbreak is no time for theatrics." Coronado furiously cranked the window down. "Amandine, I hope you know how to drive."

"A little." She scrambled into the front. "Gas. Brake. Wheel." She indicated each one in turn.

"Shifter?" Coronado crossed himself and climbed out.

"I never really got the hang of that part." She frowned and took the wheel.

The illusionist balanced on the hood with Sangria, and he gestured for Amandine to move closer to the patrol car in front of them. Amandine saw the pair exchange a few brief words before they jumped with their hands held tight. They moved like a crack of lightning. The instant they landed, Sangria smashed the window with a tent stake, and Coronado set the passengers ablaze. He wasn't nearly as sure on his feet as Sangria, but she held him steady as the car swerved, and they leaped for the next truck.

Coronado clung to the ladder on the back door of the prison truck while Sangria climbed up. She was a cat in the fading light and her sash fluttered behind her like a tail. She climbed over the truck and wrenched the driver's door open, using her ankles to rip the driver out and slip into his seat.

They were grossly outnumbered, but the three performers had decided to cause as much damage as they possibly could before they were inevitably stopped. While Sangria used her truck to smash into the patrol car in front of her, René took care of the other mounted riders, appearing in his saddle and pistol-whipping them to the ground before they even knew he was there.

Sangria's truck veered from side to side, and Coronado held onto the ladder for dear life with a lockpick pinched between his lips. Amandine moved in slowly to help, but the illusionist motioned her back. If he fell off, he didn't want her to run him over.

Coronado was about to try the lock when a curious thought occurred to him. He leaned over to look around the truck and noticed that while the leading vehicle surely must have noticed their presence by now, it had picked up speed instead of stopping.

He cursed, put away his pick, and knocked urgently on the door. To his surprise, the guard peeked outside, opened the door, and helped Coronado inside.

The illusionist steadied himself on the handrail. "*Saludos, señores.*"

About ten unshackled prisoners and a guard wearing a red scarf stared at him in confusion. "Has there been a change of plans?" the guard asked.

René didn't know what possessed him to seek out Caroline's truck. Ever since he let Amandine walk into the prison, it felt like Fortune had decided to correct his destiny with a much sterner hand. He had to make sure he wasn't dreaming when he realized that he was hiding behind a galloping horse, pistol in hand, with a bandana covering his face.

Well, would you look at that, he thought with bitter amusement. *I'm an outlaw.*

He came upon Caroline's truck and was astonished to see her at the wheel. She spotted him when he peeked over the saddle. She looked equally surprised, even with the large, loose bandage that covered half of her face. Sensing he wasn't a NAR agent, she pointed off into the distance beyond the trees. René barely had enough time to mount up properly and pull the horse back as a wall of vehicles with improvised armor burst from the tree line and rammed into the side of the procession. Amandine swerved to avoid a crushed patrol car that went spinning like a boomerang into a field right in front of her.

René turned hard and darted through the vehicular carnage back to Coronado's truck.

"What the hell is going on?" Coronado shouted from the back of the prison truck. His new friends inside seemed curious as well.

"It's the rebels!" Amandine cheered. "They are rescuing their comrades!"

A bullet whizzed past René's ear. "We'd better move before we get mistaken for NAR agents." Caroline's truck sounded its horn several times, and he pointed at it. "Follow that truck!"

"Is my mother still in there?" Amandine asked, but they were already moving and he didn't hear her. Laying low against the saddle, René gestured to Sangria, and she followed suit.

René rode up alongside Caroline again, waving his hat to get her attention. A pair of men in guard uniforms and red scarves appeared at the back of Caroline's truck and pointed their automatic rifles at him.

Caroline stared at René with bewilderment and raised her shoulders as if to ask, *"What do you want?"*

"Your daughter," he shouted.

She shrugged again and shook her head.

"Your daughter! Ta fille! Amandine!" He pointed wildly at Coronado's truck, which was gaining on them. Her face hardened. She shouted something to the men at the back, and they withdrew.

The armored ambush vehicles stayed behind, engaged in a fierce firefight with the remaining NAR agents. Caroline led the rest of the prisoners away from the battle, allowing the mysterious truck and rider to follow.

CHAPTER 15: THE REBELS

They drove for hours, weaving through a maze of hidden dirt roads until they reached a sandy path that followed a creek. The trucks crept beneath the trees down into a small, rocky canyon, and eventually the narrow path opened up to reveal a pair of colossal, steel doors set deep into the cliffs. They were eighty feet wide and painted to match the surrounding rock except where rust bled orange from the hundreds of giant bolts holding them in place. René stared up at the impenetrable wall in amazement; this was the rebels' hidden base.

The blast doors opened, groaning and squealing on their tracks to let the trucks in while more fighters came out to meet their returning comrades.

Caroline jerked her truck out of line and leaped out. She was a terrifying sight to behold— her chopped hair was wild, and all of the gore that ran down the right side of her face was poorly concealed by an improvised bandage. Brandishing a pistol, she stalked up to René before he could dismount.

"You! The one starting trouble at the back! You nearly ruined everything!" She pointed and her men surrounded the stranger. "Who the hell are you?"

René gripped the reins and walked the horse backwards. The gray Irish draught was surprisingly calm and he only flicked his ears when Caroline advanced. "*Attendez, madame!* Amandine tried to—" He explanation was cut short when he was yanked from the saddle.

"You deaf or just stupid? I said, '*Who the hell are you?*'"

René was restrained and disarmed. His grimy 1911 was given to Caroline, and she held it up to the headlights to study it. She clearly recognized the weapon, but didn't understand why this soot-blackened, French-speaking teenage had it in his possession.

"René!" He shook off the men on his arms and picked his hat up off the ground. Caroline spotted the glint of a silver thimble attached to the band, and her confusion gave way to dread. "My name is René Personne! I am not your enemy! If you doubt me, ask Amandine yourself!" He pointed to the las two trucks at the end of the procession.

Coronado jumped out first. He ignored the guards wh encircled him with their guns drawn as he helped Amandine and Sangria down from the driver's seat in turn. Familiar wit the routine, he slumped against the cab with his arms crossed while his vehicle was searched.

The sight of her daughter stole Caroline's breath, an she closed the distance between them in three quick strides.

"*Maman*, your eye!" Amandine wailed.

"My eye? Look at your eye!" With a bloodied hand, Caroline touched the blue thread that decorated Amandine's brow. "Stitched up beautifully, though. Did you do that yourself in a moving truck?"

"Yes. Well, the truck wasn't moving, and René held a mirror—"

"You dumb girl!" Caroline slapped her on the side of her head. "Stupid, foolish girl! What were you doing at the prison?"

"I was trying to get you out," she answered defensively, rubbing her head.

"You didn't have to worry about me." Caroline waved at the crowd around them. "I was taken care of by my comrades. But where is my contact? He should have been taking care of you."

"Contact?" she blinked. "*Maman*, nobody came for me. Nobody but NAR agents."

Caroline growled at this. "You need to tell me exactly what happened. He was supposed to find you at the house, tell you everything, and bring you here for safekeeping."

"Well, I've had an inquestor and a couple of police officers following me since Pearisville. Maybe he was trying to avoid them." Amandine clasped her mother's hands, desperate for more answers. "Who was your contact, *maman*? Who did you send?"

"My most loyal agent. The only one I knew you would recognize and trust without question," Caroline answered. "DJMA."

"Marc Antony?" Amandine gasped. "Yes, I think I would have known him if I saw him!"

"If he knew you were heading this way, he likely kept his head down as long as you had NAR agents on you. When he can, he avoids them like the plague."

Amandine thought back to everyone she had met along her journey. With growing amazement, she realized that she had met only one smooth-talking, rebel-linked, music enthusiast who actively avoided inquestors. Was it just a coincidence that Glorious appeared out of the blue only days after she did? Did he always volunteer to chaperone Amandine so he could keep an eye on her? Was that why Marmi sensed deception in him?

Caroline scanned the milling crowd for her contact, but instead she found the three strangers standing awkwardly against a curious black truck. A pair of uneasy youths, one dressed like a cowboy and the other like a burlesque burglar, were looking for reassurance from a weary older gentleman.

"If my agent never found you, how did you make it all this way?"

"I had help." Amandine nodded towards her companions. When she looked back at her mother, she was appalled all over again by her grisly wound. "Let's go find a doctor for that cut, and I can explain everything. Please ask your friends to be kind to mine."

At Caroline's command, everyone moved inside the bunker. The cavernous room immediately behind the blast doors was a garage full of vehicles ranging from civilian cars, police cruisers, NAR trucks, and a pair of sleek Interceptors. Amandine had to do a double-take when she saw a pin-up caricature of her mother painted on the side of a deconstructed Sherman tank.

Caroline led the way past the vehicles down a wide green hallway, following the spray-painted arrows on the walls until she reached the infirmary. When the medic saw Caroline, he turned down his dance record and leapt out of his swivel office chair.

"Cleo." He hurried towards her. He was a young man, just a handful of years older than Amandine, with loose brown hair that flopped over the left side of his square face. Strangely, he wore an apron, and Amandine thought it made him look more like a butcher than a doctor. "Looks like the clink needs a new barber."

"And he cut me a little too close," Caroline replied, pointing to the blood-soaked rag over her eye. She laid down on the examination table and grit her teeth when he peeled away the makeshift bandage. "How bad is it, Doc? I can't see out of it."

"Jehoshaphat." He brushed his hair away to get a closer look, baring a puckered, J-shaped scar that hooked across his cheekbone. "They got you better than they got me."

"And I'm only now starting to feel it," she admitted, her voice quivering in pain.

"Adrenaline is one hell of a chemical. Luckily, I've got the next best thing." Doc rummaged around in his apron pocket and administered a syrette of morphine. It only took a moment for the medicine to take effect and Caroline sighed with relief. Doc waggled a second syrette in front of her face.

289

"Want another? You can waltz on the moon while I get you patched up."

"No, thank you." She settled in more comfortably, and Doc brought her a glass of water. "I want to be awake enough to hear how my daughter found her own little pocket of resistance fighters."

Amandine sat on a nearby gurney and told her story. As she recounted the events following her mother's arrest, she took sewing supplies from her suitcase and made a red scarf to cover her mother's ragged hair and the eye that could not be saved.

Once the young medic was finished suturing Caroline's face, Amandine followed her mother to the ladies' showers. The room was already full of other freed women who were washing away all evidence of their time in prison. They greeted Caroline with admiration and respect, even when she stripped naked and joined them.

Once she was clean, Caroline put on a new jumpsuit and let another woman trim her hair into a neat pixie cut.

"Your makeup will last twice as long if you only have to put it on half of your face," Amandine chirped when someone brought Caroline some cosmetics. "Why are you putting it on in the middle of the night, anyway? You should eat something and get some rest."

"Tall-Me is due to arrive as soon as he's done cleaning up the mess on the roads," Caroline replied. "I don't want him to look at a monster when he—"

Caroline's hand shook, and her brush fell into the sink with a puff of ivory powder. The finality of her injury struck hard as her daughter's light-hearted remark sunk in. She stared at the mangled stranger in the mirror— no longer a beauty, not even a decent fighter now that she was half-blind and her rifle was lost. She reached for her eye, but couldn't bring herself to touch the bristling black stitches that were stained mustard with iodine. Putting on makeup suddenly felt as pointless as adding lace to a potato sack.

Before despair closed it's smothering grip, Amandine appeared behind her and placed a soft kiss on her cheek. Caroline blinked. The kiss was like a slap to the face, and all at once, she squeezed her daughter against her chest. What did her eye matter? She had Amandine. She was alive, safe, and had grown stronger and more beautiful than she could have ever imagined.

"You alright, *maman*?" Amandine asked, setting her completed sewing project on the sink beside her makeup.

"*Oui.*" Caroline dabbed her tears. "I just realized what a terrible, foolish mother I've been. I should have told you everything. I thought I was protecting you by keeping you ignorant, but I see now that my secrets— my pride— nearly cost us our lives. Forgive me, *ma belle*."

She reached for Amandine again, but the girl hesitated. Caroline glanced in the mirror and noted with disgust that her missing eye was still capable of crying. It was beginning to make a horrific mess, so she sopped it up with tissues and covered it with a fresh bandage before it got any worse. "*Sacré bleu*, there's no helping it! I really do look like a monster!"

Amandine didn't want her mother to dwell on her eye. "You don't look like a monster. If anything, you look very fashion-forward with a haircut like that." She tugged her own hair back and tried to envision Caroline's new look on herself. "And just think of the hats! Berets, fedoras, fascinators... You could wear them at a saucy angle on this side."

"Is that what this is?" Caroline asked, pointing to the headwrap. "*Chapeau haute couture?*"

"I was a traveling costumer, not a milliner." Amandine shrugged. "A scarf is the best I can do."

"*Dommage*." Caroline smiled. "At least it matches."

Caroline mustered up her strength much like Amandine summoned her optimism. She didn't care if she lost both of her eyes. She had survived the inquestors and led all of the prisoners to safety, which meant she could still face Tall-Me with her head held high. Encouraged, she decided to give her remaining eye a little more decoration.

"Speaking of Tall-Me—" Caroline painted a long, black wing over her eyelashes like an Egyptian queen. "I think it's important that you meet him as well."

"Gosh, really? Well then, I'd better wash up too." Amandine tugged off her soiled dress and skipped to the shower. She laughed when the water came shooting down onto her head; it was the first hot shower she had had in years. "What was I talking about before?"

"Nevermind that." Caroline tied her headscarf over her fresh bandages. "I want you to tell me more about this René."

Caroline and Amandine found René, Coronado, and Sangria in the common room surrounded by rebels. The fighters were men and women of all ages, some in NAR uniforms and some in civilian clothes. They were all watching Coronado with great amusement while he did card tricks.

"Nothing sneaky now. See?" The illusionist pushed back his sleeves and patted the table, making a deck of cards appear beneath his hand. "You, madam. Pick a card from any place in the deck, please. That's right, show it to your friends."

He shuffled the rest of the deck several times while she presented the queen of clubs.

"Put it back anywhere in the deck. Make sure it's even with the others and doesn't stick out."

She did so nervously.

He shuffled the deck one last time, revealing his top card, the ace of spades. Coronado showed it to everyone, shaking his head with disappointment. "That's not it, is it? Hmm, I seem to have done something wrong." He noticed Amandine and Caroline across the room with theatrical relief. "Cleo, I need your help. I've misplaced my card. Which one have you got on you?"

"I haven't got any cards," she answered suspiciously. "I just got here."

"Which one have you got in your pocket?"

Cleo reached in, withdrew the queen of clubs, and her face went slack with surprise. Everyone laughed and clapped.

"Ah, that's nothing." Coronado made the cards vanish into his open palm. "You should see Master René, conjurer of flames, throw fire across the room."

He put a cigarette in his mouth, held his hands open, and waited for René to take his cue. Unaccustomed to being

293

the center of attention, René momentarily forgot what he was supposed to do.

"Easy now. Just a little one!" Coronado braced himself. With a feeble flourish, René wiggled his fingers, and the cigarette in his mouth flared. There was more laughter and applause from their delighted audience.

"Or—" Coronado shouted over the noise, trying to regain everyone's attention. "Or maybe you prefer something more exotic? Watch as Miss Sangria, the world-famous Love Knot, ties herself into a bow!"

Sangria loosened herself up with a quick stretch. She performed a handstand on the table and slowly bent until she sat on her own head. The crowd murmured in amazement when she positioned her arms and legs to resemble a bowtie, then burst into applause when she sprang upright into a finishing pose.

"*Circus-people.*" Caroline huffed impatiently, but a half-smile tugged at the corner of her mouth. "Alright, that's enough! Listen to me now."

Sangria rolled off the table, and everyone turned to face their leader.

"I wanted to thank you personally for safeguarding my daughter," Caroline said to the newcomers, but loud enough for everyone to hear. "I intended for one of my own agents to look after her until I was free again, but for reasons unknown, he never found her. Since we arrived, Amandine has done nothing but tell me what good you have done. How special you are to her." She looked squarely at René. "I would like it known that these people are friends of the movement. They are to be extended the same treatment and hospitality as our comrades."

"Madame Cleo is too kind." Coronado gave an appreciative bow.

"Cleo!" Just then, a fighter came running in from the entrance, breathless from excitement and his jog across the bunker. "Boss, the rest of the convoy has returned. Tall-Me is here!"

A thrilled murmur went through the room. It appeared that many of those present had never seen Tall-Me before either. The three performers exchanged a glance before deciding to follow Caroline and Amandine through the garage.

"I take it Tall-Me doesn't visit often," Sangria said.

"I've spent a lot of time here with my crew. Tall-Me's only been here once while I was incarcerated." Caroline lifted her chin a little higher. "I'll be seeing him for the first time as well."

"So he exists after all," Coronado mused.

Amandine was still confused. "*Maman*, I thought Cleo was second to Tall-Me. How can it be that you don't know who he is either?"

Caroline quickened her pace and considered the best way to explain. Never being one for words, she eventually gave up. "I know who he is," she said as they walked out into the night. "And so do you."

Though the remaining fighters and prisoners spilled down from the trucks to join the growing throng, there was no mistaking who their leader was when Tall-Me emerged at last. He was not remarkably tall as his name implied, but his bearing still demanded respect. His black uniform was adorned with the kraken, the symbol of the NAR Navy, and he wore a red scarf, a bandolier across his shoulder, and a Mauser C96 in his belt holster. His graying brown hair and beard were neatly trimmed around his hard, serious face.

The moment he laid eyes on Caroline, they moved towards each other, and she fell into his arms. To Amandine's shock, he kissed her intensely.

"Oh, Caroline of mine, what have they done to you?" he said in a gruff, pained voice. "Your beautiful eye! Your lovely dark hair." He stroked her head and gently kissed her bandaged face again.

Amandine's throat locked. She only knew one person who used that pet name, pronouncing Caroline's name the American way.

Tall-Me broke away from Caroline to address everyone present. "Brothers and sisters, I am pleased to announce that despite outside complications, our endeavor tonight was a complete success!" The rebels cheered, and Tall-Me continued once they quieted. "Every condemned patriot in that procession was liberated and free from serious harm. Soon, every one of them can return to their families. Thanks to your bravery and sacrifice, there will be no executions at the Freedom Festival tonight!"

There was applause as the last freed rebels were unshackled and ushered inside to be doctored, cleaned, and fed. Tall-Me motioned everyone towards the bunker, but Caroline stayed rooted to the spot, waiting for her daughter to come forward.

In a voice smaller than a whisper, Amandine breathed a single word. *"Dad?"*

Tall-Me shot a look to Caroline. She closed her eye and nodded once. "Amandine?" Will Stewart's voice cracked.

He hurried to his daughter. At first he hesitated, unsure if his three-year absence had put up a barrier of resentment from the young woman that now stood before him. Slowly, he reached out. She let him hold her chin and touch the blue stitches over her swollen brow.

"My God," he choked. He kept shaking his head, struck dumb by the hundreds of questions that tried to escape all at once. Finally, he managed, "Did you use a star stitch? *On your face?*"

"I thought it would look pretty." Amandine sniffled loudly. "Hurt like the dickens, though."

"My Button!" Will wrapped her fiercely in a tight embrace. "You're so tall! You're all grown up!" He released her to look her over again. "You're already a woman!" He gathered up both Amandine and Caroline together, squeezing them close. "My beautiful ladies, how I've missed you! I have so much to ask you! To tell you!"

Amandine buried her face in his jacket and sobbed, "Daddy, I thought you were dead!"

He let out a remorseful sigh and kissed the top of her head. "I know, Button. I'm so sorry. I wanted to tell you both everything. I wanted to come home to you right away, but you were safer as long as you knew nothing. It's such a long, difficult story."

The three of them stood close, arms wrapped around each other. Meanwhile René, Coronado, and Sangria lingered some distance away, astonished by the runion they had just witnessed.

"Have you been waiting here since your mother was arrested?" Will asked.

Amandine shook her head. "I didn't know what to do when they took her. I thought that I'd better go get her, but I needed some money, so I sold the house—"

"*You sold the house?*" Will interjected in shock.

She nodded. "I sold it to the government. To an administrator. They wanted a new headquarters in town, so I took their cash, packed my suitcase, and left on my bike. I got hit by a truck and lost the bike as soon as I got to Pearisville, though."

Her report deviated so far from the plan that Will was speechless with outrage. It gave Amandine a strange mixture of happiness and concern to see him that way, and she giggled nervously before she continued. "I didn't want to spend the house-money on travel expenses—"

"What *did* you want to spend it on?" Will interrupted. "Amandine, what were you thinking, walking across the country with a pocketful of cash? You're extremely lucky you didn't get robbed or violated on the road!"

"It was a bit more than a pocketful," she admitted, holding her coat open and peeling back the lining to show the stacks of bills tacked inside. Sangria, René, and Coronado gawked at her hidden fortune. "I was thinking I'd hire a lawyer to work on an appeal. If I couldn't do that, then I thought I'd pay a guard to leave a door unlocked or something."

"You were going to bribe a guard?" her father repeated. "To release Cleo?"

"I had no idea she was Cleo!" Amandine closed up her coat. "I didn't even know she was with the resistance. I only thought she had a boyfriend at the storehouse or something."

Caroline sniffed and turned her head away in embarrassment.

"As I was saying, I didn't want to spend the house-money on my travel expenses, so I paid a visit to White's Bakery. Remember the Whites back home? Well, this was his cousin's store. Anyway, they gave me a job wrapping packages, and that's how I met René."

She beckoned to him, and he took a faltering step forward. René had never felt so vulnerable as when he was being stared down by the fearsome Tall-Me and Cleo.

"René took a fancy to me and invited me to travel to Nieuwestad with his family."

"*Took a fancy?*" As Will's anger grew, so did the southern accent he tried to conceal.

"So I wouldn't travel alone," Amandine reasoned. "They gave me a job, and I was treated very well."

Caroline tapped her husband's arm. "He's with a traveling show."

"*A traveling—?*" Will couldn't believe what he was hearing. He whirled on the last remaining person who lingered outside, fussing over a crushed Interceptor. "*Where the hell were you?*"

Inquestor Carver flinched when everyone turned on him. "*Me?* I was trying to keep up with her *and* maintain my cover *and* run my radio show! I tried to talk to her in private many times. Hell, I even took a huge risk and slipped her a note, but her friend stole it and stuffed it in her bosom!" He took a birdcage from his passenger's seat, threw it back into Coronado's cab, and pointed at Sangria. "That bosom right there, in fact!"

"That's the Inquestor!" Amandine jumped behind her father. "He's followed us!"

"Yes, I know." Will crossed his arms. "That's Marcus."

"Marcus? Radio show?" Coronado snapped and sparks popped from his fingertips. "Don't tell me... *you're* Marc Antony."

"Guilty as charged." Carver trotted over and enthusiastically shook Coronado's hand. "It's not often I get to meet a fan, what with my day job and all."

"This is too much to absorb." Amandine broke away from her parents to stand by her friends. "You're Tall-Me and Cleo. The Inquestor is actually Marc Antony, sent by you to look after me?"

"*Now* she gets it." Carver dusted his gloves and rolled his singed white sleeves up to the elbow. "I'm Marcus Carver. Ruthless inquestor by day, pirate radio disc jockey by night, all-American patriot every time in between."

"He was supposed to fetch you," Will said. "I can't wait to hear why he didn't."

Amandine felt upset and very foolish. "But he was the one who arrested *maman*!" She pointed an accusing finger at him. "I saw him do it!"

"I had a tail follow me straight to the house after my last big raid," Caroline explained. "Fortunately, Marcus was nearby, and he got me before they showed up with reinforcements."

"I love the way you say my name, boss," Carver said affectionately. "I've missed hearing you say it so badly. '*Mahr-koose.*' It's so adorable."

Will glared at the Inquestor for his audacity, but Caroline was flattered. She bit her lip, and her headscarf hid some of the blush in her cheeks.

"I had to arrest her," Carver went on. "I had to be the one to do it. That way, I could take her alive and conveniently overlook you, Miss Amandine."

"But you came back for me?" the girl asked warily.

"I did. Heard you sold the house, looked into who bought it, and learned about this crooked administrator."

"Graft?" Amandine perked. "He seemed nice."

"He was awful, really. A real sicko. He took ladies from replacement homes and used them to death. He was up to four this year alone, so I greased him."

"How did you change that story for the Chief Inquestor?" Caroline asked him.

"Easy. My report said Graft was liberating rebel-linked girls from replacement homes on the sly, and I used his purchase of the Stewart estate and failure to apprehend Amandine as proof."

Carver obviously yearned for Caroline's approval, so it was no surprise when her single nod elicited a tiny squeal of joy out of him.

"Then what happened?" Will demanded, trying to bring Carver's focus from his wife to the matter at hand. "Why didn't you get Amandine?"

Carver rolled his eyes and his posture went slack. "'*Grab her, Carver! Just get the girl, Carver!*'" he mimicked. "I've been hearing that for months! I'll tell you why I didn't 'just grab her.' I had a tail. They were watching me so closely, they were literally sitting in my backseat, taking notes."

He spoke energetically, animating his story with wild gestures. "I really needed to clean out the station in Cold River before I set off after her, but I couldn't resist doing a broadcast first. Next, I had to go to the police station to file my report on the administrator. Just as I'm trying to sweet-talk the receptionist into refilling my thermos for the road, this police captain tells me that he's honored by my presence and has a bunch of guys interested in the academy. He wanted me to take them along, show them the ropes. I made up a thousand and one excuses, but he finally called up my other boss to get his approval."

"Your other boss?" Amandine asked.

"The Chief Inquestor in Nieuwestad, name of Luther Everild," Carver nodded. "So now I had these police rookies on me, and the only car game they knew was twenty questions. 'Where are we going, Inquestor? Who are we after, Inquestor? When are we gonna shoot some rebels?'" Speaking to Will, he pointed to the trio beside him. "I followed the trail of cheese-

302

sandwich crumbs and caught up with her the very next day. Found out she got a job making costumes for these guys in a traveling show, so I let my tagalongs conduct a search. It got some more of their frustration out of their system, and I got a chance to speak with Amandine."

"'Speak with Amandine,'" Sangria scoffed. "Lay it on thick with me, you mean."

Carver tried to act offended, but he grinned despite himself. "You were laying it on pretty thick yourself, snatching up my personal correspondence to Miss Stewart and stuffing it in your underwear."

"Then what happened?" Caroline pressed, eager to hear the rest.

"I tried mentioning your name to see if she'd pick up on that," he continued. "I'm afraid she got the wrong impression. Then I thought I'd try a more direct approach. I went to one of their shows and asked Amandine to come along quietly. I dropped hints left and right. I even used my radio voice. That always gets the ladies, but she only had eyes for the fire-throwing moron over there. She wasn't having any of it."

Amandine thought back to that conversation and pieces of the puzzle began falling into place.

"Later that night, I thought I had given the blues the slip, but one of them followed me out to where I was having coffee with a nice girl. He was so mad about my light-handed approach that he scared my date off with his talk of threatening to shoot the circus-people himself. I had to use my gun."

He reached for his weapon. It was usually fastened into a leather holster over his jacket, but he had forgotten that it was gone until René pulled the missing pistol from his belt. Carver grimaced at the smudges and wiped it vigorously with his handkerchief.

"You couldn't shoot the blue officer," Caroline said flatly. "You're the worst shot in the country. How you've managed to avoid shooting yourself yet is a mystery."

"Impossible," Will cut in. "He's a high officer. The NAR requires extensive firearms training for all recruits, and he would have had to pass rather difficult tests before he could wear the black uniform."

"She's right, though." Once he was satisfied with the way his 1911 cleaned up, Carver gave it a single spin. "Couldn't hit a horse if I was riding it, so I brained the errant officer with the back end of my 45."

"And how exactly did you explain that one to the Chief?" Caroline asked again.

"With every inquestor's most favorite justification. *Insubordination,*" he replied fiendishly. "Anyway, where was I?"

To René's surprise, Carver tossed the gun back to him.

"Right. I lost the caravan for awhile after that. They didn't move very fast, but they moved all over the place. I followed the posters and checked in at my stations when I could shake the last two surviving officers. I tried leaving even more clues in the broadcasts in case she was listening."

"The officers stayed with you even after you killed their partner?" Caroline asked with surprise.

Carver nodded. "And they were the model of perfect behavior. No more chattering, no more suggestions at what I ought to do. They were loyal, obedient, and just slobbering for my endorsement."

"What happened to them?" Sangria asked.

"I'm getting to that," he smirked. "Keep your corset on."

Sangria was about to say something angry, but Coronado shook his head in warning.

"I caught the carnies on the road at night and followed them to their last camp. They seemed to have settled in pretty well. Took out a big music box, set up a grand stage. I figured I had some time since it looked like they were preparing something for the festival. I made the mistake of telling my shadows this. I thought they'd want to cut loose in the city and leave me the hell alone, but those damn dedicated patriots asked to visit IHQ."

"Marcus, you didn't take them, did you?" Will demanded angrily. "They were watching your every move! Who knows what they could have seen?"

Carver only smiled, and Will's face darkened with rage.

"*You double-crossing jackass!*" he roared. "You risk the lives of thousands of patriots and the life of this very movement with the idiotic, flippant way you guard your little charade!"

Amandine saw an immediate change in Carver, like a switch had flipped and turned him vicious.

"You obviously don't understand a goddamn thing!" He stormed up to Will, their significant difference in height making him no less intimidating. "Every choice I make is a risk! What you call '*my fucking charade*' is a balancing act on a razor's edge! One mistake on my part can mean a swift, bloody end to the patriots and a long, drawn-out death in the darkest depths of IHQ for me." The Inquestor's black eyes blazed. "*Never* assume that I do not put this movement first! If I had to *shoot that girl in the face* to maintain my cover, I'd do it without hesitation because the information I provide is far more valuable than she could ever be!"

Amandine paled and pressed close to René, whose grip tightened around both her and the 1911.

Carver stood chest-to-chest with Will and exclaimed, "The only reason why I wouldn't, the reason why I went on this fool's errand in the first place, is because *you* asked me to! *Cleo* asked me to! Who's really putting the movement at risk by sending me— an inquestor, a killer, a man now famous in the NAR for capturing Cleo— half-way across the country to pick up somebody *so stupid* that she had no idea her own parents are it's leaders?" Fists clenched, Carver glared up at him. "You don't have a clue what I have had to endure! You don't understand the weight of the choices I make everyday. Have you ever had to choose between a life and the greater good of the movement? Do you think it's easy to play along while NAR agents brutalize and murder your true comrades right in front of you?"

He jerked his head in Caroline's direction. Will looked helplessly from his battered daughter to his mangled wife. He knew Carver was right.

"How could you possibly understand? You've been twenty-thousand leagues under the sea." Carver smiled again, but this time the crazed expression made Amandine recoil in fear. "*You're dead!*"

"Will. Marcus." Caroline separated them firmly. "Don't fight. We all know what's at stake here. The survival of this cause takes priority over any of our lives, but we cannot hope to succeed if we do not trust each other." She directed a glare at each one in turn. "Every one of us has given so much to this cause. Will and I have lost any hope of returning to our old lives—"

Carver's switch had flipped again. He regarded Caroline lovingly, holding the hand she had pressed against his shirt. "I lost any chance I might have had at you by dragging this soggy sap out of the ocean."

"You were probably overestimating your chances." She took back her hand and returned to her husband's side. "But thank you for your part in bringing us back together."

Carver shrugged and shoved his hands into his pockets. He looked dejected until he backed into Sangria, and then his sly smile returned.

"As I was saying, I took the officers to Inquestor Headquarters in Nieuwestad. Chief Everild absolutely loves fresh meat. He gave them tips about the exam and the academy, asked them about what I had them do, and they spilled the beans about my rebel-linked, traveling-show theory.

307

I had to write a big report about it, and they even called in a bunch of agents from the field so I could give a briefing. I didn't get another opportunity to check on Amandine until today. Figured I'd finally get her just before the big bust went down."

Carver rooted around in his pockets and pulled out a crushed sugar packet. He dumped out its contents and smoothed the pink paper against his leg while he continued his story. "So I pulled up into their camp and got attacked by a tiger."

"Hang on," Will interrupted. "You were attacked by what?"

"A tiger." Carver pointed to long gashes on the side of his car. "You know, black and orange, long tail and whiskers?"

"A tiger," he repeated in disbelief. "Alright. And it was — what, just running loose?"

Carver nodded. "The camp looked deserted. I wasn't even out of the car yet when this giant cat flew out of the trees and smashed clear through the door. I got us out of there while the blues in the backseat were messing their pants. I gassed it back to the prison and made it there just in time for Pyro-Pierre to set the whole place on fire."

"So the boy's an arsonist?" Will glared at René. "What did he use? Petrol bombs?"

"No! That was the amazing thing. He conjured it with his bare hands!" Carver turned to René excitedly. "How did you do that, anyhow?"

"Can't say," Coronado cut in. "That stays between me and the boy."

"You sure? I'd owe you a big favor if you taught me a handy trick like that."

Coronado gripped René's shoulder proudly. "There is an unbreakable bond— a strict pact of secrecy between an illusionist and his ingénieur."

Disappointed, the Inquestor heaved a sigh.

"Don't despair, Marcus," Caroline said gently. "If you can't play with guns, then you probably shouldn't play with fire either. Finish telling your story."

Carver chuckled. "Alright, then. Well, after the fire, I told my two minions that they could have my endorsement if they hurried back to IHQ and reported the bust attempt to Everild. I knew your magic truck was hiding in plain sight, and I didn't want those two to stick around long enough to recognize it. I was planning to follow you to the ambush and try to keep you from getting shot when suddenly the warden climbs in with his nose nearly hanging off, and he wants to ride shotgun to the execution."

"Damnation," Will grumbled. "Nothing ever went to plan, did it?"

"No!" he exclaimed. "I was at wits end! I was praying for a miracle when out of nowhere, a black, phantasmic vision in tights put a birdcage through my window."

He held out his hand to Sangria. Sitting in the middle of his outstretched palm was a tiny pink rose, folded from the sugar packet paper. A new type of smile, one of spontaneous delight, broke across her face, and she accepted the little token.

With a wink, Carver wrapped up his story. "Completely shattered my windshield. She spooked me so bad,

I went right off the road. Lucky for me, I opted for every possible safety feature my car could carry, one of which is called 'a seatbelt.' I was wearing it at the time, so when the car rolled, I stayed put while the warden bounced around like a pinball and shot out the back window. When the car finally stopped, I was alright, but the warden was in really rough shape. I helped ease his passing with the spare gun in my trunk and soon one of ours came looking for me and towed me back up onto the road. Which reminds me—"

Carver abruptly turned on his heels and hurried back to his destroyed car.

Will watched the Inquestor with incredulity as he searched his pockets for keys. "I don't understand. Of all people, why *him*?"

"He's the best fighter we have," Caroline said defensively.

Hearing this, Carver shook a finger at them and shouted, "Not just the best, but the most-wanted man in the NAR that they don't even know they want!" A deep, maniacal laugh burst out of him, and he collapsed in fits on the hood of his Interceptor.

Now that Carver was through telling his tale, Amandine took the opportunity to properly introduce her friends to her father. "Dad, I know you hoped Mr. Carver would look after me, but these are the people who did. This is Mr. Antonio Coronado, a master illusionist. This is Sangria Groviglio, a talented performer and my best friend. And this..." Amandine still held René's arm, but she gave it a press to

310

show her attachment to him. "This is René Personne. He is the one who saved my life at the prison."

Will had a difficult time listening while his daughter retold her version of events. He made a face like he was getting jabbed with a fork each time he looked down and saw her holding hands with some foreign stranger. While he understood that his daughter was growing up, that particular conversation was the last one he expected to have that night and just the thought of it made him feel exhausted. When Amandine finished and looked for her father's reaction, all Will could do was sigh.

"Let's... let's all go inside."

"With your permission, sir," Coronado spoke up. "We'd like to rejoin our group. Sangria and I are performing at the Freedom Festival tomorrow evening, and we've already missed a dress rehearsal."

"Eh, I'm not sure you want to attend the Festival anymore," Carver said from across the lot as he tried to unlock his trunk.

"Why not?" Coronado raised an eyebrow. "It's not the rebels' next target, is it?"

None of the three leaders answered him.

Shocked, he exclaimed, "I thought the rebels were patriots, not anarchists. Civilians will be there! Families will be there!"

"Young, talented performers at the cusp of success will also be there." Sangria pouted and tilted her hip out to one side.

Carver chuckled. He was not oblivious to her manipulation, but he didn't seem to be immune to it either. "That's not what I meant, exactly... but I can't think of a way to explain it without everybody getting mad at me again."

"Mister Coronado, you are free to leave," Will said sternly. "However, this is only because my daughter vouches for you. I feel I must stress the importance of discretion."

"I was never here," Coronado grumbled, again proving his familiarity with the routine. He offered cigarettes to the rebel leaders and lit them both with a wave. "I needed new doves and bunnies for my act, but I got lost on my way back from the pet store."

Will didn't appreciate his sarcasm or tricks. "I'm serious. You were never here, and you were never at the prison. You have never heard of Will, Caroline, or Carver." He studied the magic cigarette before taking a long draw. "You will forget Amandine."

"If I am to forget Amandine if I leave..." René gathered enough courage to meet Tall-Me's steely gaze. "Then I will forget my life with Marmi and stay."

"I don't know you from Adam, young man," Will said curtly. "I don't care if you can build a rocket from scrap metal. If you think I'm going to let you have free roam of my stronghold and my daughter, then you have another thing coming. You'll go back to the band of tramps you came from."

"I can build. I can burn. I can shoot," René said, determined. "I am yours to command. All I ask is that you let me stay by Amandine's side."

312

"This isn't a decision to be taken lightly," Caroline put in. She had experience leading enthusiastic and sometimes misguided young people, so René's motivations were not new to her. "If you choose to fight, then you choose to die."

Ignoring the fingernails that dug into his arm, René squared his shoulders. "If that's the price, then I'm willing to pay it." He smiled sadly at Amandine. "*Je suis prêt.*"

Will sighed. "Fine. I suppose you can work on the trucks. They will need to be kept clean and in perfect working order at all times, in case of an emergency—"

Amandine couldn't listen to another word. She felt sick. René had made up his mind, but she knew she could never let him come to harm for her sake. She had feared this exact scenario would happen, and now she felt completely torn between two different worlds. On the one hand she had her family, but was doomed to face a life of conflict and violence for a cause she did not understand. On the other hand, she had René, but her presence put his family in danger. The dressmaker knew that she had to make a decision, and she had to choose right now.

Amandine tried to think, but the question René posed to her that day on the riverbank resounded like a skipping record in her memory.

Will I go or will you stay?
Will I go or will you stay?

The question was so simple, so why couldn't the decision be simple too?

Will I go or will you stay?
Neither.

313

Have you thought of another option?

Just then, a solution appeared so clearly that a bell could have announced it's arrival. Determined, she gave René's hand a squeeze and turned to face her father who was still ranting.

"—and you'll be sleeping in the garage, too, because if I ever catch you sneaking around the barracks after dark—

"Dad? *Maman*?" Amandine interrupted him. "I can't begin to tell you how happy I'm that you're both alive. I still have so much I want to tell you, but before we decide on anything else, I need to say this first: I can't stay with you." To tell them hurt and felt liberating all at once. "I cannot join the movement."

Caroline studied her daughter carefully, and Will scoffed in disbelief. "You can't go back with them," he exclaimed. "After tonight, every inquestor in the country will be after you. Do you have any idea how hard it was to get Carver back on your case?"

Carver grunted with effort as he tried to force his trunk open. "Pretty hard."

"I won't go back with them either," Amandine replied.

René searched Amandine for an explanation, but her smile told him everything he needed to know.

"I'm going to do just like you told me, dad. Starting right now, I'm going to build the life I want for myself. I won't be a fighter or a traveling costumer. I will become a nobody."

"*Personne,*" Caroline murmured. Amandine didn't choose her family or her friends. Only René.

Will didn't like that at all. He had only just reunited his family, and his daughter was already leaving him. "You would choose this boy over your own family? Why?"

"Because—" Amandine beamed with a radiance she had never felt before. This new joy came effortlessly, appearing without having to gather it up, and she knew every ounce of it came from the rugged outlaw standing beside her. "Because I love him."

René wanted to lift her up in his arms. He wanted to kiss her. He wanted to put her on the horse and carry her away somewhere, anywhere, because her words made their future together and all of its potential open wide before him. Of course he couldn't do any of those things with everyone watching, so he only closed his eyes and held her hand a little tighter.

"I don't need to ask if you're sure," Caroline said before Will could refuse her. "I can see that you're telling the truth."

"How?" Will asked.

"Just look, *mon amour*." Caroline pointed with her cigarette. "Amandine has never smiled like that before."

He knew. Will saw it long before she made her feelings known, but the unfamiliar helplessness he felt in that moment still made his temper burn. "Where will you go?" Will demanded miserably. "What will you do?"

"I don't know yet," Amandine said. "I just want to get far away from the NAR and the fighting. I want to go someplace neutral and maybe open a little dress shop there.

René wants to be a rancher. We could head west. That seems like a good place to start."

The tense silence that followed was interrupted by loud squeaking as Carver threw all of his weight into the trunk again and again. It finally gave, springing up and sending the Inquestor tumbling backwards.

"Not that anybody cares what I think—" He pulled Caroline's rifle from the trunk and rubbed his smarting backside. "But I have an idea."

CHAPTER 16: THE PLAN

August 25, 1945
Somewhere outside of Nieuwestad (formerly New York City), New York

Amandine awoke in her bunk beneath a stiff wool blanket. Fumbling for the lamp chain, she tugged it on and glaring light illuminated her little corner of the barracks. Much like everything else in the bunker, the entire room was painted green and smelled a little musty. She saw that her parent's bunk was already empty, so she decided to get dressed and look for them.

"Would you mind switching that light off when you're done?" came a drowsy voice from the bunk above her. Amandine jumped and noticed a bloodstained apron hanging from the ladder beside her. Doc yawned, scratched his side, and rolled over to face the wall. "Thank you kindly."

Amandine found her parents sitting alone at the end of a long table in the busy mess hall where two cooks worked frantically to keep food coming for the gang of fighters.

"Good morning, Button." Will kissed her head when she sat down.

"Ouch!" Amandine's brow twinged. "That really smarts."

"Sorry." Will released her with a pat on the arm while Caroline waved to the cooks to fix a plate for Amandine. "How did you sleep? A little easier than the last couple of months on the road, I'll bet."

"Actually, I never slept better than when I was on the road," she said. "It was beautiful. Morning light and bird songs came through the little windows. My bunk was loaded with soft quilts, and I could smell breakfast cooking on the campfire. If she didn't sleep in, Gia would lay there and pluck her violin. Sometimes... no, always, our cooks— these Russian acrobat brothers— would argue about anything and everything. It was funny."

Her breakfast slid in front of her on a tin tray. As she took a bite of powdered eggs, Amandine fondly recalled Sasha, Piotr, and hot *syrniki* with jam on her mosaic dishes.

"You mean it, sweetheart?" Concern creased Will's face. He didn't notice that Caroline, having only eaten scraps in prison, had already devoured her food and stole his tray while he wasn't looking. "Was it as good as you say? You're not just... looking on the bright side?"

"I really mean it, Dad," she said sincerely. "They were good people who took good care of me. I was really happy to work for them."

"Tell me about what you made," he said, eager to learn more about his daughter in his three-year absence. He knew

318

that even if she never supported the cause with the same fervor, they would always have sewing in common. "When I left, you were already a very resourceful dressmaker."

She pulled her blue journal out of her pocket and pushed it across the table to her parents. Will and Caroline sat shoulder to shoulder and thumbed through the pages, murmuring with interest at the drawings, notes, and swatches. Everything she made, from feed sack underwear to the show-stopping festival costumes, was laid out in detail. Her father noticed that the dress Amandine was wearing was in the book, so he made her stand up so they could scrutinize the workmanship.

"You're not a dressmaker." Will returned her notebook. "You're an artist."

"Thanks, Dad." Amandine beamed with pride.

Will reached for his toast and was startled to find that it had vanished. Caroline offered him an apologetic shrug and signaled for more food.

He drummed his fingertips quietly on the table while he waited. It was obvious to the others that Will wanted to say something, but it was some time before he finally asked, "Are you... *absolutely* sure you don't want to stay?"

Amandine stopped chewing.

"You don't have to fight," he added quickly. "In fact, I'd prefer if you didn't. Not unless you wanted to." He could already see her answer in her eyes, so he quickly tried a different approach. "Once all this is done, we can start over. I daresay, you've got more vision and skill than most people in the business. Can you picture it, Button? All of us Stewarts sewing together again?"

Amandine regarded him sadly. "Daddy, you know I want to, but... I can't."

"No, she mo' fertainly can't," Carver mumbled around the extra pieces of toast he had clamped in his mouth.

Will and Amandine looked up in surprise. Carver was completely unrecognizable. He had slept in the scorched remnants of his uniform, and his once perfect hair was a wild mess. Amandine thought he better resembled his chaotic radio personality, especially now that he was wearing a pair of wire-rimmed glasses.

Carver dropped his tray and an entire pot of coffee beside Amandine. "She's working for me now, remember?"

"Button, what do you know about radios?" Will asked his daughter impatiently.

"Nothing." Carver refilled Caroline's outstretched mug. "But her boyfriend sure is handy for a dimwit. I figured he could help me and my ham buddies while she could be safely tucked away in scenic Slate Plains, Wyoming. They're safe out west together *and* supporting the cause. Everybody is happy."

While Caroline enjoyed Carver's company, Will could scarcely tolerate him, especially after last night's heated exchange. His stony glower did a poor job of hiding the fact, so Carver tried to reason with him.

"What's a teenage dressmaker going to do in a bunker or pirate submarine, anyway? Besides take up a ridiculous amount of space with her fabric?" He tucked a napkin into his collar. "I once dated a girl who knitted, but I had to break it off when she started hoarding her yarn at my place. It was heartbreaking to learn she only wanted me for my storage space."

"'*Boyfriend,*'" Will grumbled, ignoring Carver's tangent.

"I like him," Caroline put in. "I thought he was a bounty hunter when I first saw him because he had Marcus's gun and Amandine's silver thimble. You should have seen him on the horse."

"You should have seen how he barbecued the blues," Carver chirped as if he hadn't been nearly incinerated himself.

"All I saw him do was put his paws all over my daughter," Will complained. "He has no spine, no concept of what is proper, and Marcus seems to think he's mentally deficient."

Carver snorted until he choked. Clearing his throat, he said, "No, he's not really a moron. At least, I'm pretty sure he isn't." He wiped his mouth with his sleeve before starting on his second cup of coffee. "He's just a French kid of fighting age, fitting the kind of profile any aspiring inquestor would die for. The magic-man fooled the blues into thinking the kid was an idiot so they'd leave him alone." Carver doctored his coffee with a little cream, and he sucked the residual sugar off of his spoon. "Which reminds me— boss, I need a new gun."

"I took care of it already," Caroline replied, pinching a bite of powdered eggs off of Will's new tray. "I visited the armory and put something that might suit you a little better in your car."

"You have your own armory at IHQ. Why do you need to root around in our supplies?" Will turned in his seat to guard his food. "You shouldn't be handing out guns like Cracker Jack prizes in the first place. They aren't toys. That dirty vagrant could shoot himself, or worse, my daughter."

"What have you got against the *maghreb*?" Caroline demanded.

"Nothing!" Will exclaimed. "Is it wrong to have high standards and expectations for my only daughter? Whatever happened to the Cordell boy back home? You remember? His family grew cotton. Didn't he walk Button home from school a few times?"

"Drafted," Caroline said.

"He took up chew and spit everywhere," Amandine grimaced.

"How about Jacob Silverman's son? Now there was a young man raised right. He was going to be a banker, like his fath—"

"Drafted." Caroline took a bottle of aspirin from her pocket and swallowed a few pills with her coffee.

"Simon called me a few nasty names once after a disagreement over what we considered to be historical fact." Amandine reached for a few pills herself. The painful throbbing in her head was beginning to make her vision go dark around the edges. "In any case, I didn't leave the house after you were gone unless I had to find food. I didn't see anybody at all, let alone any potential suitors."

Will gave up. "I never imagined you were so impulsive that you'd fall for the first boy you laid eyes on."

Amandine shrugged and shared a knowing look with her mother.

"I was exaggerating," he growled. "You mean he really is the first boy you've laid eyes on?"

"The first boy who wasn't in uniform." She smiled into her cup. "If you think I ought to shop around before I buy, Mr. Carver here tells me that the NAR has a special place for young ladies looking for a fella."

The old sailor grunted indignantly at her sass. He could command an army of patriots and the hardened crew of the Osiris, but he had no control over the people at this table.

Carver rolled his eyes. "You know, I've had such rotten luck in the romance department that I've got half a mind to just pick up a decent laundress from the replacement home." He stuffed his mouth full of eggs and added wistfully, "Though I'd gladly do all of Sangria's laundry if she'd let me take her out to dinner."

"Over your last great romance already?" Will grumbled.

Carver only bared his teeth in an artificial smile.

Amandine didn't pay any attention to their bitter exchange; she was thinking about where things stood between Sangria and Coronado. Though they were certainly closer after the party, they weren't even remotely romantic, so she thought that perhaps some attention from somebody as pushy as Carver would get Sangria to make up her mind. After all of the trouble at the prison, it couldn't hurt to have a friendly inquestor keep an eye on Marmi's group for a while either.

"If you want to see Gia, you should go to the show tonight." Amandine said. "It's her first, big, starring performance, and Glorious has got her doing some really hot numbers. It would just tickle her pink to have a fan already."

"*Ooh, can I?*" Carver spun on Caroline.

"Marcus, we have a job to do," Will reminded him firmly. "You'll be attending the festival to work, not chase skirts."

"You know, I don't remember ever agreeing to work during the festival." Carver cocked his head mechanically towards Caroline. "Do you?"

Caroline shrugged and scratched her bandage with her little finger.

"Does that mean I can't count on you after all?" Will snarled.

"Of course not, Willy. I'm your Old Faithful. You can time a souffle to my punctuality. I was just thinking aloud, because it seems that the decision to move away from resource appropriation towards high-profile assassinations was made without me." Carver smirked, clearly enjoying how easily he could push Will's buttons. "Here's a thought. How about this?" He held his hands up like a frame for his idea. "After breakfast, I head back to IHQ to get debriefed, and you three meet me at my apartment later tonight. I'll give Amandine a ride back to her boyfriend before the rest of us have to clock in, and I can watch the show and still do my part from the square. It will be easier for me to handle a bit of business for my side-gig if I'm already down there anyway."

324

Amandine had no idea what he was talking about, but Caroline seemed to follow.

"Making an appearance?" she asked.

"I need to tie up a loose end," he answered flatly, avoiding Amandine's inquisitive look. "The sooner, the better."

"What do you plan on telling Everild?"

"The truth," Carver said. "The best way to lie is to stay as close to the truth as possible. I'll simply—" He waved his fingers in the air as if the right word was floating in front of him. "—*Omit* certain details that he doesn't have to know."

Caroline reflexively touched her missing eye, and Carver's grin widened.

Will felt that he missed some important information. "Why the hell would all three of us need to go to your apartment?"

"Amandine needs a ride back to her boyfriend," Carver enunciated, peering over his glasses. "And I'm gonna need some new uniforms fit."

Caroline chuckled; she expected nothing less from the vain Inquestor.

"I have been going through suits on this mission like the president goes through mistresses, and I'm going to pick up some new ones just as soon as Everild turns me loose." He plucked at his hanging, charred collar pitifully. "Be sure to bring your big sewing kit, and when you get to my place, tell the doorman you're all tailors."

"And the doorman wouldn't find it unusual that you hired three tailors to make an after-hours house call during the festival?" Will asked skeptically.

"I've stayed at Marcus's apartment many times," Caroline answered. "Believe me, that would not be the oddest thing the poor fellow has had to let through the front door."

Carver looked very pleased with himself since nobody opposed his plan. "The other inquestors would *just die* if they knew I got my uniform fit by the man who designed them," he said smugly. "There's nothing better than going to a party in a sharp new suit."

"René and I wanted to see the show together before we left town," Amandine said amicably. "You could watch it with us if you wanted."

"Can't. When the uniform is on, I'm all business, and business dictates that I only fraternize with other inquestors and the occasional easy woman. Where's that drugstore cowboy of yours, anyways?" Carver sat up a little taller to search the busy room. "Decided he wasn't so eager to die for the cause after all?"

"He went home," Amandine replied with a sigh. When they parted ways last night, he looked exactly like the cover of a Rogue Rider novel, handsome and heroic on horseback. "He had to get some things and say goodbye to Marmi."

"His mommy?"

"*Marmi,*" she repeated. "Remember? She's the tall woman from—" Amandine paused. She never learned where Marmi came from. "She was the fortune-teller."

"Speaking of that band of bums..." Carver pressed his hands together and broke the news as delicately as he could. "They aren't exactly in the clear."

"What?" Amandine felt her stomach pitch in panic.

"Remember when I said the blues told my boss about the suspicious traveling show?" he explained. "He's got inquestors all over Nieuwestad probing the acts this week. That's why I told your friends they probably shouldn't attend the festival."

"Can't you just say, 'Never mind, they're fine, my mistake?'" Her heart sank as she imagined everyone tortured, shackled, and wasting away in a dark dungeon. Just as this picture sprang into her mind, she was struck by the realization that she never once imagined her mother this way.

Carver narrowed his eyes. "That's not— inquestors don't make mistakes. They *always* get results. They're going to expect somebody's head, metaphorically or quite literally speaking."

"Oh, no!" She paled and pressed her hands over her mouth. "Mr. Carver, you can't!"

"Unless you can think of somebody else I could nab instead, I'm going to need to get at least one person, and soon!" He threw his hands out to his sides in a helpless display. "I could have negotiated a raise if I got the French kid, but since he's off the table, my vote is for that musician. That bastard's got a record, and he was the one who set the tiger on me."

Will and Caroline watched their daughter closely to see what she'd do. Amandine imagined that this was how her mother, once just a busy tailor's wife, got started on the bloody path she was on now. She had been backed into a corner, and she had no choice left but to fight to protect the ones she loved.

"Surely there was some performer you didn't like," Carver went on. "Someone who was mean to you or thought your designs were *passé*?"

Amandine dropped her hands into her lap as a monstrous idea came to her. She suppressed her guilt before she changed her mind and tugged on the Inquestor's sleeve. He leaned close, and she nervously whispered something in his ear.

"Oh, you *wicked* little thing, you." Carver chuckled darkly. "Well, I think it's safe to say that Marmi-dearest has nothing to worry about anymore."

CHAPTER 17: THE FESTIVAL

Sufficiently caffeinated and looking perfectly wretched, Carver took his pulverized car back to Inquestor Headquarters in the city, leaving the Stewarts alone once more.

Amandine would always remember that day in the bunker as one of the best days of her life. She decided to help her father make a dress for Caroline since she couldn't wear her prison jumpsuit to the festival, but the only material on hand was some old canvas. Will agonized over the design. After so many years away, he wanted to make something beautiful for his wife, but he kept wadding up sketch after sketch. "Canvas is for seabags, not party dresses," he grumbled. "Oh, what I'd give for just two yards of gabardine."

Inspired by the challenge, Amandine took her mother's favorite drawing from Will's discard pile and added a few details she knew she could make from her scrap bag. Her contribution surprised and delighted her parents, and with a plan in place, they set to work.

While they pressed, cut, and sewed over cups of sweet tea, Amandine kept looking from her father to her mother in disbelief, wondering how the moment was possible. They were alive and all together one last time.

That evening, the train took them to the city where the Inquestor was anxiously awaiting them at his downtown apartment. He flew to the door in his bathrobe when he heard them knock.

"What took you so long?" he fussed, pushing them inside one by one. He did a double-take when he saw what Caroline was wearing.

"What's wrong, Marcus?" She floated past him and made herself at home, leaving her shoes, scarf and sunglasses at the door. "Don't you like my new dress?"

"Oh, I do." He studied it with his head tilted to one side. "I think it sure is something! I'm having a hard time working out how it can have so much going on and yet look so balanced."

"It's a combination of traditional, structured dressmaking and a little gypsy resourcefulness," she explained proudly from his kitchen. "Do you still have my hats and wigs here?"

He pointed absently down the hall. "Your clothes are in the bedroom, same place as always."

Will glared at the Inquestor like he wanted to knock him across the room.

"What?" Carver rolled his eyes. "Don't give me that. She keeps her disguises here."

"So why don't you hide them?" Will demanded.

"Why should I? If anybody ever found her clothes, I'll just say I get my kicks by dressing in drag. Goodness knows they'd probably believe it." Carver grabbed Will by the sleeve and pulled him down the hallway. "Anyway, you're worried about the wrong outfits. I was reissued three uniforms today, and we're running out of time."

"What?" Will blinked as he was led to an entire room dedicated to the care of Carver's uniforms. The room was filled with every laundry appliance, utensil, soap and solution imaginable, and Carver pointed urgently to the suit bags hanging by his trifold dressing mirror.

"You deaf, man? I need them fit." Carver dropped his bathrobe and pulled on his new trousers. "Let's see that legendary needle fly!"

Caroline appeared at the doorway, blowing on a fresh cup of coffee. She handed the mug to her husband with a smirk. "I told you he was serious, *chéri*. Better get to pinning."

Will steeled himself with a hot drink and rolled up his sleeves. Amandine came to help after she put on a dance record from the Inquestor's extensive music library. She pinned and listened to her father complain, but she noticed that he couldn't help smiling as he worked with fine material once again.

Before long, it was time to part ways, and Amandine bid an emotional farewell to her parents. She didn't know when she'd see them again but felt comfort in knowing that at least they had each other now.

"Goodbye, Button." Will held her for as long as he could. "It's not safe for either of us to write or call directly, but please let us know when you get settled."

"How?" Amandine asked.

"Leave a message with Marcus, and he'll get it to us."

Carver's head popped out from his bathroom in a cloud of steam. "That's even more dangerous! I won't do it, especially not after that wild goose-chase."

"Surely there is no harm in a single phone call," Caroline said from her place before the entryway mirror. She adjusted a blonde wig and fascinator to hide her bandages. "You could always explain it away as a wrong number."

Carver grumbled, but he couldn't refuse her. "Alright. One message, but that's it." And with that, he slammed the bathroom door again.

Satisfied, Caroline embraced her daughter. "*Adieu, ma petite jolie.* Good luck, and don't spend all of your inheritance in one place."

They left her alone in the apartment, and Amandine explored more of Carver's record collection while she waited for the Inquestor to finish getting ready. He finally emerged, groomed to the level of perfection that inquestors were known for, and he looked especially sharp in his expertly tailored new suit. She felt underdressed standing beside him, but he still offered his arm like a gentleman and escorted her downstairs.

"Seatbelts," he reminded her brightly. He pulled his new Interceptor out of the basement garage and into the busy downtown traffic.

She obeyed, gazing out of the window with wonder at the lit skyscrapers that surrounded them. "Do you know where we're going?"

332

"Of course I do." Carver sounded his horn twice, and a delivery van slammed on its brakes to let the Inquestor in. "It's my business to know everything. If I don't know it yet, then I find it out."

"Oh, really? Everything?" She thought she would test him. "What's René's real name?"

"Everything *that matters*," he clarified. "I don't care what Renoir's real name is."

"What about Gia?"

"Her real name is Blythe Greenwood, she's twenty, born in Bridge City, Pennsylvania to Chester and Myrtle Greenwood, both alive and presently occupied as field hands in Kukamonga, California."

"Ha!" Amandine exclaimed.

Carver's face fell. He had walked right into her trap.

"'Everything that matters,' my foot," she giggled. "You don't care about who's running your equipment out west, but you already know enough about Gia to start your own official fan club." She pointed to the large box in the backseat. "Is that for her?"

"Inquestor business," he grinned. "Move along, citizen."

He had to slow down when traffic thickened, and it became harder for everyone to move to let him pass. When he flicked on his lights, cars pulled up on sidewalks in a mad, desperate scramble just to get out of his way.

"Okay, Mr. Carver, if you don't want to talk about Gia, then how about my mother?"

"This festival traffic is just the worst," he whined, ignoring her.

"I suspected she had a boyfriend before she got arrested." She saw Carver's face screw up in an odd, strained expression of pain and extreme concentration. "When I saw dad again, I thought it was him all along. But after everything that was said last night, now I'm thinking that—"

With a violent jerk of his steering wheel, Carver veered down an alley and jostled his passenger quiet. When Amandine recovered, she saw that they had come to a stop right behind the bumper of Glorious's red pickup.

Carver came around the car to open Amandine's door for her. As soon as he helped her out, he crossed his arms and dropped his cheerful tone. "Alright, you. Time to get gone."

Amandine retrieved her suitcase and spied a long, flat gun case that had slid out from beneath the backseat. "Thanks for the ride, Inquestor."

He stared at her silently, waiting for her to leave.

"Take care of my parents," she added softly.

His mouth twitched into a peculiar half-smile, then he nodded once and shooed her away like a fly.

Amandine darted down the alley, dodging trash bins and avoiding the gutters in her search for René. All of the familiar trucks and painted trailers were dark except for the red shepherd's hut. Sangria was always the last one ready. Just as Amandine wondered whether or not she should go greet her friend, she spotted him.

René was standing in a close circle with Glorious, Coronado, and Nick in a final meeting. The illusionist, dressed in his magnificent white costume for the opening act, noticed Amandine first. He nudged René and pointed in her direction with a lacquered cane.

Their eyes locked and Amandine made an involuntary sound, something between a laugh and a sob. Overjoyed, they started towards each other, but Coronado caught René by the arm and pulled him into a hard embrace first. She watched as the illusionist took the stagehand by the shoulders, and they spoke privately for some time, standing almost head to head. Amandine was bouncing with impatience by the time René earnestly shook hands with everyone and said his goodbyes.

One he was finally free, he rushed for her. He swept her up into his arms, and he kissed her hard. She tried to gently push away, but he held her as desperately as a life preserver.

"Erm, René?" she mumbled.

"Yes?" He kissed her repeatedly from her collarbone to her hair.

"Ouch!" She groaned when he touched her brow. "My eye..."

"Sorry. I forgot." René relented a little, pressing her small waist against him. "I am just so happy, I could kiss you forever."

Once he had set her back down, he waved one last time to his friends. Glorious and Nick gave him a thumbs up before they turned to follow the caped illusionist towards the stage.

"There will be plenty of time for kissing later." Amandine giggled and stood on her tiptoes to whisper in his ear, "And then some!"

René's eyes went wide. He tried to stammer through a reply when a trailer door burst open, and Sangria appeared in her shimmering white costume. She eyed the couple warily.

"What do you want?"

"Nothing," Amandine replied. "Though it's good to see you one last time, Gia."

Sangria descended the short steps like a queen. Amandine noticed that she had changed her show makeup, and it bore a striking resemblance to her mother's Egyptian style. "You didn't knock just now?"

The dressmaker shook her head. "No, but I imagine whoever left those probably did." She pointed to the ostentatious bouquet of roses set near the bottom step of her trailer.

Sangria glanced up and down the alley before she stooped to pick up the gift. Attached to the vase on a black velvet ribbon was a delicate string of pearls. Amandine marveled at the presentation. It was a beautiful, dark, and expensive gift that suited Sangria perfectly.

"What does the card say?" René plucked out the note before the contortionist even noticed it. He scanned it, holding it just out of her reach while she jumped at him. "*Oh là là*, Gia's got a suitor."

"Give it to me!" Sangria snatched it out of his hand. She scanned the ivory card, mumbling the inscription to herself. "'*Good luck on your first big performance in the Big Apple. I would say 'break a leg,' but you'll need them both for dancing and dinner with me at the Office this Friday night at*

7:00. *I'll wear a tie, you tie a bow! Sincerely yours, Inquestor Marcus E. Carver.*'"

With a scoff, she tucked the card into the front of her costume. "If he thinks he can buy me with a few dozen roses and a shiny bauble, he can keep trawling the replacement homes." She tried to put her bouquet on the vanity, but it was too wide for the tiny surface, so she left it the only place it would fit: on the floor near her bunk.

René checked his wristwatch. "*Chérie*, you've got fifteen minutes until curtain."

Sangria trotted down the stairs again and turned her back to Amandine. "Fasten me?"

"You bet." She zipped up her friend and gave her a hug from behind. Sangria pretended to tolerate it, but René could see that she was smiling. "You look stunning. Break a leg out there."

"Thanks." Sangria shrugged her off. "You should get going. Try to find a decent spot before the show starts."

"*À la prochaine,* Sangria." René offered a handshake.

Sangria pressed his fingers lightly, but then she hesitated. "You were always so kind to me." To his surprise, she yanked him down to her level and planted a light kiss on his cheek. "Sorry for always being such a pill." And with that, she pranced off to the stage in a flutter of feathers and rhinestones.

The couple headed back down the alley and René tossed Amandine's suitcase into the cab of Glorious' truck. He pounded the red rusted hood proudly. "A parting gift. Do you like it?"

337

"I do." Amandine saw that the stolen police horse was tethered to the truck bed. "How ever did Glorious get you to accept it?"

"I had this rather romantic notion of us riding off into the sunset," he admitted. "But Glorious said, 'Y'all ain't gonna make that poor horse carry the two of you and a sewing machine, are you? Lord, have mercy.'"

She laughed when the horse sniffed her dress in search of treats. She stroked his velvet nose and asked, "Didn't have the heart to turn him loose?"

"No, and our new friends didn't want him either." René put on his hat and offered his arm. "Well? Shall we?"

Arms linked, they walked out of the dark alley and towards the crowded main street. The road was a river of people, and the current carried them out to the square where searchlights whirled amongst the clouds. Vendors and buskers lined the sidewalks beneath flags and strings of colorful lights that criss-crossed above them like a web. The sight made Amandine giddy, but her delight waned when her vision started swaying and made her lightheaded. Frowning, she squeezed René's arm for balance.

René didn't notice anything wrong with Amandine because he was preoccupied with the uneasy feeling that someone was watching him. He kept glancing over his shoulder until he spotted an inquestor, dogging them about twenty steps behind.

"It's just Mr. Carver." Amandine mustered up a lazy smile. "I said he could watch the show with us."

"You sure he's alright?" René pulled her closer protectively. "I am not so sure I like the thought of him going after Sangria. He gives me the creeps."

Amandine reassured him with a pat on the arm. "He's the one who is sending us someplace safe. Also, he said he'd keep an eye on Marmi for me."

"As a friend or as an inquestor?" René pulled up the collar of his jacket and drew his hat brim low as if it could make him invisible.

"Oh, you need to look on the bright side, René!" She found a little bit of energy and moved abruptly in front of him. Amandine slapped his collar back down and readjusted his hat, chiming the thimble ornament on the brim for good measure. "I mean it! Count your blessings! Say something good about what's happening right now."

René thought for a moment, looking into her bruised and beautiful face while she walked backwards. "I have my very own horse and truck."

"Yes!" She clapped. "Go on."

"I am heading out west. It's where I've always wanted to go."

"You've got it," she encouraged him. "One more!"

"And... against all odds, I am with the girl I love."

In that instant, René felt all of the fear and anxiety that had been weighing on him vanish. He no longer worried about the suspicious Inquestor, Will's disapproval, Amandine's safety, or the family he was leaving behind. They were not forgotten, but completely overshadowed by the beauty of the moment. René wondered if this was how Amandine felt all of the time. Vitalized, he exclaimed, "I am going on my first date to a big party in the city! I've never done that before."

"That's the spirit!" She skipped to his side again, lacing her fingers in his. "Good luck on that date, though. My dad reminded me a dozen times that I was raised with very high standards, and while I might be an aimless wanderer now, I should never forget my upbringing. I'm supposed to be a very tough nut to crack."

"What does it take to crack an heiress?" René grinned. "A velvet box of bonbons? A sapphire lavalier?

Amandine craned her neck when she detected a warm and sweet smell. She pointed excitedly once she'd located the source coming from a nearby vendor stall. "How about a caramel apple?"

René was happy to oblige. He had just picked an apple wrapped in shiny, blue cellophane when he felt someone press closely against his side in the crowd. It was the Inquestor. Carver didn't look at him or say anything at first, rubbing his jaw as he scanned the rows of treats on display.

"Can I get you something, Inquestor?" the vendor asked. He was just as surprised as René by his sudden appearance.

Carver pointed to the apple in the vendor's hand, the same one René had just chosen. "I'll take that one, please."

The man surrendered it. "On the house."

"Thank you," Carver said smugly. "Have a happy Freedom Festival. Hail to the Republic." He stared René down while he pocketed the treat, daring him to object.

340

"Is there anything you need from me, Inquestor?" René asked through clenched teeth. "Besides my apple?"

Carver leaned in so close that René had to tilt backwards to avoid touching him. "Mind the girl. Pretty sure she's concussed."

"Concussed?" He looked at Amandine. She was leaning against the back of a nearby food truck with a vacant look in her eyes, entranced by the canopy of lights above her.

"She was listing a bit at breakfast," Carver said shortly. "I set her upright, and I honestly don't think she noticed."

Just then, there came a shout from across the crowd. "*Marksman!*"

Carver spun away from René so fast, he knocked him back a step. "That sounds like Felix Pierce," he cried, greeting two more inquestors with his arms spread wide. "And look! You managed to drag Agent Victorin out of a bottle."

Victorin was so tall and muscular, he completely dwarfed the other officers. "It's where I'd still be if the Chief hadn't called everyone out in force tonight," he replied, shaking hands.

"I could think of worse places to do overtime." Carver let his shoulders bounce along to the music until Victorin cuffed him on the back of the neck to keep him still.

"When did you get back?" asked Pierce, the slender, drowsy-looking officer. "And who's the cowboy?"

"Beats me. Let's get out of here." Carver led his colleagues away. "That wall-eyed moron was trying to buy my caramel apple."

The Freedom Festival went on as planned, and nobody mentioned or even seemed to remember that there was supposed to be a mass execution to kick off the festivities. The official media wasn't talking about the jailbreak, and DJMA was maintaining an unusual radio silence. The scaffold was removed as soon as word of the attack on the convoy reached Nieuwestad and the space was filled with another stage. High above the packed city square in a dark, vacant apartment, Tall-Me and Cleo sat alone on the dusty linoleum floor with a radio between them.

"If a fellow's feelin' blue, his lovely wife knows what to do! She fixes Harper's in a cup! A pipin' hot mug of pick-me-up! That's right, the best housewives in the country only serve their husbands Harper's coffee. It smells great and tastes great too! Enjoy the rich, fresh taste of Harper's Coffee... if your husband has left you any!"

"We're back tonight, ladies and gentlemen, with 'How We Are in the NAR!' This is Danny Darren and Daisy Diller coming to you live from the Freedom Festival here in downtown Nieuwestad! Coming up, we have a dazzling international act just in time for the fireworks display! Stay tuned right here for details as they happen! Oh, we've seen some delightful performances here tonight already, haven't we, Daisy?"

"That's right, Danny! I really liked the—"

"My favorite was the marching band outta Massachusetts when they played the NAR favorite, 'My Home So Good To Me!' That one never gets old, does it, Daisy?"

"It certainly doesn't, Danny! I thought the—"

"How about those lovely local ladies, the Miss-Elles, doing that exciting kicking number in a line? Oh, you folks listening at home should have come out for that one! Legs for miles! Do you suppose you could kick that high, Daisy?"

"I've never tried, Danny! I could probably—"

Caroline tuned the radio to a different frequency and picked up her rifle. "I can't stand to listen to those two. Pirate radio is the only decent thing on the air anymore." She peered into her scope, scanning the crowd through her reticle. "Speak of the pirate. I see Marcus."

"What about Amandine?" Will asked. He still held onto the hope that his daughter would change her mind about leaving. "Do you see her? She was wearing that white scarf."

Caroline couldn't focus. She reflexively rubbed her right eye, only to remember it was gone. Muttering a filthy curse in French, she ripped off her wig and dug through her purse for the wrap Amandine had made. "I hope Marcus took his time on the warden. Why did he have to cut up the eye I shoot with?"

"Leave it alone or it'll hurt more. Here, give me the gun." Will gently took the rifle from her. "This is my score to settle, anyway."

Caroline scowled at him as she knotted the material around her head and tugged it down to her cheek. It didn't do much to help her appearance, but wearing it made her feel a bit more secure.

"You look beautiful, my dear. Just like a pirate submarine captain's wife."

She wasn't in the mood for teasing, so Will sang a little tune to try to cheer her up.

"Now let ev'ry man drink off his full bumper, and let ev'ry man drink off his full glass. We'll drink and be jolly and drown melancholy, and here's to the health of each true-hearted lass."

He brushed her cheek lightly with his thumb, finally coaxing a smile from her. Caroline appreciated his attempt to lighten the mood, and she moved aside so that he could take her place at the window. He propped her gun on the sill, using the spotted curtains to camouflage the long barrel.

"See them?" she asked.

Will made a sound in the negative. "Marcus seems to have found a couple of his friends, though. God, there are inquestors everywhere."

"That shouldn't be a problem." She hugged her knees like a child and touched her face through the red fabric.

"When aren't inquestors a problem?" he asked with contempt. "They're trouble, even when they're on our side."

"Stop worrying. You've spent too long in that submarine." She scooted across the floor until she sat directly behind him and leaned onto his broad back. Softly, she asked, "Does the earth still move, *mon amour*?"

"No," he replied with a smile. She tilted her head against his shoulder and relaxed with a deep sigh. "Only when you do that, my dear."

They sat together that way for some time. Colorful beams from the stage below filled the empty room through the split in the curtains and Caroline watched the lights dance across the ceiling.

"Thank you for not being angry with me about Marcus," she murmured.

Will looked up from the scope. He didn't think he could bear it if she ever brought it up, but now that it was out in the open, he was glad she did.

"I don't blame you, my dear. He may be quite a bit younger, but you are still a very beautiful woman. You believed that your husband was dead. I worried that you were lost to me until I finally met Marcus in person." He chuckled and returned his attention to the gun. "Then I didn't worry anymore."

"I won't try to deceive you, Will. We did grow very close."

"I suspected as much," he replied, trying to keep his tone light. "I will try not to be upset about what's past, Caroline of mine, but I want to know. What happened?"

"It all started about a year after we heard about the Osiris," she replied. "Amandine was starving. It would have killed you to see her, Will. She was fading when she should have been thriving, and all the while, she kept on smiling. The way she tried to glean joy out of a handful of weeds... well, it drove me into a rage."

Will drew a sharp breath and let his head fall against his hand in guilt.

"The first time I met Marcus, I was raiding the storehouse with our neighbors from Cold River. That gun—" Caroline nodded to the 50-90 Sharps in his hands. "—Was all we had between the four of us. I took it from the display in the den. Do you remember it?"

"This is the gun from the den?" He turned the weapon in his hands to examine the carved stock. It had hung over his desk for years beside some taxidermy animals that he did not kill. The interior designer had thought antique guns and hunting trophies would add a sense of rustic masculinity to the space. "I thought it was just a decoration. I had no idea it actually worked."

"Neither did I," she admitted. "Not until that night. We crept in, and I saw Marcus sitting on a crate of sugar right in the middle of the storehouse like he was expecting us. I was so startled, I took a shot at him." She smirked at the memory of him slipping on spilt sugar and stumbling for cover. "He ran and hid, and I had to talk him out. We talked for hours. I found out he was the pirate radio DJ that Amandine and I loved to listen to. He let us take whatever food we wanted and said that Tall-Me needed a reliable land crew. I didn't have a clue that it was you until just before I was arrested— that night all three of us were on the radio."

Will remembered that day well. When he heard her familiar voice, distorted through the static of the comm station, it took everything he had to keep from breaking down in front of his officers. That memory used to fill him with joy and reaffirm his dedication to the cause, but now as realization slowly crept over him, it only filled him with dread.

"Marcus found you first?" he asked with a chill in his voice. "He was waiting for you?"

"Yes," Caroline continued, oblivious to his alarm. "And I am glad he did. I never could have imagined all that we would accomplish together in those two years. After my last job, he came running to the house in a panic. He said there was no time, the inquestors were right behind him, and he had to arrest me if there was any chance of us surviving the night. I trusted him. I had to. We had a plan in place in case something like this ever happened. I told him to hit me a few times to really sell it, but he couldn't. I had to dash my own head on the fireplace before the police showed up. He had them all take me from the house quickly before anybody saw Amandine hiding upstairs."

Will was pale, and he set the rifle down to take both of her hands. "Caroline, something dreadful has just occurred to me."

"What?" Caroline stared at him in bewilderment. "William, what is it?"

"It's Marcus," he said urgently. "The amount of power he holds over us has always troubled me, but—"

"Power?" she interrupted him. "Over Tall-Me and Cleo?"

"Listen to me," he said desperately. "We might lead many capable crews, but who controls us? You and I? This cause? We are nothing without the information he gives us. He is right about being the most wanted man in the NAR that they don't even know they want. But what if this is all by his design?"

She opened her mouth to interject, but he cut her off.

"I thought it was just wild happenstance that you were Cleo. At the time I was blinded with happiness just to hear you were alive, but in light of recent events... Caroline, it's just too perfect to be a coincidence."

She shook her head again and again. He pressed on.

"Just look at how he has stacked the cards in his favor. To the NAR, he's a hero. He is their military elite. To us, he is our most vital asset. He's an inquestor with near limitless power and influence, but above all, he has information. He is playing both sides." He searched her for understanding. "That makes him not only the most wanted, but the most dangerous man in the NAR."

Caroline stared hard at him, her lips pursed as she listened. The suggestion was a chilling one that she could not believe, yet could not dismiss. She thought back to her imprisonment beneath IHQ. No matter how much Carver prepared her for the probability of torture, nothing she imagined came close to the horrors she endured at the hands of the inquestors. Like a hellish fever-dream, Carver appeared during one of her interrogations. He didn't speak, but as the others tore into her flesh, the way he gripped her arm told her many things. In that touch, she felt his fury, his anguish, and an oath to make everything right.

She also thought of the day before, when her face was crushed into the pavement at the prison. The warden's heel was on her neck, and Carver loomed just behind him. There was no smile, no wink to reassure her that everything was going to plan; there was only death in his black eyes. It was an expression she knew well after years of fighting alongside him, but as he fixed her with that look down the barrel of her Sharpes, a jolt of primal fear set every nerve alight, each one a flashing warning that screamed, "He's going to kill me."

But he didn't. He would never hurt her. He couldn't even hit her in the parlor when she asked him to. The night she discovered Will was alive was the only time he ever showed any bitterness, yet he still surrendered her without a word of jealousy or resentment.

"Will, Marcus was standing right next to me when I found out you were Tall-Me," Caroline answered stiffly. "He was just as shocked as we were."

"Marcus is an excellent actor," Will reasoned. "But which side of him is the real one? Who is he really fooling?"

She couldn't accept it. It wasn't possible, not after all they had done together. She held her husband's hands tightly. "*Mon chèr*, this is a perilous time. Every day that we get closer to our goal, the stakes rise even higher. It's too late not to trust each other."

"I don't trust him," he said angrily. "There is something very big that he's keeping from us."

"You don't have to trust him." She squeezed his shoulders. He refused to meet her gaze, so she lifted his head in both hands until she could look into his eyes. "Trust me."

Caroline leaned forward carefully, pressing her lips once to his. He remained stock-still and withdrawn.

"You think my attachment to Marcus is blinding me," she frowned. Caroline wrapped him gently in her arms and murmured, "While I still think that you're wrong, if you turn out to be right, and I must choose a side, then I will always choose you. There is no question, there never was and there never will be. You're my husband." She gently kissed him once more. "I love you, Will."

He released a long, shuddering breath of relief and pulled her into his lap. He held her close and rested his head on her chest while she ran her fingers through his hair.

"I should have come straight home," he mumbled. "If I had come home, you wouldn't be blind, Amandine wouldn't have run off, and none of us would be in this mess. What was I thinking, playing Robin Hood?"

"If you had, you'd be eating dandelion salad right next to us," she replied and felt him laugh softly. "You'd be hiding in shame, instead of making history beside me."

The radio on the floor whined loudly, interrupting their tender moment. Will sighed and took up the gun to resume watch over the events below.

"Anything?" Caroline set the radio closer to the window.

"No signal yet." Will scanned the crowd again, but a fiery streak of red on the stage caught his attention. "Was this the same group Amandine traveled with?"

"Yes, it should be." She crawled around behind him to look over his shoulder and down the gun barrel. "This is the one Marcus wanted to see."

"Oh, I recognize the magician and that little-bitty friend of hers now." He watched the performers whirl across the stage like a colorful kaleidoscope, each one a gleaming jewel on a moving stage. "Did Amandine actually *make* all of the costumes, or did she just alter them?"

"You saw her notebook," Caroline replied impatiently, pinching his ear until he nudged her off. "The design and construction was all her doing."

"Caroline of mine, you need to see this." He passed her the gun. "It's one thing to read plans on paper, it's another to see it on stage."

The two of them took turns watching the show from the scope, proud beyond words of their daughter's independent work. Caroline was moving in time to the music when she finally remembered to look for Amandine in the final act.

"Oh, there she is," she exclaimed. "She's at the very front. She probably wanted to say goodbye to her friends one last time."

"Let me see." Will went for the rifle again, but Caroline jerked it out of his reach.

"*Non,*" she snapped. Explosions as loud as thunder rattled the dusty apartment windows. "Get the binoculars and see for yourself."

Will wouldn't have appreciated what Caroline saw through the scope, so she kept it to herself with a private smile. She watched René wrap Amandine in his arms and kiss her deeply as fireworks burst in the sky. Gold, silver, and blue sparks rained down behind the electropolyharmonium as the grand finale rose into its final crescendo. It felt as if the entire

351

city was dancing, and the square couldn't contain it's boiling energy. Couples swarmed on rooftops and fire escapes. Every stair, every wall, every inch of pavement was a dance floor, and for once, René and Amandine were the only two standing still. The young couple stood pressed against each other, simply breathing, feeling, gazing with wonder at the breathtaking city around them.

That was all Will could see by the time he retrieved and focused his binoculars. Amandine looked happy if not a little tired, and Will realized that that was the best he could hope for under the circumstances. He glanced over at Caroline to guess at her opinion, but she was fumbling to get the rifle repositioned on her left side.

"Are you sure you don't want me to take the shot, dear?"

Caroline had to turn her head all the way to the right to throw him a dark look.

"I'm not doubting your marksmanship," he assured her. "I'm only thinking of your comfort. You are still recovering from a very serious injury."

"My left eye can see just as well as my right," she shot back. "And you're likely out of practice after all that time at sea."

"Horsefeathers. I'm a high officer." Will lifted his chin, pretending that she had hurt his pride. "The last time I was tested, my accuracy was scored at ninety-six percent. You're just accustomed to working with somebody who doesn't know which end of the gun the bullets come out of."

"Ninety-six percent with a shiny new Springfield, perhaps. How's your accuracy at over four hundred yards with a fifty-caliber antique buffalo rifle and a—" She glanced at a blue banner fluttering from a nearby building. "—Ten mile-per-hour wind?"

Will was impressed. Watching her settle into a new position with her giant rifle, he thought back to Paris, 1922. He could vividly recall looking across the stage, past the cascading drapes and handkerchief hemlines to a pair of dark eyes hidden beneath a cloche hat. She was eighteen, so lovely, so shy, and thankfully so charmed by his sincerity and horrible French that she accepted his impulsive marriage proposal. Though the war had been cruel to her, she emerged stronger, more beautiful, and every bit as regal as the stories told. He couldn't blame Carver for falling in love with her, and the thought made him jealous and proud all at once.

"The only time I've missed with this gun was the first time I fired it." Caroline ran her hand down the length of the barrel and felt a rush of renewed self-confidence. "*Non, chéri.* This might be your fight, but the Sharps is my gun and shooting her is my purpose."

Just then, the radio crackled to life. "Jim to Charlie, Jim to Charlie. Who orders groceries right in the middle of the festival?" said an angry voice through the static.

That was their cue. Their target was approaching fast.

Will picked up the radio. "Jim, this is Terry. That's what you get for staying open on a holiday."

"Is anyone available to handle a delivery?"

"Charlie's already out the door."

"Roger that, Terry. Don't forget to leave him a tip."

Will swept his view down to see if Carver was paying attention, and he found him staring directly back up at him. The Inquestor nodded once, then his gaze drifted up, and he pretended to watch the fireworks. Will scowled and decided to keep a close eye on this dubious character for now.

"I've got him," Caroline said. "The Admiral is surrounded by his men. He looks like he's seen a ghost."

"Keep a steady hand, and he'll be seeing a few more."

She chuckled and pulled back the Sharps' bolt with a decisive crack. "This is your last chance to change your mind."

"Absolutely not." Will readied their belongings for a hasty exit. "The Osiris has been waiting two years to settle this score."

Caroline twitched.

"And the HMS Sanctum will have justice at last," Will said, but both of them knew that he had spoken too late.

No one near the stage heard the shot, not over Big Polly and the grand finale of fireworks. The only way Amandine knew what had happened was when she looked for the Inquestor and he was gone.

EPILOGUE: THE GUN

Later that night in a crowded back alley six blocks away from the square, a freckled showgirl sobbed miserably against the wheel of her trailer. Her ankle was twice its normal size, swelling like purple over-proofed dough out of her satin dance shoes. Frantically, other showgirls tried to help her to her feet, but she collapsed in agony. "I can't dance," she wailed. "I can't even stand! It's broken, and it hurts so bad!"

"You'll dance," the showmaster slurred, tipping the last swig of whiskey beneath his moustache. "If I have to get you high as a rocket first, you'll dance."

"Have a heart, Mr. Johnstone," wheezed an exhausted old-woman who was cinching another dancer into her costume. "Let the girl get some ice and sit this one out."

"*No,*" he shouted and pitched the empty bottle onto the pavement. "That savage cow, that *Madame Marmi* everybody's so fond of, got Holloway's machine *and* fireworks for her show! *Fireworks!*"

"Codswallop," the old woman sighed. "It was just lucky timing."

"This show needs to be perfect! I will not tolerate a single gap in the line!"

"We can close gaps, but what if she falls in the middle of the routine?"

"She won't, if she knows what's good for her." The other dancers scattered like a flock of birds when Johnstone stalked towards the injured showgirl. He jerked her upright by the elbow, and she shrieked in pain. "Let's get you something for that foot from the candy cart, eh?"

He dragged her around the vehicles to the concession trailer, but he sputtered in surprise when he realized that somebody was already in it.

Carver was standing over a box of popcorn kernels that had been cut open to reveal an enormous cache of drugs. "Good evening, sir." He smiled and took a bite of a caramel apple. "Mr. Cornelius Johnstone, I presume?"

"Who the hell are you?" Johnstone slurred. He shook the showgirl until she yelped. "Who the hell is that?"

She trembled like a rabbit at the silver insignia on his shoulder. "It's— It's an inquestor," she squeaked.

Johnstone sobered, and both he and the showgirl tumbled backwards. Casually, Carver helped Johnstone to his feet. "Whoopsie-daisy. You alright?"

"Fine," mumbled Johnstone. "Don't—"

"You sure?" Carver dusted off his red velvet jacket. "If not, I seem to have found a huge, illegal stash of drugs. Something in there is bound to help with pain."

"It's for my performers," Johnstone said. "Something is always plaguing them, and we aren't always so near a doctor."

Carver nodded sympathetically. "I can see that. That poor girl looks like she needed a hospital for that foot a week ago."

To Johnstone's puzzlement, the Inquestor said nothing else. Instead, he just stood there smiling and chewing his festival treat. After a while, Johnstone managed to collect himself and clear his throat. "So, what can I do for you, Inquestor?"

"What can you do for me? Well, that's an interesting question. I suppose a better question would be, what can I do for you?" Carver reached for his pocket notebook and skimmed the open page. "Word is, you've had more run-ins with my people in the past year than most do in their entire lives. You've dealt with Agents Karlov, Brant, and Colburn…"

"How are those old bastards?" Johnstone asked with a false, chummy smile.

"Dead," Carver chirped. Johnstone's face went pale. "Brant and Colburn walked into a rebel ambush, and Karlov was shot while he was filling out paperwork in his car."

"Well, that's—" The showmaster coughed. "I'm sorry to hear that."

"Yes, yes, a real shame, all of it," Carver shrugged. "Anyway, my department got to wondering how rebels keep sneaking up on us, so we started digging around for a pattern, and can you guess what we found?" He tapped one of Johnstone's gold buttons with the end of his finger. "You, sir!"

"No." Johnstone tried to take a step back, but he tripped on the curb. "No, no, I don't know nothing about no rebels."

"Really?" Carver consulted his notebook again. "Records show that you employ civil deviants almost exclusively, with the exception of those poor ugly folks you charge people a dime to gawk at."

Johnstone crawled backwards, muttering, "You got it all wrong, Inquestor. I'm true and blue. I was trying to help these ungrateful wretches."

Carver took another crunch of his apple. "Tall-Me raided a hospital not too long ago, and this looks an awful lot like his haul. What do you think, fellas?"

Just then, Inquestors Pierce and Victorin materialized out of the darkness.

"Is this that rebel circus plot he was after?" Victorin asked his idle companion.

Pierced yawned. "Maybe. Could be. I don't think I attended that briefing."

"Right out in the open! Right in the middle of Nieuwestad during the Freedom Festival!" Carver clicked his tongue in disapproval. "Sounds awfully cocky. Sounds like something Tall-Me would do."

"I ain't Tall-Me!" Johnstone cried. "It ain't me!"

"I thought Cleo was the cocky one." Pierce used his handkerchief to clean off a spot on the dusty trailer to lean against. "What was that whole deal with you and her at the prison, anyways? I overheard the Chief talking to the Director about it."

Carver went for a case which he had set on the ground by the trailer. "I'll tell you over drinks at The Office sometime. For now, let's focus on this little pickle right here."

He tossed the applecore over his shoulder and knelt to open the case, revealing a lustrous Thompson submachine gun. His arms fell limp at his sides.

"I still love that woman," he murmured to himself, petting the blued metal. *"I love her. I love her! I want to marry her."*

Victorin whistled. "Nice chopper. That's not standard issue."

Carver clasped his hands together and sent up a prayer of gratitude before he got back to his feet. Fumbling with the heavy drum magazine, he returned to the terrified man backed against the wall. "I apologize, Mr. Johnstone." He leveled the gun at his hip. "You were saying? There's a perfectly good explanation for all the red-windowed ladies in your employ and the sixty pounds of opioids stashed in your popcorn?"

Pierce was watching with interest now. The possibility of bloodshed always stirred him from his drowsy state. "An honest misunderstanding, I'm sure."

"Wish I had a parrot feather every time I heard that line." Victorin pocketed his gloves and cracked his knuckles.

"Back off, Vinny," Carver snapped, pushing him back with one arm. "And put your gloves back on, 'cause I got this. Johnstone was just about to tell me that these drugs did not come from the hospital that Tall-Me raided."

Johnstone needed something, anything, he could use to distract the inquestors. He looked for the injured girl, but she was long gone. "I don't know nothin' about no hospital," he blubbered helplessly. "Listen, you want something good?

Something powerful? I didn't tell Karlov, but I'll tell you. The Marram Issa is right here—"

"I don't want your lies," Carver cried. *"I want Tall-Me to pay for everything he's stolen from me!"*

Johnstone bolted, and the other two inquestors groaned.

"You don't really think he's Tall-Me, do you?" Pierce asked lazily as he watched the showmaster run away. "He only barely, vaguely, fits the profile."

"No, not really." Carver pulled back the charging bolt and gave an involuntary shudder of satisfaction. "I was just hoping he'd run."

Had Johnstone gone in the opposite direction, he might have found cover behind the trailers or someone's back stoop. In his inebriated state, he chose the route that ended at a solid brick wall where there was nothing to protect him and no way even the worst marksman in the country could miss.

"Oh, yes! Please run!" Carver cackled maniacally, unleashing a cacophonous barrage of .45 caliber bullets down the alley.

Pierce stood with a stretch and shut the doors to the drug trailer. "Do you think we can get credit for this bust, too?" he shouted over the racket.

"I doubt it." Victorin wiggled his gloves back onto his giant hands, watching the carnage. "Marcus Carver always has to be the hero."

ACKNOWLEDGMENTS:

This story is like the mosaic teacup that René made for Amandine: what started as a piece of junk unearthed from garbage was carefully cleaned and repaired to become the story it is now. It took a lot of time and a lot of help to get here, and I wanted to thank everybody who gave me and this story a chance.

First and foremost, I'd like to thank everyone who has been there since the very beginning. Thanks to my husband, Mike, who always believed in Threadbare, even back when it was half an idea sitting on an old thumbdrive. I'd like to thank my kids for being so patient after so many late dinners. Thanks to my mom, Christine, for reading my first draft and being Coronado's first fangirl. Thanks to my grandmother, Joann, for giving me writing tips and for learning Google Docs just so that she could help me with my first edits. Thanks to Matt, Ashlynn, and Valerie for the earliest version of Threadbare's cover. Thanks to Safford Library, Yuma Library, and the Clark County Libraries for supporting this book by including its earliest version in your collections.

Thanks to Tam Francis for teaching me so much about America in the 1940's and for writing my first glowing review on her blog, The Girl In The Jitterbug Dress. Piles and piles of gratitude to my editor Eva Cervantes for enduring late nights and headaches on account of me and this book. Thanks to Rachel Garcia and Reyanna Jarell for shooting the beautiful new cover, and to Sage and Brian for letting them smear fake blood and soot on you!

Finally, I'd like to thank electroswing and the amazing community of eccentrics that surround it. (Especially you, Faith In The Glitch. I don't know anybody else on the planet who'd be so cool about taking a total stranger to Coney Island.) In a way, this book is a sort of vintage remix, too. Threadbare didn't truly begin to take shape until the day I first heard a clip of Parov Stelar's "Chambermaid Swing" on a drive home from work. From there, the book seemed to write itself. Caro Emerald's "Tangled" and Postmodern Jukebox's cover of "Creep" wrote Sangria. Inquestor Carver was born from Caravan Palace's "Beatophone" and Wolfgang Lohr's "Black Coffee." Hours and hours of artists like Boogie Belgique, ProletR, Skeewiff, Jamie Berry, and Peggy Suave projected each scene as vibrant as a Baz Luhrman movie in my brain. I adore every one of you for keeping the beauty of the past alive in your music.

Made in the USA
San Bernardino, CA
18 October 2018